THE SPARK

"You shouldn't do that, Kate," Hogan said after she had kissed him.

"Why not?" she whispered huskily. Her hands still lay against his chest and she could feel the pounding rhythm of his heart, which was nearly as erratic as her own. There was a yearning between them. Kate felt it and wasn't sure if it had grown from her or him. It was simply there and not to be denied. His arms curved around her, pulling her up against him. His mouth claimed hers and she made no outcry. One big hand played across her back, pulling her tighter against his chest.

She was on fire, and nothing could bank the flames except this big man with his hard, irresistible body and a need as big as hers. . . .

PASSION RIDES THE PAST

☐ **SAN ANTONIO by Sara Orwig.** In America's turbulent old West, Luke Danby, a tough lawman, vowed to exact revenge upon the vicious bandit who had raided a wagon train years ago and murdered his mother. But his plans turned to dust when Luke met his enemy's beautiful daughter Catalina . . .
(401158—$4.50)

☐ **THE GATHERING OF THE WINDS by June Lund Shiplett.** Texas in the 1830s where three passionately determined women sought love's fiery fulfillment—Teffin Dante, who was helplessly drawn to the forbidden man, Blythe Kolter, who lost her innocence in the arms of a lover she could neither resist nor trust, and Catalina de Leon, who could not stop her body from responding to the man she wanted to hate. Three women . . . three burning paths of desire. . . .
(157117—$4.50)

☐ **GREEN DRAGON, WHITE TIGER by Annette Motley.** From her barren Asian homeland to the opulent splendor of the seventh century Tang Court, lovely, indomitable Black Jade pursues passion and power with two generations of emperors, and finds her ultimate glory on the Dragon Throne.
(400615—$4.95)

☐ **TO LOVE A ROGUE by Valerie Sherwood.** Raile Cameron, a renegade gun-runner, lovingly rescues the sensuous and charming Lorraine London from indentured servitude in Revolutionary America. Lorraine fights his wild and teasing embraces, as they sail the stormy Caribbean seas, until finally she surrenders to fiery passion.
(400518—$4.50)

☐ **WINDS OF BETRAYAL by June Lund Shiplett.** She was caught between two passionate men—and her own wild desire. Beautiful Lizette Kolter deeply loves her husband Bain Kolter, but the strong and virile free-booter, Sancho de Cordoba, seeks revenge on Bain by making her his prisoner of love. She was one man's lawful wife, but another's lawless desire.
(150376—$3.95)

☐ **HIGHLAND SUNSET by Joan Wolf.** She surrendered to the power of his passion . . . and her own undeniable desire. When beautiful, dark-haired Vanessa Maclan met Edward Romney, Earl of Linton, she told herself she should hate this strong and handsome English lord. But it was not hate but hunger that this man of so much power and passion woke within the Highland beauty.
(400488—$3.95)

Buy them at your local bookstore or use this convenient coupon for ordering.

NEW AMERICAN LIBRARY
P.O. Box 999, Bergenfield, New Jersey 07621
Please send me the books I have checked above. I am enclosing $_____
(please add $1.00 to this order to cover postage and handling). Send check or money order—no cash or C.O.D.'s. Prices and numbers are subject to change without notice.
Name_____
Address_____
City _____ State _____ Zip Code _____

Allow 4-6 weeks for delivery.
This offer, prices and numbers are subject to change without notice.

TOMORROW'S DREAM

by
Peggy Hanchar

AN ONYX BOOK

NEW AMERICAN LIBRARY

A DIVISION OF PENGUIN BOOKS USA INC.

PUBLISHER'S NOTE
This book is a work of fiction. Names, characters, places, and incidents are
either the product of the author's imagination or are used fictitiously, and any
resemblance to actual persons, living or dead, events, or locales
is entirely coincidental.

NAL BOOKS ARE AVAILABLE AT QUANTITY DISCOUNTS WHEN USED TO PROMOTE
PRODUCTS OR SERVICES. FOR INFORMATION PLEASE WRITE TO PREMIUM
MARKETING DIVISION, NEW AMERICAN LIBRARY, 1633 BROADWAY,
NEW YORK, NEW YORK 10019.

Copyright © 1989 by Peggy Hanchar

All rights reserved

ONYX TRADEMARK REG. U.S. PAT. OFF. AND FOREIGN COUNTRIES
REGISTERED TRADEMARK—MARCA REGISTRADA
HECHO EN DRESDEN, TN, U.S.A.

SIGNET, SIGNET CLASSIC, MENTOR, ONYX, PLUME, MERIDIAN and
NAL BOOKS are published by New American Library, a division of Penguin
Books, USA Inc., 1633 Broadway, New York, New York 10019

First Printing, September, 1989

1 2 3 4 5 6 7 8 9

PRINTED IN THE UNITED STATES OF AMERICA

*To my lovely granddaughters,
Candi and Steffie, Jackie and Jenny,
heroines all. And to my children,
Steve and Janice, Jim and Janis,
Bob and Nancy and Laura,
and to Steve,
who started it all*

Prologue

Kate!

She was part of the premonition, part of the nagging half-dreams and disquiet that haunted his nights and even his waking hours. Yet it made no sense, for Kate was in the east and the rest of the premonition pulled him toward the north. Sometimes, when he sat in the sunshine, half-dozing, he would start and leap to his feet, taking a few steps to the north, as if his journey had already begun. Still, he couldn't forget Kate.

"It's the old restlessness come upon you, luv," Molly said, complacently crossing her arms beneath her ample bosom and sucking on the wad of snuff tucked into her lower lip.

"I tell you, this time it's different, Molly girl," Gilly answered. He was a small wiry man, his balding scalp gleaming through the straggling gray strands of hair. Once he might have been handsome, but the seasons had marked themselves in his weather-beaten face and in the squint of his eyes. His back was permanently stooped from the long hours spent hunched over a stream and a sluice box. "It's Kate I'm thinking of," he said in that vague wondering tone he'd come to use of late.

"It's gold fever I'm a-tellin' you," Molly answered. She'd taken Gilly in as a winter boarder. He'd been sick and feeble, half-starved from working the mines in the Coeur d'Alene. He'd never paid any board, but he'd warmed her bed and made her evenings entertaining and lively and she'd thought it a fair exchange. She'd always known he would pick up and leave someday. She'd never expected anything else. Now she rocked back in the old chair, one of the few things her dead husband had left her. "You'll be goin' on again soon, I expect."

Gilly made no answer. His eyes had that faraway look and he stood gripping the porch railing, his head tilted back, his nostrils flaring as if he could smell the first tantalizing metallic whiffs of gold. He'd followed the gold mines most of his life, beginning in California when he was little more than a boy, following the lure of it through Colorado, into the Black Hills, and finally here to Washington and the Coeur d'Alene. There was no place left to go north except to Alaska.

Alaska! Even its name held a promise that set him to trembling. For years, rumors of gold discoveries had been floating down from the great frozen wasteland, and some men, young and inexperienced in such things, had gone off in search of the yellow ore. But the older and wiser miners had hesitated, waiting for more substantial information. Now the pull was upon him, strong as the pull of gravity against the very center of the earth itself. Alaska!

Kate! The siren song of gold was drowned out by the rushing need to see his daughter one more time. He'd not told Molly all of his premonition. Once he traveled to the frozen plateaus of Alaska, he'd never return.

Kate! He had to see her again. Then with good conscience he could go to Alaska and search for gold.

"It's my daughter I'm thinking of," he repeated.

"Give me her address then, luv, and should you go off, I can write her myself and tell her you was here. It might ease her mind some if you don't come back." Her words slowed, then faded to nothing as she caught the look on Gilly's face. "What is it now?" she asked, a shiver running up her spine.

"I'm going to find Kate myself," he said belligerently. There had been a confirmation in Molly's words, as if she didn't believe he'd ever come back either. He saw the concern on her face and his tone softened. "I just want to see her again with my own eyes. She was a lassie when I left."

"Is she livin' with her mama then?" Molly asked slyly, nettled that he might be leaving her for another woman, even if that woman was his wife. But Gilly slowly shook his shaggy head.

"Nan died when Kate was just a little thing. That's when I got the traveling itch, and I haven't stopped much since. Kate was raised by her Aunt Petty. Like as not she's married now and has a passel of young'uns herself."

"She's that old then?" Molly asked, intrigued that he chose now to give her some information about himself, now that he was leaving.

"Kate must be twenty-six by now. She was never that much to look at, too skinny and plain, but she was right smart and a hard worker."

"She sounds real nice," Molly said wistfully. She'd often longed for a daughter. Gilly made no answer. Stepping down off the porch, he wandered toward the barn. Sighing, Molly picked up one of his shirts and began mending it. The Lord only knew when he'd find somebody else to do for him.

Aunt Petty died in her sleep, a kindly inoffensive woman who made little mark upon the world and had slipped away peacefully so as to cause the least amount of trouble for anyone. Only she had caused trouble for Kate, more than she ever could have imagined. Kate sighed and lengthened her stride. The late-August sun was growing hot upon her neck and a muggy haze was already forming at the end of the street. Taking out a lace handkerchief, she dabbed lightly at her brow and chin. It was the only concession she made to the heat. Her back was still ramrod straight beneath the heavy faille jacket. The high lace collar of her crisp white bodice was fastened to the very top button. Her bonnet, brown and drab and unimaginative, still sat precisely on her tightly braided topknot. She hadn't bought it for its looks but for its serviceability and its reasonable price. Kate had always been practical.

Good thing she'd learned early to pinch her pennies, she thought, dabbing once more at her chin. As meager as those pennies had seemed before, they were nonexistent now. She'd just visited the offices of her aunt's solicitor and found the news even more dismal than she'd supposed. Aunt Petty hadn't a penny left. In fact they'd been living these past few years on money she'd borrowed against the large stone house Uncle Jeb had left her. Kate had never guessed. Aunt Petty had never made her feel the weight of her charity. Now the house must be sold to pay back the loans.

Kate marched along Main Street, nodding now and again to those who spoke a greeting, her expression never once giving away the trepidation she felt. Her practical mind was already considering her dilemma. She would have to earn a living, and how was she to do that? She glanced around the street of imposing houses. She could become a maid for people who were once her neighbors and would be no more. She thought of the duties of a maid. They would not be unlike what she'd done to keep the great mansion up for Aunt Petty, who could not afford such a luxury. Working for other ladies wouldn't be the same as working for the dear, frail old woman who had been eternally grateful for the smallest favors.

She could teach. She glanced at the children playing in a yard nearby. She'd not been around children much, and when she had, she'd found them noisy and rude and messy. Could she handle a whole classroom full of them and somehow cram a modicum of learning into their little heads? She pictured herself in a classroom trying vainly to bring order and quiet to boisterous, defiant children. Lord, the prospect was chilling, even on a hot summer day. If she were not to be a maid or a schoolteacher, she wondered crossly, what was she to do?

She rounded the corner. Ahead lay Aunt Petty's imposing stone house with its crisp, clean lines and wide stoop. Kate stopped dead in her tracks. A vagabond was resting on the front steps as bold as you please, his legs stretched out before him, his bearded chin sunk against his chest in deep slumber.

Kate tightened her grip on her umbrella, prepared

to go forth and do battle, but something familiar about the figure stopped her. Her mouth fell open and her expression showed clearly, as it had not before, all the surprise and confusion she felt. Then, as quickly as it had come, the confusion passed. Kate's mouth curved in a smile and she went forward to greet the raggedy man sleeping on her doorstep. She had a premonition that her life was about to change forever.

1

"This was a mistake," Gilly muttered for the hundredth time.

He shifted on the hard seat, glanced at the woman beside him, and glared out the train window at the passing landscape. Although spring had already come to the Missouri River valleys, here in the Rockies snow still clung stubbornly to mountain slopes. He'd been delayed for nearly six months by a fever that had left him weak and fatigued. Patiently Kate had nursed him through the winter, nursed him and bullied him back to health. Now he chafed at the time lost. With some asperity he glared at his daughter as if it were her fault.

"I tell you, Kathleen Moira O'Riley, this was a mistake. Decent women don't go to the goldfields."

"The decision was made, Gilly. It's too late to change now," Kate answered serenely. "Haven't there been women at the other gold finds?"

"Not decent women," Gilly growled, "and I'll not have a daughter of mine mixing with the likes of camp followers that do come." Kate glanced at her father sharply. Quickly he closed his mouth, fearful she might ask how he'd come to know about such women. Surreptitiously he studied her. She would never be mistaken for one of the camp followers. Wire-rimmed glasses perched on her thin nose. Red-orange hair was pulled into a severe bun. Her appearance was drab and—he hated to even think the words about Kate—old-maidish. If she'd just fix herself up a little, maybe loosen her hair so it didn't pull her face into such a prudish, sour-pickle expression. He liked to see a woman gussied up a little, like the painted women who followed the gold camps.

Of course, that wouldn't do for Kate. Still, she might relax the stubborn lines of that obstinate chin. It testified too eloquently to the kind of woman she had become. Gilly sighed. What Kate needed was a husband. He'd have to give the matter some thought.

"What are you thinking?" Kate asked, alarmed by his expression.

Gilly started. It wouldn't do to let her know the direction his thoughts had taken. "Hrumph!" He cleared his throat. "Like I was saying, Kate. The Yukon's no place for a lady." With tobacco-stained fingers he smoothed his beard, succeeding in looking guilty when he'd meant to look self-righteous.

"You're all the family I have left," she said firmly. "I don't want to be alone." Her words touched him as nothing else could. Swallowing hard, he pulled the brim of his hat lower.

With a nod of satisfaction, Kate checked her father's appearance. He looked far better than the day he'd shown up on Aunt Petty's porch. Since that day his hair and beard had been trimmed, his clothes mended and washed, and his sunken frame had put on some flesh. He would always look as if he were recovering from a lingering illness, but she had the satisfaction of knowing he was eating better and drinking less. Once again she turned her attention to the scenery outside her window.

They'd been traveling for days now and she'd found every moment exciting and interesting, far better than being a maid or schoolteacher. She'd been hard put to convince Gilly she was coming with him. Only in the end, when she'd packed her bags and followed him to the train station, had he realized she wouldn't be denied. For a moment she'd thought he might hug her, but that wasn't the way with them. Too many years had passed between the young girl who'd idolized her father and the woman who'd learned to turn her bitterness at his abandonment into resignation and finally understanding. But now was their chance to know each other again, and she wouldn't allow him to walk away from her a second time.

"A mistake," Gilly mumbled under his breath.

"How do you know there's gold in Alaska?" Kate asked, hoping to divert him.

Gilly laid one long finger against his nose. "This tells me, sis," he growled. "Besides, there've been rumors coming out of the Klondike for years now."

"Why haven't you gone before?"

"The time wasn't right," Gilly said, shaking his head, and Kate had to be content with that.

Two days later their train drew into the King Street station in the heart of Seattle. Kate shook out her wrinkled skirts and gathered up her bags. She struggled after Gilly as he left the train and shouldered a path across the busy platform. Kate had never seen so many people milling and shoving and talking in loud excited voices. Some of them brandished an edition of the Seattle *Post-Intelligencer*.

"What's all the excitement?" Gilly asked one tipsy argonaut. Reeling into others, the man laughed good-naturedly and took a swig from a nearly empty whiskey bottle.

"Man, haven't you heard?" the fellow exclaimed. "Gold! They've found gold in the Klondike and they're bringing it in on the *Portland*. She docked yesterday."

"Are they certain or is it just another rumor?" Gilly asked, but Kate could feel the excitement mounting in him. He had little doubt about the authenticity of the claims this time.

The stampeder looked at him askance. "It's in the *Post-Intelligencer*," he cried. "It's true, man. Gold! They've found gold." His face was lit with a wild elation as he raised his bottle high and pushed off through the crowd.

"What does it mean?" Kate asked, looking around at the boisterous throng of men.

"It means every man with a hunger to be rich will be descending on this town in a matter of weeks," Gilly said. "For once I'm a jump ahead of them. Come on, Kate. Let's go find a room before they start raising the prices." Though Gilly hadn't mentioned having been in Seattle before, he seemed to know his way around. Without hesitation he led the way out of the station and into King Street. From there he set out for the nearest hotel.

Seattle was a hilly, foggy frontier town perched on the shore of a large bay which Gilly told her was called Puget Sound. In the distance a mountain peak, its base obscured by a bluish haze, seemed to hang suspended from the sky. Kate gasped in delight, but Gilly barely spared it a glance.

Dirt-and-cobblestone streets led down to the wharves. Rough warehouses and stores lined the streets. The boardwalks were so crowded with men, walking was nearly impossible.

"Gilly!" a wiry, balding man shouted, and pressed through the crowd from one of the saloons. He was dressed in much the same rough manner as Gilly and the other men.

"Uly!" Gilly threw down his bag and wrapped his arm around the other man's shoulders. Chortling gustily, they pounded each other on the back. "You old son-of-a-gun, what are you doing here?"

"Same as you, you old donkey's—"

"Uly," Gilly hastily interrupted, "I want you to meet my daughter, Kate."

Whatever the man had been about to say died on his lips. He snatched his beat-up hat off his head and bowed graciously. "Ulysses Thomas Udell at your service, ma'am," he said and, beaming, clamped his hat back in place.

"How do you do?" Kate said, but he barely heard her.

Quickly he turned back to Gilly. "They've found gold up yonder," he said, shifting his weight from foot to foot as if barely able to contain himself.

"So I've heard."

"Reckon this is the big one?"

Gilly nodded. "Reckon so," he answered. "Did Hogan come up?"

"Got here last week." Uly gestured back inside the

saloon. "Hogan, come on out here," he bellowed at someone. Raucous laughter ended abruptly and a tall dark-haired man pushed his way toward the door. Kate could see him coming even before he'd shoved aside the last group of men, for he stood a head taller than most of them. She gaped as he strolled toward them, a laughing blond woman clinging to his arm. Her flashy clothes and the suggestive way she snuggled against him left little doubt as to what she was.

Kate's lips tightened in disapproval and she turned her attention back to the tall man. As awesome as she found his height, the breadth of his shoulders was truly magnificent. He was dressed in a plaid flannel shirt with red underwear showing beneath the turned-back sleeves and open collar. Rough denim trousers hugged the thick muscular columns of his thighs. He was a giant of a man with a shaggy mane of unruly dark hair badly in need of a trim. A jagged scar marred one lean cheek and disappeared into the thick black growth of beard which covered the lower part of his face. Fresh scuffs and bruises discolored his cheeks and one eye. It was a battered, hard-used face that spoke too eloquently of the kind of hell-raising, thoughtless life this man led.

Hugging his companion against his chest, he whispered something that set her to giggling shrilly. He tossed his head back and laughed uproariously, revealing square white teeth. He seemed not to notice the people on the porch. Kate feared he meant to run them down, but he stopped abruptly and surveyed each of them with an open, candid air. His dark eyes held humor, friendly curiosity, and a touch of wariness, but then he spied Gilly and his big face broke into an even bigger grin.

"Gilly, you made it," he cried, slapping Kate's father on the back so hard she thought Gilly would surely be sent to his knees. But Gilly only smiled and pumped hands with the giant.

"Hogan, you're a sight for sore eyes. How'd you hear about it so soon?"

"I stopped by to talk to Molly," the big man answered. "She told me you were heading this way after you went off to see kinfolk." His black eyes darted a quick glance at Kate.

"Kate, this is Hogan O'Shea. He's been my partner through many a dig." Gilly grinned at the younger man. "Hogan, this is Kate, my daughter."

"Howdy, ma'am." The giant enclosed her hand in his bear-paw embrace. "I never knew Gilly had a daughter. He never once mentioned it."

Kate glanced at Gilly, who shuffled his feet and looked around. "Yeah, well, I never told you everything about me," he mumbled.

Hogan grinned, a lazy, devilish grin that brought out deep clefts on either side of his mouth. "Anyhow, I'm pleased to meet you, ma'am." He shook her hand vigorously before releasing it as abruptly as he'd seized it, spat a mouthful of tobacco juice over her shoulder into the street, and wrapped his arm back around the dance-hall girl, who'd stood momentarily forgotten and pouting.

"This is Roxanne Blayne. Say hello, honey," he coaxed the vapid blond.

"Hello," Roxanne said in a friendly manner.

"How do you do?" Kate said coldly, and made no attempt to hide her distaste for the painted creature. Her eyebrows rose disdainfully, her nostrils pinched. Every line of her body expressed her outrage at being introduced to such a low-fallen woman. Roxanne's smile faded. Hogan scowled. Gilly frowned. Kate sensed she was being rude in some manner, but made no apology. Hogan bent low to whisper something in Roxanne's ear, nuzzling her cheek at the same time. The saloon girl giggled and cast Kate a malicious glance. It was obvious he'd made an unflattering remark. Kate's chin quivered in outrage and she pulled herself up stiffly.

Hogan turned back to Gilly. "Have you heard about the *Portland?*" he asked.

"I'd have to be deaf and blind not to," Gilly exclaimed. "God Almighty, I haven't seen such hell-fire excitement since Colorado.'' The men laughed gleefully, their high spirits infectious.

"Have you got your gear yet?" Hogan asked.

"Naw, he just got here," Uly interjected.

"Come on in and have a drink," Hogan invited, half-turned toward the saloon.

Gilly glanced at Kate and rubbed his jaw. "We've got to find some rooms first," he said reluctantly.

"Go on down to the Seattle Hotel two blocks west," Uly advised. "Hogan and me've got rooms down there. They're clean and cheap. 'Course"—he glanced doubtfully at Kate—"they ain't fancy."

"We don't need fancy, Mr. Udell," Kate said crisply. "We thank you for the advice." Expectantly she turned to Gilly.

"Uh, Kate. Sis! You go on down and get yourself settled in. I'm going in here and have a drink with the boys," Gilly said.

"Right now?" Kate asked in dismay, looking from one man to another. Hogan and Uly grinned and looked away. Roxanne smirked. "What about your bags?" Kate asked stubbornly.

"I'll keep them with me." At her woebegone expression he snatched off his hat and faced her squarely. "Dadburnit, Kate, I told you when we started out what to expect from me. I told you I liked to drink with the men."

"I know, Gilly," Kate said quietly.

"And I told you not to try to pin me down. I'm a traveling man, used to being on my own."

"I know, Gilly," Kate agreed calmly. "When will you come down to the hotel?"

Gilly looked taken aback. "I don't know," he said evasively. "You can't put a time limit on a man's thirst."

"I know," Kate answered, and turned away, then just as quickly turned back. "You are coming down to the hotel, aren't you, Gilly?"

For the first time he seemed to realize her fears. He stepped forward and placed a finger alongside her jaw. "Aye, Kate, I'll be coming down to the hotel. I'll not leave you, girl," he said gently. Kate blinked back the sting of tears.

Hogan watched them intently. "Come on in, little miss, and join us." The bear paw fell on her shoulder in a friendly invitation. She could feel the heat of his hand clear through her waistcoat and blouse. Distastefully she shrugged it away.

"Obviously you've quenched your thirst several times over, Mr. O'Shea," she snapped, venting the frustration she felt toward Gilly on this big stranger.

"Kate, mind your tongue!" Gilly roared. "No daughter of mine will insult my friends."

"I'm sorry, Gilly," Kate answered calmly, but her gaze was locked with the dark-eyed glare of Hogan O'Shea. Gone were the glints of humor, the easy smile. His face was a hard, unyielding mask, his eyes black with anger. She had little doubt that if she were a man, she would be fending off this giant with her fists. "Since Mr. O'Shea is an Irishman, I thought he'd take my words as a compliment," she said lightly.

The men milling on the boardwalk mumbled among themselves. One or two chortled. Many of them were familiar with Hogan O'Shea's ready temper and flailing fists. Few wanted to test his mettle. Yet here stood a woman facing him down. They pressed closer to hear what was said.

Hogan seemed aware of the interest they'd aroused. He grinned broadly at the other men. "That I am, Miss O'Riley," he said with a swagger. "I'm Irish, the same as yourself, and I'll take your words in the spirit in which you meant them, as a compliment. Seeing as you're such a lady." He drawled the words and spat on the board near the hem of her gown. Fastidiously Kate drew her skirts aside. Gilly grinned widely. "I'll not insult you again by inviting you in." He glanced around and imperiously motioned to someone. "Zeke," he said to the thin, ragged man who shuffled forward, "here's a dollar. I want you to accompany this lady down to the Hotel Seattle. See to it she gets there safely."

"Yes, sir, Mr. O'Shea," Zeke said, bobbing his

head and licking his lips as he took the gold coin. His hands shook uncontrollably and it was obvious to Kate that the coin would soon be spent in one of the bars lining the street. But her thoughts were on Hogan O'Shea and the unspoken feud that had sprung up between them. He'd bested her, turning her insult into something else entirely. If she continued this, she'd be made to look the fool. Instead she smiled graciously.

"Thank you for your thoughtfulness, Mr. O'Shea," she said primly, and proceeded down the street. She could hear catcalls and loud laughter as the men on the porch rushed Hogan O'Shea back to the bar to buy him a drink. He'd not only established his reputation as a fearless, hard-fighting man but also shown himself to have finesse with the ladies.

Seething, Kate walked along the bustling avenue. A typical brawling, drinking Irishman who'd never amount to much of anything, she thought, chasing after some impossible dream of gold, just like Gilly. They were two of a kind! She hated to think that even now Gilly was back there drinking and talking to such an uncouth lot. Well, they'd be booking passage to Alaska soon, and Hogan O'Shea and his all-knowing, too-bold eyes would be left behind in Seattle. Like as not they would never see him again, and that suited her fine.

She managed to secure two rooms at the exorbitant price of fifty cents a day for each. Meals, she learned, would cost twenty to twenty-five cents apiece. Outrageous prices, she fumed, but a hot bath soon had her in better spirits. When she'd dressed in fresh clothes and brushed her long auburn hair and tightly rebraided it, she sat by the window to wait for Gilly. Her stomach rumbled with hunger, but she didn't want to eat alone. She whiled away the time by watching the streets below, teeming with people.

Already, opportunists were thronging into Seattle. Clairvoyants, swaddled in layers of cloth and funny dark hats, walked the streets offering to reveal to all who had a coin where the rich gold deposits could be found once they reached Alaska. Con men posing as prospectors newly returned from the goldfields sold nonexistent claims. The unsuspecting could buy maps to lost mines or any manner of equipment to help extract the gold from the ground once they found it. A Klondike bicycle could be had, or a Klondike stove, or a gold crusher.

Kate became so enthralled with the scene below that she was unaware of how much time had passed until she realized it was growing dark and still Gilly had not come. In a moment of impetuous determination she decided to brave Hogan O'Shea's ire and collect her father. She had little doubt he was even now staggering at the bar or lying facedown in the gutter in a drunken stupor. Pinning her bonnet squarely on her topknot and taking up her umbrella and gloves, she marched back up the street to the saloon where she'd last seen Gilly. Just as she feared. He wasn't there.

Anxiously she looked around; then, spying another saloon with the grand name of Paris House emblazoned over its door, she pushed her way toward it. There was a different crowd of men now, or perhaps those of the afternoon had become too inebriated to maintain the small amount of decorum they'd shown before. At any rate, they clutched at her gown and called ribald suggestions as she passed.

The Paris House was a little more elegant than most establishments of its kind. A long bar, its wood grain polished smooth by the elbows of its patrons, ran down one side of the room. Mirrors, decorated with ornate gold scrolls, were mounted on the wall behind. Green velvet panels were draped from the ceiling. On the bare walls between were garish paintings of women in varying stages of undress. Kate blushed and looked away. A smoky haze stung her eyes and made breathing difficult. A band consisting of a piano and several violins provided music.

Women, suggestively dressed, sat talking and drinking with customers. The Paris House boasted a variety of female companionship from as many as seventy-five different countries. Familiar laughter, dark and husky and wickedly intimate, claimed her attention first.

She'd found Hogan, and now she could only hope Gilly was with him. She pushed her way into the crowded room, peering around until she spied Hogan O'Shea ensconced in a corner, two dance-hall girls seated on his lap, one on each knee. His arms were around their waists and he leaned toward one while she whispered something in his ear.

"All right, darling," he said, and the other girl pouted and walked away. Hogan and the remaining girl stood up and pushed their way toward the stairs.

Dance-hall girls, my eye, Kate thought, and raised her closed umbrella high above her head. "Mr. O'Shea," she cried. "Mr. O'Shea." At first he didn't hear her. His head was bowed toward the laughing girl, his dark hair hanging over his forehead.

"Mr. O'Shea!" Kate called, and finally climbed up on a chair. "Hogan!" She used the same cry she'd used to call home the cows to Aunt Petty's garden. The room grew quiet for a moment.

Hogan O'Shea turned around and caught sight of her. "Miss O'Riley," he called gaily, and said something to the girl. With a baleful glare at Kate, she flounced off. The noise and laughter had resumed almost immediately, but Kate's cry had attracted attention. Now a man approached her, stumbling drunkenly.

"Well, look here, fellas," he called to his friends. "We got a schoolmarm standing up here ready to give us a lecture. I always had me a hankering for a schoolmarm." He grabbed for her, nearly jerking her from the wobbly chair. With a scream, Kate steadied herself and brought her umbrella down over his head with a resounding thwack. The man let out a bellow, throwing up his hands to protect himself as Kate swung her umbrella again. His friends laughed uproariously.

At the sound of their ridicule, the man swung on Kate, his face mean, his fists already clenching. Kate's face blanched and she jabbed at him with the point of her umbrella. He jumped back, then snarled a warning, preparing to leap at her. Before he could make a move, Hogan was there, his long arms encircling the man to swing him away from her. With a growl of rage the man swung at him. Hogan's big fist was there first. Almost gently he punched the man's chin and caught him as he slid downward.

"Take him someplace to sleep it off," he instructed the man's friends, and made his way to Kate. His large hands spanned her slim waist as he lifted her off the chair. She was left breathless and told herself it was the excitement of her narrow escape and had nothing at all to do with this uncouth, loutish man.

"Miss O'Riley, a lady like you shouldn't be here," he said, still gripping her waist.

"Where's my father?" Kate demanded, drawing away from his touch. He was like a great solid wall, blocking her view of the room.

"He's around here somewhere," Hogan answered vaguely. "You shouldn't have come down here. He said he'd be up to the hotel in a little while."

"A while has come and passed, Mr. O'Shea," Kate snapped. "It's far past time for supper or a decent bedtime."

"Gil O'Riley doesn't impress me as a man needing a nanny to tell him his bedtime, if you'll excuse my saying so, ma'am," Hogan offered.

"No, I won't excuse you, Mr. O'Shea. I'll thank you to stay out of our affairs. Gilly has been ill. He can't possibly get well if he's . . . if he's traipsing around in saloons with the likes of you."

The grin died off Hogan's face. "What kind is the likes of me?" he demanded.

Kate left off her perusal of the room and turned back to him impatiently. "Now, I don't mean to insult you again, Mr. O'Shea, but you must admit that you and the rest of this . . . this rabble lead . . . Well, disreputable lives."

"Disreputable lives?" he repeated. "Why, you ungrateful . . . I just saved you from these hooligans."

"Yes, you did, Mr. O'Shea," Kate said, "and I'm much obliged, but that doesn't make you any less a hooligan yourself. And I won't have you leading my father into a life of . . . of sinful ways."

Hogan stared at her in dismay, big fists planted on his hips; then he put back his head and let out a hoot of laughter. "Well, ma'am, I sure don't want to lead poor old Gilly astray."

"Where is he?" Kate demanded.

Hogan nodded toward the flight of stairs. "He's up there," he said, and glanced around for Uly. "I wouldn't wait around for him, though, he's going to be a while. Hey, where are you. . . ? You can't go up there." But Kate wasn't listening. She was already striding across the room, using her elbows as a shield to batter her way through the weaving figures. She was halfway up the steps before Hogan broke through the crowd.

"Wait a minute!" he yelled, but she never paused. At the top of the landing was a door. Striding forward, Kate knocked, then thew it open. Her shocked gaze took in the spectacle of bare flesh—skinny white shanks and hairy legs intertwined with plump white buttocks and black-mesh-clad thighs.

"What the hell?" a man yelled, and grabbed for a coverlet.

The woman shrieked and cowered, then, seeing Kate, twisted her face into an ugly grimace. "Get out," she screamed.

"I'm so sorry," Kate stammered, almost incoherent with embarrassment.

"Shut the door," the man shouted when she stood there unable to move.

"Yes, yes, of course. I'm so sorry," Kate babbled. "I . . . I was just looking for s-som—"

A strong hand yanked her away. The door was slammed shut and she was being propelled down the stairs and out of the saloon.

Only when they'd reached the street did Hogan swing her around, pushing her back against the building, the tight grip on her arm not lessening one whit as he glared down at her.

"How horrible, dreadful—the most mortifying exhibition . . ." Kate cried.

"Not horrible and dreadful, just a natural act between a man and a woman, and you had no right to interfere. What made you open that door?"

"I was looking for Gilly," she said, turning her face away so he couldn't look at her. "I . . . I didn't know . . ."

"You didn't know what the rooms at the top of the stairs were for?" Hogan demanded disbelievingly. "Lady, where in God's name have you been?"

"I . . . I thought they were rooms to let. I thought Gilly had taken one to . . . to stay in," Kate confessed, humiliated by all that had transpired. Even now the flash of plumb bare buttocks and hairy thighs swam before her eyes in a blur. She wobbled and slid down the wall. Only Hogan's grip saved her from falling into the street.

"Whoa, there," he muttered, and pulled her upright, pinning her against the wall with his big hard body while he shifted her weight. Kate feared she might suffocate in his hold. Taking a bottle from his pocket, he pressed it to her lips. "Drink," he commanded, and Kate obeyed. The raw whiskey burned her throat and stung her nose, so she coughed and gasped for breath. Patiently he waited until the weakness had passed and her wobbly knees were able to support her again.

"I'm sorry," Kate said. "I . . . I don't know what's come over me. All the travel and excitement, I suppose."

"Have you eaten anything today?" Kate shook her head. "Come on." He took her arm and guided her down the boardwalk. "You should have waited for Gilly up at the hotel. He told you he'd be there."

"I was afraid he wouldn't come," Kate confessed miserably.

"He would have," Hogan said simply.

"That's easy for you to say, isn't it?" she demanded, growing angry again. "You don't know him as I do."

"I know him well enough," he answered. His expression was grim and disapproving. Kate couldn't understand why. After all, she hadn't done anything wrong. Without consulting her, Hogan O'Shea turned into another saloon.

"Oh, no, I don't think I want to go in here," Kate protested, pulling from his grasp.

"It's all right," he reassured her. "There's a dining room in back. The food's good. Trust me." He smiled beguilingly, his teeth flashing white behind the black tangle of beard. Kate turned away from the compelling pull of his gaze, deliberately squelching the surge of curiosity about this rough-hewn man. She was tempted to hurry back to the Hotel Seattle without any supper, but she had a hunch he wouldn't allow that. Best not to cause any further scenes. Placatingly she followed him into the dining room.

Hogan plopped himself down in the nearest chair and looked at her in surprise as she stood waiting for him to hold her chair.

"What are you standing there for?" he boomed. "Take a load off your feet. Bill, bring us a couple of your thickest, rarest steaks and some of those fried potatoes and onions."

"Oh, no, I don't think I could . . ." Kate began, her stomach quivering at the thought of all the greasy food.

"Sure you can," Hogan insisted. "You haven't eaten all day. You're a little skinny. You need to put some meat on your bones."

Kate closed her mouth on any further protests, mortified at the familiarity he'd taken with his words. "Could I have a cup of tea?" she asked.

"No tea, but they've got coffee," he answered, and ordered her a cup. He watched her slender white hands fluttering from the high-necked collar to her hair, patting nonexistent loose strands back into place. Finally she fumbled with her wire-rimmed glasses, carefully removing them so she could rub her temples and the bridge of her nose. What on earth had Gilly been thinking of? he wondered. The Klondike was no place for a woman like her. She'd never last. He looked at the drawn white lines of her face and the dark circles under her eyes. Suddenly she raised her lashes and he was looking full-bore into the greenest eyes he'd ever seen. He scowled. She flushed. Both glanced away. The waiter brought their food and gratefully they fell to eating, concentrating fiercely on their plates.

Halfway through the meal, Hogan finally glanced up, a huge forkful of food poised in midair as he watched Kate slowly and precisely cutting her meat into neat little squares. "God Almighty. No wonder you're so skinny," he blurted. "You can't get enough food into you at that rate." He carried the laden fork the rest of the way to his mouth and sat chewing while he regarded her.

"Mr. O'Shea," Kate began, her tone sharp enough to shave a man's jaw, "whatever you think of my person, I will thank you to keep such overly familiar observations to yourself. No matter what rough company you're used to keeping, I must insist that you address yourself to me in a more gentlemanly manner."

Hogan's face turned red and he struggled to swallow down the half-chewed food. When at last he could speak, he took great care to enunciate each word. "It's pretty clear that you consider me a fellow of rough, no-account ways," he snapped. "But at least I'm not some skinny, frustrated old maid who doesn't know any better than to go barging in on a man and a woman's privacy."

"Ooh, you would throw that up to me," Kate cried, throwing down her napkin, "which only proves to me, Mr. O'Shea, just how ungentlemanly you are."

His chair scraped loudly across the floor as he got to his feet, dark eyes glaring. "I never claimed to be something I'm not, Miss O'Riley," he said. "Now, if you'll come with me, I'll see you back to the hotel. As I remember, when you barged in on us down at the saloon, I was about to take a woman and visit one of those rooms upstairs myself."

Kate's cheeks stained pink at his blunt words. She leapt to her feet. "I'm so sorry to have spoiled your cultural evening, Mr. O'Shea," she snapped. "I won't delay you any longer." She stalked away, the length of her stride causing her long skirts to sway provocatively over her slim hips.

Angrily Hogan tore his gaze away from the sway of her behind. "Flat-chested old maid," he muttered loudly enough for her to hear.

Horrified, Kate stopped dead-still, her hands clamped over her chest, her face livid with rage. The effrontery of him! She didn't look back. She couldn't bear to face him again. Head high, she marched out of the dining room, banging the door behind her.

Hogan's anger cooled as he watched her shove her way through the men at the bar. Several of them called to her drunkenly. Cursing under his breath, he dropped some coins on the table and hurried after her. Somehow he felt responsible for her. After all, she was Gilly's daughter and this was her first night in Seattle. He'd at least see her safely back to the hotel. Then she was on her own.

She walked faster than he'd anticipated and was already halfway down the block. Hogan started after her. She was tall for a woman, her stride long. She looked neither left nor right as she passed along the street, her ridiculous bonnet bobbing jauntily with every step, her umbrella held before her like a sword. He could imagine the stern, persimmony look on her face. Men who might have approached her took one look at her expression and the umbrella and turned away. Hogan might have laughed at the spectacle of her tall, slim figure marching along so purposefully, but the things she'd said still rankled. He followed behind until she'd reached the hotel, then turned toward the Paris House to find Gilly. No telling what the old man was up to now. All thought of Roxanne Blayne was gone from his head. Instead a pair of green eyes mocked him all the way to the saloon.

2

"Gilly!" Kate knocked on the door and pressed her ear to the wooden panel. From inside came a muffled moan. "He's hurt. Open the door immediately," she ordered imperiously, and against his better judgment the hotel clerk complied. Kate rushed in. Still fully dressed except for his boots, Gilly lay tangled in the bedcovers, his legs draped over the edge. His face was mottled and another enormous moan emitted from the mound of covers. Kate hurried forward. "Gilly!" she called frantically.

"Ah, Kate, my girl, don't screech so," he pleaded, cradling his head in his hands.

Taken aback, Kate paused. "Are you all right?" she demanded, and at his groan rushed on. "We were supposed to make our travel arrangements today and buy our gear for the trip to Skagway."

Throbbing head forgotten, Gilly glanced up, his expression troubled. "Kathleen," he began, not able to meet her gaze, "I've been thinking, I have, and I was thinking it's not such a good idea for you to try to go to the goldfields with me. We don't know what we'll find." Hunching his shoulders, he began to pull on his boots. Kate knelt to help him.

"I thought it was gold we'd be finding," she said, her expression grown wary as she watched him.

"Aye, that we will, in time," Gilly said. "But in the meantime there'll be grievous hardships, Kate, and who knows what else. Many a man ends his days in the frozen wastelands of the north."

"Then why are you taking the chance?" she demanded.

"Because I'm a man, Kate, and by God, I've never backed down to a danger yet."

"Then neither shall I," she said decisively, and got to her feet. "I'm ready when you are."

Gilly stood regarding his daughter, one eye twitching, head pounding, and he longed mightily for a hair of the dog that bit him. "You don't seem to understand what I'm saying, Kathleen Moira," he began. "We've . . . I've made arrangements for you to stay here in Seattle. There's this boardinghouse where you'll be comfortable until—"

"Stay in Seattle?" Kate flared, her green eyes studying him through her glasses. "We?"

"Huh? Oh, it was just a slip of the tongue, Kate." Gilly made himself busy looking for his hat.

Kate's face grew thoughtful as she stood with her hip against the dresser where his battered hat lay. "How will you fend for yourself all alone?" she asked. "Who'll cook for you and mend your clothes?"

"Now, Kate, I do appreciate your offer, but I've tended to myself for all these years in the gold camps. I expect I can go on doing it." He bent to look under the bed, and clamped his hands to his head in pain.

"Yes, I suppose you could at that," Kate said, and, relenting, handed him his hat. With a grateful look Gilly placed it on his head and carefully adjusted the brim as if it were the finest hat money could buy. "By the way," Kate continued innocently, "has Hogan enough money to pay his share of the grubstake?"

"He's got it and he's rarin' to go." Gilly paused and glanced at her. "You were always too smart for your old man, Kathleen, even when you were a wee lass." Kate said nothing, letting her expression speak for itself. Gilly squirmed under her stern gaze.

"It's just that Hogan and I have been partners before. He's a good man and that's important when you're out somewhere in the mountains searching for gold. You need a man you can trust, someone who won't stab you in the back or try to steal your share of the claim. You understand, don't you, Kate?" he wheedled. He smiled with that old rapscallion charm that had once fooled an adoring daughter, but no more.

"I understand perfectly, Gilly," Kate said blandly.

He smiled in relief, then looked suspicious. "You're not trying to trick me, are you?"

"Why, Gilly, shame on you," Kate replied in pretended hurt. "I'm trying to be as forthright as you are with me."

"That's my girl," he said. "I always knew you were a chip off the old block, a game girl, Kate. That's what you are." He snapped the brim of his hat. "Well, I'm off to meet Hogan so we can make up our packs."

"May I come with you?" Kate asked demurely, and, pleased at how reasonable she had been, Gilly nodded expansively.

"Sure, come along, my girl. When you see what supplies we're forced to take, you'll be glad you're staying behind." Beaming, he held out an elbow for her to take. Arm in arm they descended the stairs.

"What's she doing here?" Hogan asked suspiciously when they met on the porch. His eyes were bloodshot and he looked as if he had slept in his clothes. He looked even bigger than he had the night before, if possible. Kate refused to be intimidated by him. She held her head stiffly, trying to avoid his eyes without appearing to do so.

"It's all right, Hogan. She knows about us being partners," Gilly hurried to explain. "She's agreed to stay behind."

Hogan eyed her warily. "I'm sorry it has to be this way," he said diffidently, "but you're just not a woman who could survive up there."

"Perhaps," Kate said enigmatically. "Shall we go look at that gear?" She preceded them down the steps while both men glared at each other behind her back.

Dodging horse-drawn wagons and drunks left over from the night before, they made their way to the warehouses near the wharf, where every imaginable kind of gear was available at an inflated price. Curiously Kate followed the men as they made up their packs. It was a time-consuming task, for their goods must last them for several months in the Yukon. Although there would be a chance to add to their supplies in Skagway, the prices would be even higher than here in Seattle. And once they crossed the mountain passes, there would be no trading posts for four hundred miles until they reached Dawson. They would have to hunt and fish to supplement their food supplies. Thoughtfully Kate watched as the bustling clerks filled the miners' orders. Obviously Hogan and Gilly were experienced and knew exactly what would be needed. They stuck with basics, such as flour and sugar, rice, barley and oatmeal, nails, mercury for a temperature gauge, and medicines. She was impressed by their thoroughness.

"We've still got some evaporated eggs," the store clerk said, his eyes bright as he studied the two men.

"I don't know," Gilly said, scratching his head. "Scrambled eggs would taste mighty good some mornings. We could use them to do some baking."

"Throw in fifty pounds of them," Hogan said.

"I wouldn't," Kate said under her breath. Hogan glanced at her sharply but shrugged away her warning.

When their packs were made up and the sum figured, the two men dug deep in their pockets, grumbling at the higher cost of things. Gilly counted out his cash and looked at Hogan sheepishly. Kate could hear the two of them whispering, and now and then they looked her way. She feigned indifference.

"You let yourself get robbed by a whore?" Hogan exploded, and Gilly blushed. Once again their voices lowered to a monotone. The clerk sighed impatiently. Hogan counted out his money, then counted it again, rummaging through his pockets before shaking his head. Gilly looked crestfallen, then glanced at Kate. She bit back her smile of triumph.

"Ummm, Kate," he said, leading her off to one side. "It turns out I'm a mite short for my share of the packs. If you could just see your way clear to lend me some of that money you had left after your Aunt Petty's furniture was sold off . . ."

"Certainly, Gilly," Kate said, but she never opened

her purse. Arms crossed over her chest, she met his gaze calmly, a smile curving her lips.

"Well . . ." Gilly said, wriggling his fingers coaxingly. She made no move and he glanced up, catching sight of her expression. "Now, Kate," he said warningly, "I thought we'd agreed."

"That was before you wanted to borrow my money," Kate said firmly.

"That makes no never-mind now," he said, glancing over his shoulder at Hogan, who was watching them with a dark scowl on his face.

"You can't dump me as a partner and still expect to use my money," Kate insisted.

"I never agreed to be your partner," Gilly shouted, then quickly lowered his voice. "You just came along on your own. I never wanted you along."

Kate kept her face perfectly straight, never revealing how much his words hurt. "Then you shan't have my money. It's precious little and I shall need it until I find a teaching job here in Seattle."

"You won't need all of it, Kate," Gilly argued.

"I may." She was adamant. "Of course, if I were going along, it wouldn't matter so much. I wouldn't be paying room and board. Prices are just going to skyrocket here in Seattle. Come to think of it, I don't have a penny to spare."

"All right, all right!" Gilly snapped, his skinny jowls quivering.

"I can come?"

"If you're in such an all-fired state to come along, then yes. Just give me the money."

"You won't change your mind again?" Kate demanded, opening her purse.

"No, no," Gilly snapped irritably. "Hurry up. Give me the money."

Kate held it out to him, then snapped it back. "Maybe I'd better keep track of it," she said pleasantly. "I'm very good with figures. Shall we tell Mr. O'Shea that he has another partner?" Kate walked to the counter, where Hogan and the sales clerk waited.

"You tell him the good news, Gilly," Kate said brightly. "I have a few more supplies to pick out."

"Ah, um, Kate's going with us," Gilly said, shuffling his feet and looking at the floor.

"What!" Hogan roared, his eyes bulging, his face growing red. He glared at Kate and back at her father. "In a pig's eye, she is," he snapped. "Are you daft, man? She can't go!"

"I didn't have much choice," Gilly defended himself. "She's got the money."

"We don't want the evaporated eggs," Kate said to the sales clerk. The sly smile faded from his florid face and he glanced at the two men. "Please remove them from the pack and give us fifty pounds more of flour and sugar, thirty pounds of salt—"

"Leave those eggs there," Hogan shouted at the bewildered clerk before turning back to Gilly. "I tell you she's not going. That's final. She would never last up there."

"Why wouldn't I last, Mr. O'Shea?" Kate asked calmly, fixing him with her sternest glare.

"Because you're . . . you're too persnickety . . . too prissy," Hogan got out, his black eyes looking her up and down. He waved his hands at her. "Look at you, all got up like you're going to a tea party. How long do you think you'd keep your gloves clean digging for gold?"

"You're quite right," Kate said in her most reasonable tone. "Give me a pair of men's pants, size small, shirt, long johns, jacket, and mittens," she ordered the clerk. She could hear Hogan gritting his teeth behind her. "And take out the eggs and give us fifty pounds of cornmeal instead." She fixed the man with a steady eye. "But then, they're one and the same, aren't they? Only when it's called cornmeal, it's much cheaper, isn't it?"

"What?" Hogan shouted, his anger at Kate momentarily forgotten as he looked at the clerk. His long arm reached across the counter, his big fist knotted in the man's shirt, and he shook him roughly. "Were you fixing to sham us?" he demanded.

"N-no, sir," the man stammered. "It was an honest mistake. I'll adjust the bill. I'll even throw in the outfit for the lady." Mollified, Hogan released his shirtfront and stepped back.

"Thanks, partner," Kate said saucily, and ignored the wince of pain on both men's faces. "I guess we'd better see to our passage next. Gentlemen, we are on our way to the Klondike."

"This is a mistake," Hogan grumbled. "A woman can't go to Alaska."

"Why not, Mr. O'Shea?" Kate asked crisply, nimbly leaping over the sprawled legs of a drunk. Breathlessly she hurried to keep pace as he stalked toward the wharves. Gilly followed along behind, saying nothing but shaking his head in disapproval and resignation. They were on their way to book passage on the *Portland*, which was waiting only until goods and passengers could be loaded before returning to Alaska.

"Why not, Mr. O'Shea?" Kate insisted. "Aren't women as smart as men, as strong or as capable? Or is it just that we don't sit in the bars elbow to elbow and try to outdrink each other?"

"That's not it at all," he snapped, dodging around a post. "I just never heard of women traipsing off to the Yukon to search for gold. It's not . . ." He paused and looked at her, then at Gilly. "Well, it's not dignified, not ladylike, that's all."

"I assure you, Mr. O'Shea, I am every inch a lady," Kate said, drawing herself up grandly, and he believed her. "But a lady can do more than . . . than set a table or converse genteelly," Kate hurried on. "We can search for gold as well. You needn't worry—I'll carry my share of the work." He didn't believe that.

"It's harder work than you ever imagined possible," he said, and in spite of the press of time, he faced Gilly and her, unleashing all his charm in an attempt to persuade her that this was sheer madness. "The hardships in the North Country are like nothing you're ever likely to encounter elsewhere, Miss O'Riley," he said earnestly. Kate was mesmerized by the warmth in his dark eyes.

"Listen to him, Kate, he's telling the truth," Gilly said at her elbow.

"There's fierce cold that'll take a leg or arm faster than you can blink an eye, and bears and wolves that'll attack a man just for the food."

"It's true. I've heard those tales myself," Gilly said earnestly, returning her gaze innocently. He'd already learned that his daughter could be pigheaded and stubborn when she set her mind to something.

"There's never enough food," Hogan continued.

"I don't eat much," Kate said, casting a quick measuring glance over her shoulder at her father. They were ganging up on her.

"It's not a question of eating too much, Miss Kate," Hogan broke in. "It's a question of not being eaten yourself. There're Indians up there that eat human flesh if they don't have anything else, and men who'll kill you just for your claim. Gold camps get rough. They're not fit for women." Once again his dark warm gaze moved over her face.

Quickly Kate looked away and chanced to see a trio of gaudily dressed women boarding the *Portland*. Roxanne Blayne was one of them. A couple of besotted sailors followed behind with their baggage.

"If that's true, Mr. O'Shea, then pray tell me what those women are doing," she said sweetly. Hogan looked around, and she had the pleasure of seeing his lips tighten in anger.

"Those women aren't ladies like you, Miss Kate."

"Oh?" She looked wide-eyed and innocent. "Then what are they, Mr. O'Shea?"

He looked sheepish. "Well, ma'am, they're dancing girls sent to entertain the miners."

"I see," Kate replied dryly. "And do they not need food to eat and do they not face the same dangers?" She could see the resignation in his eyes.

"Yes, ma'am, they do," he answered. "But they're used to hardships. They've been in gold camps before. They're—"

"Experienced?" Kate asked, arching an eyebrow.

Hogan cast a baleful glare at Gilly who'd wisely remained silent.

"You might say that," he answered.

"Then I'm sure I can gain those same skills—"

"Kate!" Gilly thundered warningly.

"—in survival." Kate smiled. Hogan glared and Gilly mumbled under his breath about the perfidy of women. Without another word, Hogan strode off toward the wharf and the ticket office.

Kate chuckled to herself. She was curious about the Yukon. There had been little talk of anything else this morning at the breakfast table and in the streets. Now she was about to see the wondrous things about which the miners spoke—glaciers, great frozen rivers, bears and moose, and Eskimo. Hogan hadn't realized that everything he'd said had only enticed her more. Suddenly she felt the call that had claimed many an adventurer, the need to pit herself and her puny human strength and intelligence against a greater force than she'd ever known before.

Just think, she mused as she followed Hogan. She might have missed this. She might even now have been sitting in a stuffy classroom trying to teach Greek or mathematics, or worse yet, needlework. Cheerfully Kate opened her umbrella against the fine mist that had begun to fall and marched along behind, humming a fine lilting Irish tune.

Hogan heard the happy little hum and the muscles of his back tightened. Dad-blasted woman, he thought. How'd he ever get himself in this fix? But he knew. He needed a partner and Gilly was the best a man could wish for. Hogan had come to feel some affection and much respect for the rascally old man. Gilly was a good friend to drink with, but even more, when the drinking and womanizing were done, he was a hard-working man, never shunting his share of the digging, and he was honest. That counted for a lot when the chips were down and you had to place your trust in a partner.

Besides, Kate had the money. If he wanted Gilly as a partner, he didn't have much choice. He had to take

Kate. He glared at her over his shoulder, but she seemed not to notice. Well, he wouldn't let her put a crimp in his style. He'd continue his ways as if a woman weren't present, and if Kate O'Riley didn't like it, she could take her dad-blasted sensibilities and go back to wherever she came from.

3

At a cost of fifteen dollars each, they booked passage aboard the *Portland,* bound for Skagway. From there they would push on to the goldfields overland. To travel all the way by boat up the Yukon River would have cost two hundred dollars apiece, far more than their meager funds could cover.

Kate's enthusiasm for their outing continued through the transporting of their luggage and supply packs to the *Portland* and ended abruptly when she saw the accommodations Hogan had made. One large room without the benefit of privacy of any sort for its occupants held dozens of bunks built against the walls and even down the center, so there were only narrow walkways between. Two small portholes, one on each side, provided a meager light. In one corner sat a bucket, the only means by which the passengers might relieve themselves. The stench was terrible. Kate gasped and pressed a handkerchief to her nose.

Hogan grinned. "Sorry the staterooms were taken, Miss O'Riley," he said, strolling to one of the bunks and slapping his baggage on top with a resounding thump of ownership. Gilly had done the same. Hogan turned and studied her, the rakish, triumphant grin all too evident. "Want to change your mind?"

Kate longed for nothing more than just that, but she would not give this smug, overbearing man the satisfaction of routing her. She wouldn't fold up at the first sign of discomfort as he hoped she would. Besides, the women's room might be better.

Shrugging nonchalantly, she returned his smile brightly. "I have no intention of changing my mind," she said gaily. She caught herself as the people behind jostled forward. Hogan's grin never changed, but his eyes turned dark and she knew that once again she'd angered him with her obstinance. Her own smile widened.

Hogan nodded to the people behind her. "You'd better get a bunk, then," he ordered. "They're liable to stomp right over you."

Kate leapt aside as more people shoved forward, nearly knocking her down. Wide-eyed, she glanced back at Hogan and her father.

"That's why they call them stampeders," Gilly said, shaking his head at the crowd which quickly filled the room, racing for the bunks as if their very lives depended on it. "Get a bunk, Kate, girl," Gilly called.

"Here? With all these strange men?" she asked, turning around in bewilderment, her canvas portmanteau clutched to her chest. "Surely the women will sleep separately from the men."

"This is it, m'lady," Hogan said with a mocking bow, hand extended to the bunk beneath his. In dismay Kate looked at the shelf. Even as she hesitated, a man rushed forward to drop his bedroll on the mattress. Deftly Hogan flipped the bag away and placed one booted foot on the cross rail, his knee blocking any other squatter who meant to take up residency there. "Your chamber awaits, madam," he said with that damnable grin still in place. Kate longed to slap it from his face. Instead she looked around for another empty bunk, but all were taken.

Even now, more people spilled down the stairs, and it was obvious someone would have to sleep on the floor. Hogan was doing her a favor by holding the bunk for her, she realized, but he didn't have to be so smug, so reasonable in the face of her unreasonableness. It galled. Besides, she didn't want to sleep near Hogan O'Shea. But she had no choice. She'd set her mind on this, she reminded herself, and she'd been fairly warned. She placed her bag on the lower bunk, but he lifted it to the top.

"I think you'll be safer there," he explained, his dark eyes glinting with laughter.

"But how am I to get up there?" Kate asked, looking around for a stepladder.

Hogan held up his hand like a magician about to astound all by effecting a miracle. He heaved a keg forward against the bunkhead. "Madam," he said with a flourish. He was enjoying every bit of her dismay.

Kate forced herself to relax, and even brushed against him. "You are so kind to take such good care of me," she simpered, batting her eyelashes the way she'd seen Roxanne do.

Hogan scowled. "Just remember you'll have to take care of yourself once you're on the trail," he said gruffly.

"Oh, you needn't worry about me," Kate said as she climbed up on the keg. The top bunk was still too high for her to crawl up without swinging her knee up, which would raise her skirts and expose a considerable amount of leg to the scoundrel below. Bracing her hands against the railing, Kate tried to heave herself up, but hadn't the strength, so she teetered half up and half down, until she felt a large palm plant itself firmly on her derriere and give her a final push upward. She landed in an outraged heap on her bunk, and when she glared over its edge, her furious gaze met Hogan O'Shea's sparkling dark eyes.

"You're right, Miss O'Riley," he said. "I won't worry about you. I suspect you can always find someone to give you a helping hand."

"If you're through manhandling my daughter . . ." Gilly said, and for a moment Kate had hope that he was about to put Hogan in his place. But he slapped the big man fondly on the shoulders. "Let's go up on deck and look around," he said. Without a backward glance, the two men left, their bedrolls securing their bunks, their friendship untouched by anything Hogan might do to her. Afraid she wouldn't be able to get back into her bunk, and unwilling to suffer the ignominy of Hogan O'Shea's dubious help, Kate lay back on the bunk. The mattress was thin and lumpy, but it would do, she decided. Then the excitement of their departure faded and she fell into an exhausted sleep.

They sailed out of Puget Sound, past the green islands that protected the mouth of the harbor, and out to sea. The water was sparkling green, with small whitecaps dancing on its surface. The interminable rain had been left behind in Seattle and the sun shone brightly. Before the day was out, Kate was hanging over the railing, her hand clamped to her stomach in a paroxysm of seasickness. By the time they neared Victoria, their first stop, she was pale, weak, and fatigued.

Hogan was seemingly as robust and untouched by human discomfort as ever. Often Kate heard his ribald laughter and hearty voice in jubilant discussion with the other stampeders, and he seemed to spend an equal amount of time with Roxanne Blayne and the other saloon girls, who had managed to secure a stateroom and were taking the boat all the way to Dawson.

Kate stood pale and trembling by the rail, enjoying her first sojourn abovedeck in three days. Suddenly a familiar and odious voice sounded behind her.

" 'Morning, Miss O'Riley," Hogan O'Shea greeted her, amiably tipping his hat. As usual, Roxanne Blayne clung to his arm. She grinned and pulled her skirts aside fastidiously in a parody of Kate's behavior back in Seattle.

Gritting her teeth, Kate managed a smile. "Mr. O'Shea," she said evenly, and clamped a lacy handkerchief to her mouth as her stomach revolted. Roxanne grinned.

"I believe you've met Miss Blayne?" he asked politely.

"I don't remember, I'm sure," Roxanne said haughtily. Kate only glared. How dared he put her in this position, where she must acknowledge his doxy! She longed to give him a piece of her mind, but her stomach was rolling dangerously. When she said nothing, Hogan tipped his hat once more.

"Good day to you, Miss O'Riley."

Valiantly Kate tried not to make a sound until they

had passed out of sight, but when she heard their footsteps fade, she leaned over the rail and gave way to relieving her nausea. The ocean was heaving green motion below. She stood gripping the rail with white-knuckled intensity while dizziness swept over her. Clamping her eyes shut, Kate was certain that she would fall into the tossing waves. A moan of terror escaped her.

Suddenly, strong arms lifted her away from the railing, shoving her to the deck floor. Nimble fingers, familiar with the hooks and intricacies of female clothing, worked at her bodice and the constricting corset beneath. Kate moaned again and opened her eyes. Hogan O'Shea knelt over her, his big hands loosening her clothes.

"How dare you," she cried, slapping at him weakly. "Aren't your dance-hall floozies enough for you?" She glared up at him, too weak to stand up as she wished, and feeling the humiliation of being sprawled on the deck in full view of any who chose to pass. Her cheeks grew mottled with outrage and embarrassment.

Hogan's face darkened in anger and he sat back on his haunches. "I was just trying to help you," he snapped. "I thought you meant to jump into the sea, the way you were leaning over that railing."

"I . . . I was about to do no such thing," Kate cried. "I was indisposed. You had no right to . . . to bother me at such a moment. There are times when a person requires privacy." Hogan grinned and she knew he was thinking about the night she'd come to the Paris House. Groaning, she closed her eyes and laid her head against the rail.

"Open your eyes," he commanded.

"What?"

"Open your eyes and look at the horizon." Tenderly he smoothed the loose hair back from her flushed cheeks. His touch was surprisingly gentle and soothing. Kate opened her eyes and stared at him as if he'd taken leave of his senses. "Do it," he coaxed, and despite herself, she complied.

"Ooh, no, I can't," she sighed wearily, her hands gripping her middle.

"Trust me, Kate," he urged. "Look at the horizon. After a while your equilibrium will return and your stomach will settle. Come on." He sat down on the deck beside her, one long arm closing around her shoulders and pulling her closer. "Rest your head back against me, but keep your eyes fixed on that line of sky out there."

Kate held herself stiff in his casual embrace and concentrated fiercely on the horizon where swelling ocean and gray sky met. Perspiration trickled down her cheeks and bile rose in her throat, but she swallowed hard and willed her stomach to calm itself. She couldn't bear the humiliation of retching in front of Hogan O'Shea and his dancing girl. She glanced around, but Roxanne was nowhere in sight.

"Relax," Hogan said softly, and his voice was husky in her ear, sending shivers through her body. "Are you chilled?" he inquired solicitously.

Kate shook her head. "No, no." But he pulled her closer, tucking her under his shoulder, his big body blocking the wind from the ocean. And so they sat flat on the floor of the stern deck, their legs stretched out before them. She felt the weight of Hogan's cheek against her brow and was at once troubled and comforted by it. Anyone who came along would think them lovers, Kate realized, but made no effort to move away. Strangely enough, her stomach had grown quieter and she felt better than she had since leaving Puget Sound.

"Is it working?" he asked.

"Yes." Kate nodded and tried to pull away, but his big hand held her against him.

"Give yourself some more time," he advised. Once more she relaxed against him. Now that the nausea had passed, she was aware of the big body that supported her. It felt rock-solid. He might be a big man, but every inch of him was muscle. The thought made her blush, and she couldn't help wondering about the hard limbs and deep chest beneath the bulky clothes. His long legs stretched out along the deck; his feet, encased in rubber-soled leather shoepacs, dwarfed her own slim feet, encased as they were in modish sharp-toed, high-topped shoes.

Hogan seemed to follow her line of thought, for he shifted impatiently. "You brought some warmer boots, didn't you?" he growled.

Kate pulled her feet and the offending boots back under her full skirt and nodded. "You needn't worry about me, Mr. O'Shea," she said peevishly. "I've brought plenty of warm clothes."

"Then you'd best be getting into them as soon as we reach Skagway," he ordered. He studied her face, and self-consciously Kate tucked back a strand of hair.

"What about these?" He reached for the wire-rimmed glasses that rested against her nose. Kate's hands came up to reclaim them, but he placed them on his own nose. Curiously he peered through them. "Do you need these to see?"

Kate nodded. "I can't read without them."

"But can you see without them?" he insisted.

Slowly she nodded. "I suppose I can see well enough. It was just easier to keep wearing them."

"Try to get along without them," he advised. "You can't wear them once we reach the Yukon." He turned his head to look down at her and their glances tangled and held. Kate felt her breath catch in her chest. Her head was still tucked against his shoulder, and their lips were scant inches apart.

"Why not?" she asked faintly.

His breath was hot against her cheek. "The wire frames will freeze against your skin," he said softly, and slowly his head moved, erasing those inches that separated them. She felt the brush of warm, smooth lips against hers, the tickle of his beard against her chin and cheek. The contact startled her, causing her to jump, and Hogan pulled back.

"I'm sorry," he said, and she was disappointed. She didn't want him to be sorry.

"You take advantage of me, sir," she said pettishly. Her hands fluttered with her wire frames and finally she set them firmly on her nose again.

"Not the actions of a gentleman, I know," Hogan began, his words humble, his tone not. He straightened and pulled his arm away, glancing along the deck as he did so. Suddenly he froze, his chin jutting, his mouth grim. Feeling the tenseness in him, Kate glanced at his face and then along the deck. A man had appeared at the other end and was strolling toward them. Suddenly he caught sight of the two of them seated on the floor and paused, his face reflecting his consternation.

Kate felt a fool and made a move to rise, but Hogan was ahead of her, leaping to his feet and moving swiftly forward. The man crouched, looked in both directions, then whirled and ran back along the deck, his footsteps loud against the planking. Without a word Hogan ran after him, and the two of them disappeared out of sight. Openmouthed, Kate stared after them; then, miffed at being abandoned in such a manner, she got to her feet and shook out her skirts. She was disgusted with herself and with Hogan. Her cheeks were hot and flushed and she stood trying to compose herself, vowing never ever to speak to Hogan O'Shea again, when he reappeared at her elbow.

"I'm sorry to leave you like that," he said, slightly out of breath.

"That's quite all right, Mr. O'Shea," she said evenly. "I've come to expect such behavior from you."

He studied her face, standing with legs braced wide, hands planted on his hips in a gesture that she'd come to recognize as one of his. "What kind of behavior might that be?" he demanded. "As if I couldn't guess. Was I once again too ungentlemanly for the lady, or perhaps I was too much the gentleman?"

"What do you mean?" Immediately she was sorry she had asked.

"Perhaps I shouldn't have pulled away from that kiss. Is that it? Perhaps you'd like me to finish what I started." His hands gripped her arms, pulling her forward against his chest, bending over her so she was forced to lean against him. Only his strong arm at her back supported her. The ocean wind, cold and damp, blew against their figures and he seemed impervious to the elements, while she shivered helplessly in his grip.

"Please, let me go," she cried, trembling. She felt a lessening of the rage that gripped him, an easing of the coiled tension in his large body. Slowly he released her and stepped back. His chest still rose and fell quickly and she knew this time he was out of breath for quite another reason than before. Yet she felt confused by her thoughts, afraid to trust her instincts about this man as she so often did about others.

"Once again I've acted the ruffian," he said with an air of resignation that he'd failed in something he'd wished to do.

"Please don't blame yourself," she said quickly, and reached out one pale, slim hand to touch him, then snatched it back, clenching a fist against her chest as if to still her emotions. She straightened, stiffening her back and demeanor. "Somehow we're both to blame, Mr. O'Shea. We seem to bring out the worst in each other." She was aware of his dark eyes regarding her, but she kept her face averted, her expression aloof.

"Contrary to what you may think of me, Miss O'Riley, I'm not a bad person. I may drink hard, fight, and womanize, but I wouldn't force myself on a lady like yourself."

"I didn't mean to intimate you would," Kate began defensively.

"What?" Hogan looked at her, and a smile tugged at the corners of his mouth.

"I said I—"

"What was that word, 'inti . . .'?"

"Intimate," Kate said. "It means to imply, insinuate, accuse of." Her explanation died away.

Hogan O'Shea stood shaking his head as if in disbelief, and that familiar mocking smile grew in his eyes. "You even talk like a schoolteacher," he said. "What are we going to do with you up here?"

Kate's cheeks flushed, this time with anger. "I've told you several times, you needn't do anything with me. I am a free agent. I will take care of myself."

"You're a snapdragon, all bite on the outside and yet all delicate petals underneath. Look at your hand." He took hold of it. "So pale and thin I can almost see through it. I've drunk coffee from cups thicker than this." He held her hand up for her to see. Kate snatched it away.

"I should have known," she snapped. "For a little while you seemed nice, like a regular human being, capable of sensitivity and refinement, but you always revert to your boorish ways."

"And you, Miss High and Mighty O'Riley, always revert to your prudish, prideful, mule-headed ways." He swung about and stalked down the deck.

"Mule-headed?" Kate repeated, following him. "If either of us is mule-headed, Mr. O'Shea, I assure you it is not I. I have tried to be courteous and pleasant to you, and you in turn have been insulting and . . . and lascivious."

"Lascivious? Lascivious?" Hogan repeated, not quite sure what the word meant, but damned if he'd let her know that.

"That and more, Mr. O'Shea," Kate snapped. "I've seen how you consort with those . . . those women."

"You've been spying on me then?" He whirled, fixing her with a dark stare.

"Of course not," Kate said, unintimidated by him. "One could hardly fail to notice your comings and goings. You've been so obvious about them."

"Why would you be keeping tabs on me, Miss O'Riley? Could it be you're a little jealous?"

"Jea . . ." Words failed her. She gasped for air, opening and closing her mouth, but nothing came.

"Or is it that you're curious?" Still she said nothing, too angry to respond. "I thought as much," Hogan said, misinterpreting her silence. He jerked her forward into his arms. She was pressed against his broad chest, and before she could utter a protest, his mouth descended on hers. His lips were firm and warm, pressing urgently against hers. His tongue, a hot, moist spear, thrust against her lips, and when they parted, invaded her mouth. Kate squirmed against him, trying to free herself, until she realized her efforts were only bringing her in closer contact with his hard body. One long muscled arm shifted lower and his wide palm cupped itself around her buttocks, pulling her hips tightly against his. She could feel the hard bulge of his manhood and grew still at the wave of feeling that enveloped her.

An ache, of youth and unnamed yearnings, sprang to life deep in the core of her, spreading outward until she sighed with the urgency of it. She stopped fighting him, and unknowingly her mouth relaxed beneath his, giving him better access. Her tongue, soft and timid, met his, touched then darted away, and he couldn't coax it back. He was surprised by her earthy, passionate response. He'd expected her to remain rigid and unyielding in his embrace. Instead, he tasted the woman she could be. The discovery was heady.

Other passengers, drawn by the commotion of their verbal argument, had stayed to witness its outcome. Now they cheered mightily. Kate had grown pliant in his arms, her body bending against his like a willow. Now he felt her stiffen as she grew aware of their audience. Silently he cursed their intrusion. Slowly he released her. She turned her head away, one trembling hand pressing against her lips.

"Atta boy, Hogan. He always gets the ladies," someone called, and he saw the steel forming in Kate's jaw as she turned back to face him.

"Not quite always," she said, and brought her bag around. It was weighted by the gold pieces she'd put there for their journey. Propelled around as it was on its strap, the bag gained momentum and landed squarely against Hogan's eye. A hoot of laughter sounded from the onlookers.

"Oww," he cried, and clamped a hand to his eye. With his good eye he could see Kate winding up again. "Now, wait a minute," he cried, putting out a hand to stop her, but she twirled the bag again, and this time it thudded with deadly accuracy against his jaw. He managed to grab the bag before she wound up again.

"Kate, wait a minute," he yelled, but a sharp pain seared his shin as she kicked him with the toe of her boot. Hogan bent double, grabbing hold of his injured leg and hopping about on one foot. The other men hooted and called encouragement.

Kate whirled to face him, hands on hips, bonnet askew, head thrown back in triumph and arrogance. "I will thank you, Mr. O'Shea, never to put your hands on my person again," she said haughtily, while he gritted his teeth.

"You may rest assured it will never happen again, Miss O'Riley," he snapped. "I have a need for prickly pears only when the fruit beneath is sweet."

Kate gasped. "And I have no desire to be kissed by a man who . . . who engages in the disgusting habit of chewing tobacco." She scrubbed at her mouth as if to demonstrate how unpleasant his kiss had been. "You are truly the most loathsome and ungallant of men."

"And you are truly the one woman on this boat safest from my misguided attentions," he answered, and turned away from her outraged face. Roxanne stepped forward and put her arm around him.

"Come on, honey," she said in a loud husky voice. "I'll show you how a real woman treats a gentleman." She swished her skirts while the men cheered. Kate's face grew pink.

Casting a last glance after Hogan's departing figure, she gathered her shawl around her shoulders and turned toward the companionway. She felt shaken and ashamed of the encounter with Hogan. Somehow they seemed always to end up in an argument, and each one grew uglier than the last. She was mortified by the way she'd behaved, swinging on him like one of those horrid women in the streets. She was little better than Roxanne and the rest of her kind.

Gilly broke free of the crowd of men and fell into step beside her. "Kate . . ." he began, scratching at his jaw in a sign she recognized that meant he was about to talk to her about something that he'd rather avoid. Kate felt herself brace for his words.

"It ain't seemly for a lady to act like that," he said, nodding back toward the knot of men.

"You're right, Gilly," she said. "My behavior wasn't ladylike." She offered no apology.

"Whatever the problem between you and Hogan, you'll have to work it out," he advised her. "When we get out there in the back country, we'll need to depend on each other. We can't have hard feelings. They get in the way."

"Perhaps you should talk to Mr. O'Shea," Kate snapped. Somehow she'd known he would take up for Hogan. She walked away from him, her backbone stiff. Gilly watched her go and sighed.

"Kate, I'm just saying try to bury the hatchet," he yelled after her.

"Happily," she called over her shoulder, "and directly in Mr. O'Shea's thick skull."

Too keyed-up to go to the cabin, Kate walked along the deck and thought of the encounter with Hogan. She was mortified by the way she'd behaved, swinging on him like a fisherman's wife. She preferred not to think of the way she'd responded to his kiss or that he was probably with Roxanne this very moment.

Kate stayed in the cabin until they reached Victoria, where they stopped to pick up supplies and passengers. Then they were on their way to Skagway, which was a full five days away. Kate came up on deck for brief walks only when nausea threatened. Concentrating on the horizon at such times did seem to work, and she passed along the tip to another passenger who suffered the same response to the turbulent ocean.

He was a nice young man, about her age, possibly a year or two younger. Clean-shaven and slender, he obviously had come from a refined background, unlike most of the rowdy ruffians making their way to Alaska. She had no chance to talk to him, though, respecting his need for privacy while in the grip of his malady.

At Juneau they left the *Portland*. A stern-wheeler would carry them the rest of the way up to Skagway. Juneau was a rough frontier town with a small wharf, muddy streets, and no sidewalks. Tree stumps still stood in the main street, and although Kate wondered what Skagway must be like, sitting, as it did, farther north, she was happy not to stay in Juneau more than one night.

A small sturdy schooner carried them through the clear blue waters of the Lynn Canal. Kate stood at the rail with the rest of the passengers, marveling at the beauty and majesty of the snow-capped mountains that ringed the narrow fjord. She'd never seen anything so magnificent. Despite the seasickness and cramped accommodations, she was glad she'd come.

"They call this the Great Land," a voice said at her elbow, and Kate turned to find the young man who'd suffered from seasickness on the *Portland*. "I'm Clay Lawford. Thanks for the tip about the horizon. I think you saved my life."

"I'm glad it helped. I'm Kate O'Riley." She studied him more closely. His complexion had gained some color now and she saw that his eyes were a fine clear blue beneath sandy brows. His hair was of the same color and was combed neatly in place. His clothes, though rumpled, were of a good quality and he held himself confidently. Kate found herself smiling at the young man in approval.

"May I join you at the rail?" he asked, indicating an empty spot. Kate nodded and moved to one side to give him more room. "This is incredible," Clay Lawford said warmly. "You could never make the folks back home see the power of these mountains, not by word or picture."

"No, you couldn't," Kate agreed. "They would have to see it for themselves."

"Have you family back home, Miss O'Riley?"

"I'm here with my father. Have you?"

"My mother and sisters and a fiancée," he replied, then laughed diffidently, as if telling a gentle joke on himself. "I'm the only man in a household of women. I guess that's why I came out here before settling down. I wanted a little adventure, and if my partners and I get rich in the process, well, so much the better."

"There's nothing wrong with wanting adventure or gold, Mr. Lawford," Kate said pleasantly.

"Few ladies seem to be making this trip," Clay observed. "You're very brave." His blue gaze was admiring.

Kate blushed prettily. "Brave or foolhardy. I can't decide which." She laughed, and marveled at how easy and enjoyable it was to converse with someone who was obviously well-educated and introspective. Clay Lawford could never engage in the debauchery and depravity of women and wine as Hogan O'Shea did. They stood talking and admiring the scenery for some time, and Kate was sorry to see the journey end. But Skagway lay straight ahead. Like Juneau, the town lay in the lee of the towering mountains, although in fact they were eight miles away.

The passengers gathered their baggage, talking animatedly. The air was charged with excitement. They were that much closer to the goldfields, and within days some of them would be digging for the golden nuggets. Men stood at the rail studying the mountains and Chilkoot Pass, thirty-five miles long, rising steep and unyielding, a barrier that must be crossed if they were to reach the goldfields. Some gave up then and there and never even disembarked, while heartier souls surged down the gangplank, pushing into the tent city that served merely as a stopping-off place.

Kate stood back from the gangplank, waiting for Gilly and Hogan to catch up to her. There was no reason to shove and push, she thought, and watched the elated, impatient men.

"Kate, there you are, girl," Gilly called, and soon he and Hogan were at her side, each laden with bags and packages. The rest of their supplies were packed in crates and would be unloaded later.

"Miss O'Riley!" Clay Lawford waved to her. Kate smiled and waved back. There was little chance she'd ever see the young man again.

"Who's that?" Hogan demanded abruptly, staring after Clay.

Kate sniffed. "A gentleman I met on the boat," she answered haughtily.

"What is he, a schoolteacher?" Hogan asked, eyeing him warily.

"I believe that, like you, Mr. O'Shea, he's come to search for gold."

"A greener." Hogan sneered dismissively. "Come on, let's get off this tub." Kate followed Gilly down the gangplank, with Hogan bringing up the rear. Men were jostling and shoving impatiently. Someone bumped into Kate's back so hard she nearly lost her balance and fell. Temper rising, she turned, intending to give Hogan a tongue-lashing, certain he'd done it on purpose. To her surprise, he wasn't behind her. She could see him still on the deck above, talking to the same man he'd chased on the *Portland*. Even as she watched, he gathered the man's shirtfront in his fists and shook him. The man waved his hands placatingly, shaking his head in denial of whatever accusation Hogan had made. Finally Hogan let him go. With a last glance over his shoulder, the little man scampered down the gangplank, pushing aside those ahead of him. Kate watched closely as he shoved past her. When he reached the wharf, he paused and said something to another man, pointing back up the ramp at Hogan; then he hurried away, disappearing in the crowd.

The stampeders pushed forward, disgorging themselves on the wharves of Skagway like a school of whales offered up to the tender barbs of the fishermen, and like those erstwhile fishers, the con men of Skagway netted the unsuspecting.

Kate's quick eye caught a pocket being picked, but before she could make an outcry, the perpetrator had melted into the crowd. Other men pushed forward, offering advice and information, guiding the newcomers to saloons, stores, and gambling houses. An air of festivity reigned over the wharves and town. Snow covered the landscape and had been trampled to a dirty slush beneath their feet. The muddy streets of Skagway were lined on either side by tents and half-finished, roughly sawed wood-frame buildings. There was nothing of grace and comfort in the squat ugly collection of hovels. One building, larger than the rest, though no grander, held a crudely painted sign proclaiming it to be Clancy's Saloon.

An old prospector approached Gilly and Kate. "Howdy," he said, taking out a chaw of tobacco and cutting a plug for himself. His whiskers and the corners of his mouth were already tobacco-stained. His clothes were well-worn, as if he'd spent many a month in the wilderness. Offering Gilly a plug, he made a motion toward the milling crowd. "Ain't that something?" he asked with barely concealed glee. "Most of them fools don't even know what they're in for. Half of them ain't even prepared."

"They'll thin out fast enough," Gilly said.

The man squinted against the late sun. "You've done this before, I reckon," he said.

Gilly nodded. "Not here, but pretty near everywhere else."

"I'll tell you what," the man said. "Go on over to the information tent down the street on your right. They've got good maps, true maps. You'll need 'em once you get over the pass."

"Much obliged," Gilly said, and turned to Kate. "Tell Hogan I've gone down for some maps. I'll be needing some money."

"How much will they cost?" she asked, opening her bag.

"I don't know," Gilly said, "but give me extra, in case I see something we need."

Kate counted out ten five-dollar gold pieces and gave them to him. The old prospector shut one eye and spat a mouthful of tobacco juice into the dirty slush.

"Stay with the goods until Hogan gets here," Gilly instructed, and turned to the old man. "Which way, old-timer?" The prospector led the way down the muddy street. Kate watched until they disappeared into one of the tents.

Men milled around outside, some with pistols strapped to their hips or rifles riding easy but ever ready in the crooks of their arms. Settling herself on a packing crate, she waited. An old man, wiry and bent, his eyes still lively and alert behind his tangled hair, sidled close. Kate looked at him in alarm.

"Don't be afeered," he said softly. "I won't be hurtin' no one. I'm Axel Fredericks. My friends call me Axe."

"Hello, Axe," Kate answered, and took the rough hand he'd extended.

"Are you goin' over the top?" he asked, leaning toward her eagerly.

"What?" Kate asked in some confusion.

"The summit. Are you goin' over the Chilkoot Pass?" the old man asked.

"Yes, I believe we are," Kate said, and wondered if she should even be talking to him. He seemed harmless enough.

"I'll tote your pack over for you."

"I don't know . . ." Kate began. He looked too thin and frail to carry himself over the summit, much less tons of supplies.

"I'm stronger than I look," he said, as if reading her mind. He stood up and puffed his chest a little. He was a comical figure, and Kate was hard put not to laugh at him.

"I'll have to ask my partners," she said. "I'm sorry."

"I'm needin' some money for a grubstake," Axe said. "Would you put in a word for me with them?"

"I'll see what I can do," Kate promised. With a doff of his fur-lined cap, he shuffled away down the wharf. Kate sat wondering how long he'd been in Alaska. She didn't see Hogan until he was at her elbow.

"Where's Gilly?" he asked, dumping his packs beside those Kate guarded.

"He went up the street to get maps," she answered. "He should be back shortly. Who was that man you were talking to? Was he the same one you chased on the *Portland*?"

Hogan glanced at her sharply. "You have a quick eye."

"You haven't answered my question," she prodded.

He seated himself on the packs, and taking out a chaw of tobacco, cut himself a plug much as the old prospector had done. Glancing up, he caught sight of Kate's expression and hesitated, then with a sigh put it back in his pouch. "Yeah, it was the same man," he said. A ruckus down the street claimed his attention.

"He didn't seem to be a friend," Kate persisted.

"His name's George Sawyer. You don't make friends with that kind of man. He used to run with Fletcher Meade."

"Who's he?" Kate asked.

"A crook and a murderer. He worked all the gold camps down south, pulling one con game after another—cardsharping, shell games, whatever it took to part a man and his gold dust. If some poor soul protested too loudly, Fletch had him killed." The commotion down the street had grown. Uneasily Hogan studied the town.

"You don't suppose Fletcher Meade is here in Skagway, do you?" Kate asked, and was startled when he got to his feet.

"How much money did Gilly have?" he asked quietly. "Did you give him any of yours?"

Kate nodded. "About fifty dollars."

Hogan swore. "Stay here by the packs. If anyone comes near you, warn him away once, then point this at him and pull the trigger." He handed her a pistol. "Can you do that?" Kate looked at the gun. She'd never held one before in her life, much less fired one, but the urgency in Hogan's voice made her shake her head.

"Yes, I can do it," she said. "Do you think Gilly's all right?"

"Likely he is. He's a pretty smart, tough old bird." Hogan hurried down the street. Kate watched anxiously, cursing the fact that she must stay behind and watch the supplies. Her anxiety wasn't helped when gunfire sounded and men shouted hoarsely. Axe Fredericks walked by, and on impulse Kate waved him closer.

"Would you watch our gear, Axe?" she cried.

"Shore," he agreed, wading through the muddy slush. "It'll be here safe and sound when you're ready for it again."

"Thank you," she called gratefully, and took off at a run. More gunfire sounded, and suddenly, from one of the tent buildings, two men went tumbling into the street, clenched in combat, their fists pounding at each other. Kate stopped, recognizing one of the men as Hogan. The other man hadn't a chance. Hogan pummeled him around the face and middle with such deadly purpose that Kate held her breath, fearful he meant to kill his opponent.

Someone should try to stop this. Angrily she looked around for a sheriff. A lean, well-dressed man stood in the shadows. He wore a suit coat and tie. A wide-brimmed hat hid his eyes, but she could make out a neatly trimmed mustache. Long fingers restlessly played with a gold coin attached to a chain. Something about him made her certain he wasn't the law. He stood tense and expectant, his attention riveted on the two fighting men.

Hogan's fist landed on his opponent's nose and blood spurted down his face and onto the muddy street. Another swing of Hogan's arm and the man doubled over, an agonized groan emitting from his mouth. Groggily the man got to his feet and swung again. Hogan ducked and landed another blow at the man's chest. There was a flash of movement. Clay Lawford stood to one side, his pistol in his hand. Kate blinked and looked again, her mind not measuring what she was seeing.

Suddenly a shot rang out. Kate's gaze flew to Hogan. She expected to see him sway and fall to the ground at any moment. Certainly the man across the way expected it. He watched Hogan intently, surprise registering on his face when the big man remained standing, one fist wrapped in the shirt of the man he fought. The onlookers murmured among themselves and glanced around. George Sawyer gripped his bleeding wrist. His gun lay in the mud at his feet. Kate looked back at Clay Lawford, but he'd already disappeared into the shadows.

In puzzlement the men looked at one another. There was no clue as to who had shot the gun from Sawyer's hand, nor was there any doubt that Sawyer had meant to gun Hogan down as he fought. There were some murmurs of criticism, but most men had already learned the best rule for staying alive in a gold-mining town. They kept their mouths shut. But now most of them walked away from the tent, which sported a community-information sign in front and gambling tables inside. They'd had enough of Fletcher Meade's brand of gambling for the time being.

As the crowd thinned, Hogan picked his hat out of the mud and walked over to the tall, thin man with the coin. "I think you owe my friend some money," Hogan said quietly.

"He lost it on the wheel. He knew the chances he was taking when he put down his money," Meade answered calmly.

"Is this how you're making your money here, Meade," Hogan demanded, "running a crooked wheel?"

"You'd better be ready to back that, O'Shea, when you call me a cheat," Meade said, and his handsome face grew ugly.

"Well, I'm calling you a cheat," Hogan said, and his voice was low and quiet, but every man in the street heard him. He flicked the tails of his coat behind him and squared up to Meade. "And I'm ready to back up what I say."

Meade looked around uneasily, then feigned a smile. "Now, look, Hogan," he said placatingly. "We've bumped heads before. There's no need for us to go off half-cocked and shoot up the town. I'm a law-abiding citizen of Skagway. I know it might be a bit hard for you outsiders coming through here to understand the ways of our little town."

"I understand a fixed wheel," Hogan said. "I understand signs that mislead greeners into your establishment, and armed men who won't let them out again until they've gambled away their money."

"There's not a man around who can say Fletch Meade didn't give him a fair shake. Why, if a poor man loses his poke in my place, I provide him the money to buy a ticket home. Ain't many men who'd do a thing like that."

"That's real generous," Hogan said. "After you've fleeced them, you get them out of town so they can't raise a row against you or warn other miners of your double dealings."

"Come now, Hogan, you're too hard on an old acquaintance. Let's have a drink and talk about the old times in Colorado and Montana."

"I'm particular about who I drink with," Hogan answered. "Just pay my friend back his money and we'll be on our way."

"All right," Meade conceded, looking around the crowd. "I'll give this man back the money he lost fair and square. I don't ever want anyone to say he was cheated by Fletcher Meade. You remember that, boys, and tell your friends. Fletch Meade runs an honest house and he don't ever cheat anyone." He motioned to a man, who stepped forward and handed a bag to Hogan.

The men talked among themselves and Kate noticed that their ugly mood had shifted. The charismatic gambler had managed to sway them. She had little doubt that was the reason he was paying Hogan back, but where was Gilly? The men in front of her moved, and suddenly she caught a glimpse of her father. He lay resting against a wooden post, one foot cradled against his knee. Even from where she stood, Kate could see blood seeping from his shoepac.

"Gilly," she screamed, and rushed forward.

4

"Are you all right?" She knelt beside him, her hands fluttering over his wound ineffectually.

Hogan swore when he saw her. "What the hell are you doing here?" he growled. "I told you to stay with the supplies. Someone's probably robbed us by now."

"Oh, do be quiet, Mr. O'Shea," Kate snapped, busy tearing a strip from her petticoat and dabbing at Gilly's wound. "The supplies are quite safe. It's my father I'm worried about now."

"I'm all right, Kate, don't fuss so," Gilly said, pushing her hands aside and getting painfully to his feet. He heaved himself up along the wall so he was balanced on one leg.

"You shouldn't—" Kate cried.

"Lean on me," Hogan commanded, and gratefully Gilly braced himself against the big man's body.

"I'm sorry for the trouble, Hogan," he gasped. Beads of sweat formed on his brow, and it was obvious he was in pain. With his arm around Gilly's waist to lend support, Hogan turned toward where they'd left their packs. Gilly hopped along the best he could, leaning heavily on Hogan. Anxiously Kate followed behind.

"Like a damned fool, I walked right into it," Gilly rasped out. "Fletcher had his men posted at the door, and he wouldn't let you out until you gambled. It was a sham, those wheels, rigged so you couldn't win, but you had to go along with them or you'd get a bullet in the back. I tried to resist them, tried to outdraw one of them."

"Don't talk anymore," Hogan said. "I should have

warned you. I saw one of Fletcher's men on the boat. I just didn't think he'd move in so fast."

"I lost our money, all our money," Gilly mumbled.

"We got it back," Hogan reassured him. "We're all right. We just have to get you fixed up."

"Did you see who shot Meade's man?" Gilly asked.

Hogan shook his head. "Whoever it was, I owe him."

"It was Clay Lawford," Kate said with satisfaction, "the greener." She couldn't help making the point.

"Don't get too smug," Hogan growled. "We still don't have our gear back." He cast an anxious glance up the wharf and suddenly all his doubts about their packs pressed in on Kate and she ran ahead. Relief washed through her when she saw Axe where she'd left him, still perched on their supplies, his rifle lying across his knees. He waved when he saw them approaching.

Kate waved back and turned triumphantly toward Hogan. "It seems once again I've been a good judge of character," she said. "This is Axe Fredericks. He's a packer."

Hogan carefully seated Gilly on a pack and straightened. Kate saw the surprise and disbelief on his face as he looked at the wizened little man.

"That's right, young fella," Axe said, getting to his feet and holding out his hand. Though standing, he never even made it to Hogan's shoulders, still his manner was that of an equal. Hogan suppressed a smile and shook hands, not wanting to cut down the little man in any way.

"I'm stronger than I look and I'm in need of a grubstake," Axe explained, as if he sensed their reservations. "The missus and me wants to go back up along the river. We found us a place that looked mighty fine, mighty fine indeed. We jest plumb run out of food and had to hightail it down here to Skagway to winter out. Since then I been doin' every odd job I could find to get a grubstake together."

"I'm sorry, old-timer," Hogan said, shaking his head. "I figured on hiring Indians to do the job.

They're all I can afford." Kate saw Axe's expression drop.

"I hear that kind of often," he said in discouragement.

"Maybe you can help me get my partner and our supplies to a hotel and find me a doctor."

"A doctor? Here in Skagway?" Axe shook his head. "Ain't got a doctor yet. Ain't got a hotel, for that matter. They're just startin' the Skagway Hotel. It was one of them unfinished buildings you passed down on Main Street."

"Where are we to sleep?" Kate asked, exhausted by all the excitement of their arrival. The air had grown colder and the slush beneath their feet was freezing once again. Her thin boots were poor insulation from the icy dampness. She glanced at Gilly's white face. He needed to be someplace warm and comfortable.

"We'll pitch our tents here on the wharf for the night," Hogan was saying. "Finding someone to tend your father is a worse problem."

"I have a solution to both your problems," Axe spoke up. "I got me a shanty down there a ways." He pointed off away from town. "There's room for you to stay a night or two, and my woman's real good with injuries and the like."

"We're much obliged," Hogan said. "Are you sure we won't be putting you out?"

"Nah. We'd be real honored to have you," Axe said with a simple back-woods courtesy that was heartwarming. "My woman, May I call her, has a gift for healing people." He stooped and shouldered one of the heavy packs. "If you'll stay and guard your goods, I'll just go on ahead and bring back a sledge for your wounded friend. The missus can come with me now and get out of the cold."

Hogan hesitated, as if gauging the possibility of danger to Kate if she went with the stranger, but she brushed aside his concern. "This is most kind of you," she said, taking one of the smaller packs and swinging it over her back. Falling into step beside Axe, she waved to her father and Hogan.

Axe led her out of town toward a stand of pines. Though only midafternoon, the sun was already sinking behind the mountains, casting a ruby glow over the snow-capped peaks. Kate shivered but her discomfort was forgotten as she stopped and stared at the distant mountain range. She'd never seen anything so grand. Her breath caught as she watched the shimmering peaks.

"Pretty, ain't it?" Axe said, pausing beside her.

Kate swallowed against a sudden lump in her throat. "I thought this land was supposed to be a barren wasteland of ice and snow."

"Oh, it's that, all right, in some places," Axe said. "But most of it's 'bout the prettiest country you ever saw anyplace. The Eskies call it Alyeska, the Great Land. I guess they got it right." They'd drawn near a snug log cabin now, and Axe put a mittened hand to his mouth. "Hello, May." The door flew open and a young Indian woman stood waving at them. Her hair was blue-black and drawn neatly from a center part, her dark eyes bright and alert, her broad Indian features curved in a smile.

"May, we got company," Axe called. "Throw some more meat and taters in the pot." He saw the look of surprise on Kate's face and chuckled. "I forgot to tell you May's a Tlingit. They're one of the most civilized of the Eskimo tribes." Actually she was more surprised at May's youth than at her Indian blood. She couldn't be much more than twenty, while Axe was in his sixties.

"I'm pleased to meet you, May," Kate said, fearful she might have given offense.

May shook hands energetically. "Hello, pleased to meet you," she said in a lilting singsong voice.

"How generous you are to have us for the night," Kate continued. "I'm afraid there are more of us. My father and his partner are back with the supplies."

"One of 'em's injured, May," Axe called, swinging the packs down outside the door. "Get out your medicine bag. I'm taking the sledge back for the others."

"Ah, yes, yes. Come in out of cold," May said to

Kate, and led her into the brightly lit cabin. A fire burned cheerily on the grate and a kettle of stew hung from a rod, bubbling and sending out the most heavenly aroma. Kate's stomach growled, and only a sense of good manners enabled her to turn her gaze away. But May smiled knowingly and quickly helped Kate strip away her jacket.

"Come by the fire," she said, bustling around the cabin to arrange a rough stool for Kate to sit on and filling a wooden dish with some of the savory stew. Kate held the bowl for a moment, relishing the warmth on her fingers, then, picking up the spoon, took a bite. It was a simple stew, made with meat and a rich gravy in which rice and potatoes had simmered. Kate had never tasted anything so wonderful. As she ate, May knelt before her and began unlacing her boots.

"Oh, don't, please! I can do that," Kate said, embarrassed that her hostess should do such a menial task.

"Important to keep feet dry and warm here in Alyeska," May said matter-of-factly, and finished removing Kate's boots. She brought a heated stone from the fireplace, wrapped it in a fur, and placed it for Kate to put her feet on. She must surely be in heaven, Kate thought, and wriggled her toes in delight.

"Thank you," she murmured, but May had already moved on to another task. Taking out a bag made of some kind of hide, she sorted through several small pouches of medicines and salves and laid them on the table. Kate sat watching, and when her feet were warm, she put on her boots again.

In no time, it seemed, Axe was back with the other men. Hogan carried Gilly in and placed him on the table. Kate hovered nearby as May gently unlaced his shoepac and rolled up the pant leg. The wound had stopped bleeding, and clots had begun to form.

"Get yourself something to eat," Axe told Hogan, and Kate, unable to look at her father's mangled foot, hurried to get him a bowl of stew. He let it grow cold as he hovered over Gilly.

"How bad is it?" he asked as May washed the injury, and when she stepped aside so he could see, he cursed. "They shot off his toe," he said, and slammed a fist against the table. Gilly winced and bit his lips.

"Be careful, you'll hurt him," Kate cried protectively.

"Little toe never freeze off," May said. "Foot sore many days, but man alive."

"May's right," Axe said. "Shore not many who come up against Meade and his crowd could say that."

While the others watched, May quickly cleaned the wound and cauterized it. The smell of burning flesh rose in the room. Kate stuffed her fist against her mouth to hold back her whimpers. Gilly never made a sound as May laid the hot knife against his flesh, but sweat gathered on his flushed face and rolled unchecked into his collar. Hogan had a hold on his arm, as if to steady him and share the pain.

At last May removed the knife and examined her handiwork. Giving a nod of satisfaction, she smeared a noxious-smelling salve over the wound before bandaging it.

Gilly studied Hogan's scowling face. "I know what this means," he gasped faintly. "I ain't holdin' you to stayin' with me. I know an injured man can't cross over that pass."

Hogan moved closer and gripped Gilly's hand. "It won't be the same without you," he said huskily. His eyes were dark with pain for his friend.

"No!" Kate cried, moving away from the fire. Her eyes were wide and angry, her face stark. "Half of those supplies are ours. You can't just take them and go off."

"Kate, girl . . ." Gilly remonstrated.

"I had no intention of taking your supplies," Hogan said, and she could see by the fire in his eyes that she'd mortally offended him.

"You might need them, Hogan. Take them," Gilly offered.

"What's to become of us if you go on without us?" Kate stormed. "We can't pitch a tent and spend the summer here in Skagway."

"Why not?" Hogan declared. "You'd be a damned sight more comfortable down here than you would in the interior. What do you think you'll find once you cross over those passes? Hotels? Doctors? Hell no, Miss O'Riley. There'll be a wilderness."

"Still, we planned to go together. Can't you wait for Gilly?"

"It's madness to take an injured man into the wilderness. We'd have to pull him on a sled as well as carry our supplies. You sure can't pack much, and there's a limit to how much I can tote and pull."

Kate looked around the cabin in desperation. She saw the disappointment on Gilly's face and thought how unfair life seemed. Her gaze fell on Axe, sitting quietly by the fireplace, mending a snowshoe. "We could take Axe along as a packer."

Hogan barely suppressed a snicker as he turned away. Placing a balled fist against the rough log wall, he leaned his head against it as if thinking; his shoulders shook as if he were laughing or crying.

"This isn't funny," Kate snapped, temper flaring, and she observed that Hogan had a bit of temper himself when he swung around and fixed her with his dark glare.

"You're right, Miss O'Riley," he said from between tightly clenched teeth. "I didn't suppose it was funny. Don't you think I'm as disappointed as the rest of you? I need a partner out there, in case I get injured or lost, someone who'll watch out for me, someone I'd watch out for. This isn't the kind of country I'd want to travel alone."

Kate's anger cooled as she considered his words. "There must be something we can do," she said, and turned to May. "How long will it be before my father can walk?"

"Maybe two weeks," May answered, holding up her fingers and darting an inquisitive gaze from one man to another, as if she weren't sure of her mathematics.

"We can wait then until Gilly's foot heals well enough to travel again," Kate said coaxingly.

Hogan shook his head. "It'll take longer than that before his foot will be strong enough for those trails." Kate's shoulders drooped and she studied the floor in abject discouragement.

Axe stepped forward, tamping fresh tobacco into a pipe. "For a cheechako, you talk sense," he told Hogan. "You need a partner, but if you wait to go over that pass, you'll be caught in avalanches. There's already some danger of that. But an even bigger worry is when you get down the other side. You'll be traveling by river. Right now, while they're frozen, you can use dog sleds. Once the ice goes, you have to use boats. Some of them rivers has what the Indians call skookum water, rapids, strong currents that'll tear a man's boat to pieces. When the river breaks up, they's ice to trap a boat and crush it."

Kate listened intently. "If we go now, we could use a dog and sled, like Axe said. We could hire Indian guides to drive us."

"Kate, that'll cost money," Hogan replied, and she never even noted that he'd dropped the formal way he'd used with her name up to now.

"We have money—the gold dust you got back from Meade, and I still have some left. I won't allow my father to be left behind. He's come too far. Besides, it isn't his fault all this happened. You should have warned him of the kind of men who were here."

"Kate," Gilly said weakly, "I know what kind of men show up anytime there's a gold discovery. I've been in enough gold camps to know there's a passel of polecats. I just got careless. I was too eager and forgot to be cautious."

"Yes, you were eager," Kate cried, crossing the room to take his hand, "because you want to go on this expedition."

"Aye, that I do," Gilly said, and lay back to stare at the ceiling. "That I do."

Kate looked up at Hogan and was startled at the look of concern on his face. "All right," he said finally. "We'll hire extra Indian guides and buy a dog team and sled." He hauled out the pouch of gold dust

TOMORROW'S DREAM

and dug out his own cash. "How much money have you got left, Kate?" he asked.

Laughing, she turned away from the men and retrieved her pouch of money from beneath her petticoats and handed it over. It was little enough, but with the gold dust they'd retrieved from Meade, they'd surely have enough. Axe had once again fallen silent, going to stand by the fire while he lit his pipe. Hogan opened the bags and swore when he got to the pouch of gold dust.

"Bogus gold dust," he said, spilling it into a heap on the table.

Kate rushed forward and stared at the pile. "What do you mean?" she exclaimed. "It looks like gold."

"Brass filings and chippings," Hogan answered, raking a finger through the mound.

"Shore looks like it," Axe said. "I got a means to test it." He hurried away and came back with a glass half-filled with a clear liquid. "Pour some in there," he said. "If it's gold, it won't hurt it none." Hogan scooped up a handful and sifted it into the liquid. A dense black cloud rose from the glass.

"Damn," Hogan said, and strode to the pack near the door. He pulled a gunbelt free and strapped it around his waist.

"What are you doing?" Kate cried, running to place a slim hand on his sleeve.

"I'm going to get a crook," he answered, tightening the belt and checking the cylinder for bullets.

"You can't," she protested. "Don't you see? He'll be waiting for you, with men, just waiting to gun you down. He must have known you'd discover his bogus gold dust sometime and that you'd come back for him. He couldn't gun you down out there himself, and when Clay Lawford disarmed his man so he couldn't shoot you in the back, he set a trap for you. Don't walk into it, Hogan. It's what he wants you to do."

"She's right, Hogan," Gilly called weakly from the table. Even Axe nodded his agreement.

"I can't let him get away with cheating me," Hogan

said stubbornly. "Let me go, Kate." But she hung on to his sleeve, just as stubborn as he.

"What will I do if he kills you?" she demanded. "I already have one man down and wounded. What am I, a lone woman, to do here in a frozen wilderness? We need you, Hogan. You can't let your pride come ahead of our need for your protection and strength."

He paused. Her hand still gripped his arm and she could feel some of the tension leave his body. "We still have some money," she reminded him. "We'll get by for now, and you can settle the score with Fletcher Meade another day."

"All right," he said finally, and slowly unstrapped his belt and dropped it back on the bundle. "But, Kate, if we hire those Indian guides for your father, we won't have much money left for supplies come winter."

She looked into his eyes and saw his concern. She and Gilly had already become a burden for him, the very thing he'd said he didn't want and God knew she didn't want to be. But she saw something else in Hogan's eyes. No matter what, he wouldn't abandon them. She felt grateful to the big man for that. "We'll have money for our winter supplies," she said, forcing gaiety to her voice. "We're going to strike gold."

"It takes time," he continued bleakly, "more time than we have. We don't even know where to begin." He walked to the fire and stood staring into the flames.

"I know," a quiet voice said, and all in the room turned to Axel Fredericks. He grinned and drew on his pipe. "I know a place that ain't been touched. There's gold there. I ain't seen it yet, can't even prove it's there. But I know."

Hogan grinned. He'd heard talk like this many times before. "Why haven't you taken it out, old-timer?" he asked.

"I ain't got the money to outfit myself. I was just waitin' for spring, hoping—"

"Hoping someone like us would come along and take you on as a partner," Hogan finished for him.

Axe nodded. "I wouldn't take just anybody." He took a step forward and gazed at Hogan. "I seen your pack. You're carryin' too much, way too much. Most cheechakos do. You got enough there for an extra man and woman." He paused, letting the thought precede the words. "Make me a partner, take me along with you. I'll take you to my place."

"No," Kate said. "Gilly's his partner."

"We can be three," Axe said. "What about it? My woman here can help tend your partner until he's on his feet. I know the territory. May's Tlingit. She's good in the interior. By God, I tell you, hook up with me and you won't regret it."

Hogan looked at the old man and at Kate and Gilly. "Why would you share your gold mine with strangers?" he asked, still suspicious. Kate watched Axe's face.

"You're from the outside," he said patiently. "You don't even know yet what's out there. More gold than one man, a hundred men, could gather in a lifetime. There's plenty for everyone. I can't go get it on my own. I can't trust just any man who comes through here." He paused, studying Hogan. "I like the looks of you. You take care of your partner." He stopped talking. He'd said all he could. Now he waited for their decision.

Hogan moved across the room to the table where Gilly lay propped up on his elbows. The two men conversed in low voices. Although she trusted Axe and wasn't opposed to a new partner, Kate said nothing. She'd learned something this evening of the strong bonds between men, and she didn't want to interfere now. The decision was between Hogan and Gilly. The men talked, nodded their heads, and even before they turned, everyone else in the room knew what their decision was.

"All right," Hogan said. "We're partners." He held out his hand, palm-up, and a beaming Axe placed his gnarled hand on top. Without thinking, Kate slapped her hand over the men's, and May, giggling softly, eyes twinkling, placed her hand on Kate's. They all stood beaming at each other except for Gilly, who groaned in pain.

"This calls for a drink of celebration," Hogan said, digging a bottle of whiskey out of his pouch. "Come on, Gilly, it'll numb the pain." Gratefully Gilly took the bottle and drank down a swig before passing it along to Axe. When Hogan had finished, he handed the bottle to Kate. "You're a partner too," he said. "Drink up." Unaccustomed to anything stronger than a glass of sherry served at Christmas parties, she tipped the bottle and let the fiery contents flow into her mouth. Instantly her eyes watered and her throat burned. She swallowed and coughed and handed the bottle to May.

"Are you all right?" Hogan asked, slapping Kate on the back so that she staggered and nearly fell.

"I'm fine," she wheezed, and the men laughed, even Gilly. Seeing color return to her father's face, Kate didn't mind being the butt of their joke. The bottle went around again, but this time Kate declined.

"Come, we make our beds," May said softly, and led her to one end of the small room. Kate's happy glow extended even to the sleeping arrangements, for they were all to sleep in the tiny cabin. The women would take the bunks and the men would roll up in the sleeping bags before the fire, save for Gilly, who had already been covered and would sleep on the kitchen table. Without the benefit of a curtain or any other means of privacy, Kate elected to loosen her corset and sleep in her clothes. Settling into her sleeping bag, she closed her eyes and listened to the men talking near the fire. Their voices were already slurred from the whiskey they'd consumed. Gilly was softly singing an old Irish melody. Obviously the whiskey had numbed his pain.

Kate lay thinking. They were in Alaska. It was everything she'd expected, and more. She thought of the pass, rising high and menacing in the distance, its snow-covered trail looking impassable, yet already scaled many times by determined men. Well, she'd be just as determined, she thought. She'd give Hogan no more cause for worry. She'd show him that she and her father were not a burden. With another woman joining them on the trail, she felt strong and confident. She fell asleep to the quiet murmur of the men's voices and the lilting song her father had sung to her when she was a child.

"Hogan," Gilly called urgently, and the big man rose from his place by the fire and bent over the old man's makeshift bed.

"Are you in pain?" he asked.

Gilly nodded. "Is Kate asleep?"

Hogan glanced at the slight mound on the bed. Two red braids hanging over the edge of the cot were all that was visible of Kate. Thoughtfully he stared at them. Those two braids, free of the twisted knot in which she always wore them, bespoke a vulnerability he couldn't quite associate with Kate. He sighed and looked away. "She's asleep," he whispered.

Gilly hooked his fingers in the front of Hogan's shirt. "I've got to ask a favor of you," he said, his voice slurring badly.

"Ask," Hogan said, unhesitating.

"Kate . . . promise me if anything happens to me out there on the trail, you'll take care of Kate."

"Nothing's going to happen to you," Hogan scoffed. "You've just had a little toe shot off. You'll be fine. You'll be digging gold out of the ground by the handful."

"Do you think so?" Gilly asked, his face taking on a dreamy look.

"I think so," Hogan said warmly. "This is the big one, Gilly. The one we've searched for all along. This time we're going to find it."

"Hot damn," Gilly cried; then his face sobered. "I had a premonition once," he said. "You got to promise me, if I don't make it through on this one, you'll take care of Kate. I know she's hot-tempered and difficult and has a tongue like a whip, but underneath she gets hurt and kinda scared, like the little girl she used to be. Promise me you'll—"

"I promise," Hogan said soothingly.

Gilly lay back, the whiskey singing through his

veins. He felt no pain from his foot now. "You won't forget, will you?" he asked drowsily.

"Have I ever let you down?" Hogan asked, and was relieved when Gilly shook his head, then closed his eyes and began to snore. He tucked the covers under the old man's chin and crept back to the warmth of his own sleeping bag. Gilly and his premonitions, he scoffed; then his thoughts turned to the mound on the bed and the two red braids hanging free, and despite the whiskey, sleep was a while in coming.

5

Three days later they left Skagway. During that time Kate watched as Gilly forced himself to walk on his wounded foot, trying to make it heal faster, trying to make it whole again. His eyes burned with a zeal she had never seen before.

"Axe knows a place," Gilly said for the hundredth time. "This is it, Kate, I tell you, this is it. I feel it in my bones."

May continued to change the poultices she'd placed on the wound, and when after twenty-four hours there was no sign of infection and Gilly began to hobble around, they made their plans to leave.

Hogan and Axe bought two dog-sled teams, and once again the sourdough, as Kate had discovered the old-timers were called, proved to be invaluable. He knew what to look for in a team and how to avoid a dog that was played out or lame.

"Have dog team is good," May observed when the women ran out in the snow to see them.

"In what way?" Kate asked, happily petting the lead dog.

"If no food, eat dogs," May said matter-of-factly. Kate looked at the milling barking animals and pressed a hand to her mouth. She would never, never eat a dog, she vowed, no matter how hungry she got.

Axe also warned them of another discomfort, which seemed impossible to contemplate in the cold and snow of early spring, but they humored him nonetheless and bought cheesecloth for protection from mosquitoes and gnats later in the summer.

Carefully Hogan and Axe went over their supplies,

discarding and adding things. Leaning heavily on a makeshift cane, Gilly hovered over their shoulders, offering his own advice. Kate could sense the coil of tension and excitement in each man. Gone were the careless, hard-drinking braggarts of Seattle, and in their place were determined men willing, for the lure of gold, to pit their strength and intelligence against the vast wilderness of Alaska's interior.

If anyone could find gold, Kate thought, it must surely be these three. Under Axe's direction, much of what was in the packs was left behind in the cabin. It would be packed in later, before winter. Into the bundles went such essentials as food supplies, although not as much as Kate would have taken; basic cooking utensils—frying pan, Dutch oven, coffeepot, mixing spoon; and black gunpowder, wrapped tightly in waterproof oilskins.

The medicine chest was left behind. May took her own medicine pouch. Their clothes were sorted through and Kate was made to discard her dainty boots and don her shoepacs. She was surprised at how heavy they were, yet her feet were warm for the first time since they'd arrived in Skagway. Heavy underwear, mackinaw coat, heavy wool socks (more than needed, in Kate's estimation), woolen mittens, leather gloves, heavy overshirts, rubber boots, and felt boots—all were carefully stored for each traveler.

Needles, thread, wax, blankets, towels, rubber ground cloths, and sleeping bags were bundled into several smaller packs that would fit on each person's shoulders. With no money to hire Indian packers, they must haul their own supplies. The men could carry up to fifty pounds apiece, the women less. Each sledge would carry two hundred pounds per dog, but the men would have to pack the supplies on their backs across the Chilkoot Pass and later around the river rapids.

When they'd finished, Axe looked at the bundles and shook his head—and they all went through their packs again, discarding more things. Kate protested when he threw out the bars of lavender soap she'd packed. "They're very small," she said.

"The worst thing a cheechako can do is take too many supplies," the old sourdough admonished.

He passed on by. Hogan picked up the soaps and held them to his nose, drawing in the sweet flowery aroma. They were something from home, something for a woman to hang on to when she had nothing else. With a conspiratorial wink and a grin that made the dimples flash above his beard, he handed the bars back to Kate. Gratefully she stuffed them deep in her pack.

"Will we have enough food?" she asked later, looking around at the flour and other food that would be left behind.

"We'll hunt for fresh meat," Axe said. "We'll get by. You'll see. Man needs less than he thinks." He put aside the ice creepers, dishpan, the granite kettle and gold scale and the stove, keeping the balls of twine, spools of wire, axes, shovels, hand saw, thirty feet of rope, twenty pounds of nails, and the oakum and pitch. Kate wondered what all these things were needed for, but refrained from asking. She'd already learned to stay silent and watch and listen.

When the sledges were loaded, room had been left for Gilly. He would be spared walking the eight miles to Sheep Camp at the foot of Chilkoot Pass. It would give his foot that much longer to heal. Once they began the climb over the pass, he would have to walk like the rest of them, although none expected him to carry packs.

Kate was surprised at the number of people following the trail. Sheltered as they were at Axe's house, they'd been away from the madness of people rushing pell-mell toward the summit. As Kate watched them and the careless way in which they handled their loads, or the way they struggled to get their packs to camp, she gained an immense respect for Hogan and Axe for their care in packing their supplies.

The sun was shining brightly as they moved along, although the wind was sharp and piercing, laden with dampness.

"It'll snow tonight," Axe said. Hogan looked at the sky and Kate could see he was worried. They would spend their first night at Sheep's Camp in their tents, and he was concerned that she couldn't take a little cold and discomfort. She tightened her lips, determined he'd never hear her complain.

The dogs were fresh and ran well despite their heavy load. Kate wished she could say the same for herself. She was hard put to keep up, and found herself gasping in the cold air. Like her husband, May seemed to have unending stamina.

"How are you doing?" Hogan called. It was the second time he'd halted his team to wait for Kate to catch up.

"I'm all right," she gasped, and tried in vain to breathe normally.

Hogan regarded her somberly for a moment, dawdling to give her more time to rest. She expected to hear him make some scathing criticism about her slowing them down, but he only shrugged. "It'll come easier," he said. "You'll become trail-hardened. In the meantime, pull your scarf up over your nose and mouth or you'll freeze your lungs."

"Thanks," Kate said in relief, and they both knew she was referring to more than his advice.

This was madness, Hogan thought, turning away. He was as daft as the rest of them. What the hell was he doing packing a lame man into the interior when most partners would have balked at packing one out. And what about the women? May was all right. She was Indian. She was used to the ways of the north. Besides, she was Axe's responsibility, but Kate! Kate was a different story. She was his responsibility and she was too all-fired stubborn to listen to reason. Just like her old man, Hogan thought. Stubborn and bullheaded, and with a temper to match. Here he was worrying about her having enough room for her lavender soap and getting her lungs frozen, when he should have been thinking about the best way to get over the pass.

What did he need with a woman on this trip? he wondered for the hundredth time. God knew there would be women enough in Dawson. Even now Roxanne was on a boat traveling down the Yukon River.

She wouldn't get to Dawson before midsummer, but she'd be there. Why was he going all soft and gallant over this string-bean, fusty-old-maid daughter of Gilly's? Angrily he called to his dogs and purposely did not stop again until they reached Sheep's Camp.

It was midafternoon by the time they arrived at the foot of Chilkoot Pass, but the sun was already setting and long shadows lay over the mountains and valleys. Kate arrived in camp well behind the others, and stood, chest heaving for air, staring up at the formidable pass. Men had died up there, Axe had told her. So what would happen to a puny woman who didn't know the first thing about survival in the great north?

None of the others seemed to be contemplating the mountain. They were busy setting up tents, getting out bedrolls, and making a fire. Kate gathered her remaining strength and went to help.

May got out a Dutch oven and put beans and dried venison to soak. When Kate had finished with her chores, she went to help May and to watch and learn. She'd done all the cooking for Aunt Petty, but here in the wilderness cooking would be done over a campfire. May threw a pinch of salt and pepper over the beans and set the pot over the flame.

Kate set about making bread. When she'd kneaded the dough, May showed her how to divide it into strips and wind them around sticks. They pushed the sticks into the snow near the fire, so the bread could bake slowly.

Hogan had staked the dogs away from the camp and was now feeding them. Gilly had settled on a pile of furs near the fire, a bottle of whiskey at his side. Other travelers had pulled into camp and were setting up shelters. Other campfires were winking all along the valley. Pine forests rose behind them; ahead was the overpowering pass. Even now, as Kate watched, campfires flared all along the trail.

Axe had set them an easy pace for this first day of travel, yet all of them felt tired. After supper they relaxed around the fire, pulling their hoods tight against the cold. Axe regaled them with tales of other miners who'd come to the Yukon and learned to set their ways to the land.

"A fella come up here, I disremember his name," Axe said, cutting off a chew of tobacco and passing it around. Hogan took a piece and passed it on to Gilly. Kate shuddered. She could never get used to seeing a man spitting the dirty juice into the clean banks of snow. "Anyhow, he lost his false teeth," Axe went on. "He'd killed himself a bear and he couldn't even eat the dadblamed thing. It was winter and he couldn't get out to buy himself another set of teeth, so he made himself some. Yessir, fashioned the plate right out of wood, he did, and he set in teeth from that there bear he caught. They worked just as good as store-bought teeth." Axe chuckled and slapped his thigh. "He et that bear with its own teeth."

Everyone except Kate laughed. She shivered inside her fur and held her hands out to the fire. It was hard to know how much of what Axe told them was authentic and how much was exaggerated tales passed from one sourdough to another until they'd lost all kinship to the truth. "It's mighty cold tonight," she said, looking up at a starless black sky.

Axe looked up and grunted. "Snow before morning," he repeated.

Kate looked at the other faces around the fire. None seemed perturbed by such an announcement, so she said nothing. Hogan watched her pinched expression and spat out tobacco juice. He saw Kate shudder and avert her head, and he scowled. Leave it to a woman to disapprove of a man's little comforts, he thought sourly, and cut off another plug for himself.

"I think I'll turn in," Kate said, getting to her feet. "Good night, Gilly." She knelt and dropped a kiss on her father's brow.

His arms closed around her and pulled her tight. Startled, Kate pulled back and looked at him, wondering what had brought about this unaccustomed show of affection. "Good night, Kathleen Moira," he said. "I'm glad you're here." His unexpected words brought tears to her eyes.

"I'm glad I am too, Pa," she answered, and turned to the tent set up for May and her. At least she'd have some privacy on this trip. Carefully she closed the flap, and shivering in the frigid air, took off her mackinaw and unbuttoned her bodice to get at the corset beneath. Her breath came in a cold white vapor and her fingers were too numb to do their task quickly. She fumbled and muttered under her breath.

"You'll need another blanket tonight," Hogan said from the tent opening.

Startled, Kate whirled to look at him, her shirtwaist half up and the damnable corset strings hanging awkwardly. Her dishabille was plainly visible in the light from the fire.

"What in God's name are you doing?" Hogan demanded, staring at her middle.

"I am undressing for bed, Mr. O'Shea," Kate snapped, cheeks flaming. "Now, if you'll be so good as to leave my tent . . ."

Ignoring her words, he strode forward. One large hand yanked at the corset lace. "What is this?" he demanded. "You can't mean you're trying to wear a corset up here in this temperature and altitude. No wonder you had trouble keeping up without breathing like a spent horse."

"What I wear is my business, Mr. O'Shea, and none of yours," Kate cried in outrage, jerking away so the string fell from his big hand.

"It's my business when you fall behind and can't make it up the pass."

"I won't fall behind. You'll have no need to wait for me tomorrow," Kate stated hotly, head high.

Hogan looked at her angry face and without a word twirled her around until her back was to him. His large hands worked at the strings, ripping away the laces. "You have no need for this anyway," he snarled. "You don't have anything to hold in."

"Ooh, how dare you! Have you no sense of decency?" Kate cried, trying to evade him, but one big hand clamped down on her shoulder while the other continued to unlace her boned corset.

"When you're climbing that pass tomorrow, the air will get thin. Your heart and lungs will have to work harder for you. To hamper yourself with something like this . . ." He ripped away the offending corset and Kate screamed and snatched her shirtwaist over her camisole. It was all that preserved her modesty before this giant. But Hogan wasn't finished with her. His big hands closed over hers and effortlessly he pulled them away and stared in consternation at the thin camisole that covered her chest.

"Papa," Kate screamed, but there was no movement at the fire.

Hogan let go of her and stalked to the corner where her clothes pack lay. Rummaging around, he pulled out a pair of long woolen underwear. "Put these on now," he snapped. "You sleep in them, you wear them under your clothes. You don't take them off even to bathe. Have you got that?"

"I didn't think I'd need them now," Kate said, feeling compelled to explain her motives. "The air here isn't much colder than back home, and the coat was so thick. I . . . I was saving the long underwear for later, when I may need it more."

"We're in the panhandle here. There's not much difference in the temperature. But you need to sleep warm tonight," Hogan answered, "and tomorrow, when we start climbing, you'll feel the wind and wish you were wearing three of these."

Kate looked at him defiantly and then glanced away, realizing what he said was sensible and to ignore his advice was foolhardy. "All right, I'll put them on," she said ungraciously. "You might have explained all this to me, and I would have done as you advised."

"Would you?" Hogan fixed her with a stern gaze. "Or would it just have been another thing to fight about?"

"You leave me little recourse when you barge in on me as you did," she answered defensively. "A gentleman would have knocked."

Hogan sighed and his shoulders drooped for a moment. "Next time, I'll try knocking," he said, and stood regarding her. "While you're at it . . ." Kate's head came up in quick wary response. "Tomorrow, get rid of those wire-rim glasses."

"Anything else, Mr. O'Shea?" Kate flared.

Hogan's black gaze ran over her from head to foot in an impersonal perusal. "That's all for now," he said dismissively. Spinning on his heel, he went back to the fire, taking the corset with him. The blaze flared up as he threw the garment on the fire. Furious with his high-handed ways, Kate drew together the edges of the tent flaps.

Teeth clenched against the painful cold, she pulled on the long underwear, admitting to herself as she could not to Hogan that she'd been a fool to leave that morning without donning appropriate attire. She'd underestimated the Alaska climate. Wrapping the extra blanket he'd brought around herself, Kate climbed into the sleeping bag and curled into a ball. Soon she grew warm again. The sound of the men's voices around the fire was soothing, and she grew drowsy. She never even knew when May crept into the tent.

Sometime during the night it did snow, collapsing the canvas over their heads. "You ladies all right?" Hogan called from his tent, and when they assured him they were, he sighed and went back to sleep. Although the snow was heavy, it added to their warmth, and in the morning they dug out to meet a dazzling new world. Two feet of soft snow had fallen during the night. Climbing the summit would be even more difficult.

At the crack of dawn they had their gear packed, one tent folded and ready to be hauled to the top of the pass, where they would set up camp again. One tent would be left below and their party divided, one half to stay with the supplies below. Gilly would stay. The delay would give his wound that much longer to heal. May would also stay to nurse him. Hogan and Axe would trudge the distance back and forth, packing their goods until they were all at the top. They would stay in whichever camp they happened to be in when night fell. Smaller packs had been made, and each of them, Kate included, would carry a pack on his back. Even the dog team had been individually packed out, each dog carrying nearly as much as a man.

Kate knelt by her father, removing her woolen mittens to take his hand in hers. He felt frail and she thought of the winter months when she'd nursed him to health and of their journey to this point. She'd been at his side for months, watching out for him, but he'd never once relented in his fierce independence. She smiled at him. "I love you, Gi . . . Papa," she said softly.

He grinned. "I love you too, Kate." One gnarled hand smoothed her cheek. "You always wear your hair in braids," he said. "I want you to wear it flowing down your back the way your mama used to."

A lump tightened Kate's throat. "I will, Papa," she said huskily. "When you get to the top, I'll wear it down."

He smiled with all the old rascally charm he'd ever possessed. "I'll see you at the top." He waved a farewell.

"Let's get started," Hogan ordered, and without a backward glance to see if she followed, he started up the trail. Axe was already several hundred feet ahead.

The climb wasn't easy. Their feet sank into the loose snow that hid boulders and rocks. More than once Kate turned her ankle, until she learned where the pitfalls might be and could avoid them. Mostly she tried to stay in Hogan's tracks, but his long legs made longer steps than she could manage. They made the halfway point by nightfall and set up camp on a ledge where a campfire had blazed the night before. Without May to help, Kate hurried around to do all the chores in camp. They'd brought the leftover stew. She had only to warm it over a small kerosene stove. Wood was almost nonexistent on the mountainside, so there would be no fire to warm them through the night.

On the unprotected slopes, the wind buffeted them mercilessly, snapping at the canvas tent until Kate feared it might blow away. After a hasty supper they crawled inside its dubious shelter and curled into their sleeping bags, seeking any warmth. Sandwiched between the two men, it seemed to Kate that the energy emanating from Hogan's big body was enough to warm the whole tent. As she drifted to sleep, she wondered why she felt this awareness of the big Irishman's sprawled figure, when she gave no thought whatsoever to Axe. She slept badly and was thankful when the sun rose over the mountain peaks, lighting the world enough for them to climb again.

They nibbled hardtack and sipped water from their canteens before setting out. Up the steep incline, they trudged for mile after mile. By afternoon they'd reached the last one thousand feet. Kate was too tired to rejoice and too discouraged to celebrate when she saw the sheer wall they must scale. It seemed no one could go up that incline, but calmly Axe led the way and Hogan and she followed. Steps had been cut into the span of ice, but time and again Hogan had to turn back and take her hand, half-pulling her up the steep embankment. Even the dogs struggled to find safe footing on the sheer slopes. Several times Kate went sprawling into a snowbank. In the end, Hogan came to take her pack and add it to his.

When at last they reached the top, they lay sprawled in the snow, gasping in deep breaths of air. The wind, sharp and piercing, moaning down over the mountain ranges, soon chased them from their rest. When Kate got to her feet, the wind buffeted her, stealing her breath away.

"What are we going to do?" she cried. "Our tent won't hold in this wind."

Axe raised his voice to be heard above the wind's whine and pointed off to one side. "We'll go down a ways—there's a ledge and some overhangs that'll shelter us from the wind."

"Lead the way," Hogan called back and, bowing nearly double against the wind's fury, they made their way to the sheltered ledge. Other campers were there, and Kate spied Clay Lawford and his partners. She waved to him and he waved back. Hogan scowled.

Once more they pitched their tent, choosing a spot

well back from the other campers but still in the protection of the rock outcropping. The men gathered wood and started a fire and Kate made bread and a stew as she and May had done their first night on the trail. Kate was starting to feel quite seasoned as a camper. Soon they'd start to call her a sourdough, she thought humorously.

Now that the climb was behind her, she felt in the best of spirits. She had only to stay here and guard their goods while Hogan and Axe brought up the rest. Humming, she set the bread to baking.

It took them nearly a week to get all their supplies to the top. Hogan and Axe went down the mountain for the final load and to bring up Gilly, who would walk as much as possible. One of the sleds would be left empty. Hogan would haul Gilly to the top in it if he had to. Now Kate waited anxiously for the men and May to arrive.

Restlessly she wandered back to the ridge to watch the struggling figures as they made their way up. Shielding her eyes against the sun, she squinted, certain she'd caught a glimpse of Hogan. But where was Gilly? Then she caught sight of him, trailing behind the others. Now and then May looked over her shoulder to be sure he was all right and still moving. Kate felt a rush of love for the old man and gratitude to Hogan and Axe and May. They were all being incredibly kind to humor Gilly and take him along in spite of his injury.

A growl, distant and muffled, filled the air, and Kate looked around the mountain ridge. The sound came again, this time a rumble that seemed to come from deep inside the granite walls themselves; then the mountains were silent again. Puzzled, the people on the slope had paused and stood looking up the ridge to the west. Kate squinted, trying to see what had caused the disturbance. The slopes were smooth with untouched stretches of snow and ice.

Suddenly the mountains rumbled again, and high on a ridge snow broke loose and slowly, gracefully began its long descent down the mountain. Along the trail, figures scurried for cover. Many were right in the path of the avalanche. May had turned back down the path to help Gilly as he hobbled forward, fell, and got to his feet again. Fearfully he looked over his shoulder at the tumbling snow.

There was no danger, Kate thought in disbelief. The scene before her was too beautiful and ethereal, the billowing, onrushing snow too graceful to bring death. In wonder, she watched, neck muscles bulging as she screamed a warning that could not be heard above the roar of the mountain. She saw Gilly trying to run through the powdery snow that dragged at his ankles. Other men struggled too, but Kate saw only Gilly. She knew when he gave up, knew when he accepted the inevitability of death and turned to face the wall of snow and ice hurtling down on him.

"No!" she screamed, tears streaming down her face, but no one heard, not even herself. She saw the first snow hit him, knocking him to his knees, and then the rest rushed over him, tumbling him downward, burying him ever deeper beneath the cold white mantle.

It was over in seconds. The powdery snow rose in a white haze, then slowly settled over the new landscape the avalanche had created. Before the final wave had fallen, Hogan and Axe were struggling toward the buried trail. May had also disappeared in the white wall.

"Papa," Kate screamed, and scrambled down the sheer icy slope. The wind moaned its death chant. In a short time she was down a thousand feet, down to the edge of the avalanche's fall. "Papa," she cried, tearing at the chunks of ice and frozen snow, oblivious of the cuts to her hands or the blood that stained the pristine whiteness of the snow.

"Kate, go back," Hogan ordered, and tried to catch hold of her, but she twisted away. Unwilling to relinquish her loved one, she tore at the mountain with a vengeance. Suddenly her hands clawed at something soft, something warm and alive. May! The Indian woman's dazed eyes stared up through the thin layer of snow.

"May," Kate cried, frantically brushing away the crushing weight of snow; then Hogan and Axe were beside her and in no time May was free. She groaned and sat up, shaking her head in bewilderment.

"May, where's Gilly?" Kate cried, grabbing the woman's jacket and shaking it frantically. Sadly May shook her head. "Where's Gilly?" Kate demanded, and turned away, running along the edge of the blocked trail.

"Kate," Hogan called, and took hold of her arm. "Stay with May. Axe and I will look." But Kate only ran on, clambering over piles of snow, digging until her nails broke and bled and her hands turned red, then white with cold. Everywhere around her, men were burrowing into the snow, trying to find partners or other men trapped beneath the avalanche.

Kate lost all sense of time. Tirelessly she dug, sometimes weeping and calling to Gilly, but there was no answer. Finally an exhausted numbness fell over her and she crouched in the snow, head bowed as she cried brokenly.

"Come on, Kate." Strong hands lifted her, arms cradled her against a broad chest.

"No, I want to stay. Gilly needs me," she sobbed, fighting against Hogan's strength.

"It's too late," he said wearily. "If we found him now, he'd be dead, smothered by all that snow. You can't stay here. There's danger of another slide."

"No!" Kate wept, but Hogan gathered her up in his arms, cushioning her face against the warm hollow of his throat. He carried her back to a makeshift camp on the trail. Hot coffee had been made for the rescuers and survivors. Hogan pressed a cup to her lips, forcing her to drink.

"He never had a chance with that lame foot," Axe said glumly.

"He isn't dead," Kate cried, rising. "He's still alive. I know it." Hogan pressed her back down on the bedroll.

"If you'll stay here with May, I'll go out to look some more," he said, and silently Kate nodded. She wore no headgear or gloves, only the mackinaw she'd thrown on when she'd run to look for them. She seemed not to feel the cold. Hogan wrapped a woolen scarf around her head, tucking it beneath her chin, and peeled off one of the pairs of mittens he wore. With one last worried look at Kate's stoic face he turned away. He knew of no way to ease a woman's grief, except to let it have its time.

All night Kate sat in the tent, watching men come and go, seeing the stack of dead bodies grow beyond the flaps of the tent. Slowly came the acceptance of Gilly's death. Axe's words echoed in her mind. With his lame foot, Gilly hadn't had a chance.

When May had recovered, she helped hand out coffee and later stew for the rescuers. There were few survivors left, and as the night dragged on, fewer and fewer cries of triumph as a lucky miner was unburied still alive. One hundred men were saved, pulled from their icy graves, but sixty more perished beneath ten acres of snow, buried thirty feet deep.

Kate ate nothing, only sucking on a little snow and ice to cool the fever inside. A fever of hatred grew for Fletcher Meade. If not for his wound, Gilly might have gotten away. One day, she vowed, one day she would see Meade paid for his evil deeds.

At first light, Hogan and Axe came to the tent, and silently May and Kate followed them back up the trail to their camp. Nothing was said, but Kate knew they hadn't found Gilly's body. Exhausted, they fell into their bedrolls and slept straight through the day. When the others rose, they found a fresh pot of stew and baked bread waiting for them, and Kate, solemn-faced and withdrawn, sitting beside the fire. Somberly everyone ate, save for Kate. Hogan watched her anxiously. Her face was too pale. She seemed too controlled, too calm, like a spring wound too tightly.

Laying aside his plate, he cleared his throat and began what he knew would be unpleasant. "I'm sorry, Kate, for what happened to Gilly," he said gruffly. "I guess he was just about the best partner a man could ever have." She made no answer. He'd expected none. "I'll take you back to Skagway tomorrow."

"No." Kate's head came up, her eyes fierce. "I'm staying."

"You can't stay out here," Hogan said in surprise. "Gilly's gone. We're never going to find him."

"I know that," Kate said evenly. "But Gilly was a partner and he wanted to go find that gold mine." She paused, clenching her hands tightly while she fought back a surge of tears. When she had her emotions under control, she met his gaze. "I'm going in his place."

"Kate," Hogan began, helpless as to how to persuade her she'd be better off back in Skagway. She had a lot of her stubborn old man in her. "We'll send you Gilly's share of the gold when we strike. Trust me."

"It isn't a matter of gold," Kate said. "It wasn't the gold itself, it was the excitement of looking for it. If I go back, it'll be like Gilly was never here, but if I go on, if I help find the gold . . ." She paused and smiled softly. "Don't you see? It's for Gilly."

Any argument, he thought, any argument but this one. He could have fought, could have reasoned with her, could have ignored it. He got to his feet and walked away from camp to stare out at the mountains. They lay cold and uncompromising on the gray horizon. Turning back to Kate, he tried to sway her, and realized his attempt was weak and futile. "Gilly died on the mountain yesterday," he said. "How do you think I'll feel if you die out here too? It's too much responsibility, too much of a chance. I have to live with myself too, Kate."

She left the fire and came to put a slender hand on his sleeve. He could feel the slight weight of it and it made him feel all soft and uncertain inside. "I know," she said gently. "You were very kind to my father and me. I absolve you from all responsibility for me, Hogan. If you don't want to take me, I'll understand. We've held you back enough. You and Axe can go on without me."

"What will you do?" he asked warily. She'd capitulated too easily.

"I'll go down to Skagway and find some Indians to help me pack my gear, and I'll go on by myself," she answered with such quiet determination that he knew she meant it.

"Kate," he growled helplessly, but he knew he was beaten. He thought of the promise he'd made Gilly, the promise that he'd take care of Kate. Swearing softly under his breath, he walked away, shoulders slumped. She watched him go and turned back to the fire. She wasn't surprised when he returned sometime later and stood staring down at her, his dark eyes filled with misery.

"We'll go on together," he said hoarsely.

"Thank you, Hogan," she replied gratefully.

"You'd best get married," Axe said. He'd been sitting quietly by the fire watching as things transpired. Hogan and Kate looked at him in dismay. "She's a white woman out here in the wilderness, without the benefit of a husband or father to protect her. She'll be fair game."

"She has me to protect her," Hogan growled.

"Make it legal," Axe said, "elsewise she'll be treated no better than a whore by some."

Hogan looked at Kate in disbelief, his eyebrows V-ing in comical testimony to his dismay. Yet there was no laughter. The time was too somber, too near death. Kate wanted to deny Axe's suggestion. She'd never dreamed her wedding would be on a windswept mountain to a stranger, with her father dead below. She shook her head in denial, then was still. They were far from civilization. Here in the harsh Alaskan wilderness she must adapt if she were to survive. She saw the resignation on Hogan's face and knew his thinking had run in a similar vein.

"There's a preacher down below. I'll fetch him," Axe said, and rose. Kate stood staring at Hogan across the campfire. All her dreams of what a bridegroom would be were ended here. There was no refinement, no fine manners to charm a lady, and there was no love, but there was kindness. She had to cling to that.

What the hell was he doing? Hogan wondered. He hadn't ever intended to get married, and certainly not to a woman like Kate O'Riley. She was pushy and bossy, with a tongue that could cut a man to ribbons at twenty paces, stubborn, set in her ways. He liked a woman like Roxanne, who knew how to make a man laugh. Kate just made him mad most of the time. What the hell was he doing? Gilly had been his partner, true, and he had made a promise to him, but a man couldn't be expected to give up his freedom on a promise. Hogan rubbed the back of his neck and paced along one side of the fire.

Rough, Kate thought, eyeing him surreptitiously. He'd never be anything else. There would be no discussions of the classics with him, no sharing of poetry. Could he even read? He would constantly offend her sensibilities. He had thus far. Perhaps she could do something with him, teach him things so he would act more like a gentleman and less the ruffian. She sighed. The task seemed herculean, but she'd have to try. She glanced at him again. He needed a haircut. Lord, that beard! It would have to go first thing. Hogan spat tobacco into a snowbank and Kate sat down abruptly. How could she marry a man who looked like a bear and chewed tobacco?

Hogan whirled from his pacing and pointed a finger at her across the fire. "You can't change me," he thundered. "Don't even try."

"No, of course not," she answered mildly. "I wouldn't dream of it."

"I'm my own man," he went on, pacing restlessly. "I always have been, always will be. You can't tell me where to go and when to come back. And don't ever . . ." He whirled and pointed his finger again. A log shifted in the fire and sent up sparks, lighting his dark roguish features. "Don't ever come looking for me like you did Gilly."

"I wouldn't," Kate said quietly, but the corners of her mouth crimped stubbornly.

"I'm a man who likes his whiskey, and I'm not going to have a woman telling me I can't."

"I won't." Kate's gaze was steady on his, and when she was sure he was finished, she rose. "I have a few rules as well, Mr. O'Shea," she said primly. He groaned and made a face. Like as not she'd tell him not to belch in front of her and to clean his nails.

"This marriage is obviously one of convenience. I appreciate the protection you offer me while I'm here in the Yukon. But once we've struck gold, our need for each other will be gone. I propose that in the meantime we conduct ourselves with each other as if we were merely acquaintances."

Hogan listened to her words as if having trouble understanding. "You mean there'll be no . . ." He waved his hand back and forth, trying to find a word fit to be said in front of a lady. "No hanky-panky, no man-and-woman stuff," he finally got out.

"No hanky-panky, Mr. O'Shea," Kate snapped. "No connubial bliss, no consummation of our marriage. It will be just words on a piece of paper, somewhat like a business contract."

"Well, I'll be a—" He bit off what he was about to say and scratched his head. "You're a pretty cool customer," he snapped.

"I'm practical," Kate replied serenely.

"Practical!" His dark eyebrows rose in a V. "'Unnatural' is more like it."

"I found the preacher," Axe said, leading a thin, timid man into the circle of light. "This here's Reverend Talbot."

"How do you do, Reverend?" Kate said graciously, extending her hand. "I'm Kathleen O'Riley."

"How do you do, Miss O'Riley? Are you the bride? And this must be the lucky bridegroom." Hogan stepped forward and wrung the little man's hand. The preacher winced and quickly withdrew. Digging out a well-worn Bible, he thumbed through it, looking for the wedding passages.

Hogan glared at Kate. "It ain't fair to take all a man has to offer and give nothing in return," he hissed.

"I am not one of your dance-hall women, Mr. O'Shea," Kate whispered furiously. "Trading my services for something from you." Troubled, Reverend Talbot ducked his head so he wouldn't hear their conversation.

"I never said you were," Hogan snapped. "And stop calling me Mr. O'Shea. I'm just plain old Hogan."

"Let's be truthful with each other, Mr. . . . Hogan," Kate said crisply. "I do not find you physically attractive." The preacher glanced up, startled. "And you've made it very clear I'm not the kind of woman with whom you're used to consorting."

"Consorting?" Hogan's face was a study in puzzlement. His big lean jaw clenched and the cords in his neck quivered. "You beat all I've ever seen!" he shouted.

"Uh, if we could gather around," Reverend Talbot said, and Axe and May came to stand behind Kate. Hogan stalked forward, and glaring mightily, took his place beside her. The bride and groom seemed out of sorts with each other, the reverend thought mildly. Perhaps it was wedding jitters. He'd seen plenty of those before.

"It's true," Kate replied in an undertone only Hogan could hear. "I find a man of your caliber"—she let her gaze sweep over him scathingly—"not of my preference. Had I a choice in the matter, I would have picked a man of some taste and refinement."

"And if I'd had a choice, I'd not be getting married," Hogan snarled. The preacher stepped forward and they both smiled at him. "Anyhow, I'd have chosen someone soft and womanly with hips and breasts," he muttered. Kate's face flushed, her temper rising.

"If the bride and groom will join hands," Reverend Talbot said serenely.

"You are truly one of the crudest men I've ever met," Kate flared. "I've a half-mind not to marry you."

"That'd suit me just fine, lady," Hogan cried. "You . . ." Whatever the insult he'd been about to hurl at her was left unsaid as the preacher stepped forward to bless them.

"What a joy," Reverend Talbot said with a kindly smile, "to perform such a pleasant task as a wedding after the tragic circumstances below. In the midst of death, there is life, continuing with faith and confidence in the future." Kate and Hogan looked at each other shamefaced, remembering Gilly and the reason they were going through this wedding in the first place. They glanced away and stood silent and repentant.

"If the bride and groom will join hands," the reverend reminded them gently, and Hogan took Kate's hand in his. He seemed to engulf her with the warmth of his palm. From beneath her lashes she glanced up at his dark profile. His chin was held high. He looked straight ahead at the preacher.

"Dearly beloved, we are gathered here . . ." Reverend Talbot began, and Kate felt her knees go weak.

Somewhere down the mountain a lone wolf howled, its long sad cry riding on the wind. Kate shivered, suddenly cold. What was she doing here in this frozen wilderness, wedding a man like Hogan O'Shea? She slumped forward and feared she might fall, but Hogan's hand was at her elbow, steadying her. She felt the strength of him and was reassured. Gratefully she glanced up. His dark eyes were watching her with such intensity that, try as she might, she could not turn her gaze away as the wedding ceremony continued.

"I now pronounce you man and wife," Reverend Talbot intoned. "Whom God hath joined, let no man put asunder. You may kiss the bride." Uncertainly Hogan turned to Kate. Sighing gently, she pitched face-forward into the snow.

6

She felt cold, a numbing, piercing cold that weighed down her limbs so she could no longer command them. She lay frozen and inert, able only to shiver. With immense effort she thrashed out, trying to overcome the frightening icy bindings that held her captive. Images invaded her dreams, of mountains rising endlessly to the gray winter sky, and white walls that tumbled downward threateningly. She screamed and tried to run away, but something white and wet and cold held her fast. A roar, low and ominous, grew in intensity. The sound filled her head.

Suddenly, on a ledge above, Gilly appeared. Smiling, he held out his hand to her. He looked young and happy and she knew he'd found the gold mine. But the roaring in her head grew and she cried out a warning, pointing back at the falling wall of ice and snow. Gilly only threw back his head and laughed. Then the snow was upon them. With a scream and a roar, it rushed downward in an icy swirl that carried everything before it. The ledge was empty, but she could hear Gilly's laughter fading down the mountainside. She tried to run after him, but her feet were frozen fast. Try as she might, she couldn't move. Weeping piteously, she called to Gilly. Suddenly an immense black bear reared up from the ledge and silently enclosed her in its embrace. Darkness closed over her, and blessed warmth, and she slid down the mountainside into oblivion.

Kate opened her eyes and looked around. What was wrong with her room? Where were her favorite curtains and her old chest? There was no sunlight streaming through the window. Rain must be falling.

Painfully she turned her head to look out the window, and found a strange man seated in her bedroom. Dear Aunt Petty would have a fit. She'd best tell him to leave. But her mouth was dry and she couldn't speak. She blinked, and suddenly her old room was gone and she was staring at the slender sapling trunk used as a support pole and the gray-green canvas stretched across it.

Puzzled, she turned her head and recognized Hogan sitting on his bedroll on the other side of the tent. His knees were drawn up, his elbows resting on them while he cradled his head in his big hands. He looked to be asleep, but even as she studied him, he opened his eyes and glanced at her. Startled, he crawled across the tent to kneel beside her.

"Kate," he whispered wonderingly. "We thought we'd lost you." His dark eyes were filled with joyous lights, but she could see the dark circles and the fatigue in his face. His dark beard seemed flat and drooping instead of its normal exuberant bushiness. A fine white line encircled his firm lips. He looked as if he hadn't slept in days.

"What happened?" she whispered. "Where are we?"

"We're on the other side," Hogan answered, and smiled, his teeth flashing white against his dark beard. "You've had a fever."

"A fever," Kate said weakly, and looked away, weak tears rolling down her cheeks. "Gilly didn't make it, did he?"

Hogan looked alarmed at her question. Had she forgotten so much?

"No, he didn't," he said reluctantly. "We'd begun to wonder about you as well. We weren't sure what brought this on, until May said she'd observed you eating snow and ice along the trail."

"I was thirsty. I thought I could save the water in the canteens for later, when we might need it."

"Don't ever eat the snow or ice without melting it first. It'll freeze your insides, give you fevers and chills, even kill you if you're not careful."

"I'll remember next time," Kate said with something of her old sass. Her face was incredibly pale, the cheekbones prominent and fragile. Dark shadows hollowed her cheeks. Hogan brushed a bright strand of hair from her brow, unaware of how it gave him away. Kate read the relief in his eyes. He'd been afraid she wouldn't make it, she thought. Yet if she'd died, he wouldn't have to take her along on this dangerous trek into the Yukon. Looking at his strong face, she knew he would never seek such an easy answer. He could simply have ordered her back to Skagway, and in spite of her threat to the contrary, she would have had little choice but to turn back. Gratitude flooded through her as she thought of all he'd done for Gilly and her. Then the memory of their wedding ceremony came to her and she looked at him in dismay.

"Reverend Talbot? The wedding?" she asked, barely able to remember the proceedings.

Hogan nodded. "What about them?"

"Are we . . . ? Did we get married?"

He nodded curtly and turned away, his back and shoulders rigid. Silently Kate studied him, guessing how such a man as Hogan must hate the thought of being wedded, even if as a matter of convenience. She would, she vowed, make every effort not to behave like a wife to him, nor to demand more from him than she was entitled.

The tent flap parted and May entered. "You awake!" she said in surprise, her bright eyes studying Kate.

Axe was right behind her. "Feeling better now?"

Kate smiled thinly. "Feeling better," she echoed faintly. "Thank you, May, for your care."

"Not me. Hogan take care. Do everything he can think make well. I get food now."

Kate listened to May's clipped speech while a growing horror settled over her. She was lying in her bedroll in only her long underwear. Who had taken off her clothes? Certainly not the diminutive May. When the Indian woman returned, Kate asked her.

"Hogan good doctor," May said with a warm smile.

TOMORROW'S DREAM 99

She spooned broth until Kate could take no more and waved it away. "Hogan work hard so you not die. Have chills, he hold, warm with body. Have fever, he wash with melted snow. Work hard to make better. He say his fault Gilly die, not let you die too."

"That's enough, May," Hogan growled.

Taking the cue, Axe turned toward the tent flap. "Come on, May, we'll go back to our tent and start packing up. We need to push on as soon as possible."

"We'll start first thing in the morning," Hogan said. Axe grunted his agreement, and with a last nod at Kate accompanied May from the tent.

"If you'll leave so I can dress, we can go immediately," Kate said, sitting up, the covers clutched high under her chin. In her embarrassment she didn't look at Hogan. She didn't see him reach for her until she felt his hands, large and warm, on the bare flesh of her arms.

Firmly he laid her back on her bedroll and smoothed the covers over her. "We leave in the morning," he said, and when she opened her mouth to protest, held up an admonishing finger. "For me, not you." Once again she noted the fatigue around his eyes and mouth. The ugly zigzagging scar on the side of his face seemed to stand out more boldly against his gray-tinged skin. With a slight smile she relaxed against the bedding, grateful she didn't have to move yet. She felt tired and weak.

Hogan opened his sleeping bag and sat down to tug off his boots. In consternation, Kate watched him. She'd assumed he would return to the other tent to sleep, but now she remembered Axe's words to May. She'd be sharing this tent, then, with Hogan. She could understand Axe and May's assumption. After all, Hogan and she were wed, but they both had set the rules for that marriage.

Kate closed her eyes, too tired to argue. Fiercely she concentrated on the sapling supporting their tent. She'd never shared a sleeping room with a man before, save for Gilly when he was sick with the fever and she'd sat by his bed through the night, dozing. Would

Hogan take off his clothes? she wondered, and kept her eyes rigidly averted until she heard the whisper of bedclothes and his tired sigh as his head settled against a pillow. Only then did she venture a look, and saw to her horror that he had indeed shed his outer clothes. Now he lay with one arm flung across his eyes. The sleeves of his long underwear showed above the covers.

Kate lay back, trying to calm her outraged thoughts. She was married to Hogan O'Shea. There was nothing wrong with his undressing in her presence or in their sharing a tent. The old conventions of propriety were behind her once and for all. Deliberately she turned her thoughts to other matters and remembered something else May had said.

"Gilly's death wasn't your fault, you know," she said out loud.

Hogan looked at her sharply, one eyebrow rising slightly the way it did when he didn't know how to answer and was about to hide it behind an insult. Please don't, she silently pleaded. As if he'd read her thoughts, he sighed.

"I shouldn't have let him come, not with his foot like that," he said finally, his voice low and ragged.

"He was there because he insisted," she reminded him quietly. "I insisted, so I suppose I'm to blame too. But the man most responsible is Fletcher Meade. If Gilly hadn't been wounded, he might have gotten away." Her voice cracked.

"Don't do that, Kate," Hogan said, rising on an elbow to peer at her through the gloom. "You'll drive yourself crazy thinking about what might have been 'if only.' "

Shakily she wiped at her tears. "Gilly was so afraid he'd be left behind. You were kind enough to do what most men would have refused." Kate's heart contracted at the thought of Gilly's futile struggle to avoid death. "He would have wanted to die like this." She spoke softly. "I saw his face just before the snow hit, and he wasn't afraid."

"He was a scrappy little Irishman," Hogan said, and Kate heard the affection in his voice.

"How did you meet up with him?" she asked, suddenly curious about the relationship of the two men.

"He was in a saloon fight with a gang of big guys lined up against him. He never backed down once. I just didn't think the odds were even enough, so I gave him a hand. We were outnumbered and took a terrible beating. I finally had to haul Gilly out of there myself. He didn't want to quit. You had a right to be proud of the old man. He was like a father to me. I always kind of figured if I could be a little more like him, I'd be a better man."

"I never knew him very well," Kate said, suddenly jealous of the time Hogan had had with her father.

He seemed to hear something in her voice, for he turned in his pallet and studied her across the half-darkened tent. "He spoke of you often."

"He did?" Kate scrubbed at her eyes with the heels of her hand. The fever had made her silly and weepy.

"Uh-huh. He used to tell me how feisty you were as a little girl, how you had all that fiery red hair and a temper to match, and about how you'd stick up for littler kids when the older ones tried to bully them, and how you'd drag home dogs and cats to tend."

"He told you about all that?" Kate asked in surprise.

"He also told me about the bird you found and how you tried to mend its wing, and the questions you used to ask. He thought you were just about the smartest kid he'd ever seen."

Kate swallowed a lump.

"I always kind of envied you having an old man like him," Hogan went on. 'My pa, well, he wasn't much account, just a whiskey Irishman who couldn't hold his liquor. He used to stop off at the bar on payday and drink up all his wages. It was Ma who held the family together, taught us manners, and made us go to school. She wanted us to have a better life than she and Pa had."

"Us?" Kate prodded softly, moved by the love in his voice when he talked about his family.

"Yeah, I've got a brother and sister. Dory married a doctor, and my brother, well, he went on to become a lawyer. He always liked school." He glanced at Kate with a sheepish grin. "I'm the black sheep in the family. I was too restless to settle down back there, so I came out west, knocked around a little, worked on the railroad for a while, then got to looking for gold." He shrugged self-deprecatingly. "I'm a roamer. Guess I'll never change."

And now he was married to her, Kate thought, tied down to a woman as weak as one of those kittens she used to drag home. Well, it wouldn't be forever. Soon they'd be able to go their separate ways. Now she studied the big man's profile. He really was quite good-looking if not for that horrid beard.

"I know you think me a rough man, Kate," he was saying reflectively. "But the plain truth is, I've been living rough for some years now and keeping rough company. It just sort of rubs off, so a man forgets the things he's learned at his mother's knee."

"Rough company like your father?" Kate asked quietly, wondering about her in-laws. His mother sounded lovely, but his father was quite impossible. Something of her feelings must have sounded in her voice, for Hogan was quick to answer.

"Pa wasn't so bad," he said softly. "He was just a poor starving Irishman who came over here thinking he'd find streets paved with gold. What he found was slums and dirty, backbreaking work at pitifully low wages. There was no way to break away. Maybe if he'd left the city and come out west, he might have found what he was looking for." He paused and turned to look at Kate. "In his way, I suppose he was somewhat like Gilly. Both men were looking for a pot of gold. Only with Gilly the gold wasn't all that important. It was the search that kept him going. He often talked about going back east to spend some time with you, but he just never seemed to get back there."

"No, he never did," Kate said, her throat clogging with the old hurt.

"He was afraid to go back, you know," Hogan said gently. "Your mama wasn't there, and I don't think he could face that all over again."

Kate looked at Hogan's outline in the waning light. Somehow she felt better for his words, knowing that Gilly had carried that love and pain for her mother right to the end. She was able to forgive him a little for leaving her alone to deal with her loss. After all, she'd had Aunt Petty, who'd been like Mama in some ways. Suddenly Kate was glad Gilly had had someone like Hogan as a friend. She would hate to think of him being all alone these past years. Lying back, she stared into the dark shadows.

"Thanks for everything, Hogan," she said softly, speaking of more than his nursing her through the fever.

"Good night, Kathleen Moira," he answered, rolling the words in a broad Irish brogue the way Gilly had. Easy with each other for the first time, they lay in companionable silence until sleep claimed them.

Somehow Hogan had managed to get her down the mountain during her illness, so they could camp in a protected hollow where it was warmer. Now, standing in the dazzling sunshine, waiting for the dogs to be hitched to the sledge, Kate craned her neck and stared up at the mountain. It had claimed Gilly's life and, thanks to her own foolishness, had nearly claimed her own. Surely nothing they encountered after this would be as brutal and dangerous. Hopefully Kate turned her face toward the north.

In the days that followed, her premonition seemed to be coming true. The trail was deceptively easy. The dog teams raced over the snow, packed hard by others who'd surged ahead while she lay ill.

They reached the head of Lake Linderman, where they halted to rest. Kate was breathless and shivering with cold, but she said nothing. She'd insisted on walking behind the sleds as May did. She hadn't regained as much strength as she'd hoped. She put a mitten to her nose, trying to warm it. It felt as if it might fall off her face any moment.

"Pull it, Kate," Hogan called. Taking his hand out of his mitten, he tugged on his nose gently. Kate followed his example and was relieved to feel some warmth returning. "Do it often," he called, "or your nose will freeze."

"Thanks," she answered. She'd come to respect every bit of advice he and Axe passed along. Now she watched as he crouched beside the dog team and checked the bindings and the leather snow socks that had been tied over their footpads.

"Ice looks pretty solid to me," Axe said, studying the terrain ahead. "We'll put up the sails."

Hogan nodded and the two men went into the woods to cut down slender saplings for masts. Quickly they fashioned sails from the extra canvas and fastened them to the two sledges. In wonder Kate watched. Hogan had ordered a fire, and now May set about melting snow. The water was poured over the wooden runners until they were slick and smooth. Then the goods were lashed down again.

"Okay, ladies, climb aboard," Hogan said with a grin and a bow. He helped Kate settle on top of their supply packs, then climbed up beside her.

"Ready?" he called, glancing at the other sled. Axe nodded and May giggled with anticipation. Hogan raised the sail. With a jerk that nearly unseated Kate, it caught the wind. The sled leapt forward, skimming across the frozen lake so swiftly their eyes teared. Axe and May were right behind them.

Kate laughed at the illusion of flight. Hogan knelt above her, the rigging line gripped firmly in his gloved hand. His head was thrown back and the wind whipped the dark hair across his broad forehead. Eyes gleaming, teeth flashing white against his black beard, he laughed and whooped his delight to the wintry sky. Raising one fist jubilantly, he shook it as if in a challenge to the gods that thought to control men's destinies. Let lesser, punier men bow to the vagaries of the fates. Hogan O'Shea would not. He was a man bigger than life, vibrant and alive. He made all others seem colorless by comparison.

Kate studied his unguarded expression, which reflected the confidence and ebullient vitality of a man able to take care of himself, able to meet any challenge offered. Her heart caught in her throat. Be careful, she warned herself. Though he was in name her husband, there was little else between them, and never could be. She'd meant it when she said he was not the sort of man with whom she wanted to spend the rest of her life. Their backgrounds were too different, their goals for the future too far apart. She might enjoy his company, as she would a frisky pup playing in the sun, but she must never feel more than friendship for him, if indeed that.

Yet she was bothered. Hogan could never be compared to something so tame as a frisky pup. He would never be one of her wounded animals, one of her causes needing attention. Certainly he was too self-sufficient ever to need a woman. It seemed strange to her to be in the role of accepting help and kindness from another human being. She was too independent herself.

Kate sighed and put all her thoughts behind her, giving herself over to the sheer pleasure of gliding over the ice. But the wind off the ice was chilling, and long before they'd reached their destination, she pulled her hood tightly about her and huddled down on the packs to doze.

It took only two hours to cross Lake Linderman to the mouth of the Yukon River. There they set up camp. Kate climbed off the pack and walked around until the stiffness had left her limbs. The men had already started setting up the tents. Breathing deeply of the cold, crisp air, Kate looked around the wintry wonderland of their surroundings. Tall slender pines rose toward the sky, their branches weighted down by the heavy accumulation of snow. Low-lying bushes were smothered beneath mounds of snow. The sun, gleaming low in the sky, set the mountaintops aglow with a silvery light. A quiet stillness lay over the landscape and echoed the loneliness that rested in Kate's heart. Shivering at the stark isolation, she turned back toward camp and the sound and sight of other human beings. The men had already set up the tents, so Kate hurried to help May gather firewood.

Hogan dug his rifle out of the pack and filled his pockets with ammunition. "We're going to find some game," he said. "We're out of fresh meat."

Kate nodded, aware suddenly that May's stews had held more beans and fewer chunks of meat the past few days. She watched as the men tied on their snowshoes, then trudged off toward the timberline. While they were gone she and May set about making a fire and putting a pot of coffee to boil. They'd fallen into an easy work routine between them. Now, as they settled on the edge of a sled and sipped coffee, Kate smiled at the younger woman.

"How long have you and Axe been together?" she asked, giving way to the curiosity that had plagued her about the mismatched couple.

"Long time," May said. "Two moons after May become woman." Kate stared at her in dawning horror as the realization came that May was much younger than she'd thought.

"Why . . . why did you choose to mate with Axe? I mean, he is a good deal older than you."

May giggled at Kate's words. "Axe many summers."

"Why didn't you marry someone from your own tribe?"

May's eyes widened, then grew sad. "When May girl, bad winter. No food. Men go hunting. No come back. Tribe wait many days. No hunters. No food. Few men in tribe. Come time of May's second moon. May woman now. Time get ready for marry." She shrugged. "But no friend to make May ready. Father, Mother, take May to next village. Seek kind friend who make May ready."

Kate's face was crimson as she listened to May speak so frankly of her monthly cycle and of the Eskimo custom of giving a daughter to a friend for her first intimate encounter. Biting back her censorship of such a barbaric custom, she listened quietly as May continued. "No find mate. No want young man. Too bossy. Axe come village. Have gun. Kill much game. Feed village. May choose Axe." She finished with a flourish. Throughout the telling, her mobile face had reflected numerous emotions—fear, sadness, and joy. Obviously May felt she'd made an excellent choice for herself, and perhaps she had, Kate thought, in spite of their vast differences in age. Axe was kind and considerate of May and always treated her with respect. Kate grinned to herself. She'd never once heard him boss May.

When the chores were done, Kate wandered along the frozen lakeshore and came upon a small area where the ice was already melting. A pair of trumpet swans floated on the still, quiet pool of water, their long necks arching gracefully over their heavy bodies. Breath held for fear she might startle them, Kate watched the majestic birds. They must be among the first of the migrating birds returning from the warmer climates, she guessed. It made spring seem that much closer, and she wondered what this vast land would be like when the snow and ice were melted. Would it be as breathtakingly beautiful, as wondrous and isolated as it was now? Thoughtfully she made her way back to camp.

The men had returned empty-handed. Kate could see worry etched in their faces. Meat was an important part of their diets, for the cold soon took its toll on a man if he weren't eating properly. Morosely Hogan and Axe sat down on the packs to sip the coffee May poured.

"Spring is coming," Kate said brightly, hoping to cheer them from their depression. "I saw a pair of swans back there a ways." She nodded in the direction she'd taken earlier.

Hogan looked at Axe. "Swans make good eating," he said.

"They shore do," Axe cried, grabbing up his rifle. The two men leapt up and ran off toward the lakeshore.

"Where are you going?" Kate cried. "What are you doing? You can't kill the swans." But they didn't even look back. Kate ran after them. "Wait," she cried. Panting, she caught up with them as they crouched behind snow mounds. Hogan put a finger to his mouth to gesture her to silence.

"You can't kill a swan," Kate cried. "They're too beautiful."

"They're food and we need meat right now."

"I won't eat it," Kate declared.

"The rest of us will," Hogan said absently as he raised his rifle and took aim. Kate could see the finger settling on the trigger and squeezing ever so gently.

"No," she cried, and reached for his rifle barrel. She'd left her mitten behind in camp and her hand was bare.

"Don't grab the barrel," Hogan shouted, jerking the rifle away before she could grab it.

Kate whirled on him in a fury. "You can't kill those swans," she snapped.

"That was a damn-fool thing to do," he shouted at her. "Don't ever grab a rifle barrel, especially in this cold. Your hand'll freeze right to it."

"I don't care," Kate declared. "You can't be so brutal as to kill these beautiful wild creatures. If I'd known this was what you intended, I never would have told you about them."

"Kate, we have to eat," Hogan replied patiently.

"Not the swans," she answered stubbornly. They faced off, staring at each other. It seemed neither of them meant to give way. Suddenly Kate whirled and ran along the shore, taking off her coat and waving it wildly while she called shrilly. At last, startled by this strange apparition, the swans opened their great wings and rose from the water. Gracefully they soared through the air, their heavy bodies revealed to the hunters below. Kate looked back. Hogan was already standing, legs braced, rifle to shoulder.

"No," she screamed, and raced back along the path. Without slowing her speed, she plowed into him, sending him tumbling backward. His rifle spun out of his hands and buried itself in a snowbank. Kate lay sprawled across Hogan, her petticoats flying, her legs and arms thrashing as she sought to hold him down. She could hear Axe fire and curse. He'd missed, and now his gun was jammed.

Hogan wrestled with Kate, surprised by the strength of her slender body. Of course, he'd held her down often during her fever, but now was different. Now she was conscious and fully aware of what she was doing. As he tried to capture her wrist, she wriggled it out of his grasp while keeping him pinned down with her body. Her hood fell away and loose flame-colored tendrils feathered around her face. Hogan stopped struggling. He was breathing heavily. He could easily wrest her off him, but he found himself enjoying the spectacle of a prim Kate wrestling him to the ground.

Her green eyes were glowing with anger and determination. Auburn tendrils framed her face. Her cheeks were bright with color. One pale hand grasped his above his head, while his other hand was pinned between them by a soft mound of breast. Eye to eye, they stared. Hot breaths mingled as they gasped from their exertions. Hogan saw in her eyes sudden awareness of the way their bodies were pressed to one another, and surprisingly enough, he felt his own response to a soft warm female in such close proximity. His body acted of its own accord and he saw the start of surprise as she felt the burgeoning evidence of his response against her leg. Quickly she moved, scrambling off him. Regretfully Hogan got to his feet and looked for his rifle, retrieving it from the snowbank and wiping at it with his gloved hand.

"You can't kill them," Kate cried again, looking at the sky in search of the swans.

"You don't need to worry about that now," Hogan said disgustedly. "My gun's got snow in the barrel."

"I missed 'em too," Axe swore. "My dadblamed rifle jammed."

"We might as well go back to camp. Looks like we have flapjacks tonight." Dejected, the men turned toward camp. Kate tagged along behind, sorry she'd gotten snow in Hogan's rifle, but happier that she'd saved the swans.

"You get swans?" May asked eagerly when they returned. She already had out a Dutch oven. Her smile faded when they told her what had happened, and for the first time since they'd started out together, she frowned at Kate. Kate glanced at their accusing faces and felt defensive and angry. How could they possibly have wanted to eat such beautiful creatures? she wondered, and turned her back on them.

But their censure wasn't over. As they huddled around the fire, Kate on one side and the three of them on the other, she felt the oppressive weight of their disapproval. They were used to the wilderness and the demands it made in order to survive. She was not, and she began to wonder if her fine principles had been properly placed after all. Silently they ate their meager meal and readied themselves for bed.

Once again Hogan and Kate shared a tent, and mindful of his response when she'd wrestled with him, Kate crawled into bed in her clothes. When Hogan came to bed, she breathed deeply, feigning sleep.

When they woke in the morning, deep cracks had formed in the mirror surface of the river ice. "Guess we'd better stay right here till it's out," Axe said. "No sense in taking risks."

Hogan nodded in agreement. "We'll do some hunting then," he said. "Maybe we can find some game." He glanced at Kate, but she looked away. "You won't have any objections to that, will you, Miss Softhearted O'Riley?" he asked, gathering up his snowshoes and rifle. His tone wasn't entirely angry.

"Certainly not," Kate replied, "as long as you don't kill swans."

"We may get a goose or two," he shot back. "Is that going to offend you?"

"*You* offend me, Mr. O'Shea," she declared grandly, and turned her back on him. She didn't watch as the men trudged toward the woods. While she and May waited for the men to return, they mended the canvases and watched the river ice break up.

The men returned late in the day with two geese and a small caribou. Kate tried not to show her queasiness as May and the men set about cleaning the game. Instead, she busied herself dragging in more firewood, although the stack was already high enough, and bringing clean snow to be melted for drinking water. In no time May had a plucked goose roasting over the coals. The men cut up the venison in smaller chunks and buried it in a cache beneath the snow.

Hogan had refrained from saying anything to Kate about their kill, but that night as she feasted heartily on roast goose and rice, he smiled knowingly across the fire. Kate flushed and wished she had the willpower to dash the meat into the fire, but the plain fact was that she was hungry. She was aware too of how she must look, with her hair windblown, her skin red and chapped, her chin and fingers smeared with grease, but she didn't care. She took another bite of the succulent meat and suddenly smiled back at him.

With a nod of his dark head, he raised his own plate in a silent salute. His black eyes reflected the firelight with a provocative glow that warmed her blood. Unbidden came the memory of his hard body beneath her and the swell of him against her leg. What would it be like, she wondered, to be loved by a man like Hogan?

She thought of Roxanne with her adoring gaze and smug, sensuous smile. Oh, yes, he would be an experienced lover, as knowledgeable in that as he was in most things, she thought crossly. But she wasn't Roxanne, simpering and admiring of him and his manly accomplishments. Abruptly she set her plate down in the snow, although it still bore a fat, juicy piece of goose.

Across the fire's glow, Hogan wondered what had caused the mischievous smile to be replaced by her customary scowl. Sighing, he turned to stare into the fire, and his thoughts turned to Roxanne as well. He missed her. That was the reason for these disturbing feelings. He must truly be more desperate than he realized, if for one brief moment he'd found that sour old maid beautiful and desirable.

The following day the men cut down trees and whipsawed lumber for two boats. In fascination Kate watched as they worked on the roughly made crafts. When they were completed, she wondered if indeed they could hold all four of them and their supplies, but the men serenely ignored her question and went into the woods to find a pine tree and collect its resin to mix with their tar and pitch and thus waterproof the boats.

The days were growing perceptibly longer. The bright sun burned away the ice, and in a matter of days they were able to start out again, this time in their rough boats, which the men alternately poled and rowed. The sledges had been lashed to the sides. The dogs rode inside the boats, restless and snarling at first, then settling down on the packs to sleep. At the mouth of the Yukon River they turned northwest. They would travel four hundred miles down this winding waterway, moving ever deeper into the interior. They continued to meet other travelers on the river. They called hearty greetings to one another, but no one halted long for a visit. They hurried on, each intent on reaching the goldfields first. With their single-mindedness, Kate could understand why they'd been dubbed stampeders. They were not unlike a herd of cattle in mindless stampede.

Although they'd waited nearly a week to ensure that the ice was out, still ice caps lined the shore, some of them breaking loose now and then to drift by with a deceptive languidness that belied the dangers they presented to the flimsy boats. It became the job of May and Kate to keep their eyes open for such ice floes and push them away before they could plow into the boats, overturning them or ripping holes in the sides. Now and then they caught a glimpse of wrecked boats washed ashore and packs of goods floating in a backwash, evidence that some travelers had not been lucky enough or wise enough to avoid the dangers of the ice caps.

"Dang fools started out too early," Axe said when

they passed some travelers stranded on the shoreline. "Got caught by the ice."

"Aren't we going back to help them?" Kate asked, feeling sorry for the men who stood watching resignedly, their hopes for the gold mines squelched for the moment.

Axe shook his head. "No room in our boats. Besides, don't do no good with some of 'em. They got to learn to help tharselves."

"Don't worry, Kate," Hogan said. "They'll get tired of waiting for someone to rescue them and build another boat or start hiking through the woods."

"If they ain't got the gumption to do that, then they'd best head on back to civilization," Axe called. He chewed on his tobacco and spat.

"Axe is right." Hogan nodded. "You offer help where help is truly needed, not where a man's being lazy."

Kate thought about his words. The land was harsh, pitiless, and she supposed it took sorting out priorities if one were to survive. Still, she wished they'd stopped and offered help of some kind.

They traveled down the river all day, and late in the afternoon it seemed the current grew swifter. Kate could tell by Hogan's expression that he was growing worried.

"Axe, what's going on?" he called.

The old sourdough shook his head. "I don't rightly know," he answered. "I ain't never seen the river like this either."

They pushed on, growing ever more tense and watchful. A hum seemed to fill the air. Kate heard it and glanced at Hogan, who sat with head raised, dark eyes wary and thoughtful. He turned toward Axe, but the old man and May seemed not to notice anything out of the ordinary. Suddenly Hogan went stiff, his eyes widening, alarm growing in his expression.

"Head for shore," he shouted, paddling wildly. "Axe, make for shore. Now!"

Some of Hogan's intensity made itself felt, for the old man turned his clumsy boat to the riverbank. Already the current had reached such strength that they were forced to struggle against its pull. The hum had turned to a menacing roar. The air crackled with danger. Hogan angled the boat upstream, and Axe followed.

Sitting in the prow, Kate watched the two men straining against the river and she wondered how Axe, with his thin old body, could find the strength to row against the river's current. May was using her hands to help move the boat along. Kate did the same, and gasped at the coldness of the water. She could hear Hogan grunting with his efforts at the paddle, and still it seemed they moved in slow motion. Slowly the riverbank grew closer, and Kate felt relief sweep through her as the boat hull brushed against gravel. Hogan flung himself out of the craft and heaved it safely up onshore. Then he raced into the river again, his long legs churning the cold water to a white froth as he grasped Axe's boat and tugged it onshore. For a moment he rested there, leaning over the prow, chest and shoulders rising as he gasped in air. Then he raised his head and all four stared at each other as they listened to the loud, wild roar of the river.

"Let's walk up the bank a ways and see what's happened," Hogan said, and they started out. They didn't have to go far. Rounding a bend, they stopped dead in their tracks and gaped. Before them spread the awful tale of how close they'd come to death. An ice jam had formed at the bend, the ice cakes racking up on each other along the river's edge until a narrow chute had been formed. Water rushed through it at a dangerous speed. They might have survived that, riding the icy rapids successfully, but at the end of the chute an ice wall had built up, blocking the passage of any boat. The rushing river water was forced beneath the ice floes. It would have carried their boats to a watery grave.

No one said a word. All three turned to look at Hogan, and he read plainly on their faces how grateful they were. He'd saved their lives. With a final look at the treacherous river, they made their way back to their boats.

"Might as well set up camp," Hogan said. "We'll have to wait until that breaks up." The men hauled out the canvas tents and set them up. Automatically Kate went to help May gather wood. What had seemed drudgery before seemed a blessed and sweet privilege now. They were alive, despite the trap set for them by the river.

Kate thought of others who might not have understood what the racing current and thundering roar meant. Had they been swept to their deaths? How many men would this land claim before it yielded up its treasures?

"We have to warn others," she said to Axe when she'd returned to camp. "There's no telling how many men have already perished."

"Aye," he said. "Hogan's already set a bonfire back there a ways. It'll give 'em more of a warning than we had."

Kate looked at Hogan, who was busy unpacking the provisions. He seemed to think of everything before anyone else. She could see the growing respect in Axe's eyes for this big, capable man. Now he rose lithely and carried some packs to the fire.

"We'll take turns watching until nightfall," he said. "Then we'll light bonfires. Likely no one'll travel at night, but we won't take a chance. We'll need more firewood." Without a word of protest, Kate hurried off to search for more dead wood. Hogan looked at her strangely, then dug out his ax and followed. Still shaken by their close brush with death, the four of them were somber as they ate the rich caribou stew May had prepared. Darkness was falling rapidly, and although they expected no passersby this late in the day, still Hogan lit the bonfire. No one felt like telling stories or joking tonight. Quietly they stared into the flames and contemplated this adventure they'd undertaken.

Suddenly the sound of men singing and laughing came to them. In disbelief and mingled horror they stared at each other. Hogan leapt to his feet and rushed down to the river's edge, followed by Kate and the others. A boat glided quickly into view. It was dangerously overloaded with three men and their supplies.

"Hey, hey," Hogan shouted, waving frantically.

"Dang fools are ignorin' the bonfire," Axe said.

"Stop, come to shore," Kate cried, jumping up and down as she waved her arms above her head. The men in the boat couldn't hear their words above their own singing. Cheerily they waved back and sang more gustily.

"There's an ice jam," Hogan shouted, pointing downriver, but the boat never faltered in its course. It swept majestically downstream, while its passengers called and whistled a greeting, then began another song. Kate screamed until she was hoarse, but to no avail.

The boat disappeared around the bend. The roar of the river swallowed up the sound of singing. The people onshore fell silent, staring at the spot where the boat had disappeared. Hardly breathing, they stood listening. There was no sound of screams, no cries of distress, no brave song, only the river roaring its displeasure at puny, thoughtless mankind.

"Come on," Hogan cried, and led the way along the riverbank. Dread filled them as they thought of what waited beyond the bend. But when they reached the ice jam, there was no shattered boat, no bits of goods buffeted by the churning foam; all was still and quiet, as if no men had passed this way. Kate shuddered uncontrollably.

The boat had been swept under the ice and the men had gone to their graves, a joyous song on their lips. Still, in those final moments before death, they must have known, must have realized what lay ahead. Surely they hadn't been such fools that they'd failed to recognize their fate. As she turned away, she spotted a movement in the water and cried out.

"What is it?" Hogan demanded, running to her. Kate pointed a shaking finger at the churning water. A lone head had bobbed to the surface, and even as they watched, a man threw out an arm to grasp the rough edge of an ice floe. The current sucked at him greedily, but with superhuman effort he hung on. With bated breath Kate and the others watched his valiant struggle. It seemed certain that any moment the current would suck him away from his precarious hold and spin him away under the ice. But one leg was thrown over the edge of the ice cake and the man hung half in and half out of the water, while he rested and tried to gain strength for the final effort. At last he heaved himself up on the ice, rolled over onto his back, and lay still.

"He's dead," Kate whispered.

"If he's not now, he soon will be," Hogan said.

"Yup, he'll die of exposure out here, sure enough," Axe observed, looking at the darkening shadows.

"You have to help him," Kate cried.

"He on other side. No way get him," May said with asperity to Kate.

"We can't just leave him there to die," Kate insisted. "There must be some way."

Hogan stood looking up and down the river. "We could take one of the boats back upstream and cross over where it's safe," he said, as if considering, "but it would take too long, half the night, before we got him back." He turned downriver. "We could—"

"Don't think about it, boy," Axe broke in.

"But the ice jam seems steady enough now. We could cross over that."

"That jam could go any minute," Axe said. "When it does, anyone out there won't stand a chance."

"Don't do it," Kate cried, and wondered at her fierce protectiveness. She was dependent on Hogan, she told herself. If he were killed, she would be alone in this dangerous wilderness except for an old man and his Indian wife. "We don't even know if he's alive." She paused. They all knew the unconscious man on the ice cake was alive. They'd watched his brave struggle and had been touched by it. Now Kate fell silent before the look in Hogan's eyes, for she knew nothing she could say would sway him. He followed a code of his own, a code that allowed him to turn his back on stranded careless travelers onshore, but compelled him to help a brave man, no matter what the risk to himself.

"I'll cross over alone," he said to Axe. "You'll stay with the women."

Axe nodded in agreement, and Kate knew it wasn't out of fear for his own life, but because if anything happened to Hogan, Axe would be needed to take Kate and May back to civilization. "I'll get some rope from the packs," the old man said. "It might help."

"It might," Hogan said curtly. Quickly the rope was brought. One end was tied around Hogan's waist and the other end secured around a tree onshore. Hogan paused only for a moment, clamping Axe on the shoulder in some unspoken message that only men seemed to share; then his gaze swung to Kate. For a moment his dark eyes held hers; then he was gone, running down the riverbank. He disappeared for a moment or two, then was on the ice, agilely making his way across the stacked ice cakes. Sometimes he had to climb; always he picked his way with care. Breathlessly Kate stood watching the lone tall figure, and it seemed that her heart had stopped beating.

Hogan had reached the other side now, and as he raced out on the shelf where the unconscious man lay, the ice shifted and he fell to his knees.

"Hogan!" Kate screamed, and ran forward.

"Stay here, girl," Axe ordered roughly. For a moment they all held their breath, their muscles tensed as if they lay on the ice themselves. Would it shift again? Would the river at last wash away its frozen waste? Kate pressed her cold, trembling hands to her lips and prayed. She was unaware that tears rolled down her cheek and froze in icy runnels.

Her breath came now in vaporous gasps, soughing in relief as Hogan got to his feet again. Running to the fallen man, he took no time to examine him, only raising his long lean frame and slinging it over his shoulder. Bent under his burden, he started back. With a loud grating sound the ice shifted again. Hogan staggered, but stayed on his feet.

"Hurry, boy," Axe said under his breath. "The ice is going any minute." Kate felt her heart constrict, but she made no more outcry. She wanted to do nothing that might distract Hogan from what he was about. The ice moaned and the roar of the river seemed to change in pitch, growing higher, like a whine now. Hogan had left behind the flat ice shelf where the man had taken refuge and was directly over the raging water of the chute.

Kate gripped her hands so tightly her fingers turned white, but she never noticed the pain. "Don't let it go now," she prayed fiercely.

Then he was beyond the chute, picking his way over the stacked ice, climbing slowly, carefully, but steadily with his heavy burden. He disappeared for a moment and Kate waited for him to reappear below them on the bank. Suddenly the ice thundered, cracking loudly, and the river screamed. In horror Kate watched as the ice moved, then slowly began to twist and roll in the current. Everything was motion and loud deadly noise. Kate screamed and heard no sound of it in the roar of the river and ice. Only the aching muscles of her throat assured her of her action. She screamed again and again while memories of another man's death flashed before her.

She saw the rope tighten and strain and then go slack, and she turned away from it, away from the river and the ice that had proved a man's cunning and strength a lie. Hogan had been outwitted by the river. Like Gilly, he'd lost his challenge to the great white wilderness. She thought of him the day they'd sailed across the lake, with his hair blowing and his laughter ringing out boldly. He'd been so alive and vibrant, so strong and invincible, but the river had won the battle. Kate pressed her fist to her mouth and bowed at the waist, sobbing with despair.

"I could use some help down here," a voice gasped from below the bank. Kate whirled to look at Axe. He stood transfixed, as if listening to a voice from the dead. But now a dark head showed above the edge of the bluff. Kate and Axe rushed forward to help haul the man off Hogan's shoulders.

"Hogan," she cried as he scrambled up the bank. Without thinking, she flung her arms around him and felt herself enclosed in a fierce bear hug. Then Axe and May were there, laughing and talking all at once. A moan brought their attention back to the man Hogan had risked his life to rescue.

"He's in pretty bad shape," Hogan said.

Axe laid the man out on the ground and crouched over him. May hurried to examine him. But Kate had no eyes for the unconscious man. She stared at Hogan.

"We thought you were caught in the ice," she said wondrously.

Hogan glanced up from his patient. "That rope saved me," he said to Axe. "I swung the last few feet to shore. Got my feet wet some, but I'm all right."

"You was sure lucky," Axe said fervently. "I thought you was a goner."

"I thought so too," he answered, and glanced at Kate. His dark eyes studied her tear-streaked face. "Why, Kate," he said in a soft voice. "Are those tears for me?" When she made no answer, he reached out a rough hand to gently wipe at her cheek. "I've never had a woman weep for me before." He brought his finger to his lips to taste the salty tears, and forced a half-mocking smile, as if his words had meant nothing. But she'd seen the trembling of his hands, and suddenly she wanted to fling her arms around him again. Their gazes held and she knew without words just how frightened he'd been. The revelation shook her, for she sensed that this big brave man seldom let anyone see very far inside his soul.

7

May knelt beside the still body. There was no sign of life. Not even the man's chest rose and fell to indicate breathing. It would be a miracle if he lived after this harrowing experience. Sorrowfully Kate glanced at the handsome young face, noting the deathly palor, then gave a small cry.

"What is it?" Hogan asked anxiously. "Do you know this man?"

Kate nodded. "He's Clay Lawford, the man who saved you from being bushwhacked back in Skagway." Any other time Hogan might have given a small grin at the way Kate was adopting the western slang, but now he just grunted and looked at the still figure. May had brought a blanket and wrapped it around Clay.

"If we don't get those wet clothes off, he's going to freeze. Let's take him back to the fire," he said, and bent to gather up the slender form. May had already rushed ahead to open her medicine pouch and pick out bundles of herbs. They settled Clay Lawford on a pallet near the fire and stripped away the icy outer garments. Working quickly, they wrapped him in some of Hogan's clothes and extra blankets. May brewed an herb tea from her medicine pouch, and patiently the women took turns spooning it into his half-open mouth and stroking his throat muscles to force him to swallow. Hour after hour they worked with their patient. Hogan and Axe hovered nearby. At first Clay lay pale and unresponsive, and Kate feared it might already be too late, but as the night wore on, he began to toss and cry out, lost in a delirium of fever.

Unperturbed, May gathered rocks from the riverbank, heated them, then wrapped and placed them at her patient's feet and sides. Kate struggled to keep the covers over Clay as he fought his way through the chills that racked his body. And when the fevers came, she bathed his arms, legs, and face tirelessly to cool his body. At Kate's insistence, May went off to rest for a while before taking another turn at nursing. Hogan crouched by the pallet, studying Kate as she tended Clay.

"How's he doing?" he asked softly.

"He's pretty bad." She wrung out the rag and placed it over Clay's forehead. "He just can't die, Hogan," she cried. "Look at him. He's so young and beautiful and brave. It would be a tragedy if he didn't make it."

Hogan glanced at her sharply. He couldn't understand the jealousy that coursed through him at the softness of Kate's voice or the concern on her face when she looked at Clay Lawford. True, he was young and handsome and brave, although he was also foolhardy. Look how he and his friends had ignored the bonfire warning and sailed blithely to this disaster. He was a tenderfoot, a pilgrim, a cheechako of the worst sort. If the circumstances hadn't been so tragic, Axe would no doubt be laughing at him now. The thought gave Hogan little comfort. It was what Kate thought that bothered him. Sighing, he went off to gather more wood for the fire. They'd have to keep it burning hot all night long.

Toward morning the fever broke and at last Clay slept quietly. Exhausted beyond anything she'd ever known, Kate slumped beside him, unable to get up and go to her sleeping bag. Shivering, she huddled near the fire. Strong hands gripped her shoulders, pulling her to her feet. She could feel Hogan's large body behind her, and for a moment she leaned against it, grateful for his support.

"Go to bed," he ordered. "I'll sit up with him now." Firmly he guided her to their tent.

"I think he's going to make it, Hogan," she said tiredly.

"He should," Hogan agreed. "You and May did a good job."

Kate smiled at his words. In spite of her fatigue, the smile seemed to light her face with a special beauty and warmth. Beneath her aloof, oh-so-proper exterior, Kate O'Riley was a passionate, caring woman. Never mind that she'd shown this side of her nature over another man, Hogan told himself. Yet it rankled. Long after he saw Kate safely to the tent, he sat before the campfire and thought of the past few weeks. Death had brushed by them several times now, and yet somehow they'd managed to elude its sharp clutches, but could they the next time? He had little doubt there would be a next time. Thus far, the land had only tested them. Next time, would it break them? He studied Clay Lawford. What was this man to Kate?

Light touched the eastern rim when he finally pulled his blankets around himself and hunkered down for some rest. Clay was sleeping easily. The fever had passed. He'd been lucky. They all had.

"I can't tell you how grateful I am that you saved my life," Clay Lawford said the next day, holding a hand out to Hogan. His clothes had been dried over the campfire and he was dressed now, although his face was still pale and showed the strain of his ordeal. When he'd awakened earlier and they'd told him of the fate of his companions, he'd walked down to the bend and stood staring at the tumbling river. The ice jam was gone, as were most of the ice floes, washed away toward the Bering Sea, hundreds of miles to the west. Sadly he'd made his way back to camp and sought out Hogan. "Kate told me what you did," he said, his eyes clouded with emotion, his face earnest.

Hogan shook hands, wanting to dislike him, yet finding himself drawn to Clay. "From what I hear, it was something I owed you. Thanks for disarming Fletcher's man back in Skagway."

Clay smiled diffidently. "I never liked to see someone dealing underhandedly. If death must seek us out before our natural time, it seems somehow ignoble to come from the bullet of a coward."

"Thanks again," Hogan answered gruffly, and turned back to inspecting the boats.

Clay stayed where he was on the riverbank, studying the swirling water below. "I guess it's not much better to die from being a fool," he said quietly.

"Didn't you see the bonfire?" Hogan asked. "Didn't you hear us hollering?"

Clay shrugged. "We were feeling pretty euphoric. We'd crossed the Chilkoot safely. We figured the worst was behind us. We could handle anything. We just hadn't considered the force of this river." He paused abruptly and turned away.

"What will you do now?" Hogan asked to get his mind away from the death of his companions and on the very act of surviving. "We've got some extra supplies. We can give you enough to get back to Skagway."

Clay wiped at his eyes and faced Hogan. "I'm much obliged, but I think I'll try to go on to Dawson."

"Man, that's foolhardy." Hogan's eyebrows shot up as he scowled at the younger man.

"You have reason enough to think that," Clay observed. "But I've set my sights on Dawson. I noticed that some of our gear washed ashore on the other side. If you'd ferry me across the river, I'll take stock of what I have and make a final decision then."

Hogan nodded. "I'll take you across." He watched as Clay Lawford walked back to the campfire, and was struck by the similarities between him and Kate. Both had a foolhardy disregard for common sense at times, yet each possessed such staunch spirits, such indomitable reserves of character that Hogan began to believe that Clay could reach Dawson. Swearing, he turned back to loading the boat.

Hogan did ferry Clay across the river later that morning. Together they dragged several bundles of gear back to camp. Many of Clay's belongings had been swept away, but the remaining packs held foodstuff, a rifle, and some heavier clothes.

"Better than I'd hoped for," Clay said. "If I'm careful with my supplies and have luck with hunting, I'll have plenty of food."

"We can spare you some," Kate said. She had crouched nearby to help sort out and dry the retrieved supplies.

"Hogan's already offered," Clay said. Kate glanced up at Hogan and smiled her thanks.

"I'm sorry you won't be going on," she said to Clay.

"Actually, I will be. I've decided to push on to Dawson. I can buy more supplies there."

"They'll be twice what you paid back in Seattle," Axe reminded him.

Clay shook his head in understanding. "I know, but I don't want to turn back. Not now." His pale blue eyes turned to Kate, who blushed prettily. Hogan stared at the two of them and felt a flush of anger wash over him. He bit his tongue, unwilling to reveal his anger when he didn't understand the reason for it.

"I have an idea," Kate said brightly, looking around at the circle of faces. "Clay can join us." Axe reared back on the log he'd chosen as a seat. One hand thoughtfully combed through his long graying beard. May watched Axe, looking for a clue for how she should respond, and Hogan just plain glared at Kate.

"We don't have enough room in our boats as it is," he protested.

"He ain't got much to tote. I reckon we could squeeze in one more person if we had to," Axe said, sucking on the tobacco wad in his mouth.

"I wouldn't want to put you out," Clay said, thereby securing Kate's and May's votes. Even Axe seemed to like the young man, not treating him the way he would any other cheechako. Hogan gritted his back teeth. Hellfire, he liked Clay too, but it didn't mean he wanted to wet-nurse him all the way to Dawson.

"We aren't going to Dawson directly, Mr. Lawford," he replied. "We'll be stopping along the way to pan for gold."

"I understand that, Mr. O'Shea," Clay answered.

"I'm not in any hurry. If I'm careful I can make my supplies stretch for some time. I'd appreciate your company on the way, though."

"Then it's settled," Kate said with such enthusiasm that Hogan thought for a minute she intended to throw her arms around Clay. He smiled at her and it seemed to Hogan that an unspoken message passed between the two of them.

Getting to his feet, Hogan doused the campfire. "Let's get moving, then," he said gruffly, and stalked away.

Startled, Clay Lawford looked after his retreating figure. "Perhaps if Mr. O'Shea doesn't want me to join you . . ." he began tentatively.

"Don't you pay any attention to Mr. O'Shea," Kate said. "He behaves that way toward me as well. His manner is just naturally gruff." Hogan heard her words but he didn't look back. He didn't care what Kate had to say about him, he decided, or what Clay Lawford thought. If the two of them wanted to sit around grinning at each other like a couple of fools, then let them. He had come to look for gold. But as he lashed down the canvas over their supplies, a thought came to him and he paused, glancing along the bank.

Clay Lawford was busy helping Axe with the lashings on his boat. Hogan watched him work. He wasn't a shirker. He seemed a well-meaning young man. Hogan wondered how he'd react if he knew Kate was married, and resolved to make him aware of that fact as soon as possible.

Deliberately Hogan placed Clay's supplies in his boat, so Clay was left to ride with Axe. With the added weight, the craft rode dangerously low in the water. Axe and Hogan stood considering, and of one accord reached for the sleds. With the snow fast melting, they wouldn't be needing them until fall again. By that time they could make new ones, so they left them behind. The dogs were unhitched and allowed to follow onshore while the men called to them now and then to keep them on track.

Gaily Kate waved to Clay, calling out to him to notice a bird or animal onshore. When the boats swung close together, they would share some observation that would invariably bring laughter. Kate seemed so light and carefree, and Clay seemed as pleased with her company. Hogan tried to ignore them, but as the afternoon wore on, his dark gaze registered impatience and his mouth grew tight-lipped and sullen. Kate couldn't imagine what was wrong with him and blithely ignored his grumpy mood. Without the danger of ice floes, the trip downriver was far more relaxed. Languorously she leaned back in the prow of the boat, a dreamy, relaxed look on her face. Her cheeks were pink with excitement, her green eyes sparkled. She looked very pretty. Hogan was irrationally annoyed and wished she'd put her wire-rimmed spectacles back on.

Late in the afternoon the river's current increased again. Uneasily Kate sat up and looked around. "Do you think it's another ice jam?" she asked anxiously, but Hogan merely shook his head, unperturbed.

"We're near the rapids," he said, and signaled to Axe to go ashore. Quickly they made camp and hiked downriver to look at the churning river.

"The White Horse Rapids," Axe said.

Kate could see why they'd been named thus. The water curled and churned in foamy wisps that resembled a sea of horses' manes tossing in the wind. She shivered. "Will we have to ride down these?" she asked fearfully.

"Some men have." Axe spat tobacco juice in mute declaration of what he thought of those same men. "We'll portage our goods around and send the boats through empty."

Hogan nodded in agreement. "Let's get back to camp," he said. "While the ladies make supper, we can take some of the supplies around tonight." The other men followed him back along shore. Kate and May built a fire and set a kettle of stew to simmering.

"Have time for bath," May said, and Kate looked at her in surprise. She longed to have a hot bath and to wash her hair, but how were they to do that out here? She could never stand to bathe in the cold river water. But May had something else in mind. Motioning to Kate, she walked down to the river and selected several good-sized rocks, which she placed in the hot coals. Pulling a large, tightly woven basket from her bundles, she scooped up river water and placed it near the fire. When the rocks were glowing, May removed them and dropped them into the basket of water. They hissed and snapped and a vapor rose as the water was heated. When it was steaming hot, May took out the stones and once again placed them in the coals.

"You go first," she said, pointing to the hot water.

"Are you sure?" Kate asked even as she moved forward to claim the basket. Happily May nodded and Kate gratefully agreed. She longed for a bath, a real bath in a tub, where she could soak away the aches and pains of her muscles and wash away the grime of traveling in such primitive surroundings, but this precious basket of warm water would have to do. Carefully she carried it to her tent and dug out the lavender soap, remembering Hogan's kindness in letting her slip it into her pack.

In spite of the chill, she stripped to the waist, dipped her precious soap and a clean cloth in the warm water, and began her makeshift bath. As the sweet flowery scent of lavender wafted up to her, reminding her poignantly of home, she thought of Hogan. Sometimes he could be wonderfully sensitive to a woman's needs in ways she'd never known from other men, but then, she grimaced, she wasn't exactly experienced when it came to men. Still, she'd watched how the men back in Missouri had treated their wives and she'd often been mystified at their careless disregard of their wives' feelings. They'd seemed more like ill-behaved, selfish little boys than mature men who'd pledged to protect and care for their wives.

In some ways Hogan was like that, and yet he was different. Tender when she most needed it, as if he sensed her fears; gruff and impossibly rude at other times. His shift of moods was quite puzzling. Like today, for instance. He almost seemed to dislike Clay Lawford, for he'd certainly scowled often enough when he saw Kate talking to him. She sighed. Perhaps when Hogan knew Clay better, he would like him as well as she did. In the meantime, she'd take extra care to be friendly to Clay to make up for Hogan's behavior.

Her bath completed, Kate undid her braids and washed her hair as well, rinsing it in unheated water until her teeth chattered. Feeling fresh and clean again, she pulled on clean clothes, and leaving her hair streaming unbound down her back, emptied the basket and carried it back to the fire for May to have her bath.

The stew was nearly done by the time the men returned. Kate had made sourdough bread and baked it on sticks over the fire, and fresh coffee waited on the edge of the fire. The aromas were enticing. Eagerly the men went down to the river to wash up. Hogan was the first one back up the bank, and he paused, his dark eyes suddenly still, his breath held as he caught a glimpse of Kate squatting to stir the contents of the kettle. Long auburn strands flowed over her shoulders, their color rivaling the dancing flames of the fire itself. It was the first time he'd ever seen her with her hair down and he was mesmerized by the fiery curls, which semed to possess a flaming life of their own. Blazing sunrises and dazzling sunsets were there in Kate's hair. He longed to touch it, to run his fingers through the brilliant silken strands, to feel the warmth of it against his face. Her face was turned away from him, half-hidden by the silken red-orange curtain. Then, as if she'd sensed him there, she glanced up, green eyes dancing with laughter, face glowing in the firelight. The soft smile faded. For a moment she looked uncertain.

"Oh, I thought you were Clay," she said in a small voice. Hogan's heart lurched in his chest and his big fists balled the hand towel he'd been using.

"Kate, you look smashing," Clay said, coming to the campfire. His pale blue eyes were bright with admiration. Kate blushed and glanced back at the fire, but Hogan could see the smile was back on her face.

Snorting disgustedly, he flung the towel onto a tent pole and strode to the fire. Picking up a plate, he held it out to Kate.

"Is the stew any good tonight?" he asked roughly. He didn't look at her again. Looking at her made him feel kind of queer, as if he'd gone all week without eating and was hollow and empty inside.

"I hope you like it," Kate said softly, ladling up a plateful for him. Her tone was friendly enough, but when he ventured a glance, he saw her face was serious and closed-looking. That sure wasn't the case when Clay approached with his plate. She was all smiles again.

Dishing up his stew, she made a point of seeing he had big chunks of meat on his plate, and even got his bread for him. Hogan had been left to get his own. Even Axe had May to get his food and fuss over him. Well, Hogan thought, he'd gotten this far in life without a woman, he surely could go on now. But it rankled and he felt an urge to remind Kate she was his wife, even if in name only.

Scowling, he seated himself on an upended log and fell to wolfing down his food in his customary fashion. On the other side of the fire, Kate had gotten herself a plate, and now she settled herself near Clay. Daintily she ate, using her fork and knife as if she were in the finest hotel in Seattle. Beside her, Hogan noticed Clay doing the same thing, and all the time they ate, they talked. The murmur of their voices and their low laughter was as irritating as the pesky flies that would come to plague them later in the summer. Suddenly Hogan's pleasure in the good-tasting stew was diminished and he put aside his plate.

"You coming down with something, boy?" Axe asked from his place by the campfire. Quickly Kate's head came up; her green eyes studied Hogan. But even that show of concern was short-lived, for when he nodded a denial, she turned back to Clay. A lot she cared, Hogan thought, and couldn't put away the memory of Kate huddled over Clay's pallet just the night before. Vexed without knowing why, he stalked off into the dark shadows and spent some time pacing along the riverbank, staring at the dark boiling water below. Now and then Kate's laughter, light and silvery, came to him on the night breeze, and he wondered what Clay could have said that was so all-fired funny. He took small satisfaction in wondering what Clay would think when he saw Kate sleeping in his tent. His ire cooled somewhat as he made his way back to camp.

"Hogan, I'm glad you're back," Kate said in a low voice, coming to stand close to him. He felt his spirits rising. "I've put your things in Axe's tent," she rushed on. "Clay will sleep with you men, and May will sleep with me."

"Why the change?" he demanded, feeling the anger rise again.

Kate shrugged, but Hogan noticed that her eyes didn't meet his. "I just thought this would work out better, since we have an extra man and no place for him to sleep. You don't mind, do you?"

"Why would I?" he snapped, and stalked toward Axe's tent. At least she hadn't suggested Clay sleep in the same tent with her, he thought bleakly, and knew he was being unfair. Her arrangements made the most sense, and yet he would have preferred to stay in his own tent tonight and watch Kate sleeping with her flame-colored hair fanning around her face. The image stayed with him long into the night as he twisted and turned on his bedroll.

The morning air was brisk and cold, but the rising sun was already bright above the treetops. Branches dripped incessantly with melting ice. The snow had turned soft beneath its crusty surface. With labored breaths and straining leg muscles, the men slogged through the slush and mud until all their goods had been packed around the rapids. Finally they untied the empty boats and watched as the racing current swept them through the churning boulder-strewn waters.

Standing onshore with Clay, Kate thought how fragile these roughly made vessels looked as they bobbed in the churning foam. Sometimes they were completely submerged beneath the raging water, but somehow eluded the river's clutches and resurfaced. Like children, Kate and Clay ran along the shore, trying to keep up, the dogs howling and running along behind as if they thought this were a game, and well it might have been. But Kate was heartily glad they weren't riding the boats down.

Hogan was already below the rapids, ready to retrieve the boats. There was surprisingly little damage. Everyone waded into the swirling icy water to help haul the boats onshore. Hogan and Axe smeared on more pitch to tighten the seams, and they reloaded their supplies. With yet another difficult part of the journey behind them, their moods lightened.

Kate could sense a growing excitement in the men, as if they knew they were closer to the goldfields. Even Clay seemed caught up in the same feverish anticipation. That night, as they sat around the campfire, they talked of little else. Names like Forty Mile, Circle, and Bonanza Creek punctuated the conversation. The men spoke of rockers and panning. Kate was reminded of Gilly. He'd once sat around fires like these men, talking and dreaming of finding the big strike. How few of them actually succeeded, and yet the lure of gold was so strong it pulled men from their jobs, their homes, their families. Saddened by this thought and piqued at Clay's preoccupation, Kate went to bed early, never noticing the grim look of satisfaction on Hogan's face. He was tired of watching Clay and Kate huddle with their heads close together every evening, talking low and privately.

He glanced at Clay Lawford across the fire. He couldn't help liking the young man. He had to admit he was a worker, willing to carry his share, and he'd been unfailingly courteous, even in the face of Hogan's surliness. In a surge of brotherhood Hogan passed him a plug of chewing tobacco. Clay declined. Scowling, Hogan spat in the snow. It left an ugly splotch.

While the men talked on, Hogan sat contemplating the ugly smear of tobacco juice and spittle. He couldn't help remembering Kate's words the day he'd kissed her on the boat. She found his tobacco chewing a disgusting habit, but what did he care what she thought? What did it matter if she preferred this namby-pamby shirtwaist from back east with all his fine manners? If not for Hogan, she'd still be an old maid. Never mind that their marriage was in name only. She was his wife. He didn't have to please her and court her. Hadn't he warned her he wouldn't change in any way? Well, this was just one more disgustingly filthy habit that set him apart from Clay Lawford. Kate would just have to get used to it.

And while she was about it, she should begin to conduct herself as a married woman instead of hanging on to Clay Lawford's every word. It didn't look right. More than once Axe had looked at Hogan quizzically. Even if they weren't a real man and wife, she should show some propriety. He was surprised at her.

Self-righteously he cut off another plug, but it had lost its appeal. It was hard to sit talking about gold mining when just a few feet away Kate was undressing in the dark, letting her hair down so it was all loose and hanging over her shoulders in silken scented waves. He thought of how it would be to bury his face in the vibrant mass and kiss the soft white skin of her neck. He'd watched her bending over the fire earlier, squatting and rising effortlessly as she stirred the kettle of stew or moved the coffeepot closer to the flames. She didn't exactly move like other women, all short-stepped and mincing. There was a lean, graceful rhythm to her tall slender body that belied the crimped, ladyish airs she put on. Strip away the gown and petticoats and he'd wager she was as warm and giving a woman as Roxanne and the best whores he'd known.

An ache rose in his loins and raced outward. Then, realizing where his treacherous thoughts had taken him, and that he'd had the gall to compare Kate to a whore, Hogan swore under his breath. Kate was a lady, every inch of her, and not the kind of woman he needed or wanted. He hoped they reached Dawson soon and that Roxanne and the other women were already there. He'd saved up a passel of need over the past few weeks.

Hogan was surly the next morning when Kate bent close to pour him a cup of coffee. Growing used to his surly moods, she ignored him and moved around the fire to sit beside Clay. He greeted her cheerfully, his pale blue eyes studying her face as she talked. That day they passed an Indian village. Kate crouched in the bow of the boat and stared unabashed at the brush-and-skin huts. They seemed woefully inadequate for the people who must live in them year-round. Indians, dressed in ragged furs, hid behind trees and stared with unblinking black eyes as they passed. Axe paddled closer to Hogan's boat.

"Athabascan tribe," he said.

"Are they dangerous?" Kate asked in a low voice, as if they might hear her fear and be sparked to some violent act they might not otherwise have undertaken.

Axe shook his head. "They don't cause much trouble now," he said, "although they've been known to eat one another when the food gets scarce."

Kate shuddered and held a hand over her mouth. "How dreadful!"

Hogan's hand inched toward his rifle. "Should we worry?" he asked.

"I don't think so," Axe answered. "The poor devils are fairly peaceful. They eat their own, and only when they're facing starvation. It's comin' on to spring again. Game's gettin' plentiful. We'd be better off to worry about our supplies when we make camp tonight." The boats passed on, and by late afternoon they'd reached the mouth of Lake LeBarge.

"We'll camp on one of those islands," Hogan called. "They'll provide some protection if the Indians try to come into camp." Axe nodded in approval and they made for the small grassy islets. The shores were rocky. Stunted trees, their branches rising in stark, naked supplication to the clear sky, provided firewood.

Quickly, with the precision of numerous rehearsals, they set up camp; then Kate and May went to search for gull and duck eggs. Swans and geese floated in the river nearby, and although the men had taken their guns, Kate had little worry that Hogan would shoot a swan. She tried not to think of the geese that squawked and flew away at the first sound of gunshots. May knew just where to look for nests, and soon they'd gathered up several eggs. Carefully they carried them back to camp and stored them deep in the flour bags for later use.

Everyone was jubilant when the men returned to camp with two geese, which were quickly plucked and placed over the fire. Kate felt none of her former queasiness as she watched the fat bubble and the skins turn a crisp golden brown. They'd run out of fresh meat two days ago and the monotony of their stews had been unrelieved by the dried caribou strips they'd been forced to use. Her mouth watered as she hovered near the fire, basting a goose so it wouldn't burn. May's face lit with laughter as she watched Kate. The Indian woman had spread one of the oiled ground cloths to one side, and now she sat sewing a shirt for Axe out of tanned caribou hide. Hogan and Axe were retarring the boats. Clay was cleaning his rifle. An air of domesticity lay over the camp.

"Hogan!" Axe said it quietly, but the tenseness in his voice brought everyone's head up. When he had Hogan's attention, he pointed to the far bank. Two Indian canoes had put off from shore and were now making their way toward the islet.

"Do you think they mean trouble?" Hogan asked, laying aside the tar stick he'd been using.

"I don't see no women or children," Axe answered. "It could be a war party."

Hogan glanced at his rifle, propped nearby, but he made no move to pick it up. He knew it was loaded and ready. He kept it that way. Likewise, Axe's rifle was handy, but Clay's gun lay in pieces. Out of the corner of her eye Kate saw him fumble to reassemble it. Metal clunked against metal and Hogan waved him to silence, his eyes never wavering from the approaching canoes. Taking more care, Clay continued to put his gun together. Hogan eased his way over to the packs and laid out his pistol and ammunition.

"If the Indians attack, you women get into those trees as fast as you can," he ordered. Kate nodded, already rooted to the ground by fear.

Swiftly the canoes approached. Now they could see the Indians seated inside.

"Looks like a sorry lot to me," Axe said, and spat nervously.

"Best not to take a chance," Hogan said. The canoes bumped against the bank and the Indians got out. They wore leggings of rawhide with attached moccasins. Some were wrapped in robes of beaver pelts and wore fur hats, but the furs were dirty and the caribou skins old and thin in places. The Indians' hair hung down in greasy strands around their faces. Their black eyes were fierce and missed nothing, from the roasting birds to the guns and ammunition laid ready. They carried deadly-looking spears. Sharp bone-handled knives were jammed into their waistbands. Axe stepped forward.

"Howdy," he said, holding out his hands palm-up to show he carried no weapon.

"Howdy," one of the Indians answered in a like manner. The other men shuffled around their leader. "Me Chief Lean Elk," he said.

"I am Axe, chief of this tribe." The old man made a sweeping gesture. "We wish only to pass through on our way to Dawson."

The Indians regarded him and talked among themselves. Slyly their eyes moved to the bundles of goods and the food cooking on the fire. "Have many goods. Share with Lean Elk and his people?" the Indian asked.

Axe shook his head. "We have only enough supplies for ourselves," he said.

Watching their lean, hungry faces, Kate felt a welling of sympathy. Surely they could give up some food. Impulsively she moved forward. Her movement caught the attention of the Indians and they turned on her with ferocity. She stopped dead in her tracks, the words she'd been about to utter stilled by the wild panic that rose in her breast.

The Indians talked among themselves until, with one impatient gesture of his arm, Lean Elk silenced them. His gaze pinned Kate where she stood, even when he moved closer. From the corner of her eye she saw Hogan reach for his gun. The other Indians raised their spears and held them poised menacingly. Even May drew back in fear, her dark eyes rolling from side to side.

"That's far enough, Lean Elk," Hogan ordered, but the savage chief had already reached Kate. He put out a grimy hand and tugged at the flame-colored strands of hair that had escaped her hood. Kate whimpered and drew back. She could hear the click of Hogan's rifle as he drew back the hammer.

"Wait a minute, son," Axe cautioned. "He ain't hurt anybody yet. He just likes the color of her hair." Everyone waited, hearts pounding, muscles tensed as the Indian ran his hands through Kate's hair, holding the strands up to let them fall through his fingers. His face held a childlike wonder. Suddenly the wonder changed to sternness and he stepped back, although his black eyes still scowled at her. Using his own language, he spoke with somber formality.

Axe scratched his chin and shook his head. "I can't understand you, Chief," he said.

"He say"—May stepped forward—"he want fire woman. He trade for her."

Shock settled over Kate as she realized the Indian was referring to her. Helplessly she looked at Hogan. His dark eyes were nearly as fierce as Lean Elk's. He shook his head. "My woman, no trade," he said.

Again the Indian chief spoke, this time more vehemently. "He say trade," May interpreted.

"Careful, son, we don't want to anger him," Axe muttered under his breath.

Hogan stepped forward until he was facing the chief. "What do you have to trade?" he asked, and Kate thought she saw a glint of humor in his eyes. If she weren't so scared, she would be furious with him. Instead, she remained silent.

Once again May translated. "He say trade spear, knife, and two wives," she said, her eyes enormous as she looked at Kate. Lean Elk had made a most generous offer and she had little doubt that Hogan would agree.

Indeed, Hogan paused as if considering the trade. Slowly he circled Kate, looking her up and down as if she were a horse on an auction block. She fully expected him to ask her to open her mouth so he might inspect her teeth. There was definitely a glint of mockery in the dark eyes that met hers. Kate's ire rose. Her cheeks stained with color. She opened her mouth to speak, but Hogan held up a hand to warn her to silence. Turning back to Lean Elk, he studied the knife and spear that were eagerly proffered, testing their sharpness and the straightness of the shaft. Finally he laid the weapons back in the chief's hands and shook his head. "No trade," he said.

With a growl, Lean Elk took a step forward, his spear raised.

"Would you like some food?" Kate said loudly and in some desperation. "We have a whole pot full." Her heart was pounding wildly.

"Potlatch?" the Indian chief asked, and his eyes lit.

"Potlatch? What's that?" Hogan asked, his body tense, his eyes never leaving Lean Elk's face.

"It's a party," Axe said. "There's food and dancing and gifts given."

"Potlatch," Lean Elk repeated, waving to his men. Kate leapt aside as the Indians surged forward. They squatted around the campfire and with dirty hands tore at the roasted birds. In silence, Kate and May watched them. Even the men said nothing, only swallowing back their own saliva, for they were hungry themselves and had looked forward to having fresh meat. In no time the carcasses were decimated, not one scrap of meat remaining on the bones. Replete, Lean Elk and his men sat back wiping at their greasy chins with equally greasy fingers.

"Dance, sing," he ordered, and Hogan and Axe looked at one another.

"I reckon we'd better do something," Axe said. "Seeing as how that's the way a potlatch goes." He took his harmonica out of his back pocket and blew on it. Lean Elk sat up, his eyes round in wonder. Axe broke into a lively tune.

"Dance," Lean Elk ordered, and his men got up and began to weave around the fire. "Dance," Lean Elk commanded imperiously to Kate and Hogan and the others. Hogan took hold of Kate's hand and swung her around. His arm slid around her waist as he led her into a waltz. Stunned, she tried to follow. She'd never thought Hogan knew how to dance; now she was surprised at how light-footed he was as he led her through the swaying steps.

She could see Clay and May dancing as well. Lean Elk nodded his approval. The snow had long since been trampled beneath their feet and the ground turned to mud that sucked at their boots, and still Hogan moved her around the fire in a graceful dance. Kate forgot about the Indians, forgot about the primitive, harsh setting. She saw only Hogan, his head bent over her, his broad shoulders hunched a bit, as if to protect her, his long legs moving rhythmically. In the warmth of the late-afternoon sun, he'd laid aside his heavy coat. He wore only his long underwear and the flannel shirt over it. Beneath the fabric she could feel the muscles of his shoulders as they bunched and expanded. She could see the graceful sway of his lean hips. She'd never been more aware of the overpowering manliness of him.

Tilting her head, she glanced at his strong face, suddenly wishing he weren't wearing the heavy beard so she might see his jawline. Slashing the bushy beard was his mouth. His lips were firmly molded, the lower lip slightly fuller than the top. Kate remembered the feel of those lips against her own and suddenly wished she could pull his dark shaggy head down so she might kiss him.

She couldn't, of course. It was unthinkable under

the best of circumstances, and these were not the best. She pushed away her sensuous thoughts and concentrated on a spot dead center on his chest. But even there her wayward gaze found trouble, creeping upward to the crisp dark hair curling over the edge of his shirt. She could feel the heat of his body, and somewhere inside were awakened the old devils of temptation and pure lust. Kate blushed and tripped.

Hogan paused. "Are you all right?"

"I . . . I'm just dizzy from dancing so much," she replied.

"Don't stop now," he advised, and pulled her closer while his long legs moved into the dance circle again. Now Kate's cheek was pressed against his chest, and with every trembling breath, she drew in the scent of him. He smelled of fresh air, campfires and the outdoors, and under all that, a healthy, sensuous man smell. She had no willpower to pull away. She wasn't sure she wanted to, so they danced around the fire to the wail of Axe's harmonica and the guttural chants of Lean Elk's Indians. Kate lost all track of time.

It seemed they danced for hours, and indeed they did. The eastern horizon was growing light when Axe finally laid aside his harmonica and drew a weary breath.

Lean Elk and his men grinned amiably. They'd had a wonderful time. Now it was time for the next phase of the potlatch. "Gifts," the chief said, holding out his hands expectantly.

"Uh-oh," Axe muttered. "We'd better give them some of our food. Have you ladies got any trinkets? May, get out your shiny beads."

Kate crossed to her own bundles and dug inside until her fingers met the hard square of her soap. She couldn't give that, she thought unhappily, but she had nothing else of any real value. Across the way, May took out the strung beads she held in such high regard and passed them over to Axe. With resignation Kate took out one of her bars of soap. Lean Elk and his braves were pleased with the gifts. He hung the beads around his neck and turned Kate's soap over and over

TOMORROW'S DREAM

in his hand. He sniffed it, eyes gleaming as he offered it to his men. They too smelled the lavender soap. Finally Lean Elk took a bite of it, his grin fading briefly as he chewed, then returning as he offered the soap around to his men. Each took a bite, until the soap was gone. Expectantly Lean Elk waited.

"Now what?" Hogan asked.

"He's wantin' something more, but I'm not sure what," Axe said.

Suddenly Lean Elk strode forward and grasped Kate's fiery locks, nearly yanking them from her head. "Trade," he insisted. His expression would brook no more delay. Hogan strolled across the circle and took the knife from Lean Elk.

"Hogan, no," Kate whispered, but before she could move, he grabbed a strand of her hair. The knife flashed through the air and a shank of flame-colored hair fell into his hands. Holding it aloft, he turned for all the Indians to see. The light from the campfire caught in the bright strands, echoing its fiery colors. The Indians oohed as Hogan turned back to Lean Elk.

"Trade," he said, and grandly handed over the bright strands. Eyes gleaming, Lean Elk took the locks and with abrupt decisive movement tied them into his own hair so they fell forward onto his shoulder as they had with Kate. Chin lifted proudly, he turned and preened so his men might see him. At last the Indians were satisfied. Gathering up their gifts of flour and beads, they moved toward their canoes. They left behind one bone knife in return for Kate's hair.

Silently she watched as they left, and only when their canoes were well away from shore did she put up her hand and feel the jagged edges where Hogan had lopped away her hair. Although he'd taken a small portion near the front, she felt bereft, incomplete. Turning, Hogan caught a glimpse of her face.

"Don't worry, Kate. It'll grow back," he said lightly. His matter-of-fact tone was all she needed to unleash the tension of the past hours. It was her hair, wasn't it, and he hadn't even asked.

"How dare you?" she cried.

"I had no choice," Hogan said defensively. "Would you rather I had traded you off instead?"

Kate stamped her foot. "That's beside the point," she snapped, and knew she was being unreasonable. "I didn't see you cutting hanks of anyone else's hair."

"Lean Elk didn't want anyone else's hair," Hogan said, his temper rising in the aftermath of the danger they'd suffered through. "And he wouldn't have wanted yours if you hadn't been flaunting it."

"Flaunting?" Kate cried, outraged. "I wasn't!"

"Weren't you?" Hogan asked quietly, and stalked away, his back rigid with disapproval. Suddenly Kate's cheeks were flaming. She had been flaunting her hair. She'd done everything she could to make Hogan notice her, and she'd thought she'd failed. But he'd known what she was about and he'd been disgusted at her fumbling attempts. They had made a pact between them at the very start of their marriage. She'd known where she stood. If he had tried to cross the lines drawn, wouldn't she have felt the same contempt for him?

The answer that came to her wasn't the one she wanted. She wouldn't have felt contempt. She would have been ecstatic if Hogan had tried in any way to make their marriage real. What was happening to her out here in this wilderness? Back home she would never have considered a man like Hogan O'Shea, yet here she was using every feminine wile she could think of, and ineptly at that. She placed her icy fingers over her hot cheeks and crouched by the fire. The flames had burned down to a few winking embers that could never give enough heat to warm the chill that had settled around her heart.

8

The pale gray light of dawn lay over the Yukon River, turning it to a silver band. As weary and hungry as they were, the shaken travelers quickly packed their supplies and headed downriver again. There was no sense in taking a chance on Lean Elk returning with more of his men. Next time the Indians might demand precious food supplies that would mean the end of their journey and possibly death by starvation.

Kate huddled miserably in the bow of the boat. Her stomach rumbled with hunger and she thought fleetingly of the succulent golden geese the Indians had devoured. How she longed for one little snippet. She cast a quick glance at Hogan's stony face. He hadn't said a word to her since their earlier argument, and she could tell by the grim slash of his mouth and dark stormy eyes that he was still angry with her.

Well, so be it, she thought, raising her chin in defiance. She might feel a little bit sorry for her outburst, but she couldn't swallow her pride enough to tell him so. True, he'd saved her from becoming one of Lean Elk's wives, and what was a little hair compared to that? Yet some thread of resentment still smoldered deep within her.

He'd never even noticed her hair when she'd worn it down, and without a qualm he'd cut it away as if it had no value to anyone. But it was his words that were the most hateful of all, for they'd made her take an honest look at herself and her feelings for this rough, unschooled man. Thrown together with him every day and forced to rely upon his strength and wilderness experience, she had begun to admire Hogan O'Shea, to overlook his crudeness.

With horror now she saw how the wilderness had begun to warp her principles. Well, she thought, sitting straighter, she would not let that happen again. She'd already bound up her hair in tight braids and wound them into a bun on top. She would not again forget she was Kathleen Moira O'Riley, and she had no need of any man, much less one so uncouth and unlearned.

He'd hurt her pride. He could see that. Perhaps he shouldn't have spoken so plainly in front of Clay Lawford, Hogan thought as he pulled against the oars. But her behavior with Clay had rankled. Oh, not that anything she'd done was unladylike. Kate was a lady in all ways. It was just the way she leaned close to Clay when she laughed at something he'd said. Hogan could never remember her laughing in quite that way at anything he'd said. She'd only poked fun at him and let him see how insensitive and dull she found him. Well, maybe he hadn't the wit of Clay Lawford, but at least he was keeping them alive. He wouldn't apologize for cutting her hair, no, nor for the things he'd said. He dipped the oar deep and pulled hard, burning his anger out in action. The boat shot ahead and disappeared around the bend.

Around midday they halted to exercise their stiff muscles and relieve themselves, but they were still too close to the Indian village to linger, so they ate some jerky and climbed back into the boats. That night they made camp on the riverbank, huddling close to the fire while they downed a soup made with boiled jerky and barley. They were desperately in need of fresh meat, but the men were too exhausted to hunt. Besides, they didn't want to leave the camp unguarded. Lean Elk and his men might have followed them and even now be waiting to creep into camp and steal the rest of their food and guns. They would just make do with flapjacks and the rest of the dried caribou meat.

"I'll take the first guard," Hogan said, laying aside his empty bowl. "Clay, I'll wake you for the second shift. That leaves the early hours for you, Axe. If they're out there, it'll be morning when they try anything."

"Shore nuff," Axe agreed, and laying aside his bowl, went off to the men's tent.

"Do you think they're out there?" Clay asked, peering into the dark shadows anxiously.

Hogan glanced around. "They're out there," he said quietly. Picking up his rifle, he checked to see if it was loaded, and disappeared into the shadows. Kate's heart was in her throat. She longed to call out a warning to be cautious. What if the Indians crept up in the dark and killed him? He seemed to give no thought to danger to himself. Without any fuss or bravado, he shouldered whatever responsibility was required of him. Suddenly the loss of her hair seemed a petty concern indeed, and she was sorry for her harsh words.

As if she weren't feeling bad enough, May crept close to her. "No mad at Hogan anymore," she said in wheedling tone. "Hogan smart man, Hogan good man. Lean Elk think you shaman with much power from your hair. Hogan give him some hair. Lean Elk think you share your power with him."

"I know I've behaved badly, May," Kate said miserably. "Hogan was right to do whatever he had to in order to save us. I don't know why I get so angry with him."

"Kate have strong feelings for Hogan," May said with a knowing twinkle in her dark eyes.

"No, no, of course not. That isn't it at all," Kate denied hotly. "Hogan . . . is just not the kind of man I'm used to. He's rough and boisterous and . . ." Why was it getting harder and harder for her to find bad things about him? "He's just not like the men back in Missouri," she finished lamely.

May sat quietly contemplating Kate's words, then rolled her eyes in puzzlement. "Missouri men must be very good, be better than Hogan," she said, shrugging. Before Kate could reply, she went off to bed and Kate was left sitting at the fire alone. Clay came out of the tent and sat down near her. Somehow Kate wished he hadn't. She wanted to be alone.

"I couldn't help overhearing part of what May had to say," he began. He rolled his fur hat in his hands nervously. "I hope you meant what you told her, that you didn't have strong feelings for Mr. O'Shea."

"No, none," Kate said, irritated beyond belief that she must explain her feelings when she didn't know them herself.

Clay gave a deep sigh of relief. "I'm immeasurably pleased to hear that," he murmured, "because these past few weeks of traveling together have made me . . ." He paused. Kate looked at him sharply. "Well, I've never quite met a girl like you, Miss Kate, and although I have nothing to offer you, now, no prospects here in Alaska, I am of a good family and . . . I know I have a fiancée back home, but I can't help having some feelings for you."

"I'm married," Kate blurted, not wanting him to go on. She cursed herself for not telling him sooner. Now he fell silent, his eyes round and disbelieving.

"I . . . I beg your pardon, Miss Kate?"

"I'm sorry I didn't tell you," Kate said. "It just didn't seem important enough." Her words sounded lame to her ears.

"Didn't seem important enough? I . . . I don't quite understand," Clay stammered. She could see anger growing in his kindly blue eyes, and she couldn't blame him. She'd acted in a most callous fashion, using him to try to make Hogan notice her and, yes, trying to make Hogan jealous. She'd given little thought to what effect all this was having on Clay. After all, it wasn't as if she were a raving beauty who swept men off their feet.

"When I first met you on the boat, I wasn't married," Kate said, "but when Papa was killed on the trail, Mr. O'Shea married me to protect me from . . . oh, I don't know, men who might want to take advantage of a lone woman in the gold camps. It was Axe's idea, and at the time it seemed the necessary thing to do. Mr. O'Shea didn't really want to do it, but I assured him I wouldn't hold him to his marriage vows. As soon as we find gold, I'm returning to Missouri with, I hope, enough gold to buy back Aunt Petty's house. I suppose I'll teach school or something." Kate twisted her hands together in her lap as she rushed through her explanation.

"You mean once you've all struck gold, Mr. O'Shea won't continue with the marriage?" Clay asked with disapproval.

"I want it that way too," Kate hastened to say. "After all, Mr. O'Shea and I aren't exactly compatible. We could never be a real married couple."

"I see," Clay said slowly. "Then it's a marriage in name only, a marriage of convenience."

"Yes, I suppose that's what you'd call it," Kate replied, and got to her feet. "Now, if you'll excuse me, I'm quite tired."

"Of course, Miss Kate." Clay scrambled to his feet. "Good night."

"Good night," Kate said, and walked to the tent she shared with May. She felt as if she'd been dragged behind a team of mules. All she wanted to do was go to sleep and find herself back in Missouri in Aunt Petty's cozy little house.

Marriage of convenience, hell!

Standing in the shadows, Hogan listened to the two of them talk. He should move away or at least make his presence known, he thought, even if it meant risking Kate's slashing tongue. But Clay's words caught him, and so he stayed and listened. She'd finally told him about the marriage. He found little solace in that. She'd been so matter-of-fact, so cut-and-dried, as if she were discussing a business deal. What had she said about them? They could never be a real married couple, they were just too incompatible. Another way of saying she didn't think he was good enough for her.

Hogan took out his tobacco and cut a piece, then in disgust flung it from him. Kate O'Riley, old-maid schoolteacher from Missouri, and here he was mooning over her like a kid, jumping whenever she got her temper up, and trying to please her every whim. Well, enough was enough. He'd never let a woman get a hold on him yet, and he wasn't about to start now. He sure as hell hoped Roxanne had arrived in Dawson by the time he got there. He spent the rest of his watch enumerating the dance-hall girl's charms, but the memory of lush white breasts and soft thighs had paled somewhat and he couldn't help thinking Roxanne was a mite on the plump side.

Lean Elk made his move at dawn, just as Hogan had foreseen. On silent feet his men moved toward the boat and supplies. Axe sat tense and watchful, letting his instincts tell him where they were. Close! He could almost smell them. Should he fire a warning shot to alert Hogan? Perhaps it would scare Lean Elk. Axe snorted at his own foolishness. Lean Elk was too desperate to be scared off. No doubt his tribe needed the food supplies as much as the rest of them did, but Axe wasn't going to let the Indians have them. Slowly he inched back the safety catch. Suddenly there was a movement behind him and a hand fell on his shoulder.

"It's me," Hogan said quietly, and slid down beside Axe, his gun drawn and ready. He leaned his rifle against a log and peered through the darkness. "They're out there."

"Yep," Axe said, and spat nervously. Carefully he sighted along his rifle barrel and squeezed the trigger. There was a soft yelp from the direction of the boats and a shadow slunk away. Axe lowered his rifle and looked disgruntled. "My eyes ain't what they used to be," he said. "I just wounded him."

"Here they come," Hogan said tightly. "Let's keep them away from the tents." Crouching low, he disappeared into the darkness. Long shadows moved stealthily across the open snow. Once again Axe took aim and fired. He could hear Hogan's rifle and a pistol. Clay must be up and out. He smiled grimly. By damn, it was like the old days.

Hogan hunkered down and waited for the big shadow to move again. He'd be willing to swear this was Lean Elk himself. The Indian was hidden now by the dark shadow of a tree trunk, but Hogan had caught a glimpse of movement and now he waited calmly. It was as if the chief knew who was watching him, and the thought made a cold shiver run up Hogan's back. Lean Elk hadn't come just for food. He was after Kate as well. Hogan cursed himself for not thinking of it sooner. He should have taken her into the woods and hidden her until this was over, but like a fool he'd kept her near, thinking he could protect her better if she were at his side. He blinked, straining to see through the darkness. Suddenly the shadow behind the tree moved, loping across an open area where he could be clearly seen. Hogan raised his rifle and took aim.

Too easy, he thought even as his finger tightened on the trigger. Lean Elk had made himself too easy a target. A cold chill ran through him. Unless this wasn't Lean Elk, but a decoy. And if it weren't, then where was he? He squeezed the trigger, but didn't stay to see if the Indian fell or not. He was already skimming over the fallen tree trunk and running on silent feet up the riverbank toward the tents.

A dark figure loomed at the entrance. Without breaking his stride, Hogan fired high lest he hit Kate. The Indian jerked around. Kate screamed and Hogan prayed she'd have sense enough to remain silent in the dark so the Indian couldn't find her so easily. Lungs bursting from the need for air, Hogan topped the last rise and paused, taking careful aim. Lean Elk threw his spear at the same time Hogan squeezed the trigger. The hammer came forward on an empty chamber. The spear caught Hogan in the side, spinning him around. Unable to stop his fall, he slid down the snow-slicked bank. Above him, Kate screamed again, then all was ominously silent, not even the sound of shooting from Axe and Clay.

"Hogan, they got Miss Kate," Clay cried from somewhere nearby.

Groaning with pain, Hogan pulled the spear from his side, praying it wasn't poison-tipped, and clawed his way back up the bank. May huddled at the door of the women's tent.

"Where's Kate?" Hogan shouted before he'd even

reached her, and silently May pointed back toward the river. Cursing himself for not going there first, Hogan half-ran, half-slid back down the bank. The Indians had come by the river; they'd have to leave that way. He raced along the bank, his eyes straining to catch any movement, any sound that would lead him to Lean Elk.

A blur of white caught his attention. Kate's nightgown. Suddenly he was ridiculously happy for the persnickety ways that led her to change into a nightgown each night instead of sleeping in her drawers the way the rest of them did.

Held tightly in Lean Elk's grasp, Kate was struggling for all she was worth, and Hogan didn't know if he was glad for that or not. At any moment Lean Elk might plunge a knife into her to still her struggles; on the other hand, her desperate fight was occupying the Indian's attention, so he didn't hear Hogan's approach until he was upon him.

Knife drawn and at the ready, Hogan took a flying leap at Lean Elk. As his big body collided with that of the Indian, Kate was thrown to the ground. She rolled clear and got to her knees, crouching near a tree as she watched the two men tangle. Lean Elk was a wily fighter, fast and experienced. He twisted out of Hogan's grasp, at the same time drawing his own knife.

Warily the two men circled in the slippery snow. With the coldness of nightfall, the slush had refrozen and was slick and treacherous beneath their feet. Suddenly Lean Elk lunged, barely missing Hogan's ribs. For a big man, Hogan was graceful and agile. He sidestepped Lean Elk's thrust and circled again, gauging his adversary's weak spot. When he lunged forward, he knew just how Lean Elk would respond. Quickly his knife point eluded Lean Elk's parry and buried itself deep in the Indian's chest. With a cry the chief fell to the ground, his death mask horrible in the growing light of dawn.

Chest heaving for air, hand pressed to his wound, Hogan bent over the Indian. When he straightened, a hank of red hair dangled from his fingers. "Miss Kate,

I got your hair back," he said, and fell to his knees in the snow.

"You're hurt," Kate cried, scrambling to her feet.

"Aye, that I am," he gasped, weaving dangerously.

"We have to get you back to camp," Kate cried leaning her hip against his broad shoulder. His head was on a level with her chest, which seemed an inviting place to lay it. His face burrowed against her small soft breasts. His breath, still coming in hot labored gasps, seared her skin through the heavy flannel gown, but Kate gave little thought to that now.

"Axe, Clay," she screamed, and heard men rushing along the bank. She could only pray it was not more of Lean Elk's men. Axe swung into view, followed close behind by Clay.

"Hogan's been wounded," Kate cried. Immediately they took hold of him and, half-supporting, half-dragging, got him back to camp. Kate followed behind, and she never even felt the cold snow against her bare feet. They got Hogan into one of the tents, lit a lantern, and May set to work on his wound.

"I'm all right," he grunted. He'd gotten his second wind now and the dizziness had passed. "There's some whiskey in my pack."

Kate hurried to get it for him. When she brought it, Hogan fixed her with his black eyes.

"Woman, get some shoes on," he bellowed. She blinked, opened her mouth to make a retort, and closed it just as quickly. Without a backward glance she went to her tent and dried her feet and legs with a rough towel until the skin was warm again, then donned thick dry socks and her boots, concentrating fiercely on her task so she wouldn't cry. But bitter tears stung her eyelids.

Certainly she knew the importance of keeping her feet dry and warm. Axe had impressed upon them often enough that they could lose a limb if they didn't, but that was no reason for Hogan to shout at her in front of the others. He almost seemed angry with her, as if he blamed her for the Indian attack. But that was unfair. She couldn't help it if Lean Elk had come after her. Still, the truth was, she did feel guilty, and her guilt didn't fade any when, after a short while, Hogan was up and walking around, his wounded side tightly bandaged. He stopped by the fire where she sat, the hank of auburn hair still clutched in his hand. The strands were dirty and tangled now, not at all like the shiny red mass that hung down Kate's back.

Hogan's mouth curved in a humorless grin as he held it out to her. "Your hair, Miss Kate."

She shivered and turned away. "Take it away."

"You don't want it?" he asked. "I went to a lot of trouble to get it back for you."

"You're being truly hateful, Mr. O'Shea," Kate snapped.

"I thought you might want it, seeing as you made such a fuss over it."

Goaded beyond endurance, Kate snatched the hair from his hand and threw it into the fire. "That's all I care about it, Mr. O'Shea," she said, eyes glittering like green ice as she rounded on him. "I know you think me responsible for all this trouble and your wound, and I am truly sorry, but I will not have you mock me."

"That wasn't my intent at all," he said. "I don't know what you're getting so all-fired het-up about. I just saved your life back there."

"As you have done many times on this trip," Kate snapped, "and as you have taken great pains to point out to me at every turn. Well, I won't be beholden to you, Mr. O'Shea."

"I surely wouldn't want you to be beholden to me," he growled, "so the next time an Indian takes a liking to you and that hair of yours, I'll just let him have you."

"Thank you very much, Mr. O'Shea," Kate flared.

"You're welcome, Miss O'Riley," Hogan said, and spun on his heel.

" 'Mrs. O'Shea,' if you please!"

"What?" Hogan said, caught off guard.

"I am no longer Miss O'Riley. I'm Mrs. O'Shea." Kate's head was flung back proudly. Her hands were anchored on her hips; her green eyes flashed fire. Speechless, Hogan allowed her the last word and stomped away, but what she'd said followed him as he stalked to the boats and began loading them. Mrs. O'Shea. He'd never thought to see a woman wear that label because of him, and yet he'd given it to one of the meanest, most cussed women he'd ever met. He tossed some more bundles into the boat, and Axe winced, wondering if the bottom would hold up under such an onslaught. Wisely he remained silent, as did Clay. They'd all learned that when Kate and Hogan were going at it, it was best to stay out of the way.

"We'd better get going," Hogan said, glancing upriver. "Lean Elk's men might come back." Hastily they drank down scalding coffee and ate leftover corn cakes from the night before. With Hogan wounded, it was decided that Clay would ride in his boat and Kate would join Axe and May in theirs. Though it made perfect sense, Kate felt hurt by the decision, as if she'd been banned from Hogan's boat on purpose. Without demur she settled on the packs in Axe's boat and she and May took turns poling while Axe pulled at the oars.

In spite of their sketchy breakfast, they made no stop for lunch, chewing on the last of the jerky as they traveled. Late in the afternoon Hogan angled his boat close to Axe's.

"We have to stop and hunt for some meat," he said. "We can't go on like this."

"Dare we take the chance?" Clay asked. His young face looked pale and troubled.

"Hogan's right," Axe said. "We'll have to take the risk." He glanced around. "That bend in the river up ahead looks a good place. We can hide the boats and put Clay as a lookout while we hunt."

"Good," Hogan called, and let their boats drift apart. Swiftly they drew around the bend and into a little cove, where snow-laden pines grew close to the riverbank and offered some cover. Hogan and Axe got out their guns and ammunition and settled Clay in a good lookout position.

"We'll leave our supplies and tents in the boat," Hogan ordered. "Just take out the sleeping gear."

"Surely we aren't going to sleep out in the open," Kate said in dismay. A light snow had started to fall, and she pulled the drawstring of her hood tighter.

"Sure, missy," Axe said, glancing at the sky. "I've siwashed it many a time, sometimes in weather thirty degrees below. It ain't bad tonight. It's warm enough to snow." With a final wave, Hogan and Axe started off for the dense timberline farther back from the riverbank. Doubtfully Kate watched them go, and couldn't help the shiver of fatigue and apprehension. With almost no hot food over the past days, and little sleep, she wondered if any of them could go on.

"We be okay," May said with so much cheer and confidence that Kate felt ashamed of her fears. May motioned her to follow and led the way into the huddle of pine trees. With a sharp knife she cut some boughs and hollowed out a place in the snow at the base of a tree. "We be warm enough. You see," she insisted. "Sleep together, stay warm." She flashed Kate a mischievous smile. "Sometimes, too warm." Once again Kate wondered why such a young woman had chosen to live with an old man like Axe. Yet May seemed devoted to him, her first concern on the trail for his comfort.

Scooping another hole, much smaller and deeper, May built a fire, taking care that it couldn't be seen from upriver. Carefully she chose wood that was seasoned and would be less likely to give off smoke. Placing stones around the coals, she set coffee to boil. Gratefully Kate huddled on a log, cradling a cup of the hot liquid between her hands.

Shadows lay long and dark along the river before the men returned toting a fur-wrapped bundle. They dumped it beside the fire pit. The men had dressed out the meat and cut it into smaller pieces, easier for carrying.

"You find bear?" May asked, eyes gleaming.

"Bear cub," Axe said. Hogan shot him a warning

glance, then looked at Kate. Her face was drawn into a grimace.

"A baby bear? You shot a baby bear?" she demanded accusingly.

"I know," Hogan said, looking shamefaced. "It's not something I liked doing, but we need food, Kate. He wasn't exactly a baby, closer to a yearling." As they talked, May and Axe had set about cutting the hunks of meat into smaller pieces to be cooked and smoked. Now May arranged lean bear steaks over the heated stones.

"Bear cub tender, make good steaks," she said, glancing up from her work.

"I couldn't possibly eat a bite," Kate snapped, although her stomach was aching from lack of hot food. Unperturbed, May set about making bread from her sourdough pot and placed it to bake as well.

With troubled eyes Hogan studied Kate, then settled on the log next to her. "I know how you feel," he said with surprising gentleness. His dark eyes studied her face and she felt herself grow warm. "But we couldn't find the mother, and if we had, we couldn't have left the cub to fend for himself. We had no choice." He winced, and Kate was reminded of his wound.

"Are you all right?" she asked quickly.

He nodded. "Just promise me you'll eat some of this meat," he said. "We have to take what we can, Kate, or else we can't survive out here."

"I know you're right," she said, gripping her hands tightly. "I'm sorry to keep imposing my old beliefs on you. I'll eat some of the meat . . . and thank you, Hogan, for getting it for us." The look of surprise and gratitude on his face was such that she thought he meant to give her a bear hug himself.

Instead he got to his feet and spoke with feigned gruffness. "I'd better relieve Clay for a spell."

"Hogan," Kate said as he turned away. He glanced back at her. "I didn't thank you for saving me this morning. I'm sorry you got hurt and . . . and I'm sorry I acted the way I did about my hair."

"I understand, Kate," he said. "You were scared like the rest of us." He swung around, and with a loose-hipped grace that belied his size and height, strode away down the riverbank. Kate sat where she was, thinking of how gentle his voice and manner had been, almost refined. His dark eyes were really quite handsome, and his nose and mouth strong and masculine. In spite of his roughness, he was a most virile and engaging man. Then she remembered his words about flaunting her hair and her lips tightened. Handsome though Hogan O'Shea might be, she must be very careful not to lead him into thinking she was interested in him. Still, she couldn't help wondering what his strong face looked like under the bushy beard.

Kate! She'd been as soft as the mist rising from the river, as sweet as the first golden pear of summer. Her smile had been like the dawn light breaking over the trees. How soft her voice, how warm her eyes, how dear and earnest her face as she listened to him. How unlike Kate!

Why couldn't she be like this all the time, cooperative and understanding and willing to change to his way of thinking? Instead she fought him on everything, always willing to take offense, mule-headed, always talking about her rights, as if women had as many rights as men. Well, he supposed they did, or if they didn't, they should have. He wouldn't like not having the same freedom and respect he commanded now. He hiked along, thinking of how it must be for a woman, alone and dependent on others.

On the other hand, women didn't have the responsibilities of men. Kate should be grateful she had someone like him to watch out for her, to provide her food and protect her. How warm and soft her voice had been when she'd thanked him—as if she really meant it.

No, if he'd come to know anything from this journey, he knew Kate. It wasn't like her to accept anyone's help. No, she was probably making fun of him, probably thinking that's all he was good for, to hunt and chase Indians through the dark and, yes, to take knife wounds. She hadn't nursed him and worried over him the way she had Clay Lawford, and he'd been wounded trying to rescue her. Was she grateful when he brought back her hair? Of course, he shouldn't have needled her so by returning the dirty hank of hair, but he'd still been riled over her tongue-lashing. Hadn't she realized how much he'd hated cutting away part of her beautiful hair? No, she'd yelled at him and thrown the hair on the fire, and now she'd tossed the whole thing off with an apology and a simple thank-you. If it had been Clay wounded, she would still be sobbing by his side. Even now she was probably back at the fire getting Clay's food ready so he wouldn't have to wait when he returned.

Hogan stomped up to the fallen tree where Clay crouched watching the river. "You'd better get on back to the campfire and get something to eat," he growled. "Likely as not Kate's got it waiting for you."

Startled, Clay glanced at the big man's gruff face. "You don't think much of me, do you, Hogan?" he asked, glad for this time alone.

At first Hogan said nothing, and Clay thought he meant not to answer. Hogan burrowed himself a place against the snow-covered log, carefully set his rifle at the ready, and finally turned to look at the other man.

"I don't have anything against you," he said roughly.

"But still you don't like me," Clay persisted. "You think I'm a greenhorn and pretty helpless up here in the Yukon."

"That's about it," Hogan admitted. "But I don't dislike you."

Clay considered the blunt words and studied the open face. He'd seen men like Hogan O'Shea before, fiercely independent spirits who followed no man. He admired the Irishman and wished he was more like him, but he could never tell him that.

"I appreciate what you're doing for Kate," he began.

"Let's leave Kate out of this," Hogan said, and turned his gaze back to the river.

"Sure." Clay studied the stern profile. So that's the way of it, he mused. Thoughtfully he made his way back to the clump of trees where a delicious aroma of roasting meat drew him.

When the bear steaks were cooked, May clamped them between hot pieces of sourdough bread. Kate thought she'd never tasted anything so wonderful in her life, and tried not to think of a tiny fur ball of a cub. Hogan had said a yearling, which would have been a good size already. When she'd eaten her fill, she took a hot sandwich and a cup of coffee to Hogan at the lookout. It wasn't because she was concerned about him unduly, she reminded herself. It was just that he had, after all, done the hunting and hauled the food in, and now he was out guarding them so they could eat.

"I brought you something to eat," she said, smiling cheerfully.

"I'm much obliged," Hogan said shortly, taking the food. Then he turned his back to her as if intent on something upriver.

"Have you seen any sign of Lean Elk's men yet?" Kate asked, not wanting to go back to the campfire so soon.

"No," he answered gruffly without looking at her. His manner was not encouraging, and she wondered what had happened to the warmth he'd shown her earlier.

"Do you think they're still following us?" She squatted beside him. Hogan shifted a little, but didn't look at her.

"I don't know," he answered finally. "They might. After all, I killed their leader."

"How's your wound?" she asked, nonplused by his coolness.

"For God's sake, Kate, stop fussing over me. Get back to the campfire and see if May needs any help."

"I always help May," Kate said, stung by his words. "I carry my share of the load."

"Maybe you do. I'm not saying you don't," Hogan answered. "But you're not doing anybody any good sitting here jawing."

"Jawing?" Kate snapped. "Well, I never . . . I was just trying to be friendly, but I can see you don't know the first thing about socializing or . . . or just plain being nice."

"You and I just aren't compatible enough to be friends," he snapped, remembering what he'd heard her tell Clay.

"And I surely don't want to be friends with a . . . a gloomy Gus like you," Kate snapped.

"A gloomy Gus?" Hogan repeated derisively. "You can't even swear properly."

"A lady doesn't swear," Kate sniffed, "but if you have trouble understanding my meaning, let me put it another way. I'd sooner try to be friends with that mama bear when she finds out what you did to her cub than I would with you."

"Likely you'd have better luck, since you're two of a kind," Hogan retorted.

"Oooh," Kate stormed, "and to think I came all the way out here to bring you food because I was worried about you. I wish I'd left you to starve. It might have improved your temper."

"What improves yours?" Hogan called, but Kate was already stalking back toward the fire, her back ramrod straight, her booted feet flying. Sighing, Hogan resettled himself at the log. Yep, this was the real Kate, with a tongue like an adder. He'd better remember that the next time he started getting all soft-kneed over her.

Later that night, as Kate lay sleeping with May and the men in the scooped-out hollow, she felt bodies shift. Axe rose and went to stand guard while Hogan, exhausted and cold, lay down beside her, careful to keep his distance. She lay stiff and awake, feeling him shiver long after he'd fallen asleep. Impulsively she curved her arm around him and moved closer, letting her body heat help to warm him. It seemed strange to be lying beneath the open sky, her arm around a man like Hogan O'Shea. Still musing about it, she fell asleep and woke in the morning to find he had turned in the night and clasped his arms and legs around her.

Two days later they made Five Finger Rapids, so named because the river split into five separate channels.

"God Almighty, look at that," Hogan exclaimed, pushing his fur-lined hood back from his face as he stared ahead. Kate swiveled around in the boat. To the right of the rapids a wall of ice rose majestically for approximately thirty feet in the air. Its hard surface was a clear sparkling green. In awed silence Kate and the others stared at the reflecting shield of ice. It seemed you could look deep into the heart of the emerald crystal, where lights and shadows danced and beckoned like a witch's spell. The men had stopped paddling and sat gawking. Silently the boats drifted past the enchanted place, while the passengers sat as if under a spell.

"Watch out for ice," Hogan cried suddenly, and using the paddle, pushed away from the nearly submerged ice floe.

"These don't move," Axe called out. "They're fastened to the bottom. Watch they don't rip out the bottom of your boat." But already the prow of Hogan's boat was rising.

"Kate, get down," he cried, throwing himself forward. The boat reared higher, and he clambered over the side.

"Hogan," Kate screamed as he fell into the ice-cold water. But he was already standing on a submerged ice cake, bearing down with all his might on the boat.

"Kate, get in the bow, hurry," he called, and she clambered forward. The back of the boat had already begun to sink, and more water was pouring over the transom. With a mighty heave, Hogan pushed down on the bow, struggling to maintain his footing on the slippery ice. Kate balanced in the boat, trying to keep as far forward as possible, and so they hung, unable to move, fighting with the swirling icy waters to keep their boat afloat.

"Hang on, boy. I'm coming," Axe hollered, snubbing his boat alongside.

"Keep your prow off the ice. It'll buck you up," Hogan shouted in warning. When they were close enough, Clay threw himself onto the submerged ice shelf. With his added weight the boat was anchored fairly steadily, but it had taken on a great deal of water.

"Kate, get into the boat with Axe and May," Hogan ordered.

"What about our supplies?"

"Never mind that now. Get in the other boat."

Stubbornly Kate shook her head. "Axe, can you bring the boat alongside? I'll hand over some of our gear."

"Get in the other boat, Kate," Hogan yelled. "Do as I tell you." She ignored him. They couldn't afford to lose their supplies. When Axe brought the boat alongside, she began passing bundles to May. Quickly the women worked, stacking the gear in the space normally used by Clay. When the water was high on the sides of the boat, Kate waved Axe away. Pulling hard on the oars, he made for the nearest shoreline. To her surprise, Kate caught a glimpse of a campfire, and a boat had already pushed off and headed their way. Two men pulled alongside, and Kate handed over the last of the gear.

"Now, then, little lady, I think there's room for you in here as well."

"What about the men?" Kate yelled. She could see the strain on both Clay and Hogan, but it was the pinched white look around Hogan's lips that bothered her the most. She knew his wound must be bothering him a great deal.

"Go on, Kate. We may not be able to hold this much longer," Hogan called. "It'll be easier without your added weight."

Kate wasn't sure whether to believe him, but she followed his instructions nonetheless. She'd done all she could, and Axe was already making his way back. The two strangers dropped Kate and the supplies onshore, then hurried back to the ice floe. Anxiously she stood watching as the men secured the half-submerged boat between the other two and dragged it back to shore. Only when Hogan was safely inside a boat was Kate able to draw an easy breath.

"My land, you're soaked to the bone," a woman said and, whirling, Kate saw what she thought must surely be the best surprise of all. A tall middle-aged woman hurried down the bank, her wide skirts billowing when she walked so Kate could see the rough shoe-pacs and long woolen underwear beneath. The woman was robust in appearance and attitude, her dark eyes flashing with good humor and old-fashioned common sense. "Come on up here to the fire and get them wet things off," she commanded, and Kate willingly complied. May was already huddled in blankets near the fire, her clothes spread to dry nearby.

"My land, we thought you folks weren't going to make it when your boat rode up on the ice like that. We thought surely you'd sink. Bud and Quentin, that's my husband and my brother out yonder, run to give a hand. Seemed like it took 'em forever. By the way, I'm Iris Garrett."

"How do you do? I'm Kate O'Ri . . . O'Shea."

"Pleased to make your acquaintance," Iris said. "Good thing my men and me was camped here. We was just on our way back to our trading post. We come down here to trade some with the Indians." Kate looked around and noticed a rich stack of furs to one side. "I ain't never seen anything as brave as you, girl, out there trying to save your supplies when you should of been savin' yourself." On and on Iris talked, and all the time she was helping Kate peel away the wet, ice-stiffened clothes. In no time Kate was seated before the fire wrapped in warm blankets.

"I don't know why it was I made up more stew than we needed. Sometimes seems like a body knows, before our heads do, what's going to happen, so we're prepared for the unexpected. Now, here, child, you eat this." Iris handed around bowls of delicious hot stew. Kate fell on her food like a ravenous beast, gobbling it down with manners that once would have appalled her. May was silent as she ate hastily. The men came into camp, and with the same unstoppable line of chatter, Iris Garrett tended their needs, and soon all five of them sat around the fire looking like little mummies wrapped in their blankets.

9

"Now, you men just rest and get dry. I'll have some supper ready in no time." Introductions had been made all around and now Iris turned her attention to the kettles over the fire. For all her quick movements and continuous chatter, Iris Garrett was not a nervous kind of woman. Her tall rawboned figure was lanky and graceless but never quite clumsy. Silver strands laced through the blue-black hair and her long face was not unattractive. It bore a look of cheerful acceptance of the hardships of the trail. Kate guessed her to be somewhere in her fifties, as she bent easily to stir a kettle or fill a coffee cup from the blackened pot. Indeed, so cozy a mood did Iris set that it seemed to Kate they were almost as comfortable as if they were sitting in a kitchen back in Missouri. She liked the woman at once, and from the quick friendly smiles Iris bestowed upon one and all, it was obvious she met few people she didn't like.

"We're lucky you were here," Hogan said, sipping from his tin cup. "We're much obliged for the help, Mr. Garrett."

"My name's Harold, my friends call me Bud," Garrett said. Like his wife, he was tall, although a paunch had added some girth to him. Now and then he pushed his fur cap back to smooth a few wisps of black hair over his balding dome. Like his wife's, his dark eyes were lively and friendly and wise. Kate sensed a wariness in him that Iris didn't exhibit. "We're mighty glad we could help," he was saying now. "We nearly run aground on one of them things ourselves."

"I should have been more alert," Hogan answered,

swirling the dark liquid in his cup. "I just got caught up looking at that wall of ice."

"That's sure something, ain't it?" Iris said, coming back to the fire. "Hope you folks like stew. Gets kind of tiresome, the same old grub on the trail, but it fills you up."

"It was delicious," Kate said, thinking of the bear-cub meat. She'd happily eat stew rather than that again, as good as it had tasted when she was nearly starving. "But we hate to eat your food."

"We'll have enough," Iris replied. "The men'll go hunting tomorrow. The Lord always provides."

Bud Garrett approached the men with a bottle. "Would you like a spot of rum in that coffee to help warm you?" he asked, and all three men held out their cups.

Still thinking about Iris' generosity and the remaining bear-cub meat, Kate eyed the bottle of liquor "Have you plenty of that rum, Mr. Garrett?" she asked.

" 'Bud,' little lady, and yes, I've got a couple more bottles in my pack. It warms the body of an evening." He winked. "Just pass your cup over here."

"Oh, not for me," Kate said, laying her hand over the rim of her cup. "I was wondering if you'd be willing to trade some bear-cub meat for a bottle of that rum."

Bud Garrett looked from her bright face to Hogan's somber one. "Well, shore, I reckon I can," he answered cautiously. He didn't want to cross the big man who sat silently staring into the fire.

Hogan was looking surprised, his black brows raised questioningly, his dark eyes gleaming in the firelight as they regarded her. But he nodded a go-ahead. Holding her blanket tightly, Kate crossed to the packs and drew out several packages, one of them the spare outfit she'd bought back in Seattle. Unrolling the bundle, she shook out a pair of men's breeches, a heavy plaid shirt, and her last clean pair of long woolen underwear. Crossing to the Garretts' tent she quickly dressed, then returned to her packs.

Hogan was already there and had pulled out the spare bear meat. "What do you need the rum for, Kate?" he asked curiously. "You're not a drinking woman."

"You'll just have to wait to find out. A woman likes to keep some secrets." She smiled up at him, green eyes sparkling, red tendrils of hair gently weaving around her face, and he caught his breath at the fire and beauty of her. She was like that ice wall, magnificent and awesome. Then the moment passed and she was plain old Kate, peering up at him sassily. Shaken, Hogan got to his feet and went back to the fire, but he couldn't help edging around to look at Kate again. This time he noticed the breeches. They hugged her long slim legs and boyish figure. The top button of the woolen plaid shirt was open in a V that revealed her graceful white neck. Her long hair had been combed into one fat braid that hung down her back. The side where he'd cut away a hank was too short, so it fell forward over her cheek. Impatiently she pushed it back behind her ear. She'd taken some sugar from their pack, and now, as she bent over a kettle beside the fire, Hogan noticed how the breeches tightened provocatively over her round buttocks.

The only place she was round, he tried to tell himself, and imagined Roxanne in the same outfit, with her full bosom straining at the shirtfront and her full hips revealed in the breeches. Somehow, by comparison the dance-hall girl came out looking overblown. Kate looked clean-limbed and youthful and incredibly vulnerable. Hogan glared into the fire, lips tightened in anger at himself and his wayward thoughts. But even there he found Kate, the thin delicate planes of her face, the white skin with its smattering of freckles like a dusting of gold across her nose and cheeks, the high cheekbones, the mouth, prim and proper and disapproving one moment, then soft and full and inviting the next. He remembered the way she tasted when he kissed her on the boat, like ginger and exotic fruits he'd tasted once. The taste of her was still with him. With a gesture of disgust he tossed the contents of his cup into the fire. The liquid sputtered against the hot stones, causing Kate to raise her head like a startled deer. Christ, couldn't he ever stop thinking about her? He stalked off to the boats and busied himself assessing the water damage. Before long Clay and Axe came to join him.

"Are the boats able to go on?" Clay asked anxiously.

"Aye, we'll tar the seams again," Axe said. "They'll float for a little while longer."

"Supper's ready," Iris called. "Come get it while it's hot." Reluctantly Hogan left his packs and returned to the fire. May had also dressed, and now she helped Iris dish up the food.

"Save a little room, men. Kate's got a surprise for us," Iris said as they all settled around the fire. They had no sooner taken their first bite than a call hailed them from the river.

"Halloo, the camp!"

Hogan and Bud Garrett glanced at each other, recognition growing on their faces. "By gum, I do believe that's Uly," Bud cried. "Ma, set another plate."

"Uly!" Hogan yelled, leaping to his feet. He ran down the bank, laughing and waving as the old sourdough paddled his boat to shore. "By God, you old flea-bitten raccoon, where've you been?"

"Hogie," Ulysses Thomas Udell shouted gleefully, springing out of the boat with a vigor that belied his years. The two men embraced, slapping each other on the shoulders and back much as Kate had seen her father do back on the sidewalk in Seattle. "You're shore a sight for sore eyes," Uly said, stepping back to study Hogan. He glanced up the bank at the line of people watching him. "Bud, Miz Garrett," he called by way of greeting. "Where's Gilly?" he demanded.

Hogan's grin faded and he glanced away, scuffing the toe of his boot in the mud. "Gilly didn't make it," he said quietly.

"What? You mean he didn't come?" Uly cried. "I'll bet he stayed back there to be with his daughter. Remember he always talked a fool about her?"

"He was caught in the avalanche at Chilkoot," Hogan said.

"Ah, man, no." Uly's voice broke. The two men wrapped their arms around each other and stood sharing a moment of grief. "Wasn't no better man than Gilly O'Riley," Uly said in eulogy, and Kate felt the tears streaming down her cheeks. Once more the men slapped each other on the shoulders.

"Come on up to the fire," Hogan said, wiping at his cheeks. Uly smiled and hailed Bud and Quentin.

"You old buzzard. You out here cheatin' all them Eskimos," he called, "or have you finally given up bein' a peddler and started huntin' gold?"

Good-naturedly Bud shook his head. "I'll leave the gold hunting for you fellows. I'm just a trader. Won't ever be anything else."

"You'll probably go home richer than any of the rest of us," Uly said, and accepted the bowl of food Iris handed him. His keen old eyes fell on Kate. "I'm real sorry about your pa," he said, recognizing her at last. He looked the same as he had that first day Gilly and she had met him in Seattle.

"Thank you," Kate answered, and sat looking into the fire as Uly filled them in on his whereabouts since their last meeting.

"I had me some bad luck with my partner too," he said around a mouthful of stew. "He drowned when we come through the rapids. Guess it was a damn-fool thing to do, ridin' those rapids down, but a couple of Englishmen went down in front of us without mishap. I buried him back up there along the river. When I get to Dawson I'll write to his next of kin and let 'em know." He laid aside his bowl and wiped his mouth on his hands, then took out a pipe. "In the meantime I'm lookin' for a new partner. You wouldn't happen to know of anyone wantin' to hook up, would you?" He fixed Hogan with a somber gaze.

Clay sat straighter. He'd been quiet most of the evening, caught in his own thoughts. Now he looked at Uly. "I'm in need of a partner," he said calmly.

Uly swiveled around to study him. Cheechako, he

thought, and spat into the fire, but his gaze never left the younger man. Clay waited until Uly was through with his perusal. He'd learned sometimes it wasn't what a man said that told so much about him as his demeanor. "First time to Alaska?" Uly asked.

"Yes," Clay answered.

"What do you think of 'er?" Uly bit on his pipe stem.

"She's harsh and mean," Clay answered truthfully.

"Why don't you go back?" Uly demanded idly.

Clay shrugged. "I came to find gold. Besides"—he glanced around—"I like it here."

Uly shook his head. "I'm of a mind to hook up with you," he said, and held out his hand. Looking slightly dazed at the swiftness of events, Clay shook it.

"Well, that's nicely done," Bud said, passing the bottle around. Everyone laughed and relaxed. A feeling of goodwill had settled over all. "We need to celebrate a little."

"Land's sake, we forgot Kate's surprise," Iris cried, and everyone turned to look at Kate.

Blushing slightly at the attention, Kate rose and got the kettle she'd placed near the fire earlier. "Plum duff!" she declared grandly, taking the lid off with a flourish. "And rum sauce to go over it." Everyone's face lit up, lips were licked in anticipation, bowls were passed, and Kate dished it up with a generous hand until all was gone. Quiet reigned over the camp while they ate. Darkness had fallen around them, but in the circle of firelight they were safe and warm and well-fed, and sharing the moment with old and new friends. Contentedly they finished their desserts and settled back against the logs and boulders to rest a bit. Shivering against the penetrating cold that always returned when the sun went down, Kate wrapped her blanket around herself again and sat staring into the fire.

"Quent, break out some music," Bud called, and Iris' brother hurried off to his bedroll and returned with a fiddle and bow. From the moment the quiet man set his bow to the strings, he was changed; his blank expression became animated and his eyes gleamed happily. His foot tapped a rhythm so spontaneous that Bud Garrett leapt to his feet. "Come on, Ma, let's dance a bit."

"My land, Bud, you do beat all," Iris said, but she rose and went into his arms. They raced around the fire, the mud flying from beneath their feet. Kate glanced at Hogan and then quickly looked away.

"Would you care to try it, Miss Kate?" Clay said, and smiling to hide her disappointment that it wasn't Hogan who'd asked, she rose and followed his lead. When she whirled around, she saw that Axe had led May out as well, his short bandy legs pumping energetically. May laughed and tried to follow his lead, but she'd never had much experience with the white man's way of dancing. Next Uly danced with Kate while Clay claimed Iris and Bud danced with May; then they changed again and with each dance grew freer in their steps, each man trying to outdo the others. Kate danced until she was exhausted, but never once did Hogan come to dance with her. It didn't matter that he also did not dance with Iris or May. She'd hoped he would dance with her. Finally so tired out they were ready to drop, they banked the fire and went to their bedrolls. Their evening of gaiety was too quickly over. Tomorrow they must continue their journey.

"I hope to see you again soon, Miss Kate," Clay said, standing before her, his eyes sad, his smile strained. He and Uly were striking out on their own.

"Be careful, Clay," Kate said, taking his hand.

"I will. You . . . well, I hope all goes well with you. This is mighty hard country for a woman to be in."

"I know," she said, smiling up at him. "But Hogan will take care of me."

"Hogan's a lucky man." She felt his fingers close around hers tightly and she knew he wanted to say more, but he was bound by honor and by what he'd seen between Kate and Hogan. It had been part of his reason for taking up with Uly. Each day it had become harder to see the woman he loved and admired turn to another man as Kate did, without realizing it. Should he tell her his suspicions about Hogan? he wondered, but then decided against it. Fair play worked only so far. Why should he help another man win Kate? "If you ever need me," he said instead, "get word to the mayor in Dawson. I'll check with him every time I get there."

"Thank you, Clay," Kate said with a smile. "I hope you find another El Dorado."

He laughed and released her hand. "The same to you, sweet Kate." Placing his fur-lined cap back on his sandy head, he turned toward the boats where Uly waited. Kate turned to wave good-bye, and her smiling gaze tangled with Hogan's. His face was twisted in a dark scowl and his glance was scathing. Now what had she done? she wondered, and waved as Uly's boat drifted out into the current and the two men picked up their oars and began to paddle downstream.

"See you in Dawson," Uly called back.

"Tell Roxanne I'm on my way," Hogan shouted, and shot Kate a triumphant glance. Her heart lurched painfully and her smile faded as she glared at him.

"Not too much longer, Mr. O'Shea," she said with mock sweetness, "and you'll see your trollop again."

"Trollop she may be, Mrs. O'Shea," Hogan answered, "but at least she doesn't stand in broad daylight holding one man's hand when she's married to another." Color soared in Kate's cheeks.

"I expect you're right, Mr. O'Shea," Kate answered tartly. "Everything Miss Blayne does is done in the dark." Chin high, she strode away.

"Well, whatever she does in the dark is done very well," Hogan called after her, but Kate was already singing a little song about a dove. From the smirk on her face, he guessed she already knew that was a name often given to whores and dance-hall girls.

"Come see me at the trading post, you hear now?" Iris said as they separated and went their ways.

"I will," Kate called from her boat. "Thanks for everything." She seemed sad at the parting, and Hogan guessed she missed seeing other white women. She'd been warned before she came on this trip. Now she'd have to bear it. Still, she hadn't complained and he was sorry he'd angered her. Sometimes it would be nice just to be friends with Kate, so he could share things with her. He liked the way her eyes lit up when she learned something new or saw something unexpected. Like green ice, he thought.

They traveled without event now. The ice floes were gone. Their bodies had become trail-hardened. Game seemed more plentiful the deeper they moved into the interior. They shot a moose one day, which gave them enough meat for several weeks. But now the days were growing ever warmer. The snow had nearly disappeared even from the high banks, and they were forced to take time to smoke their meat to preserve it. They passed the mouth of the Pelly River and turned northward once more.

As the snow melted and ran down to the swollen rivers to be carried out to sea, the sun warmed the exposed earth for a depth of a few precious inches, nurturing the tenacious plants that managed to survive the harsh winter. Tufts of grass and sedges peeked through the lingering patches of snow. Gray-green clumps of lichens, dormant for months beneath the snow, slyly reached crinkly, crusted fingers of leaves toward the warming sun.

Tiny cones formed on the hemlocks and spruce trees, and buds burgeoned on the cottonwood and alder trees. In the sandy, barren places the yellow-flowered dryas grew in thick mats, the salmonberry plants thrust up their thorny leaves, and the tiny forget-me-nots, so beautifully blue they brought tears to the eyes, found footholds in crannies between the rocks. As June came, welcomed by an unexpected snowfall, clumps of dwarf alpine rhododendron spread their knobby branches so their rose-red blossoms shone vividly against the patches of white. And in the rocky places where it seemed nothing else might grow, the arctic poppy poked out its delicate yellow petals and spindly stems.

"I never thought there would be flowers here," Kate said in wonder. At first she picked the tiny, delicate blossoms, but they withered so quickly that she soon gave up the practice and simply enjoyed looking at them wherever she found them.

Not only did the face of the land change as they moved closer to Dawson. So did the population. Often they passed permanent cabins. Miners came out to wave to them as they passed, and there was more traffic on the river itself, boatloads of cheechakos come to find fortunes in gold. Sometimes they stopped to visit with some of Axe's acquaintances, sourdoughs who had for years been searching the streams that fed the Yukon. They were rough, hardy men with a common look of the Yukon wilderness, bearded faces, wiry, hardened bodies, and colorful names like Broken-Assed Davis, River Dan, China Joe, and Caribou Johnny. It seemed each name was given as a sign of affection and acceptance of a man, and he wore it with pride, using it as a means of identification in place of his real name. Often these colorful pseudonyms were cause for one of the endless tall tales the sourdoughs loved so much.

One afternoon as Axe led the way around a bend, he was hailed from shore. "Hey, Axe, *mon ami,* you are back," a burly, bearded man called with a heavy accent.

"Hello, Frenchy," Axe shouted back. "You're still here? I thought you were leaving."

"No gold yet, my friend. But many men, they strike it rich. I think maybe Frenchy be lucky soon, eh?" The bandy-legged Frenchman roared with laughter as if the joke were on him. "You stop here, have supper, eh? I kill a fresh caribou today. You need fresh meat, eh? Come on in." He waved them ashore, his face beaming, his white teeth flashing against his black beard. Axe glanced at Hogan, and at his nod of agreement paddled in to shore. As the two men tied off their boats and helped the women alight, Axe turned to Hogan.

"Watch the women and the supplies," he warned. "Frenchy never gives anything without expecting something in return." Hogan glanced up the bank at the gusty Frenchman, and his hand tightened on Kate's arm.

"You bring company. Is good, *bon*," Frenchy said, waving them up the bank. At first he didn't recognize that the tall slim figure dressed in men's breeches and shirt was a woman, until Kate took off her beaver hat and her long red braid fell down her back. His dark eyes studied her; then his broad face broke into a roguish grin.

"You have brought a woman," he laughed, "and such a woman." He let his gaze run up and down Kate's figure, wagging his eyebrows in approval. Normally Kate would have been offended by such behavior, but he was so obviously good-natured and high-spirited that she found herself smiling back.

"*Bon, très bon,* this woman has much courage, and humor besides. It is an honor to welcome you to my humble home." He took her hand and with a gallant bow placed a loud smacking kiss upon it. All his gestures were so broad and outrageous that Kate thought him a harmless buffoon. But Hogan scowled and deliberately brushed between Kate and the Frenchman. Frenchy's quick glance followed Hogan as he dumped his gear.

"*Monsieur,* you have a very beautiful wife," Frenchy said, and Kate wondered how he'd guessed their relationship so accurately. Next Frenchy turned his attention to May, bowing and kissing her hand until she giggled. "You are like one of the tender delicate flowers that bloom on the mountainside," he said. May laughed again and her bright gaze met his boldly.

"You will sleep in my cabin tonight," their host continued. "We men will sleep outdoors. How you like that, eh, to sleep in a real house again?"

"You are most kind," Kate said, staring up at the small cabin perched in a stand of spruce trees, "but we don't want to put you out."

"Pah! Come, I will take you up and you may do"—he waved his hand vaguely and waggled his eyebrows—"whatever it is ladies like to do." He looped an arm over May's shoulder in a casual gesture that seemed meant only to guide her. Quickly Kate glanced at Axe, who appeared surprisingly calm. Hogan continued to scowl.

"I, Frenchy LaRoche, will prepare supper tonight," he continued as he started toward the cabin. Kate followed.

"We are grateful for your hospitality," she said, trudging up the slight incline. But when they'd stepped inside the small filthy cabin, Kate began to regret his offer. A rough cot had been built at one side, and a stove occupied the other. In the corners lay piles of fur, so hastily tanned they stank of rot. Trying not to breathe the rank air, Kate turned to May and the other men, forcing a smile to her face.

"Not so grand," Frenchy said, as if he guessed her disappointment, "but it is dry and warm, *n'est-ce-pas?*"

"Y-yes, it will do nicely," Kate said. Her glance went to Hogan, who backed toward the door.

"I'll set up the tent right outside here," he said, his gaze filled with sympathy and a little bit of mocking humor. Kate's chin shot up.

When the men had left the cabin, May looked around. "Frenchy need woman," she said. "Clean for him, cook." Something about her words bothered Kate.

"You're right," she answered, and looked around the cabin. "Since there's only one cot, May, I'll stay in the tent."

"*Bon!*" May said with the same exaggerated emphasis Frenchy had given the expression. Once again Kate felt troubled. It was obvious the Frenchman possessed a great deal of charm. She hoped May hadn't been swept off her feet. Compared to Axe, LaRoche was a young man. Perhaps May had grown tired of Axe.

True to his word, Frenchy prepared supper, roasting hunks of caribou steak over a campfire and boiling up a pot of rice. Kate was glad they'd be eating outdoors instead of in the dank close cabin. She was not surprised to see several other miners come in to join them, for it seemed to be the code of the Yukon to share when one had an abundance of meat. Altogether there were ten of them seated around the campfire, and when the meal had been consumed and jugs were passed around, the men began to tell of their luck, good or bad, in searching for gold.

"You folks have any trouble with Indians on your way down?" one man named Windy John asked.

"Aye, we did," Axe answered. "Hogan there killed one of their chiefs."

"Man, that's not wise," Frenchy said, his dark eyes rolling dramatically. "The Indians are looking for a reason to cause trouble for us miners. The Northwest Mounties are quick to bring a man in if he breaks the law."

"I'll be happy to talk to a mountie," Hogan answered. "It was done in self-defense."

"He did it to save my life," Kate said quickly. "Lean Elk was trying to . . . to kidnap me."

"Well, that puts a different light on things," Frenchy shouted, and refilled Hogan's cup.

"The devils have been gettin' bolder," a man called Kenzie said. "Two of 'em chased old Ned Davis when he was trying to get home after a hunt. Ned had to leave his game behind. Just barely got away by making a toboggan out of his moose hide, just slid on down that mountainside away from them Indians, slick as you please."

"I heard me about a fellow up near Circle who . . ." And so it went. Each miner had his favorite tale about the Indians, the weather, their gold finds, and each story got wilder than the last.

"I lost a couple of my partners a few years back," Windy John said, leaning back and drawing on his pipe with a somber air. Kate could see how he'd gotten his name. Of all the miners, he seemed to love to talk the most. "I had me an awful time figuring out what to do with them dadblamed bodies. I didn't want to keep them in the cabin with me all winter. They'd get to stinkin' right bad. I figured if'n I put 'em outside, the wolves might get 'em. That warn't no decent thang t'do." He paused and fussed with his pipe as if it weren't drawing properly while the suspense grew.

"What'd you do?" someone asked finally.

"Well, sir, I pondered on it some, I can tell you," Windy said, "and finally I come up with a plan. I froze 'em down till they was real solid, and I stood 'em on their heads. Then I sharpened 'em with an ax till they was right pointy on they heads. I just drove 'em into the ground like stakes. I figured that made a right comfortable burial for 'em."

Gagging, Kate leapt up from the fire and ran off into the bushes. Reluctantly Hogan followed.

"What's the matter with you?" he asked when he caught up with her.

"That awful man," Kate cried, swallowing back the bile. "How could he do such gruesome things?"

"Kate, he didn't," Hogan said gently. "Don't you know these are just tall stories that don't mean anything? If you ever want to get past being a cheechako, you have to learn to listen and not be taken in by these sourdoughs. They like nothing better than poking fun at a greenhorn."

"You mean they were lying?" Kate asked.

"Well, they're not exactly lying. Everyone knows it's just something they made up. It's part of the camaraderie between the miners."

"I'm sorry. I didn't understand."

"Can you come back to the fire? They'll think you were offended, or worse, that you don't like them."

"Yes, all right. Just give me a minute."

"Go look in my pack and get that bottle of whiskey I've got stashed there. Drink down a slug of it and then bring it back to the fire."

"Thanks, Hogan," Kate said, grateful for an excuse for leaving the area. Impulsively she stood on tiptoe and kissed him on the cheek. She'd meant it to be a simple gesture of friendship, but he stood so tall, she had to sway against him. One hand splayed against his broad chest to brace herself. She caught the warm masculine smell of him and felt his smooth cheek against her lips. Slowly she drew away, her gaze troubled as she looked up at him.

"You shouldn't do that, Kate," he said softly, and she felt his hot breath on her cheek.

"Why not?" she whispered huskily. Her hand still lay against his chest and she could feel the pounding rhythm of his heart. It was nearly as erratic as her own. There was yearning between them. Kate felt it and wasn't sure if it had grown from her or Hogan. It was simply there and not to be denied. His arms curved around her, pulling her up against his broad body. His mouth claimed hers and she made no outcry. She had, she realized, wanted this ever since he'd kissed her on the boat. His mouth moved over hers, gently at first and then with a growing hunger that awakened her own forbidden passions.

One big hand splayed across her back, pulling her tighter, so that her breasts, their nipples taut and aching, flattened against his hard chest. The other cupped her buttocks intimately, lifting her, grinding her hips against his so she felt every long, hard line of him. The rigid bulge of his passion pressed insistently against her soft mound, awakening a hunger that threatened to consume her. She was on fire, and nothing could bank the flames of her raging desire except this big man with his rock-hard body and a need as big as her own.

Intuitively Kate bent one knee, winding one leg around his. The movement didn't feel wanton or unnatural as Hogan's big hand slid along the length of her slim thigh and lifted her against himself. Now the hard bulge of his arousal pressed against her more intimately, and Kate thought she might swoon from the pressure. She writhed in his embrace, straining against the confines of the coarse material of the clothes that kept them apart.

"Kate, my sweet, sweet Kate," Hogan said against her mouth. He was breathing heavily, his large body trembling. He arched his back, drawing back his pelvis, then thrusting forward. Kate felt hot flames lick through her. His hot tongue speared her mouth in a tantalizing forerunner of the act his hips were trying to perform.

"Hogan," Kate whispered, and her hands were in his hair, holding his shaggy head so she could return his kiss. Suddenly a shout of laughter went up from the campfire and, horrified, Kate returned to reality. The wantonness of her behavior shamed her, and with a cry she tore herself from him, lowering her legs. But Hogan's knees were slightly bent, the better to support them, and now Kate's legs were tangled with his, held apart by his knees.

"Please, let me go," she whispered brokenly.

"Why, Kate? We both want this."

"Not I," she declared angrily. Then, feeling shamed, she pushed against his broad shoulders. "I'm not one of your whores, Mr. O'Shea, to be handled in this manner."

"I wasn't thinking of you as such, Kathleen," he answered, and his voice was still soft and coaxing, although she detected an edge of anger to it. "I was thinking how lucky I am that you're my wife."

"In name only, Mr. O'Shea. That was the agreement between us." He still held her against him, not willing to relinquish the passion she'd aroused in him.

"And what of the rest that's between us?" he asked stoutly. The softness was gone from his voice.

"There is nothing else. You kissed me, and because you were kind, I allowed it. You've taken liberties with me I . . . I had not expected. Now let me go. Haven't I been shamed enough?"

"Shamed?" Hogan demanded, releasing her at last. "Do you think these feelings between us are a cause for shame, Kate?" He glared at her. "Are you ashamed of the feelings of a woman?"

"I'm not that kind of woman," Kate cried. "I . . . I'm a lady."

"Aye, you are a lady," Hogan said, "but can't even a lady admit her needs for a man? You have them, Kathleen Moira."

"No that . . . that wasn't me. I was carried away for a moment. I admit I kissed you back, but . . .

but . . ." She paused, not knowing how to extricate herself from this. "I could never feel that kind of need for a man like you," she said halfheartedly, wanting to wound him, to drive him away, for he'd frightened her with the depth of passion he had awakened within her. "I could never give myself to you."

"Because I'm not good enough, is that it?" he demanded, and she was too miserable herself to hear the hurt in his voice.

"You're a good man, Hogan," she said lamely.

"But not good enough for an educated lady like you," he said flatly.

"I'm here to find gold, nothing more," Kate answered. "I want nothing from you."

"And you shall have it," he answered. He'd drawn himself up in anger so that it seemed to Kate he'd grown in height and breadth. He towered over her, and she longed to throw back her head and challenge him, but she was too shamed, too shaken by all that had passed between them. She stood with her head down. Now, at his words, she glanced up quickly.

"You promised to protect me," she said raggedly.

"You'll have my protection, Mrs. O'Shea," he answered, "and you'll not have to worry that I'll bother you again. Now, if you'll get the bottle of whiskey and return to the fire as I asked you . . ." He whirled on his heel and stalked away. Kate saw him take a seat among the other men. Someone made a ribald remark about his absence, and he answered in kind.

Kate blushed, imagining what he'd implied and knowing that whatever he'd chosen to say wouldn't have been a lie. She'd done everything but let him take her standing upright leaning against a tree, like an animal rutting in the woods. What had happened to her? she wondered. Placing her chilled hands on her flushed cheeks, she fled down the riverbank to the boats. She was grateful for the cold night air, for it cooled the longing she still felt for the big rawboned man. That she'd wounded his pride cruelly was obvious, but she couldn't go back to explain. If she couldn't control her own passion for Hogan O'Shea, she must goad him to hostility so he stayed away from her, for the next time he pulled her into his arms, heaven help her, she'd never be able to resist.

Finally she calmed herself enough to take the bottle of whiskey back to the campfire. With a cheerful roar the men welcomed her back.

"I hope I didn't offend you none, ma'am," Windy John said as she passed around the bottle.

"Not at all," Kate said. "In fact, your tale reminded me of the time the town banker died in our town. He was, of course, held in the highest esteem. It was summer, and usually the custom of the undertaker to bury a body immediately, but knowing there would be many people wishing to come to the funeral from some distance out, he decided to wait a day or two. In order to keep the body"—she took a breath and glanced around the group as if she were about to tell them the most shocking thing of all—"the undertaker placed him in the icehouse overnight, and the next day, after the banker was buried, the iceman delivered that same ice to all the good citizens of the town." Her eyes widened and rolled dramatically. "Aunt Petty and I had a chuckle or two out of thinking a tiny bit of the banker might have been served up with their iced tea." Kate slapped her knee in a facsimile of what she'd seen the other miners do and waited expectantly for their response.

The men looked at her, waiting for the end of the story, the truly outrageous ending that made a tall tale worth repeating, and when they realized she'd finished, they glanced at each other in surprise and then in understanding.

Watching her face, Hogan felt like snickering. Kate's words had hurt him more than he'd ever imagined, and he longed to hurt her back. Yet, listening to her innocent tale, he realized how inexperienced she was in the hard ways of the Yukon and the people who lived here. Suddenly his anger vanished.

In spite of her years, she was naught but a young girl, as unlearned in her way as he was in his. She was trying, trying with her pitifully innocent tales and her hard work around the campfire and, yes, even when she'd kissed him on the cheek in gratitude. It had been he who'd carried it further, who'd forgotten she was a lady, a dried-up old maid.

He stopped at that. He could never again think of Kate as a dried-up old anything. She was too alive, too passionate beneath those prim-and-proper ways of hers, and he, crude as she claimed he was, had pushed her too hard and too fast. He had to give her time to sort out her feelings. He needed time himself, for he knew beyond anything that if he mated with a woman like Kate, he'd not be free to walk away as he could from Roxanne and her kind. Was he ready to give up that freedom? Now he was glad Kate had pulled back, and as he watched her face, with its disappointment growing because the miners had not been entertained by her tale, he felt a softening toward her.

Throwing his head back, Hogan began to laugh, clapping his hands together as if in the throes of humor over her story. Glancing at one another and at the red-haired lady, the other miners did the same out of politeness, feigning glee they did not feel at first. Then, as the humor of the situation with the lady cheechako settled over them, they hooted with genuine enjoyment and passed the bottle back along the line to Kate.

Laughing nervously, she wiped at the bottle top with a handkerchief and took a large swig, coughing as it burned her throat. Good-natured slaps landed on her back, making her cough more. Eyes shining, she glanced around the circle of men and drank again before wiping her lips on the back of her hand in a swaggering motion. Gratefully she glanced at Hogan and was surprised to see the anger had left his face. He smiled at her, his eyes gleaming with the dark secret of what had passed between them earlier, and Kate blushed, unaware of how the color stained her high cheekbones prettily.

The whiskey had put a shine in her green eyes that brought many a man's gaze back to her. Yes, she was a real lady, most of them thought, but she knew how to be a real person too. Nostalgically they thought of homes left so long ago and the sweethearts and wives they'd long since left. Many of them had native wives now, as did Axe, wives better suited to the wild, adventurous lives they led. Still, they gazed into the fire for a time and dreamed of home.

It was late when they went off to their bedrolls. Kate longed to sleep in the tent Hogan had placed outside Frenchy's cabin, but after what had happened between them, she was leery. May hadn't come to the cabin yet, and Kate hoped she was with Axe, for she'd noticed how Frenchy's eyes strayed to the little Indian woman.

Reluctantly Kate made up a pallet on the floor behind the stove. The fire had burned down to a few coals, giving off a lovely warmth, and soon she grew drowsy. Much later she heard May at the door, giggling softly, and a man's rough growl followed by a lengthy silence. Then May giggled again and entered the cabin, closing the door firmly behind her.

Troubled, Kate lay feigning sleep as May prepared for bed and settled on the cot. What would Axe think of May's behavior? she wondered, and felt sad. She liked the old man, and although she'd often wondered what had kept the young woman at his side, she was now out of sorts with May. She had no right to hurt Axe like this. He was kind to her. Yet kindness wasn't always enough, especially when there was such a difference in their ages.

Kate thought of Hogan's kiss and the passion that had flared between them. Was that what was happening between May and the Frenchman? She rolled on her side and tried not to picture the two of them together, for if she did, she would wonder how it would have been with Hogan if she hadn't pulled away. She shut her eyes tightly, scrunching them up until her eyelids hurt, and curled her long legs up to her chest. She would not think about Hogan O'Shea. She would not allow her traitorous body to remember the aching need for him. She would not admit that need even to herself. It took much concentration not to remember, and the following morning she arose from her pallet grumpy and tired.

"Come on, May," Kate called, tying up her bundle and preparing to take it down to the boats. But the little Indian woman had already left the cabin. Kate glanced around and saw her talking to Frenchy La-Roche. Frenchy touched her shoulder and May giggled as she looked up at him with adoring eyes. Not knowing what to do, Kate hurried on down to the boat and stashed her gear. She kept her eyes lowered so she wouldn't have to look at Axe or Hogan. Hogan watched her closed expression and wondered if she were still angry about the night before. By rights, he should be, he thought. After all, she was the one who'd hurled insults at him. Vowing to say nothing until she did, he clambered into the boat and picked up his oars.

Standing by his boat, Axe glanced up the bank. "May, are you comin'?" he called, and Kate stood half in and half out of the boat, her breath held as she waited.

May appeared at the top of the ridge, the Frenchman beside her. "I stay," she called down to him. For a long moment Axe said nothing. Kate could see his shoulders rise and fall as he took a deep breath; then without another word he climbed into his boat and pushed away from shore.

"May!" Kate called.

"Get in the boat," Hogan commanded, and after one look at his scowling face, she did as he ordered.

"How can she do that to him?" she fumed as Hogan pulled on the oars. "Axe has been kind to her. He doesn't deserve this."

"Maybe she thought Frenchy was a better prospect," Hogan said flatly. "That *is* what you ladies look for, isn't it?" He knew his words were unfair to Kate, but anger at May's treatment of Axe had awakened his resentment of her cruel words the night before.

"It's not the same thing," Kate said, reading Hogan's thoughts. "May and Axe have been like a real husband and wife. You and I have made no such pledge. Neither of us wanted that." She stared at him earnestly, and suddenly she wanted very much to hear him deny what she said. Suddenly she wanted to be committed to Hogan and to have him feel the same way toward her.

Instead, he nodded his head. "You're right," he said. Kate's shoulders sagged in some unnamed defeat. "No entanglements. We're free to come and go as we wish. A wife and children are not in my plans for the future." He dipped the oars and the boat shot ahead.

10

"This is it!" Axe shouted, holding up his hand. He angled his boat into a stream that fed the Yukon. "Sweetwater Creek!"

"Are you sure this is the right place?" Hogan called, pulling hard on his right oar to turn the boat and follow the old man.

"Aye, it looks like it," Axe said. Seated in the bow of the boat, Kate studied the wizened little man's set shoulders. Since they'd left the Frenchman nearly a week before, Axe hadn't said one thing about May, nor had he indicated by the flicker of an eye that he missed her or wished her back. Men! Kate thought disgustedly. They were all alike, thinking only of themselves and their pursuit of gold.

The week had not been an easy one for her either. Hogan had remained surly and aloof, and with May gone, much of the work around the camp had fallen to Kate. She missed May, if the others did not. She missed her shy smile and quiet companionship and her happy giggle. Now their evenings around the campfire had become silent, stiff affairs, with each of them avoiding the other's eyes, eating quickly, and retiring early to bed. Last night had brought about a change, when Axe had stated he thought they were close to the place where he'd found his gold. He and Hogan had sat with their heads together, discussing the likelihood of his claim having been found by someone else. Now, as Axe paddled his clumsy boat up the stream, Kate could feel the tension building. They floated some distance before Axe pulled over to a sandy spit that jutted into the stream.

"Let's give it a try here," he said, and Hogan pulled in beside him. Getting out of the boat, he waded to the front and tugged it further up onshore. Kate got out and looked around. It was a beautiful spot, with a dark-shadowed, mature forest to their back and a wide mountain range facing them. The sky was close and cloudless, so the sunlight spilled into the tiny clearing, sparkling gold and silver in the rippling creek.

"We'll set up our tents over there on the knoll," Hogan said, and began pulling out the supplies. Kate gathered up some bundles and headed toward the incline. Much to her surprise, Axe pulled out the saw they'd brought and began cutting down a tree. Hogan looked around at him.

"You're that certain, then?" he said.

Axe nodded. "Aye, that certain. It's here in this creek bed." He laid a long gnarled finger against his nose. "I smell it, just like I did before."

Hogan smiled. "Hadn't we better do some panning first?"

"You pan if you need to," Axe said, and went back to his sawing.

Hogan watched him for a minute, then dumped the supplies. "No, no, I don't need to." He went to help Axe. By noon they had set up wooden floors and partial walls that rose a couple of feet high on three sides. Then they pitched the tents over each wooden frame and tied them down. Kate watched in wonder. Except for their brief night at the Frenchman's cabin, this was the closest she'd come to a permanent dwelling since Skagway. She felt like weeping with delight. Hogan moved Kate's supplies into her shanty and turned to watch her. Her face was alive with excitement, her eyes sparkling. Happily she smiled at him.

"I'll be staying with Axe from now on," he said.

The smile faded from her face. "Yes, I suppose that would be best," she said, tilting her chin high and looking down her nose in a way he found particularly irritating. "Thank you for your help. You've been most kind." She held out her hand with an air of condescension that infuriated him. Hogan had half a mind to take the hand and yank her into his arms and kiss her until she surrendered to him as she had that night at the Frenchman's, but he gritted his teeth and turned away.

Kate dropped her hand and looked at him in surprise. He had been stiffly polite to her for days now, and she supposed he would go on with his pouting as long as she wasn't willing to melt into his arms and submit to his lust at every opportunity. Well, he would just have to pout. They had struck a bargain at the beginning, and she had no intention of satisfying his baser needs. She was a lady!

Yet somehow the refrain had become somewhat ragtailed, and no longer gave her comfort. Now, as she watched Hogan stride away, she wondered what had prompted him to move in with Axe now. They must be close to Dawson, she realized, and that meant saloons and dance-hall girls and Roxanne. He hadn't meant to be thoughtful of her at all. He was only making it easier on himself. Living with Axe, he could come and go as he pleased. Well, good for him. It mattered naught to her.

Kate set about rearranging her belongings in the small one-room shanty. It didn't take her long. She had no bed, no chairs, and no table, but it was the first home she'd had in weeks, and it pleased her mightily.

When she'd tired of arranging her sleeping bag and other supplies, Kate wandered outdoors and down to the stream. Both Hogan and Axe were there, catching up water and sand in flat metal pans. Carefully they swirled the water, then tipped it out. Idly Kate picked up a pan and joined them. Suddenly Hogan straightened, staring intently at the sand and gravel in his pan.

"Axe, Kate, come here," he cried, and they splashed out into the shallow stream where he stood. "Look at this!" he called excitedly, and held up several small nuggets. "It's gold, just lying here on the bottom of the creek."

Axe examined a nugget. "Aye, it's gold, all right," he said, and his eyes gleamed.

"Look at this, it's everywhere," Hogan said, pointing into the water.

"Gold! It's really gold?" Kate cried, scooping up panfuls of sand. She was too excited to feel the coldness of the water. "We're going to be rich, Hogan, rich," she cried, dancing around excitedly. His laughter boomed, nearly drowning out Axe's dry cackle.

Hogan swooped Kate up in his arms and twirled around. "We're going to be rich," he echoed, and threw his head back. His teeth flashed white against his dark beard and laughter boomed from his chest. The sunlight sparkled off his hair and face, and Kate couldn't take her eyes off him.

"If only Gilly could be here," he cried, catching her arms. He swept her up with his enthusiasm, so they pranced like children, splashing each other with water that had never quite warmed far above freezing and scooping up bits of gravel and sand in their pans. Each new nugget found was an occasion for much cavorting and cheering. Finally, worn out from the excitement, they moved back to the creek bank and collapsed on the ground.

"You know this is only the beginning," Axe said. "Many a man has found a little gold in a creek bed and it's meant nothing."

"I know," Hogan said. He was lying flat on his back, eyes closed, chest heaving. Now he sat up, his face somber. "Your memory was good, Axe. But now the real work begins. We'll sink a shaft, go down to bedrock, wash out what we find, and see if it's worth staking a claim."

"It's worth it," Axe said. "I keep telling' you, I know." His hat had fallen off in their madness, and now his thinning white hair stood up in untidy peaks. He fixed Hogan with his pale blue eyes and nodded. "This is bigger than Eldorado or Bonanza Creek. When they talk about big finds, they'll put Sweetwater Creek at the top. You mark my words."

Hogan looked at the old man and felt the blood leave his head, making him slightly dizzy. "I've never been this close before," he whispered tensely. Watching the two men, Kate realized that as exciting as finding gold was to her, it meant a good deal more to them, just as it would have to Gilly. She could never know or understand the intensity that drove these men forward.

"We'd better make a rocker next," Hogan said, and Axe nodded. Suddenly the two men slapped each other on the shoulders, and getting to their feet, hurried off to find the proper tree to cut down for their rocker. Kate felt slightly left out. Why would they suddenly want to make furniture after their discovery? she wondered. But later, as she watched them construct the boxlike affair set on rockers, not unlike a baby crib, she began to understand. It was a device for finding gold. Water and dirt would be dumped into the box, the water would wash the dirt through, but gold, being heavier than water, would sink and be caught in the blanket below. When the men had set up the rocker at the edge of the stream, they got out shovels and picks and chose a spot to begin their digging. Standing over it, the two men shook hands, and quickly Kate thrust her hand between them.

"Don't forget I'm a partner as well," she said.

"I'm not forgetting that, Kate," Hogan said.

"Of course, I intend to do my share of the work."

"It's hard work, Kate. I don't think you'll be wanting to do that."

"I insist," she said, chin high, that glow of determination in her eyes.

Hogan shrugged and handed her a shovel. "All right. You can start right now by digging here."

Kate took the shovel and without a word went to work. "How deep do you want the hole?" she asked, working quickly.

"Go all the way down to bedrock. Could be ten feet, could be thirty." Hogan refrained from winking at Axe.

Kate halted in throwing a shovelful of dirt on the growing pile. "Thirty feet?" she repeated uncertainly.

"Thirty feet!" Hogan said firmly.

Kate continued digging, but before the shovel had

TOMORROW'S DREAM

gone too many times into the ground, she hit something hard. She scraped around and cleared the dirt away, then looked up at Hogan triumphantly. "Bedrock," she said smugly.

He reached into the pack of tools and pulled out a pickax. "Frozen ground," he said. "You'll have to use this to loosen it." Hesitantly Kate looked at the pickax, glanced at Axe, then took it and hacked ineffectually at the ground.

"You'll have to swing harder than that, Kate," Hogan said, leaning back on his packs, hands behind his head. "Bring the pickax back behind your head, and watch your toes when you come down." Kate paused, then raised the pickax high and swung it down as hard as she could. "Want me to show you?" Hogan offered, and Kate stepped out of the shallow hole. "Of course, if you want to shovel out what I loosen, we could go faster."

"If you insist," she said, grateful to be allowed a graceful way out. All evening they worked, taking turns shoveling and hauling creek water to the rocker. Hogan and Axe showed Kate how to work the device, swing the pickax, look for gold on the blankets, and so on. And when they stopped to make supper, all three worked as the team they'd become. Kate was exhausted by the unaccustomed labor, but she made no complaint. After supper she rose stiffly and hobbled to her shanty.

"Are you all right, Kate?" Hogan asked, concern etched on his face.

Kate merely nodded and kept walking. If she stopped now, she'd never make it to her bed. Every muscle in her body was racked with pain. She'd never get to sleep. But her head had no sooner hit the pillow than she was out. Sometime during the night, she was awakened by a callused hand on her cheek.

"Kate, wake up," Hogan whispered. "You're moaning in your sleep."

"Ooh, I hurt," she mumbled, rolling over painfully.

"I figured as much," he said. "If you weren't so

all-fired stubborn, you would have told me about it last night."

"What are you doing?" Kate demanded when he threw the covers off. She sat up and grabbed for them again. She wore only her white flannel nightgown, and although it was high-collared, without undergarments beneath, she felt half-naked. "How dare you?" she said, shivering suddenly, whether from the night chill or the presence of this big man at her bedside, she wasn't sure.

"Calm down. I'm just going to rub you with some of this. It'll take away the aches and pains so they won't be so bad."

"You needn't bother," Kate protested, but Hogan brushed her words aside.

"If you want to be able to walk in the morning, we have to do something," he said. "Now, lie down and roll over." He shoved her back on her bedroll and she made no more fuss.

Hogan poured the contents of the bottle into his palm, slathered his hands together to spread it, then bent over her. When his hands first gripped her bare calf, she jerked and drew up her foot, nearly kicking him in the jaw.

"Be still," he ordered, and began massaging the liniment onto her legs, his strong fingers kneading out the knotted muscles. When he finished her calves, he moved up to her thighs, and once again Kate stiffened.

"I don't think you should . . ." she began, but he ignored her and his warm hands kneaded and massaged the backs of her thighs until she felt her tense muscles relax. Hogan raised the hem of her gown, shoving it high on her back.

"Please, I'm not wearing drawers," Kate said, but he was already drawing the covers over her hips, adjusting them so only her back was bared to him.

"Your modesty's been preserved," he said lightly. "It's too dark to see anything." His hand trembled slightly. True, he hadn't been able to see much of Kate's slender pale form lying before him, but his fingers had brushed against the satiny plumpness of her buttocks and he longed to touch her again. He poured some more liniment into his hands and smoothed it onto her back, marveling at the delicate slimness of it. He should never have let her dig like that today, no matter how much she insisted. He'd thought she would quit long before, but she'd held out to the bitter end and then had attempted to make supper by herself.

"Besides, I've seen a woman's backside before." He talked to keep his mind off the way her warm, pliant skin felt beneath his callused hands.

"I'm sure you have," Kate sighed. "Roxanne Blayne's, no doubt."

"It wouldn't be gentlemanly of me to tell," he said, and wondered if he'd detected a note of jealousy. Languidly he smoothed his big hands over her back until he felt her resistance fade and she relaxed under his hands. "You don't have to prove anything, you know, Kate."

"What do you mean?" she asked dreamily. He could swear she was purring under his ministrations.

"You're a woman, and this work is too hard for you. Don't feel you have to force yourself."

"I want to do my share," Kate said.

"There are other things you can do," Hogan said, enjoying the satiny feel of her slender body beneath his hands. "Things only a woman can do." He felt her go stiff again, and wondered what had brought it about.

"That's quite enough, Mr. O'Shea," she said icily. He lifted his hands from her back.

"What's wrong now?" he asked in bewilderment.

"I am not Roxanne Blayne," Kate said, struggling to pull her gown down and unable to roll over and face him until she'd done so. "I am not just a woman to fill your . . . your lustful needs, Hogan O'Shea."

"My lustful needs. Is that what you think I was talking about?" he demanded in outrage.

"Weren't you?" Kate muttered, twisting to reach her gown, still tucked high on her shoulders.

"No, Kate O'Shea, it was not," Hogan said, yanking her gown down for her. "But there would have been nothing wrong if I had meant that. Rest assured that I do not lust for your . . . your skinny beanpole body as much as you'd like me to."

"As I'd like you to," Kate squawked, trying to extricate herself from the covers. She poked her fanny into the air as she tried to rise, and all the time her mouth blazed out an angry tirade of words. "You conceited, egotistical, boorish, opportunistic man."

Hogan couldn't resist the slender mound of fanny presented to him. His broad hand came down on it with a resounding slap. "Don't forget 'lustful,' 'lascivious,' and 'ungentlemanly,' " he growled, and getting to his feet, stalked out of the shanty. He could hear Kate's squeal of anger and pain, but he didn't look back. Stalking into his own tent, he threw himself on his bedroll and breathed deeply, trying to calm his anger. He could hear Kate mumbling in the next tent, and he thought he heard words that only the men used when they were seated around the fire and thought no women could hear. The furious rise and fall of her voice went on for some time before all became quiet again. Hogan lay thinking for a long time, and part of his thoughts were of the smooth perfection of Kate's long slim legs and delicate back and the sensuous plumpness of her trim buttocks. He groaned. He had to get to Dawson soon. It was imperative. He was startled when Axe spoke out of the darkness.

"I had me a woman like that once," the old man said quietly, "with red hair and a temper to match. She was a glory, that one, a glory." Hogan heard the drag of loneliness in the old man's voice.

"What happened to her?" he asked gently. There was a long silence and he thought Axe meant not to answer.

"She died a-birthin' my son," he said finally. "He died later on. I ain't never found another woman like her, not even May." It was the first time he'd spoken May's name since she left. Sighing, the old man turned on his side and went back to sleep, and Hogan lay on thinking about the red-haired woman with the temper to match in the next tent. Was she a glory woman too? He remembered her passion and somehow knew she could be. The thought scared him more than nearly anything else he could think of.

In the days that followed, they dug their shaft deep, all three working in much the same way they had that first day. While two of them dug and picked at the resisting frozen earth, the other washed out the dirt to see what their labors had yielded. Though hard, the work seemed to go quickly. The sun was warm on their backs, the creek gurgling cheerfully.

At night they built fires in the pit to thaw the earth and help speed their work, and during the day they worked steadily, stopping only long enough to hunt for food. Even Kate took a stab at hunting, although the first time she pulled the trigger she was knocked flat on her fanny. Still, she'd gotten up and tried again, until she'd learned to brace herself against the gun's recoil. Hogan still hadn't gotten used to seeing her in men's breeches, and often during the day his gaze would wander to the sight of her slim hips and long legs or her trim backside as she bent over the rocker or the campfire. It seemed to him that all he'd been doing lately was watching Kate.

He tried never to let her know how she drew him. No doubt she'd mock him or rail at him, calling him a lustful animal, and maybe he was, but he couldn't seem to remember Roxanne's face or the feel of her skin beneath his hands or her plump body, while that was all he could think about around Kate. Whether she was bent over the campfire or reaching to fill his cup, his glance caught some part of her he wanted to explore. He wondered what her breasts looked like beneath that thick flannel shirt and heavy union suit, and if her belly was satiny smooth as her back had been. His thoughts were driving him crazy. Maybe he should just go to Kate and demand his connubial rights. After all, she was his wife, and she certainly enjoyed many privileges of being his wife. Didn't he provide for her and protect her? What had he gotten in return except a lot of sass? She hadn't even noticed that he'd given up chewing tobacco.

It wouldn't work. He could imagine the tongue-lashing she would give him. He wasn't afraid of Kate's anger. He wanted something more than that. He just wasn't sure what. He thought of appealing to her sense of fairness. If Kate were anything, she was fair-minded. He could point out that they were two people out here in the wilderness, alone together, except for Axe, and he, Hogan, had a powerful need for a woman. Why couldn't they enjoy each other and go on their way without strings, just as they'd agreed in the beginning? No one need ever know. No. That wouldn't work either.

His mind grappled with a hundred arguments, and each one seemed inadequate when it came to presenting it to Kate. She had a sense of what was right and wrong for her that was absolutely unshakable. So the days passed into weeks and they worked on their claim. Suddenly their pleasant days came to an end.

"Look," Kate called one day, pointing to the sky where a black cloud drifted quickly over the treetops. "What is it?"

"I don't know. You'll have to ask Axe," Hogan said, preparing to slide down into the pit. Axe had gone off to hunt some much-needed game. Hogan worked for a couple of hours in the pit before Kate called down to tell him Axe was returning. Wearily he laid aside his shovel and climbed out. His startled gaze took in Kate. Her face was swollen and blotchy with small bites. With tears in her eyes, she slapped at her face and neck.

"What's wrong, Kate?" he asked, feeling sorry for her plight, whatever it was. Obviously she was in discomfort and upset.

"No-see-ums," Axe said. "That's what the Indians call 'em. Mosquitoes so dadburn small you can't hardly see 'em. Too small to fry, so they ain't much good for nothing 'cept to make a man's life miserable during the summer."

"What can we do about them?" Hogan asked as Kate continued to slap at her neck and face.

"I got just the thing," Axe said, and laid down the

face. She looked madder than a wet hen, he thought, and ducked his head to look out at the creek again. "Seems like I've never felt any other way."

"It won't wash, Hogan," Kate said tightly. "Save your sad stories for someone else. They won't work with me. I have no intention of fulfilling Roxanne's duties until you can get to Dawson." Quickly she got to her feet and stalked away.

"Kate, wait. I didn't mean that," Hogan called, but she didn't look back. In disgust he picked up a pebble and flung it into the creek. Well, not exactly, he amended. He had been feeling her out, checking to see if she would consider ending this constant feuding between them. But ultimately, what had he hoped to gain? He thought of Kate's body beneath his in the sand, her long legs thrashing against his in her struggles to free herself, and of her face all flushed and happy with laughter and mischief.

No, he didn't just want to end the feud. He wanted more, much more, and he sat puzzling over his newly acknowledged feelings. What was so different about Kate that made him want her so? She hadn't changed much at all since they started out. She still had the same foul temper, the same cussed stubbornness, the same arrogant air when she addressed him.

Finally he decided it wasn't Kate he wanted, it was a woman, any woman. He wasn't a monk, never had pretended to be. He was a lusty man with a need for a female. Roxanne would sure fill the bill right now. Groaning, he pushed down the throbbing need that rioted through his body. By God, he was going to Dawson as soon as he got that shaft dug down to bedrock. He had a shaft of his own that needed to be buried, and damn soon, or he wouldn't be responsible for what happened.

Hogan was surly for the next few days, and Kate was withdrawn. She prepared the meals, filled his coffee cup, worked beside him and Axe digging and washing out the gold. Carefully she collected their findings, disappointing as they continued to be, but she never looked at Hogan or laughed with him. Their rough play must have been more offensive to her than he'd realized, he thought, watching her bend over the rocker.

He'd gotten so he watched her without realizing he was doing so, although he was careful to look away so she wouldn't know he watched her. He enjoyed the sight of her pants, the round trim backside sticking in the air as she worked, her red braid falling over her shoulder, the way she pursed her lips to blow away a gnat or a wayward strand of hair, the way she stood with long slender legs planted wide apart, hands resting on hips as she watched a red squirrel gathering spruce cones or listened to the silvery notes of a thrush. The more he watched her, the more it seemed she became a part of the enchantment of the forest and sky and water. She was a rare forest creature, adapting itself to the days of the midnight sun, storing up radiance for the long dark winter that would follow. Kate! She was like a song within him.

They reached bedrock and they'd found no deep river of gold running through the frozen soil. Hogan scooped the last of the dirt into the bucket, yanked on the winch, and Kate cranked it up and threw it into the rocker. Even she seemed to have lost heart. Climbing out of the pit, Hogan noted how her slim shoulders slumped wearily. He knew how she felt; he was just as disheartened. Axe was nowhere in sight. Hogan knew he'd gone farther upstream to scout for a better prospect. He hoped he'd found something; otherwise they'd pick up and move on downriver, with far fewer prospects than they'd had coming here. Kate dumped in a few pails of water and rocked the cradle that divided the dirt from its heavier metal. Examining the blanket, she gathered up the bits of gold nuggets and chips and stored them in a small pouch that was only half-full for all their hard work. Hogan could tell by the matter-of-fact way she handled the bag that their luck had not improved. Bending over, she washed out the rest of the dirt, her backside bobbing invitingly with every movement. Throwing a leg over the rim of the pit, Hogan succumbed to the temptation and landed his broad hand on her neat fanny in a resounding swat.

"What?" Kate screeched, straightening up. Eyes blazing, she rounded on him. "You . . . !" she raged. "You hooligan, you ruffian, you . . . you bully."

"Kate, don't get so mad. I just meant it as a joke," Hogan said, trying to calm her. "You looked so dejected."

"I *am* dejected," Kate cried, "and why shouldn't I be? For weeks I've traveled in this godforsaken, lonely country. I've dug, I've hauled, I've cooked over a campfire until my eyebrows were singed. I've worn men's breeches and smeared bear grease on my face and picked lice out of my hair." Tears rained down her face. In fascination Hogan watched, thinking he hadn't seen Kate cry since Gilly was swept away down the mountain. Now she seemed so vulnerable and angry. Kate was furious!

"I've gone without genteel company, intelligent conversation, or stimulating companionship," she continued, not tending to the tears that streaked the black bear grease. "I've worked until my hands were raw, my back near breaking, my feet aching. I've been hungry and dirty and scared, and I've never complained. I've tried to pull my share of the load. But one thing I will not tolerate is to have a man like you pawing me anymore."

"Kate, I'm sorry. I didn't mean to offend you."

"You do offend me, Mr. O'Shea, at every turn."

Hogan's temper started to rise. "What do you mean by 'a man like me'?" he demanded. "I've hunted for food for you to eat, saved your hide when you got into trouble, massaged your muscles when you were tired. I even married you to protect you from the likes of Frenchy and the other low-life scum that frequent these gold camps, and what do I get in return? A persnickety old maid who thinks she's better than I am. Every time I try to pay you a little attention, you round on me."

"No lady would welcome the kind of attention you've tried to press on me," Kate snapped.

Hogan put his hands on his hips in outraged disgruntlement. Toe to toe, they stood glaring into each other's eyes. They looked more disreputable than either had ever thought possible, he with his mud-encrusted clothes and grimy face, she with her breeches and the black bear grease smeared on her face.

"How do you know I'm not meaning the best kind of attention? How do you know I'm not trying to court you, woo you a bit?" he demanded, and his face was filled with self-righteousness. Kate had not treated him fairly.

"Is *that* what you're doing?" She hooted in disbelief.

"Of course. What else are you thinking?" he fired back. "Now, Kate, who's being low-minded?"

She snickered, which deflated his chest somewhat. "You wouldn't know how to go courting a lady," she snapped. "Not the first thing about it!"

"Well, maybe I'm not so fine-mannered as some of your other gentlemen callers." He sneered, trying to imply that she had no other callers. "But some seem to find my courting effective."

"Roxanne?" Kate scoffed. "She can have you. I'll not have a man who slaps me on the backside and thinks that's all that's needed."

"What else is it you're wanting, then?" Hogan demanded angrily. His black eyes were fierce in his grimy face.

"I want a man who brings me flowers and talks nicely to me about the weather or other everyday pleasant things. I want a man who looks like he takes a bath once in a while and uses manners when he eats, and calls me 'ma'am' and holds my chair for me and doesn't chew and spit tobacco, and . . . I don't know." She raised her hands in frustration and caught a glimpse of her grimy arms. It was the last straw. "I want a bath," she shouted, and stalked to her tent. Pulling out her bag, she rummaged for the dwindling bar of lavender-scented soap and took out one of the rumpled gowns she'd brought from Seattle. Carrying her belongings down to the creek, she laid them over a bush and began unbuttoning her shirt. Hogan still stood where she'd left him.

"Go away, Hogan," she shouted, slinging her shirt off her arm. For weeks she had struggled to find privacy, dodging into tents and behind bushes to dress and undress. Now, in her anger, she began removing her clothes. Let Hogan do his share to maintain decorum. She was tired of doing all the worrying.

For his part, Hogan was stunned when Kate began unbuttoning her shirt, and when she slung it away from her and shouted him a warning, he straightened. By the time she had the buttons undone on her breeches and they were sliding down her hips, leaving only the long underwear beneath, he was headed for the woods.

What the hell was the matter with her? He grunted to himself. He'd never seen a woman get herself on a high horse faster than Kate, and all because he'd slapped her fanny. He wandered through the sun-dappled spruce trees. His steps made no sound on the moss-carpeted floor. Hands in pockets, he stopped to watch a bald eagle soaring high and free above the mountain peaks. The serenity of the forest calmed him as nothing else could. With his head stuck down in that pit from morning to night, he'd lost sight of the beauty around him. Now he looked his fill and thought about where he'd been in his life and where he was headed. The years had been long, crammed with brawls and daredevil adventures, but they'd been lonely as well—he'd been telling Kate the truth about that—and somehow aimless.

His wanderings carried him back to the creek, upstream. Thinking of Kate bathing farther down, he stripped his clothes off and waded in. The water, warmed by a sun that shone for more than twenty hours a day, was pleasant to the touch. Using sand to scour away the dirt and grime of the pit, Hogan rolled over on his back and floated, staring up at the cloudless sky. Kate came drifting back into his thoughts, and he no longer tried to resist. She was a woman a man could settle down with if he was of a mind to.

"Ho!" Axe called from far up the creek. "Ho, the

camp." If Hogan hadn't come upstream to bathe, he wouldn't have heard him.

"Ho, Axe!" he called, standing up and waving his hand. The old man paddled his canoe over to Hogan.

"This is it, son. I know we ain't had much luck on this creek, but I'm a-tellin' you, I've been smelling the gold. I just couldn't figure out where it come from. Look, look at this. I think we've found it this time. Look." Axe dumped out the pouch lying on the bottom of the canoe. Large gold nuggets, some of them as big as a man's fist, glinted up at him.

"Good God Almighty," Hogan breathed. He thought of how excited they'd been over their first gold find and how insignificant it really was. In a few hours Axe had gathered up more gold than they had mined in six weeks. "Kate'll never believe this."

"It ain't that far up," Axe said.

"Kate! Kate!" Hogan shouted exultantly. Grabbing up his clothes, he tried to put on his pants as he ran along the creek, falling into the water in the process. It didn't matter. He wanted to see Kate's face when she got a glimpse of what Axe had. "Kate!"

Seeing him running along the creek, shirtless and shoeless, Kate could think of only one thing. Indians were attacking them. She ran to their tent and grabbed out a rifle and with fumbling fingers tried to load it. She couldn't hit the broad side of a barn with it, but she could have it ready for Hogan. Shoving a shell into the chamber, she ran to meet him, heedless of the splash of water on the hem of her gown.

"Hogan!" she cried, holding the rifle high for him to grab it. She could see Axe paddling for camp. Thank God he'd come back safely, she thought. Hogan was to her now, but instead of taking his rifle, he swooped her up in his arms and twirled around with her. "We did it this time, Kate. We've struck gold!" he shouted.

The meaning of his words washed over her, and Kate pushed away from him, shoving the rifle between them. "Fool! Let go of me," she cried, twisting away. "I thought Indians were attacking."

"No, wait until you see what Axe has," Hogan said,

laughing. Grabbing her arm, he jerked her over to the canoe the old sourdough had just pulled up onshore. "Show her," he commanded, eyes gleaming. Axe flipped back the fur pelt, revealing the nuggets.

Silently Kate stared at them. "What does this mean?" she asked.

"It means we've found gold," Hogan declared happily.

"We discovered gold here," Kate said, and looked at the small bag of nuggets. She didn't have to say more.

"It's not the same thing," Hogan said persuasively. "This is better, Kate, I promise you."

"How do you know?"

"Axe knows."

"Axe *thinks* he knows," Kate said adamantly. "He was so certain when we came here."

"He was mistaken," Hogan said. "Every man makes a mistake now and then."

"I've found the source of the gold that washed down here," Axe said.

Hogan turned gleaming eyes toward him. "The mother lode?" he whispered reverently.

"I don't reckon there is a mother lode," Axe said, "but it's near enough to one to make me damned glad I found this stream again. I scooped up these pieces of gold in just a few minutes."

Kate looked from one to the other, knowing they were excited and wanted her to be too, but already she was disillusioned with gold mining. "What are you going to do?" she asked.

Axe glanced up and down the stream. "When word gets out about this, we'll have miners down this stream like a school of salmon. We're going back up there and pick our claims, one for each of us. Then we need to build a couple of cabins for ourselves."

"Let's not take the time for that right now," Hogan said eagerly.

Axe shook his head. "Son, we've got about six weeks more before winter sets in here again. We'll take turns mining and building, and then we'll go register our claims."

"Hot damn! Dawson!" Hogan said, clenching his fist, and Kate knew he was thinking of Roxanne.

11

Kate was less than enthusiastic as they moved their belongings from one campsite to the other. This time they traveled farther upstream, away from the mouth of the creek where it flowed into the Yukon. It seemed to Kate they were getting farther away from people or the possibility of seeing them. At least on the river there had been other people traveling to Dawson or to Bonanza Creek in the hopes some unclaimed area was still available. But here there was no one except Hogan, Axe, and herself. Axe was seldom in camp. That left just Hogan and her, and the strain of always being thrown together with him was beginning to tell. It was because they were so incompatible, she told herself, because they didn't like each other, because . . . because . . . The becauses made her head ache, so she was grumpy as a wounded old bear, or so Hogan was quick to point out to her.

After her initial rebellion, Kate had once again donned her breeches and blackened her face with the bear grease, for the gnats were worse than the mosquitoes, and both were biting something fierce. As always, Kate did her share of work, toting and lifting, and never a word of complaint, although Hogan discerned she was quieter. Something was bothering her, and he wasn't sure what. He hadn't much time to think about it, for he started felling trees for the cabins. They would build two. One for Kate and one for the men, and unlike the shanties, these would have real roofs over them, with whipsawed boards laid across roof beams. Hogan thought Kate would be happy, but she said barely a word, turning back to her chores.

She'd been gathering berries and putting them out to dry in the sun and checking their supplies. If they were preparing to spend a winter here on the creek, they'd better make sure they had plenty of food. She remembered the miners they'd met along the way talking about the near-starvation some had faced the year before. She should have planted a garden, she thought idly. Although the summer was short, a few plants might have grown in these long days of continuous sunshine. Kate no longer panned for gold. Her gold fever seemed to have burned out.

In their spare time from building, Hogan and Axe panned for gold. They easily filled two bags, and then a third. Hogan no longer attempted to show Kate his findings. He sensed her aloofness from him, and it troubled him more than anything else about her. It enraged him as well, for he felt helpless. He was used to a peppery, sassy Kate, not this quiet, docile creature. What had he done? He thought back over all their fights, all the times she'd raged at him, all the angry words they'd flung at each other, and he had to admit she had cause to be angry. But she'd never held a grudge before. Why now?

Everything about her was tamped down. Her eyes were dull and uninterested when he spoke to her. And although she would answer courteously enough, there was not the old biting wit that kept him on his toes. Even the brilliance of her hair seemed to dim to match her mood.

Well, he wouldn't have this sulking, Hogan thought angrily. He'd be damned if he'd spend all winter with a sullen, pouting woman. He'd tell her so, by God, just as soon as he finished building this bed for her. After the bed, he built her a table and two stools, and then some rough shelves. He also cut a window and stretched a tanned caribou hide over it to let in light if not air.

A thought occurred to him. "Do you want to return to Seattle?" he asked one day.

Startled, Kate looked at him. "Are you trying to get rid of me?" she asked.

"No, I'm not trying to take your share of the gold claim, if that's what you mean," he said, dark eyes studying her closed face. "I just thought you might be tired of the hardships and . . . and loneliness. You don't have to stay here, you know. Axe and I will send a third of anything we find."

Kate's aloof expression wavered for a moment; then she put her chin in the air and glanced down her nose at him. "I'm not here for the gold. I'm here because this was Gilly's dream. I just want to share it for a little while. Does that cramp your style too much, Mr. O'Shea?"

"Not in the least, Mrs. O'Shea," he snapped out of habit. "I was just trying to look out for your best interests."

"That's not necessary," she answered dismissively, and gritting his teeth, Hogan stalked away. But later, when he had time to examine his feelings, he had to admit that he wasn't nearly as angry as he'd thought he was. In fact, he felt kind of relieved, but he couldn't for the life of him understand why. Kate's staying only meant he had to worry about her all through the winter. The thought of spending the winter with the increasing tension between Kate and himself was disheartening, the possibility of spending the winter without her unthinkable.

"We'd better go to Dawson," Axe said one morning, puzzled that Hogan had continued to delay the trip.

"Maybe I'll have a chance to see Iris Garrett again," Kate said with quickening interest as she prepared for their journey. In anticipation she dug out a gown and shook it. Using the mosquito netting from her cot, she fashioned a veil of sorts, so she could do without the bear grease.

Hogan handed her into the boat and picked up the oar. Axe was already pushing away in his boat. They'd decided to take both boats in order to haul back supplies. Kate had her list tucked securely into her bag.

All day they paddled, halting only when darkness forced them to. Hogan set up a tent for all of them to share and laid out their bedrolls while Kate gathered wood and started a small fire for coffee. She'd brought cooked meat and cold beans for their supper. The smell of the campfire and the earthy forest behind them reminded her of those early days when they'd started out on this adventure. How excited the four of them had been—Axe, May, Hogan, and she. Now the summer was nearly past, and May was gone. They'd found their gold, but somehow it had come too easily and pointed out too clearly to Kate that gold brought little happiness to its seekers.

She glanced at Axe, chewing on his wad of tobacco. He'd never mentioned May in her presence, but she sensed he missed the young Indian woman. Hogan himself looked pretty morose as he sat staring into the fire. What was he thinking of? she wondered. Roxanne Blayne, no doubt! Her heart seemed to turn over in her chest and she wondered if the dance-hall girl would be in Dawson. If she were, Hogan's mood would be greatly improved on their trip home. Kate felt no comfort in that thought. In fact, she had a weepy feeling that Aunt Petty used to counteract by feeding her chamomile tea and hugging her a lot. Kate wrapped her arms around herself. She could stand to have one of Aunt Petty's hugs right now, or one of Gilly's clumsy pats. She'd never felt so lonely before. She glanced at Hogan, his long legs stretched out before him, the firelight reflected in his dark eyes, and remembered how he'd spoken of his loneliness. She had an overwhelming desire to go to him, to offer him whatever comfort he sought from her, and in the giving, gain a bit for herself. But of course she couldn't. They were on their way to Dawson, and within a few hours Hogan would be with his trollop again, rip-roaring drunk, no doubt, and embroiled in every low vice the town had to offer.

"I'm going to bed," she said abruptly, and left the sterile light of the fire. Without a word, Hogan watched her go, and once again turned his attention to the leaping flames. This time tomorrow night, he'd be in Dawson, and if Roxanne wasn't there, other women would be, available women who'd laugh with him for a while and cuddle on his lap and make him feel loved, at least until his gold ran out.

Dawson City! It was a ragtag town, birthed by the discovery of gold, forgotten by God, and wallowing in its own greed and corruption. The town had been built on a sphagnum bog at a bend in the Yukon River, and its streets were rivers of mud. Mules and horses struggled to pull wagons and sleds through the mire. When they broke a leg or dropped from exhaustion, they were simply shot and left in the street, the stench of their rotting carcasses adding to that of human waste and other filth.

No one had time to clean up the streets or worry about the consequences. In one summer the town had burgeoned from five thousand to thirty as the discoveries of the Bonanza and Eldorado were followed by equally sensational finds on Dominion and Sulfur creeks. Even the hills themselves—Gold, French, and Skookum—yielded up their treasures.

Lots fronting the Yukon River that had been worthless a few weeks before now sold for five thousand dollars a front foot. Few took time to build permanent dwellings, simply pitching tents near existing cabins and hurrying off to the creeks to find unstaked ground. The detachment of thirty Northwest Mounted Police had been increased to eighty, and even their presence barely kept a lid on the lawlessness. Men made fortunes during the day and lost them at night on gambling, watered-down whiskey, and women. Diamond Tooth Gertie, Glass-Eyed Annie, and Virgin Mary were but a few women who'd arrived in Dawson penniless and were quickly growing wealthy.

As Hogan and Axe tied off their boats, Kate held her nose and looked around in dismay. Dawson was nothing at all like what she'd expected, yet she didn't know why she was surprised after seeing Skagway. A few log buildings sat along the streets. Most were saloons; from one came the plink of a piano. She hoped they had a general store.

"Kate, here's some gold to buy supplies with," Hogan said, handing her one of the bags. "I put in extra to pay for our share." He'd already given Axe his, and the old man was even now loping off down the street. "The rest is yours to spend however you want."

Kate glanced around. "I'm sure that won't be hard to do," she said with some of the old mockery. A shout of ribald laughter came from a saloon.

"Look, Kate . . ." Hogan fell into step beside her. "I think I'd better walk you down to the general store, and afterward, well, maybe the storekeeper will let you stay there for a while. It's not safe for you to wander around alone here."

"I see," Kate said, and wondered just how long she'd be forced to sit like a piece of forgotten baggage before he left his whore and came to collect her. Pride stiffened her spine. "You needn't worry about me, Mr. O'Shea," she said firmly. "I'm sure I can amuse myself until we leave. What time do you wish me back at the boat?"

"Kate, this is no time to get all huffy and stubborn about things," Hogan began.

"My land, I'm shore happy I came down today," a familiar voice interrupted him, and Kate swung around to find Iris Garrett bearing down on her. She hurried forward to greet the woman. With unrestrained affection Iris threw her arms around Kate and hugged her like a long-lost friend.

"Hello, Mr. O'Shea. You just gettin' here?" she demanded, and tucked Kate's arm into her elbow possessively.

"Yes, ma'am, we did," he answered. Kate grinned, happy to see the gregarious woman again. In spite of Iris' bustling take-over air, Kate liked her.

"Well, you just come along with me, Kate. I'll show you where the general store is and where a few ladies meet afterward to get a bit to eat and visit while their men are"—she paused significantly, casting a disdainful glance at the nearest saloon—"otherwise occupied."

"Thank you, Mrs. Garrett." Hogan's relief at getting rid of her was all too evident. Kate's lips tightened in anger. He could barely wait to find Roxanne.

"I'll be happy to spend the day with you, Iris," she said stiffly, and without a backward glance stalked away. Hogan watched her go, liking the swing of her hips beneath the dark skirts. As much as he enjoyed the sight of Kate in breeches, it was nice to see her in a gown again.

Sighing happily, he turned away, meandering along the boardwalks and muddy streets to look in the store windows. He'd thought he would hurry right to a saloon for a drink, but now he found it was too early for him. The stores were filled with supplies now. Steamships had made it down the Yukon a few weeks before, bringing desperately needed food as well as other gear. Before the ships' arrivals the miners had been reduced to a flour-and-water diet. Peering into one store, Hogan halted and stared in delight at an object sitting proudly on display. It was just the thing for Kate and her new cabin, he thought, and, knocking the worst of the mud from his boots, he stepped inside.

Kate was still smarting at Hogan's obvious haste to get her off his hands. Her ire was soon turned to something else as she made her purchases. Flour was an unbelievable seventy-five dollars a twenty-pound sack and eggs eighteen dollars a dozen. She debated long over butter at five dollars a pound, and finally bought a pound. If she were careful with its use, she could make it last awhile. When she'd finished shopping, the supplies had taken a sizable chunk of the gold in her bag. Still, there was enough, and Kate turned to the back of the store, where a few bolts of bright calico lay across a table.

"How much is it?" Kate asked, fingering the material.

"That'll brighten a cabin on a dreary day," Iris said, and impulsively Kate ordered a length cut off for a tablecloth and to make cushions for her stools. She might even have enough for a ruffle at the top of her window. The purchase brightened her spirits considerably, and happily she followed Iris along the street toward the small log cabin set aside for visiting ladies.

"Kate!" She turned at the sound of her name and saw Clay Lawford hurrying toward her. He was dressed in rough miner's garb, but his hair was neatly combed and his jaw freshly shaved.

"Clay," she cried in delight, holding out her hands. He took hold of them and for a moment Kate thought he meant to pull her into his arms. Her cheeks blushed brightly and her green eyes sparkled with pleasure. "It's so good to see you again."

"Miss Kate, you never looked prettier," he said, his young face eager and alive. "I've worried about you."

"There was no need," she answered with some dismay. "I'm in good hands. Hogan is quite capable."

"Yes, that's true," Clay said. "I guess what I meant was that I thought about you a lot."

"Well, we've thought about you and Uly," Kate said earnestly. "Somehow it wasn't the same after you left." She didn't notice how his eyes gleamed at her words. "May left too." She stood in the middle of the street filling him in on the news since they'd last parted. So intent was she on the exchange, she didn't notice that his hands still gripped hers or that he bent over her with a proprietary air. The sun was warm on their heads. Clay was as witty and endearing as he'd always been. Kate stood gazing up at him, laughter mingling with his. She'd forgotten Iris, who waited on the sidewalk, nor did she see Hogan as he came out of one of the stores.

Hogan saw her, though. He saw how lightheartedly she laughed, how she peered up at Clay almost coquettishly, and his big fists tightened. He was tempted to stalk into the street and tear Kate away from him, but pride kept him from it. Angrily he made his way toward a saloon and ordered his first whiskey of the day. His first, but not his last, he vowed. While he was mooning about the stores, buying gifts for Kate, she was standing out in the middle of the street for all of Dawson to see which man she preferred over her own husband. He waved the bartender over to pour another drink. "Have you got a woman called Roxanne Blayne working here?" he asked.

"Hey, Roxy. Someone asking about you," the bartender called, and the blond-haired woman glanced up, her face lighting when she caught a glimpse of Hogan. Patting the cheek of the man on whose lap she sat, Roxanne whispered a few words that caused him to laugh uproariously. The hand he'd run up the inside of her thighs patted her slightly and withdrew. Roxanne rose, shook out her skirts, tugged her tight bodice so her full breasts were only a little better covered, and turned toward the bar. Her face registered her pleasure in seeing Hogan again. It had been a long time since Juneau, and she'd thought of him often.

She seldom considered giving up her career as a camp follower, but when she looked at his hulking shoulders and darkly handsome features, the thought flittered through her mind. She'd never had a more satisfying lover. He was gentle, considerate, and experienced. Those elements, coupled with his physical strength and stamina in bed, were a heady combination.

"Hogan!" she called now as she flung herself into his arms.

"Roxanne!" He swung her high and twirled with her, then set her back on her feet, a quick kiss planted on her mouth.

"Ummm," she said, tugging his head down to deepen the kiss. He complied, his tongue delving into her mouth with expert mastery. Roxanne felt herself go weak against him, but Hogan pulled away. His dark eyes studied her in bewilderment for a moment, and then the look was gone. He threw back his head and laughed.

"Bartender, bring us a bottle," he commanded, and grabbing up the bottle and two glasses in one hand, he circled Roxanne's waist with the other and led her toward a makeshift table and stools. He pulled Roxanne down on his lap and poured her a drink. "How've you been, Roxy?" he asked, and slapped her on the fanny. "You don't mind if I do that, do you?" he asked, and at her giggling permission, he lightly slapped her backside again. " 'Course you don't," he growled. "You're not some highfalutin lady putting on airs, are you?"

"I'm whatever you want me to be, sugar," Roxanne said in her sultriest voice. She brushed her breasts against his chest and looked invitingly into his eyes. Boldly Hogan let his gaze roam over her ample wares, absently patted her behind, then stood up, nearly dumping her on the floor.

"What's wrong, baby?" Roxanne exclaimed, smoothing his shirt across his back.

"I'm sorry, Roxanne," he said, pushing his dark hair back with an impatient brush of his hand. "I guess I'm just not in the mood for a woman right now. It's not fair for me to take your time."

"My time is just for you, Hogan," she said soothingly, unwilling to give up on him. She'd sensed something was different with him, but she wasn't quite sure what the problem was. "Why don't you come up to my room and let me put you in the mood?" she offered.

Hogan glanced at her, slowly nodding his head. "All right," he said, and followed her up the rickety steps to her tiny room.

Once there, Roxanne unbuttoned his shirt, letting her fingers roam upward through the crinkly dark hair that covered his chest and swirled most enticingly downward to disappear into his trousers. Roxanne knew just what the swirl of hair led to, and the thought of Hogan aroused and demanding was exciting.

Breathing deeply, so the tops of her breasts rose and fell, she pushed him down on her bed and filled his glass. Standing in front of him, her gaze locked with his, she slowly and seductively removed each piece of her clothing, until she stood pale and nude. She knew she was beautiful. Men had told her so often enough. Hogan refilled his glass and gulped down the raw whiskey, his dark gaze raking over her body.

But there was something missing, Roxanne sensed.

TOMORROW'S DREAM 217

There was not the hunger, the frank, uncomplicated need in him. At least not for her. Was there another woman in his life? she wondered briefly, and brought up her hands to grasp her full white breasts and thrust them forward temptingly. Her fingers captured the already taut nipples and rolled them gently. She arched her back in simulated response, then thrust her hands toward him, flexing her fingers in an unspoken invitation.

Hogan stayed where he was, watching her, his eyes black and unreadable, a half-smile on his face that told her nothing. Roxanne bit back her vexation at his seeming coldness and half-turned. Lifting her hands high above her head, she arched her back and rotated her hips suggestively. He was playing hard-to-get, she thought, and pushed down her own impatience. Many men were like this. They wanted the woman to be the bold one, to entice and seduce them.

With a pout she threw herself at his feet and slowly began to unlace his boots. When she had them both off, she removed his socks, then trailed her hands up his trousers until she reached his waistband.

Hogan's fingers stopped her. "I'm sorry," he said, and wondered what in the hell had happened to him. When he looked at Roxanne, he pictured Kate's slimmer figure and what it must look like under those damn trousers and petticoats and nightgowns she wore.

Stunned, Roxanne looked at him, slowly dragging her fingers away from his pants. "We can just talk if you want," she said, and wondered at her own patience. Hogan was a man worth it. If she could just get him to open up to her the way he had back in Seattle . . .

"Tell me about your trip out here," she said, wrapping a robe around her naked body. She should be downstairs making money, she thought, but settled into a chair. "Was the pass dangerous? Have you and your partner found gold yet?"

He started talking, hesitantly at first, then with increasing fervor as he told of the hardships and danger he and the others had faced. Carefully Roxanne listened. Through it all, one name appeared with more frequency and occasioned more reaction on Hogan's mobile face than any other. Kate! Kate O'Shea! Hogan's wife!

"I wouldn't like to be that young man if Hogan catches him mooning over you like that," Iris said tartly when Kate had rejoined her.

Surprised, Kate glanced at her. "It wouldn't matter to Hogan," she said, and explained the arrangement of her marriage. Still the other woman looked disbelieving.

"I think you might be surprised at what your husband feels for you," Iris said cryptically.

"What do you mean?" Kate asked, puzzled.

"Why, it's just as plain as the nose on your face that the man has feeling for you," Iris said, staring at Kate as if she were truly a dunce not to see it herself.

"Oh, no, Iris, I'm afraid you're wrong this time. Why, right now Hogan is at one of the saloons looking for Roxanne Blayne, a dance-hall girl he met in Seattle. So you see, he couldn't possibly care anything about me . . . nor I for him," she hastily added. "That was our agreement."

"I could be wrong," Iris said doubtfully. "I sure thought I seen . . . Well, no matter. I expect you know what you're doing." She opened the door of the women's cabin.

"Ladies, this here's Kate O'Shea," she cried. "She and her mister are in town for the day. They just come up this summer. Kate, this is Ilse Talbot, our new schoolmarm, and Ethel Johnson, her and her man are mining down on Dominion Creek, and Leona Hollis, who just come a few days ago. She's been doing wash and making doughnuts and the like until her husband strikes a claim."

"I'm glad to meet you all," Kate said, looking around at the women seated on benches and stools, baskets of needlework and food sitting at their feet.

Kate settled herself on a stool and took out the length

of calico, thread, and needle she'd purchased and began hemming it. All the while she answered the women's eager questions about where she was from and how she'd gotten here. They were hungry for news from home and the chance to share feminine confidences, so that talk flowed with seldom a pause. At lunch the ladies laid out their baskets of food on a common table and shared recipes with one another. The hours passed quickly. When the shadows were long in the little cabin and someone rose to light a lamp, Kate gathered her things.

"I'd better find Hogan and Axe," she said, knowing they wanted to return some distance upriver before making camp for the night. Bidding the women good-bye, she and Iris set out for the boat landing. What if Hogan and Axe weren't there? she wondered. How would she go about finding them? She remembered how she'd searched out her father back in Seattle, and Hogan's admonition on their wedding day that she never do that to him. Well, she wouldn't, she thought. If Hogan and Axe didn't show up, she'd bed down in one of the boats. The nights were still warm enough to do that.

Her dilemma was solved as she passed in front of the Lucky Lady Saloon. Suddenly the door was flung open and a man tumbled out onto the porch. He would surely have pitched forward into the muddy street if not for the blond woman supporting him with her shoulder. Kate's lips tightened as she recognized Hogan. He was laughing so hard he could scarcely stand, even if he hadn't drunk half the whiskey in Dawson. Roxanne's thin laughter echoed with his as she propped him up against the side of the building and pressed herself to him. She wore only a shiny satin gown of gaudy blue, trimmed with black lace and shiny black jet beads across its low-cut bodice. A black feather rose at a discordant angle from her untidy coiffure. She looked as if she had dressed hastily, and Kate had little doubt as to what she'd been doing for the past few hours.

Roxanne wound her arms up around Hogan's neck

and swayed slightly, letting her full breasts brush against him suggestively.

"Come on, baby," she wheedled. "Let's go back up to my room."

"C-can't," Hogan said, and laughed again. "I . . . I got to meet . . ." He paused for a long time, as if marshaling his thoughts. "Kate," he finally got out, and with obvious self-satisfaction that he'd managed that much.

"Let the old maid wait." Roxanne sneered. "I found you first. She doesn't know how to satisfy a man like you. I do. Remember? Remember, baby?" She rubbed her body against his, pumping her hips suggestively.

"Disgusting," Iris Garrett snorted derisively, and Kate's cheeks flamed with embarrassment in spite of the fact that she'd already told Iris the truth about her marriage.

"Mr. O'Shea!" Iris hailed him before Kate could stop her. Not for anything had she wanted Hogan to know she'd witnessed such a lascivious display. Bleary-eyed, he looked around.

"Hello, Miz Garrett," he slurred drunkenly, waving a hand at her.

"Your wife is here, Mr. O'Shea," Iris continued, casting such a withering glance at Roxanne that Kate wondered why she didn't melt on the spot. But Roxanne seemed to feel no such embarrassment. She made no move away from Hogan. Her arms were still around his neck.

"Mr. O'Shea is indisposed at this time, ladies," she said brassily. "Why don't you come back later?" Her blue eyes glittered with malice.

"His wife is waiting now," Iris began angrily, but Kate forestalled her.

"Let me handle this," she said, and walked up on the porch. She paid no attention to Roxanne whatsoever. Her green eyes met Hogan's unwaveringly. "It's time to start back," she said quietly. "Are you ready?"

Hogan nodded, his head wobbling on his great neck.

"Ready!" he said, and tried to straighten, but he leaned to one side dangerously.

"Lean on me," Kate said, and stepped forward. Roxanne still clung to his neck. Now she glared at Kate with a spiteful grin, issuing a challenge.

"Maybe he don't want to go with you," she snapped. "Not when he can stay here with a real woman who knows how to please him." She brought a finger up and ran it along one side of her pouty lower lip. "And I do know how to please him."

"I'd be surprised if you didn't," Kate answered mildly. "I understand you've had a great deal of experience in pleasing men."

Roxanne stiffened. "You bet I have. I've been in nearly every gold camp between here and South Dakota."

Kate looped her arm around Hogan's waist, pushing his flopping arm over her shoulder. "I'm sure your credentials are the best," she answered blandly, and by her very failure to show anger or jealousy, infuriated Roxanne more than she ever realized.

"What's Hogan doing with a woman like you?" Roxanne jeered. "You're not even his kind. You must have tricked him into marrying you."

Impatiently Kate met her gaze. "The point is, he did marry me. Now, let go of my husband," she said with more force in her voice than she'd intended.

"And if I don't?" Roxanne asked haughtily.

Kate looked at the cheap prostitute and felt anger at Hogan for spending the afternoon with the likes of Roxanne Blayne. Without a word she doubled up her free hand, drew back, and socked Roxanne squarely on the chin. Taken unawares, Roxanne was knocked off balance. Teetering on the edge of the porch, she emitted a high-pitched scream and fell backward into the muddy street. Her cry brought men running from the saloon, and now they crowded onto the porch.

"Why, you . . . you . . ." Roxanne sputtered, floundering up. Her feet went out from under her and she fell again, this time face-forward. Kate had already turned Hogan and propelled him off the other end of the porch and headed for the river. Behind her she could hear men guffawing and Roxanne's outraged screams, but she never looked back.

"That was the neatest piece of comeuppance I've ever had a chance to see," Iris Garrett said, coming to Hogan's other side. "I knew you were a woman of spirit, Kate O'Shea. You're just the kind of woman we need up here." She glanced at Hogan. His head lolled on his shoulder and his eyes rolled. His legs were so unsteady under him he could barely walk, and he emitted a ghastly groan. "You're just the kind of woman a man like Hogan O'Shea needs," she observed. "Take him in hand, Kate. I've got a feeling he'd make a good husband if you could tame his wild ways."

"That wasn't my agreement with him," Kate answered. "I don't have the right to force him to change for me."

"Why not? You love him, don't you?" Iris demanded. Kate looked at her in stunned surprise. Hogan's legs folded under him, saving her from having to answer. They were at the boats now, and Kate lowered him into one.

"Good-bye, Kate," Iris said. "I see Bud waitin' for me." She nodded toward the little steamer they used to ply their trade along the river.

"Good-bye, Iris," Kate said, hugging her. She hated to part with the older woman. God only knew how long it would be before she'd see her again.

"Just keep in mind what I said about Hogan," Iris reminded her, and with a final wave hurried away.

Axe stepped out of the shadows "How's he doing?" he asked.

"Not too well," Kate answered. "I don't think he can handle a boat tonight."

"Yesh I can," Hogan said, forcing his legs to support himself. "I'm jush fine."

"I ain't too crazy about bedding down here," Axe said, looking back along the street. "Too many drunks. Someone might decide to have a go at our supplies."

"You're right. Lesh go. I can paddle. Never met a

bottle or a woman who could keep Hogan O'Shea down."

"I can help with the oars," Kate said. "But I left our supplies up at the general store."

"Hogan and me brought 'em down earlier, along with our things," Axe said. "I've been guardin' 'em, waitin' for you two to come back."

"I didn't know," Kate said apologetically. From beneath her lashes she observed the old man. Although his attitude was as reserved and self-contained as always, she sensed an underlying agitation. Was he angry that he'd been left in charge of the boats and hadn't been given a chance to enjoy himself as well? Her conscience was stricken. "Didn't you want to have a drink or something?"

"Naw, I didn't," Axe said quietly, and picked up his paddle.

"LaRoche ish bastard," Hogan muttered as he fumbled with the oars. Kate took them from him and set them in the oarlocks.

"Did you see Frenchy in town?" she asked. Axe pushed off from shore without answering.

"Yep," Hogan said, sitting upright with almost comical rigidity. "I hit him." He grinned like a child who'd done something of which he was eminently proud. "Knocked out his gold tooth." He chuckled.

"Was May with him?" Kate asked, but Hogan didn't answer. He was concentrating fiercely on coordinating his rowing so both oars went in the same direction at the same time. "Was May there?" she repeated.

Hogan stopped paddling and sat pulling in deep breaths of air, as if his puny efforts had already exhausted him. "No, I didn't shee May," he gasped finally. Kate waited for him to take up the oars again, but he slumped forward, his head hitting the prow of the boat with a sickening thud. He seemed not to notice. With a little chuckle he began singing a ribald song that would have made Kate's ears turn red if she weren't so angry with him.

"Move over," she said impatiently, pushing at his heavy weight so she could get at the oars. They were in the middle of the river now, with Dawson's sights and sounds and smells receding somewhat.

"Kate," Hogan crooned drunkenly, and ran his hand up her leg beneath her skirt, caressing the curve of her calf before moving up to the warm flesh of her thigh.

"Remove your hand from my leg, Mr. O'Shea," Kate commanded. "At once!"

Her sharp tone seemed to cut through his whiskey haze. He let his hand drop. "Hard woman, Kate," he mumbled. "Hard wo—" A snore cut across what else he'd been about to say. Kate pulled against the oars with all her might. They were going upriver and it took more effort to maneuver the clumsy boat. She wished they'd fashioned a canoe for themselves, as Axe had done.

As if summoned, Axe emerged out of the darkness. "I found a place for us just upriver a piece," he said. "It's not far. Throw me that rope and I'll help tow you." He looped the rope over his bow and began paddling. The boat skewed around, but Kate managed with the oars to keep it straight and aid a little in their forward progress. They pulled the boats deep into the foliage that lined the riverbank, so it wouldn't be immediately noticeable to passersby. Then the two of them struggled to get Hogan out of the boat and up the bank. His big body was deadweight for them. As they neared the tree beneath which they would siwash, Hogan surged forward on his own steam, staggered a step or two, and fell flat on his face.

"Leave him there," Kate snapped, and all her exasperation was evident in her tone. Axe brought up their bedrolls. Kate relented and threw a blanket over Hogan, then settled beneath the tree in her own bedroll. The events of the day flashed by her. It had been a pleasant day until she'd met Hogan and Roxanne Blayne. Now anger whipped through her as she thought of Hogan's drunken lewd behavior and Roxanne's malice.

She could picture Hogan holding Roxanne and kissing her with the same passion he'd shown her. He'd never made any secret of the fact that he needed a woman nor hidden the hard arousals he's gotten when he kissed Kate. Well, now he'd had a chance to satisfy his lust with that lewd creature. Kate could imagine them locked in an intimate embrace. But the thought of Hogan's lips moving across Roxanne's mouth the way they had hers awakened a rage in her such as she'd never known. She wished she'd hit the dance-hall girl again, or that she'd scratched her eyes out or . . . She put aside her vengeful thoughts. She shouldn't blame Roxanne Blayne. She was only there to fill the needs of undisciplined, lust-riddled men like Hogan O'Shea.

And what about herself? She was hardly any different, brawling in the streets with a whore. Her cheeks burned at the thought. A whore that Hogan had deliberately sought out for the afternoon while she had sat sewing with the ladies and talking about her man as if Hogan really were. She was mortified beyond tears.

It had been embarrassing enough to run across Hogan with his trollop in front of Iris, for she was fast becoming a kind friend, but what if any of the other ladies had seen him? And Dawson was probably no better than any other small town. Everyone knew everyone else's business. Were people even now laughing at her pretending to be Mrs. Hogan O'Shea?

But the biggest hurt of all was the memory of Roxanne in Hogan's arms, pressing herself to him shamelessly. How brazen the woman had been. Was that the kind of woman Hogan wanted? Kate sniffed. She could never be like that. She never would be. Not she. Not for any man. Not even for Hogan O'Shea. Never.

But the plain fact was that Hogan had no care for the kind of woman she was. He'd blatantly ignored her for weeks before they came to Dawson. He'd had no need for her once he knew he would be seeing Roxanne again. But what of the desires he'd awakened within her? Kate pushed the thought away. She had no need of Hogan. She could live without his arms around her, without his big hard body and his hot kisses. Life was better without those things, less complicated.

Kate pulled the covers over her head, but she

couldn't shut out the sight of Hogan holding Roxanne in his arms, and the thought made her sick to her stomach.

Dawn was breaking over the eastern trees when she awoke. Axe was already up and had a pot of coffee boiling over a small fire. Hogan hadn't moved. Kate went down to the river and washed her face, then filled a bucket of water and took it up the bank for Hogan. "Wake up," she said, prodding him with the toe of her boot. Not even his eyelids flickered. "Hogan," she called, booting him more sharply and taking a visceral pleasure in the act.

"Uhh!" Hogan started. His eyes popped open and closed again without having focused on anything. A soft snoring started again.

Hunkered by the fire, Axe glanced up from the flapjacks he was making. "Throw the water over him," he advised.

Kate grinned. "Of course, why didn't I think of that?" she said serenely, and taking up the bucket, flung the water into Hogan's face.

"What the. . . ?" Hogan sat straight up, eyes bulging, nostrils flaring as he gasped for air. He shook his head, flinging the water off his hair and skin in tiny iridescent droplets. His eyes focused at last and he glared up at Kate.

"What the hell'd you do that for?" he bellowed. His black brows were drawn downward in a mighty scowl that only infuriated Kate more.

"You needed it and deserved it," she said airily, dropping the bucket beside him. "I have no intention of rowing all the way home myself."

"There's an easier way to wake a fellow, Kate," he said plaintively. Throwing the blanket to one side, he tried to rise and fell back to the ground, face grimacing, hands clamped to his head in agony. "Oooh, Holy Mother Mary," he exclaimed, rocking back and forth.

"I'll thank you not to further compound your sins by cursing, Mr. O'Shea," Kate said crisply. Hogan cast her a telling glance, but remained silent, willing the pain to leave his head. It was as uncooperative as Kate.

"Just bring me a cup of coffee, will you, Kate?" he begged.

She turned from her task of folding the bedding. "I'll not be bringing you anything, you . . . you great lout," she snapped. "If you've been foolish enough to drink yourself sick, then you must suffer through it on your own without any sympathy from me."

"It's not your sympathy I want this morning," he mumbled from behind his hands. "I just need a little wifely concern."

His words were a red flag. He could almost sense her pawing the ground in her rage. "Wifely concern!" she said with ominous quiet. "Where was your wifely concern last night when you were with that tramp, that dirty dove?"

"*Soiled* dove." Hogan corrected her automatically, then flinched, wishing he'd kept quiet.

Kate snorted. "Soiled dove, indeed," she said scathingly. "I'll have nothing to do with you, Mr. O'Shea. Not after you spent the day with the likes of her. Get your own coffee and fold your own blanket." She pitched the sodden cover at him.

"I don't know why you're on such a high horse this morning," he said, tossing aside the blanket and getting to his feet. He staggered only a bit before firmly anchoring his feet and squaring off at Kate. "You got no call to complain after the way you stood out in the middle of the street in broad daylight holding hands with that pantywaist Clay Lawford."

"You were spying on me?" Kate declared. "And you hadn't even the decency to come over and speak to Clay, after he traveled with us all those weeks? You're a mean-minded man, Hogan O'Shea."

"Well, I didn't figure you wanted me to interrupt you," he said rather lamely. How was it Kate always had him feeling in the wrong? Besides, he never would have gone to Roxanne Blayne if he hadn't seen Kate with Clay. He'd just about decided to go find Kate and spend the day with her. But he wasn't about to tell her that now. Like as not she'd just make that derisive sound she always did and flail him with her tongue. Well, he was tired of it. He'd never kowtowed to a woman before and he wasn't about to start now. "And I wasn't spying on you," he shouted, snatching up his wet blanket. "What do I care what you do with Clay Lawford?"

"Precisely what I'm asking myself about you and Roxanne," Kate snapped heatedly, moving with quick, angry steps from the tree to the boat with her bedding, "except that it was up to me to see you got back to the boat."

"I didn't ask you to wet-nurse me," he yelled, refusing to feel apologetic. He wished she'd stand still.

"You were too drunk to get there under your own steam, and Miss Blayne was more interesting in getting you back up to her room." Kate stopped and glared at his face. "I didn't mind getting you back to the boat nearly as much as I minded having to fight off your paramour."

"You fought with Roxanne?" Hogan asked uncertainly.

"Yes," Kate snapped, bending to pick up the rest of her bedding.

"You mean you actually fought physically?" Hogan asked, to be sure.

Kate glanced over her shoulder disdainfully. "I socked her with my fist," she said flatly, "and she had it coming."

Hogan stood staring after her ramrod-straight back, his brows pulled down in puzzlement. Then his expression cleared. A big grin split his face. Snatching up his blanket, he tossed it high in the air. "Whoopee!" His shout rent the quiet. Axe glanced up.

"What's wrong with you?" Kate asked, startled. Her eyes were huge and green in her thin face. She looked as if she were ready to charge up the bank if he but said the word.

"Nothing!" Hogan said happily.

Kate's look changed to one of exasperation. "I recommend you not drink any more of that hooch thy sell down in Dawson," she said. "It's made you addle-pated."

"I believe you're right, Miss Kate," he said cheerfully. His dark eyes were bright and unreadable and eminently disturbing as they looked at her. "I do believe you're right."

Disgusted, Kate got into the boat and waited for him to join her. Hastily Axe doused the fire, wrapped the flapjacks that no one but him had eaten, and walked down to the canoe. Without another word they cast off, and although Hogan retained a cheerful look all day, he said little. But later that evening, when they arrived back in camp, Kate found a shiny new stove sitting in place in her cabin and a small bouquet of flowers placed on her pillow.

12

The man was trying to court her! Kate was certain of it. He brought her flowers. When she went to the creek to fetch water, he was there taking the bucket out of her hand as if she were too delicate to carry it back to the cabin, though she'd done it for weeks now. He told her often how fetching she looked, even if she wore breeches and had bear grease smeared on her face. The first time he'd done so, she'd nearly lambasted him with the shovel, but there'd been no glint of mockery in his eyes.

He'd taken to pointing out things in the forests, a special animal or flower, or rushing to her cabin after she'd gone to bed to hurry her out to see the moon and to explain with great patience and in some detail why their location so far north made it possible to see the moon for only a few minutes each night. In the winter, he'd hastened to point out when she'd turned back toward her cabin, it would be the same way with the sun.

Sometimes he took her hand to help her over a log she'd stepped over fifty times before. Addlepated, she'd called him. Imbecile, she'd called herself for enjoying the extra attention he was heaping on her. How could she ignore his dalliance with Roxanne?

Winter was not far away now. They could feel it in the northern winds that poured down onto the plateaus from the mountains, by the frantic scurry of the red squirrels shucking spruce cones to get to the seeds, and by the clustering of geese and other water fowl as they prepared to migrate south. The three of them redoubled their efforts to dig out the frozen gold-laden earth. Fires burned day and night as the men drove a deep shaft reaching for bedrock. Kate washed the dirt, lugging pails of water from the creek, tending the rocker as if it contained a precious life instead of the glittering gold she sought in the bottom.

In the evenings Kate prepared meals for all three of them on her new stove. She loved the ease of cooking on its top instead of the back-aching labor of cooking over an open fire pit. The stove would warm her cabin in the winter as well as provide a cook top. She was grateful to Hogan for his thoughtfulness, yet some perverse thought plagued her that he thought of her as a kitchen person and Roxanne as a bedroom person. She found the comparison unflattering, and didn't speak to Hogan for a whole day while he pondered what new blunder he'd committed.

Axe seldom joined them for the evening supper. The rest of the time he managed to be in the woods hunting for game or off in his canoe. Kate guessed that he was lonely, but she didn't know how to help him. One night when she managed to catch him in camp and insist he come for supper, he sat stiff and formal at her table, obviously on his best manners. Kate had carefully set the table with her new calico cloth, their tin plates and cups, and with a bouquet of late-blooming dandelions, wild fuchsia, shooting stars, and graceful fronds of lady ferns she'd gathered from the creek banks.

With some little ceremony for the occasion, Kate served up a caribou pot roast with boiled potatoes and wild onions. There was also fresh bread and some of the precious butter she'd bought in Dawson, as well as berry jam from the sparse fruit she'd so painstakingly gathered. When the men had finished their meal, she filled their cups with hot black coffee, passed them a whiskey bottle, and settled back in her chair to listen to the talk about the mine.

"We'll continue to dig through the winter," Hogan was saying. "We're washing out about two hundred dollars a day."

"How can we wash out the dirt and gold during the winter?" Kate asked doubtfully.

Hogan shook his head and poured a drop of whiskey into his coffee. "We can't," he said. "The water'll freeze, but we can keep on digging. We're nearly down to bedrock now, and we'll start two or three more at a time. That way, while the fires thaw the ground in two, we'll dig in the other."

"Aye, good thinking," Axe said, cutting a plug of tobacco and passing it on to Hogan. Glancing at Kate, Hogan declined with a shake of his head.

"I'm figuring on going to Dawson one more time before bad weather sets in," Axe said. "I forgot a few supplies."

Hogan glanced at him in surprise, then at Kate, his eyes telegraphing a message. "If Frenchy's there, be careful, Axe," he said.

"It's not Frenchy I'm wishing to see," Axe said, but didn't elaborate.

Emboldened by this much of a confidence, Kate couldn't help asking, "Do you think May is there, Axe?"

"She's there," he answered.

"Did you see her?" Kate demanded in surprise. "Why didn't you say anything?"

"Nothing to say," Axe answered, and Kate could have strangled him for his reticence.

"What did she say? How did she look? Was she all right?" she asked all at once. "Is she coming back?"

"I saw her down the street a ways," Axe said. "I called to her, but when she saw me, she took off. She wouldn't look back. I reckon she's happy with La-Roche." Axe stood up. "I'll just go out for a bit now, Kate. Thank you for the meal."

Kate watched his thin stooped figure until he closed the door behind him, and then she turned to Hogan. "He's still pining for her," she said softly.

"He loves her," Hogan said, watching Kate's austere face soften with sympathy for the old man. He wondered if she'd ever feel anything for him but cold disapproval.

"He never told her so," Kate said sadly, suddenly afraid to meet Hogan's gaze now that they were alone together. Her cabin was cozy and seemed far too intimate. "Maybe if he'd told her, she wouldn't have stayed with LaRoche."

"Sometimes it's hard for a man to voice his feelings," Hogan answered. His husky voice set shivers to racing along her arms. Kate rubbed them briskly, as if she could rid herself of these feelings he awoke in her.

"Sometimes a man's actions speak louder than words," she said flatly. He knew she was thinking about Dawson, and cursed himself anew for what had happened that day.

"Sometimes, but sometimes a man acts like a fool because he doesn't know how to say what he's feeling. He gets all mixed up inside, and ashamed about what he is and has been, wishing he was better so the woman he wants will think well of him."

"That shouldn't be any problem for a man like you, Hogan," she answered, and her voice was so soft he had to strain to hear.

"A man like me?" he repeated, studying her face closely. Red-gold lashes lay against the freckled skin of her cheekbones. He wished she would look up.

"Especially a man like you, Mr. O'Shea," she repeated, and leaping to her feet, began to clear the table.

Hogan stood up. "Let me help you, ma'am," he said quickly, picking up a coffee cup.

"I don't need any help," Kate said, and whirled on him. "And why do you keep referring to me as 'ma'am' in that ridiculous manner?"

Puzzled, Hogan set the cup back on the table. "I'm just trying to be a gentleman, ma'am," he answered, gritting his teeth not to snap back at her. He didn't want to undo all his headway so far, but he couldn't understand the source of her irritation now.

"You needn't bother," Kate snapped, stepping briskly toward the stove. In her haste and agitation, her boot caught against a piece of firewood and she pitched forward, hands outflung to catch herself against the hot metal. Strong arms wrapped around her waist. For a moment she was held against a rock-hard chest. The familiar smell of his skin and hair came to her; then he released her and stepped back.

"I'm sorry, ma'am," he stammered. "I didn't mean to grab you like that. I was afraid you'd fall against the hot stove."

"Yes, thank you," Kate answered, putting a shaking hand up to straighten her hair. It pulled the bodice taut across her breasts, and Hogan thought of Roxanne's movements, designed to show off her body. Kate wasn't even aware of how her movements enticed a man.

Discouraged, he turned toward the door. "I'll be leaving you now, ma'am," he said, opening the door. "Thank you for supper. I'm much obliged."

"You're welcome," Kate answered as the door closed behind him. Her hand closed around the cup he'd set down, and for one dreadful instant she wished it were china so she might have the satisfaction of dashing it against the door. Even as the thought crossed her mind, the door opened again and Hogan stood there, a sheepish grin on his face.

"About that day in Dawson, ma'am . . ." he began.

"I really don't want to hear about it, Hogan," she said quickly.

"I think I ought to tell you, ma'am. I'd feel better if you knew Miss Blayne and I never . . . well, we didn't . . . uh . . ."

"It's of little interest to me," Kate said quickly, the color high in her cheeks.

"All we did, Kate, was have a few drinks and talk." She remained silent. "I couldn't . . . I mean, well, I only went in there after seeing you and Clay Lawford standing out there so cozy and friendly."

"That's all it was between Clay Lawford and me," Kate said, "friendly."

"That's all?"

"Uh-huh!" The smile on his face made it hard for her to breathe, much less talk. He was grinning ear to ear and she could tell she must look just about as silly, but she couldn't stop smiling.

"I'm right glad to know that, Kate," he said, fumbling once again with the door. "Good night."

"Good night." This time when the door closed she stood staring at it with a bemused look on her face. Picking up the cup, she carried it to the stove and, as carefully as though it were the finest china, placed it in the pan of warm water. He hadn't been intimate with Roxanne that day in Dawson. He'd only shared a few drinks with her, and only because he'd seen her with Clay and been jealous. He could be lying, one little part of her mind thought, but she pushed it away. She knew. He'd told her the truth. She felt it deep in her bones.

The first snow fell, softly, gently, covering the hemlocks and spruce, the mosses and lichens, the wildflowers and fragrant pine needles, with a carpet of white. Kate stood in her doorway and watched the still-unfettered creek waters tumbling past banks of pristine white. Axe was getting ready for his trip to Dawson, packing up his bedroll and rifle. Kate had a hunch he was going to find May.

"I may be gone several nights," he said. "Don't worry if I don't get back."

Hogan and Kate waved farewell from the shore, then faced each other with some trepidation, recognizing, perhaps for the first time, that they would be alone together. Suddenly feeling awkward, they hurried off to do the day's chores. Imbued with new energy, Kate gathered up all the dirty clothes, hauled water up from the creek, and heated it. Scrubbing the clothes until her knuckles were nearly raw, she hung them on a rope she'd stretched behind her stove. Then she swept and cleaned her cabin and started a special supper.

By late afternoon the clothes were dry and Kate folded them neatly, dreamily smoothing the collar of Hogan's shirt. It was a wifely gesture, she realized. Why not? After all, she was Hogan's wife. What would it be like, she wondered, to live as a real man and wife, here in this cabin, to cook and clean for him and to share the narrow bed? Her cheeks blushed as she remembered the passion he'd aroused in her. She was getting as twittered as those goose-headed girls back in Missouri when they contemplated marriage. Besides, she knew how it would be with Hogan. She'd felt his passion and her own answering desire.

Flinging a shawl around her shoulders, Kate gathered up the clean clothes and carried them to the men's cabin. Fires were blazing strongly at the new shaft Hogan worked. She glanced at the pit. It was nearly down to bedrock now and she could no longer see his head as he dug. She felt guilty that he worked on alone, and resolved to help him as soon as she'd put away the wash. Pulling the latch string of the men's cabin door, she stepped inside, then caught her breath in surprise.

The light spilled in through the open door and gilded the figure of Hogan O'Shea. He'd heated water over the outdoor fires and now he stood naked in the center of the room, the buckets of warm water at his feet. Mesmerized, Kate could not back away. Boldly she gazed at his body, feeling the heat churn up from her stomach and fill her breasts. She'd known he was muscular and strong, and at times a wayward thought had crossed her mind of what that big rawboned body looked like beneath the rough clothes and all-covering union suits. She had never guessed how beautiful he was, how virile and masculine the lines of his body, from the strong jawline to the sloping long legs.

His torso seemed sculptured by the hand of a master, the broad shoulders and chest curving and dipping with well-defined muscles, the flat stomach and slim hips and the long muscular thighs and calves all perfectly proportioned. Even the graceful arch of his long feet did not escape her notice in that brief glimpse. He was pale where the sun had never touched, like fine white marble. A silky mat of black hair lay against his pale skin, swirling across his stomach and loins, to the juncture of his strong thighs, where the hair grew thicker and crisper, cradling the darker-skinned bulge of his manhood. He took her breath away.

"Kate," he said, and snatching up the piece of linen

he'd laid out to dry himself, held it in front of his loins.

She should feel ashamed, Kate thought, but didn't. She should act ashamed, but didn't. Her emerald gaze held his for a heartbeat that made the blood roar through his body, so now he held the towel tightly to shield his arousal from her.

He held his proud shaggy head high, his dark eyes never wavering from hers. He saw the flush on her cheeks, saw the desire in her eyes. He saw her gaze sweep over him again, felt the heat of her glance, and unconsciously his chest expanded. He wanted to fling aside the towel, to show himself to her, to reveal the hot passion she'd aroused just with her presence. He wanted to strip away her calico gown and lay her naked body against his. He wanted to kiss her and make love to her, but he stood and waited.

"I'm sorry," Kate said, and it seemed her voice came from a long way off. She set the folded clothes on a packing crate. "Supper will be ready soon," she said, and went out. The words were inane, utterly and completely senseless. He must think her a fool, a rigid, unthinking, unfeeling fool.

She closed the door of her cabin behind her and leaned against it. Eyes closed, heart pounding, breasts aching, body clamoring, she stood remembering everything about him, the way he looked standing before her. She wanted him, she thought, and whimpered with the pain of the admission. She wanted him with the same abandon that Roxanne or any other whore might show. She wanted him without shame or remorse or hesitation. If he came knocking at her door at this moment, she would fling it open and offer herself to him.

"Please come," she whispered. "Please know I want you. Please want me too."

By the time he knocked on her door, she was once again primly in control. "Come in," she called, and busied herself at the stove so she wouldn't have to look at him.

"Ma'am, Miss Kate, I'm sorry about that. I should have warned you I was taking a bath."

"That's quite all right, Mr. O'Shea," she said firmly. "It is I who must apologize to you. I had no right to enter your cabin without knocking first."

Mr. O'Shea. His heart sank. They were back to that. It seemed every time he made some headway with her, something happened so he went backward. He'd never get anywhere this way. "It wouldn't make sense for you to knock at a cabin you thought was empty, ma'am," he said stiffly.

"Perhaps we'd best forget about it, Mr. O'Shea," Kate suggested, stirring the kettle of food so vigorously her skirts twisted and danced about her.

"Maybe you're right, ma'am," Hogan agreed, crossing to one of the stools at the table. Kate started dishing up the food, then settled herself across from him, arranging her skirts with fastidious care. Solemnly Hogan waited while she draped a napkin across her lap.

At last it seemed there was nothing else to claim her attention. She picked up her spoon, dipped it into the hot stew, and lifted it to her mouth, at the same time raising her eyes to Hogan's face for the first time. What she saw caused her to draw in her breath sharply, so the hot broth caught in her throat. Coughing and sputtering, she fought to regain her breath.

"Are you all right?" Hogan asked, leaping to his feet and pounding her back.

"Yes, yes, I'm fine," Kate said at last, waving him away. Her gaze went back to his face. "What happened to your beard?" It had, she realized, been gone before, but she'd been too distracted by his nude body to note the difference.

Now Hogan ran his hand along his smooth jawline. "I figured I'd shave it off. Now that it's snowed, the mosquitoes and gnats won't be bothering me anymore. You said often enough you didn't like it."

"You needn't have shaved it off on my account," Kate said, studying his face. It was a beautiful face, a strong face. The long ugly scar that had disfigured one side and ended in his beard had faded somewhat with the months. The face was perfect for him, handsome and strong and robust and wonderfully manly. The skin was shiny and smooth, and Kate wanted to touch his cheek, to slide her hand along that stern jawline and trace the molding of his firm lips. She jerked her gaze away, trying to discipline her wayward thoughts.

"Don't you like it?" Hogan asked, somewhat uncertain. His dark eyes looked hurt and she longed to throw her arms around him and kiss his lids.

"It's fine," she stammered inadequately. "You'd best eat your stew, Mr. O'Shea, before it gets cold."

Looking disappointed, he took a mouthful and chewed. Try as he might, he couldn't think of anything else to say. In silence he took a second spoonful, and unable to sustain the stiff politeness that had fallen between them, he set his spoon down and stared at Kate, wishing she would give him some sign, some idea of how she felt about him.

"You're not eating, Mr. O'Shea," she said with far more calmness than she felt. "Isn't the stew to your liking this evening?"

"I . . . I guess I'm not very hungry this evening, ma'am," he said stiffly. Kate took a deep breath, a sigh, wistful and sad. Hogan listened to it and his fist tightened where it lay on the table. "I guess I'll turn in now," he said, and rose.

"Good night, Mr. O'Shea," Kate said, striving to keep the disappointment out of her voice. He went out without a backward glance, and listlessly she rose and cleared away the table, dressed for bed, and poked up the fire, then sat with the stove door open, staring into the flames.

What would he have done if she'd told him of her feelings, she wondered, if she'd said she desired him, that she had a terrible hunger for him? Would he have thought her too bold, would he have laughed at her, would he have held her as she needed him to do? She would never know now. She'd let the moment slip by. She'd have to wait now for another such time and hope it came.

In the dancing flame she saw again his naked masculinity, saw the hard muscles rippling beneath the smooth pale skin, saw the curl of his member nesting against the dark hair, and she had trouble swallowing. Abruptly she slammed the stove door closed. The fire had scorched her cheeks and kindled a disturbing flame deep in her belly. Restlessly Kate paced the cleanly swept floorboards, her agitation growing.

She would go to him, now, tonight, and offer herself and hope he wouldn't laugh or refuse her for all her cruel taunts to him. She paced to the door and whirled away. What would happen when they had mined their gold, when they went back to civilization? What if he didn't want her then? She paced away from the door. What would it matter? That was months away from now, months in which she could try to make Hogan love her as she loved him. She paused, drawing in her breath. She loved him. She'd loved him from nearly the moment he'd stepped out on that porch in Seattle. She'd been captured by the robust vitality of him, the sheer masculinity of that tall capable body, and more, by the humor and kindness and fairness of him.

She loved him! And with that recognition of love came a new recklessness, a new willingness to risk her pride and stubborn independence for the chance that he might return that love. After all, hadn't he spent the past few weeks in a rough courtship? He must feel something, he must! Eyes shining, Kate grabbed up her shawl and ran across the room. She flung open the door and stopped dead-still on the doorstep. Hogan stood on the other side, his shoulders hunched against the wet snowfall that had begun again. A fine smattering of flakes glistened in his dark hair.

"Kate!" he said in surprise.

"Mr. O'Shea," she answered breathlessly, and drew her shawl tightly about her.

"Kate, I came over here to . . . to . . . Where are you going?" His dark gaze captured hers.

"I . . . I wasn't going anywhere," Kate said, glancing from side to side. "I thought I heard something, an animal or something."

TOMORROW'S DREAM

"And you opened the door just like that?" he demanded. "Wait, I'll get my rifle and check around for you."

"Oh, there's no need. I'm sure whatever was out there is gone now."

"It'll just take a minute," Hogan insisted. "Close the door and latch it." He waited until Kate did as he'd ordered. She could hear his footsteps crunching in the snow as he went back to his cabin for his gun. Angry with herself over the silly lie, Kate moved the coffeepot to the front of the stove and added more wood. The temperature was dropping.

"I didn't see anything out there," he said when she'd opened the door again and invited him in. "What did it sound like?"

"Oh, I don't know," Kate said, taking a deep breath. "It was just a sound, probably my imagination." She laughed uneasily. "Would you like some coffee?" Hogan studied her in her long prissy nightgown, a shawl thrown over it and her brilliant red hair hanging loosely around her shoulders. His voice was too ragged to speak, so he shook his head and turned back to the door.

"Hogan," Kate said quickly. "Uhh, I'm sure I heard something. What if it was a bear? What if he comes back? I'm frightened. Can you stay here in my cabin tonight?"

Hogan's mouth tightened. How could he sleep in the same room with Kate, he wondered, and keep his hands off her. "I'll get my bedroll and sleep on the floor by the door," he said, and went out with admonitions that she close the door behind him. Kate hurried to the mirror to fluff her hair and pinch her cheeks. Her eyes sparkled with some purpose and light of their own. Did Hogan find her pretty? she wondered, and hoped he did.

He was back in no time, his presence filling her cabin so that there seemed too little room for the two of them. Hogan spread his bedroll and sat down on it to remove his boots. Shucking his coat, he unbuttoned his shirt and hesitated. "I'd better turn out the light, ma'am," he said, reaching for the lantern to turn down the wick.

"No, don't," Kate said, and her voice was husky. Hogan glanced over his shoulder, and the look in her eyes made him tremble.

"Kate," he whispered raggedly. "Kate, girl." In two bounds he was across the room. He stood before her, not touching her, his eyes boring into hers. "What is it you want, Kate?" he asked gently, and she knew this moment depended on her, on what she said and did.

Her eyes closed briefly, the delicate white lids looking transparent in the lamplight. Suddenly her eyes blinked open, the green irises dark with emotion. He read the want in her eyes, but he waited. She had to voice the wants. He had to know she was sure of what she felt.

"Kiss me, Hogan," she whispered, and stepped into his embrace as he threw his arms around her and molded her slender body to his.

"Kate," he cried in wonder; then he set her aside. Shock and hurt washed over Kate's face until she looked into his eyes and understood. They'd both fought this moment, and now that it had come, he would not rush through it. He would savor each moment of discovery between them. Her heart beat so fast she thought she might faint. She gripped Hogan's hand, glorying in the hard reality of him. He was better than any maiden's dream.

"I love you, Kate," he whispered. One finger traced along her cheekbone and down the hollows of her beautiful face. He felt the satiny warmth of her skin, put out his tongue to touch a freckle, slid his fingers through the fire of her hair. In wonder he looked his fill, seeing finally as a whole all the composites that made up his Kate. He touched her shoulder, marveling at the delicate bones. His big fingers tangled in the buttons of her gown while he pressed his lips to her smooth, rounded brow, slithered a kiss along her jaw, nudged at the corner of her mouth with his tongue. He forgot the buttons for a moment as he pulled her pliant body against his. His tongue teased her lips, and when they parted, delved deep into the warm moistness beyond. Kate moaned, feeling a languid pleasure wash over her.

His hands tangled in her hair, fanning the satiny strands through his fingers. He held the fiery curls to his face, breathing in the gingery, spicy fragrance that was Kate. His hands shook as he caressed her. He could hardly believe she was here in his arms, that he was free to touch how and when he pleased. Her acquiescence was like a gift to him. He savored it, peeling away each wondrous layer until the very core of Kate lay before him. Not for them the quick lusty mating of a lonely man and a whore.

He wanted more, so much more, and deep in the glistening emerald crystals of Kate's eyes he found what he sought. He read the love in her eyes and was renewed by it. He read the trust and trembled with the magnitude of it. He read the passion and was consumed by it.

His hands brushed at the fabric of her gown, and when it caught, Kate rose and pulled it over her head and stood before him much as Roxanne had done, yet innocently, oh so sweetly innocent. There was no coquetry in her pose. She stood facing him squarely, her eyes unflinching as his gaze roamed downward over her body. Red-gold curls, heavy and silken, brushed her shoulders and covered one breast. Its bright color was aflame against her ivory skin. Hogan brushed the strands aside to reveal her small, perfectly formed breasts with their taut nipples. Had he once thought her flat-chested? Fool, that he hadn't seen the fineness of her. But later he had. She'd been a flame inside him.

His hands were warm on her skin as they brushed over the delicate ribs to her small waist and the flat planes of her stomach, smoothing and touching much as a sculptor would caress a beloved piece of work.

He'd thought her figure boyish. Now he saw the womanly flare of hips and thighs, the red-gold curls of her mound, the sweet swell of her breasts, the tantalizing dark areolae of her pert nipples.

"Kate," he breathed, and laid his head against her breasts, inhaling the womanly scent of her. Like a reed she bent to him, arching her back, unthinkingly straddling his legs where he sat on the bed. His chin was smooth against her flesh. She ran her hands along his jaw. His lips closed around one nipple, and Kate gasped in ecstasy as he suckled. Never, never had she known such pleasure. It was like a silvery pain running through her. His lips nibbled, and then his teeth, gently, greedily claiming her.

Kate groaned. One slender hand lay against the side of his face; the other buried itself in his dark, unruly curls. His mouth came back to hers. Readily her lips parted. Readily they gave of the nectar within. Hungrily he kissed her. His mouth was everywhere, nibbling at her shoulder, teasing the corner of her lips, spearing deep inside her mouth, suckling at her breasts, sliding over her ribs to bite lovingly at the softness of her belly. He pressed her back against her pillow. His hand glided along her sides, over her buttocks, and down the slender columns of her pale thighs. Gently he parted her knees, his fingers brushing through the red-brown curls to the pink, moist center of her. Tenderly he caressed her, readying her, preparing her, delighting her as nothing else in life ever had done. His thumb touched the small button of her desire, drew away only to touch again until she thought she might cry out. She could feel a fire curling inside her.

"Hogan," she pleaded softly, trying to draw away from his touch, knowing there was more than this for him, there must be, and not wanting to go ahead into this world of sensuous pleasure without him.

"Shh, my dearest," he whispered, unrelenting in his caress of her. "Relax and enjoy." Kate felt the flame spread outward like a flower uncurling before the sun. Still she resisted, for she wanted to touch Hogan, to see him as she had when he bathed, to share this world of light and color and sensation.

Her fingers fumbled at his belt. Impatiently he stood and drew off his clothes until he stood before her nude.

Her gaze never wavered. Her soft hands slid over his skin, and Hogan closed his eyes. Down his hard middle, over the trim stomach, to the hard spear thrusting at her. Her fingers curled around the hot smoothness of it.

"Ah, Kate, love," he groaned. "I'd thought to pleasure you more, to ready you for me."

"I'm ready for you, my love." She smiled at him, her eyes loving and giving. Hogan's heart swelled. Slanting his mouth against hers passionately, he lowered himself to her, letting his shaft rub against the hot womanly moistness of her. She rose up to meet him, and unerringly he entered her.

He met the resistance of her maidenhead and she winced at the pain of its giving. He cradled her for a moment, letting the pain pass, then moved against her gently, slowly, until he was sure she was ready again. Then, able to wait no more, he surged deeply into her.

They raced the rapids, scaled the mountaintops, and reached for the midnight sun. Their mingled cries echoed through the silent snow-covered wilderness, and finally, their passion spent, they lay still and sweating, their chests heaving, their faces alight with love for one another. Smiling, their bodies still connected, they slept.

Wrapped snugly in Hogan's arms, Kate watched the gray light of morning creep into the cabin. She should rise and put wood in the stove so the cabin would be warm when Hogan woke, but she stayed where she was, loath to disturb the wonder of waking beside his large body. She'd never known such joy. She looked at the handsome face pillowed beside hers. In sleep there was a softness, a vulnerability that he never wore when he was awake. She couldn't resist touching the clean-shaven chin. Already a blue-black stubble had roughed his jaw. Lightly Kate ran her fingertips over it, feeling the unsettling tingling effect deep inside herself. She'd never felt so completely possessed by anything in her life.

Through the night Hogan had loved her, barely giving her time to rest before reaching for her again. He'd taught her, dismayed and delighted her, and finally teased from her every ounce of reserve she'd ever possessed, so she had responded as passionately and wantonly as he. A small chuckle escaped her. She was a lady no more, she thought, stretching sensuously. For a lady would surely never have done or experienced the things she had during the night. It was a title she gave up willingly. She would give up anything and everything of her old life to have Hogan beside her always.

As if he'd been awakened by her thoughts, Hogan opened his black eyes and stared at her. Kate met his gaze, and reading the wicked intent in his bold gaze, laughed outright.

"Again?" she murmured. He took her hand and guided it under the covers. Kate caught her breath, her fingers curling familiarly around the hot, hard shaft. "How are you able always to do this?" she mused, moving her hand intuitively.

"Waking beside you makes it possible," Hogan said, leaning on one elbow to stare down at her. His body smelled warm and sleepy and sexy, all at once. "The question is, lady, have I pushed you too far?" He waited for her answer, one large hand settling possessively over one breast.

Kate laughed and spoke her earlier thoughts. "I'm afraid I'm no longer a lady."

The devilish lights in his eyes faded for a moment. "You'll always be a lady, Kate," he said. "You were born and bred that way. But here in bed, you're a woman, my woman."

His breath was hot against her skin as he dipped his head to kiss her deeply, awakening every nerve ending, every passionate, desirous corner of her being, so she pressed upward against him, her hand on his shaft more urgent. "Then your woman is ready once again," she said huskily, boldly holding his gaze. A light leapt in his eyes so intense Kate felt its searing heat deep in her soul. She opened herself to him, feeling the sensuous brush of his sleep-warmed skin against her own. Then he was there against the swelling moistness of her, thrusting deep inside, and she closed her eyes against the ecstasy of it, no longer a part of the cabin and the snow outside or of the world itself.

"I'd like to take the day off," Hogan said later as they lingered over the breakfast she'd prepared. She'd used the last of the eggs bought in Dawson, made sourdough biscuits, and fried some bear steaks. He'd eaten an enormous amount, while she'd pecked at her food, too happy to be hungry. His hand clasped hers across the rough table he'd built for her. "I'd love to stay here with you all day."

"Why don't you?" Kate asked, curling her fingers around his. Would she ever have enough of him, enough of the feel and sight of his big body and his handsome battered face? Not in this lifetime.

"I need to dig out the dirt that's already thawed," he said, shaking his head. "No need to let it freeze again. And as long as I have to be out there, I might as well relight the fires."

"You're right," Kate said reluctantly. "I'll help you."

"Oh, no. I want you to stay snug and warm here in the cabin," he ordered sternly.

"If I help, you can be finished that much sooner," she argued, but he was already getting to his feet with an air of finality.

"Stay in here," he growled, and pulled on his boots and parka. At the door he paused to look at her, then tromped across the room to capture her face between his big hands and plant a kiss on her lips. "I love you, Kate," he said, and then, as if embarrassed at his words, hurried out of the cabin.

Kate sat as if thunderstruck. The newness, the compelling wonder of loving and being loved was simply too much for her. Tears slid down her cheeks, and yet she was smiling, laughing, in fact, deep inside at the sheer glory of it. Hogan had called her his woman, and surely she must be, for he'd awakened her to that wonder.

The wind picked up late in the morning, whipping

the snow around the little cabin with a mighty force, yet the woman inside the cabin and the man toiling over the gold pits paid no heed to its bitter sting, lost in a radiance of their own. Quickly Kate did her chores inside, then, unable to bear being apart from Hogan, donned her outdoor clothes and pushed her way past the snowdrifts to where he stood in a hole knee-deep.

"I told you not to come out here," he yelled above the whine of the wind.

"I want to help," she shouted.

"Go back in, Kate, where it's warm," Hogan commanded, glaring up at her.

But his glares no longer intimidated or angered her. "It's not warm in there without you," she answered, and just that quickly his scowl was replaced by a grin.

"Build a new fire here in this pit and I'll start on the next one," he ordered, and pulled himself up out of the hole. Kate nodded and staggered to the woodpile to carry back an armload of wood. When she had enough piled beside the shaft, she lowered herself into it. Hunkered down inside, she could see why Hogan had worked so hard to get the shafts started before the snows hit again. The holes were deep enough now to close out the driving wind.

She laid the kindling in the icy mud and coaxed a flame and patiently added twigs and small branches, building the fire bit by bit until she had a hot bed of coals. Laying the logs Hogan and Axe had cut in the summer, she climbed back out of the pit and hurried to the next one.

Hogan had already dug out most of the thawed mud, flinging it up on the rim of the pit. He stood, cold and muddy, chest heaving for breath, but when he caught sight of Kate he smiled. "Last one for the day," he gasped.

"And it's still daylight," Kate said meaningfully. He grinned again and bent to retrieve the pickax and shovel. Kate hurried off to the woodpile. Together they built the last fire, then stood looking upstream.

"It's getting colder," Hogan said, looking at the leaden sky. "We won't be able to dig much longer.

We'll have to stop for the worst part of the winter. Looks like the river might freeze anytime now."

"What about Axe?" Kate asked worriedly. "How will he get back?"

"He'll have to wait and mush out with a dog team." He looked at her. "Don't worry. He'll be all right. He'll lay over until he's sure travel is safe."

"You mean we may be here alone for some time?" Kate asked with a significant leer.

Hogan laughed and put an arm around her. "Would that bother you?" he asked, nuzzling her ear.

"Come inside, let me warm you and show you how much it would bother me," she murmured.

Together they walked back to her cabin, stopping only to gather up armloads of wood so they wouldn't have to come out again. While Hogan took off his boots and parka, Kate poked up the fire and moved the stew kettle and coffeepot over the higher flame.

"We won't be needing that for a while," Hogan said, coming up behind her to cup her breasts. Kate melted back against him. He could feel her nipples swell against the confines of her shirt. Tugging the tails of the flannel shirt out of her waistband, he slid his hand underneath, pausing in disappointment when he encountered the thick wool of her long underwear.

"I know a way we can stay much warmer," he said huskily, and smiling dreamily, Kate turned away from him and walked toward the bed. She kicked off her boots and unfastened the waistband of her breeches. Her glance caught Hogan's. He was busy doing the same. They grinned, their fingers flying over buttons and fasteners, racing to shed the unwanted clothing, and all the while their gazes held.

When the last fragment of cloth had been tossed aside, they reached out for each other, their naked bodies melding, pressed thigh to thigh, chest to chest, hungry mouth to hungry mouth. They fell across the bed, loath to break contact with each other even to pull the covers over themselves. Kate wrapped her legs around Hogan's waist, pulling him down to her tightly. He entered her silken flesh, groaning her name as her warmth enclosed him. Surging against her, he felt a roaring like that of a river thawing in the warmth of spring. Hoarsely he called her name and heard her answering cry, and then they were rushing together toward ecstasy.

13

Axe didn't make it back before the river froze. The creek had already fallen captive to a blanket of ice. Each day, Hogan had to chop through the ice to get water, and Kate had taken to scraping up snow from the nearest snowpile. The next morning, standing on the banks of the creek, Hogan called to Kate. Hurriedly she drew on her parka and went to join him.

"Listen," he said, cocking his head. Kate pulled off her hood and strained to hear. The snowfall had deadened all sounds save for the wind soughing through the trees. The sun was shining warmly, but the temperature had dropped during the night. Suddenly a booming sound rent the air. Startled, Kate looked at Hogan. "It's the river ice," he said. "Come on." He held out a hand to her and led the way along the creek toward the river. It was hard walking, for the snow had already accumulated in high mounds. Soon they would need snowshoes to get around at all.

Long before they reached it, Kate could see great slabs of ice building up. The rushing current pushed against the new ice cakes, turning them in the slushing waters, pushing them near the shore. Mouth open, gasping for air, Kate watched the awesome power of the ice and water. Had she really forgotten so quickly the raging icy river they'd fought in the spring? Suddenly the thought of the winter they must face in the wilderness seemed overwhelming and she trembled until Hogan took hold of her hand. His dark eyes held hers.

"We'll be all right, Kate," he said reassuringly, and she believed him because she believed in him. She trusted his strength and intelligence. She was not alone. Hand in hand they made their way back to the cabin. Sunlight glinted on the snow-laden spruce trees and on the high mountain peaks. A tiny snowbird trilled its exhilaration at the world in general, and Kate felt better for its sweet reminder that she was not alone. Beneath the frozen water, fish still ran swift and silent. High in the snowy mountains, caribou and sheep survived. Man's presence here was no less precarious than that of those creatures, and like them, Hogan and she would manage to survive.

Hogan moved his belongings into Kate's cabin. "What will we tell Axe when he comes back?" Kate asked later that afternoon as she lay curled beside Hogan, naked and replete from their lovemaking.

"We won't have to tell him anything," Hogan answered drowsily. "He'll understand."

"He'll be lonely," Kate said sadly. "I hope he finds May. He misses her."

"Ummm!" Hogan mumbled, burying his face in her hair. He didn't tell her that Axe had suffered a much greater loss years before, the loss of his glory woman. May had cooked for him and taken care of his needs, and it was obvious Axe felt some affection for the young Indian woman, but it wasn't the same. A man gave himself, heart and soul, only once in his lifetime. Hogan tightened his hold on Kate. God help him if he ever lost her.

"You're crushing me," Kate whispered in his ear, and he smothered any further protests with urgent kisses that soon led to Kate's being on top, straddling him, her hot flesh encasing him, her slim hips undulating until he thought he might go quietly and joyously mad. In their delight with each other, they forgot about Axe.

But Axe had not forgotten about them, nor had he succumbed to the ruthless river. As Hogan had predicted, he weathered over in Dawson, and storing his canoe, bought a dog team and sled, loaded his supplies, and mushed his way upriver, followed by Hans Nielson, a big Swede who had earned the name Thor

TOMORROW'S DREAM

by the simple virtue of his size. So greatly had the snow and ice altered the landscape that Axe almost missed the mouth of the creek.

Kate saw them first, as she was hauling firewood to the pits. "Axe," she cried. "Axe is back." Hogan threw down his shovel and climbed out of the shaft. They raced down to the frozen creek bed, which had once again become their throughway.

"Son of a gun, it's good to see you," Hogan cried, slapping the old man on the back.

"I had to wait till the ice got solid," Axe explained. "Had to buy me a dog team to make it back."

"I figured as much," Hogan said, and paused as another sledge and dog team hove into view. "What's this, Axe? You brought back company?" Kate could see that Hogan wasn't too happy with the intruder.

"I know I shoulda waited to talk it over with you, Hogan," Axe said. "But Thor done me a favor back there in Dawson and I owed him." He fell silent as the other sledge came to a stop before them. "Hogan, meet Thor Nielson. Thor, this is my partner, Hogan O'Shea, and his woman, Kate."

"Hello, pleased to meet you," the man said, holding out a great paw. Kate could only stare. She'd thought Hogan was a big man, but he was dwarfed beside this giant. Thor's big face was clean-shaven. Blue eyes twinkled good-naturedly from behind pale lashes. Even his brows were pale. His features were pleasant enough, and he smiled readily. But Kate couldn't help gaping at his height and size. Hogan shook hands with him, although his expression remained reserved.

Snatching his hat off his shaggy blond head, Thor turned to Kate. "I am pleased to make your acquaintance also, Mrs. O'Shea," he said in his pleasant singsong voice. Once again his paw shot out, and Kate placed her hand in his. Smiling beatifically, Thor shook it until she thought her arm might fall off at the shoulder.

Hogan rescued her, reclaiming her hand and holding it at his side possessively. "What's brought you out here, Mr. Nielson?"

"Please, you call me Thor, *ja?*"

"Thor," Hogan said, and waited for an answer.

Thor shuffled his feet and smiled again. "Mr. Fredericks vas kind enough to ask me. He knows I haf no place to go."

"I figured I'd tell him about the creek, and if he was of a mind to come up here and stake a claim and work it, I wouldn't be caring none."

"I don't care about the claim," Hogan said reluctantly. "But a man gets kind of particular about who his neighbors are." Kate was startled at Hogan's rudeness, but Thor seemed not to take offense. He nodded his head.

"*Ja,* is goot," he said. "I'll not stay if you don't vant me here. I vas yest glad to find a friend." His big hand made a sweeping gesture toward Axe.

"He's a good man, Hogan," Axe said. "He saved my life back there in Dawson."

"Oh, Axe, what happened?" Kate demanded.

"Did you have a run-in with Frenchy?" Hogan asked tersely.

"Aye, I did that," Axe said, "but I couldn't prove he was the one who waylaid me in a dark alley later that night. Thor came along just in the nick of time and scared off whoever it was. I kinda figured he could stay in my cabin with me, since you'll be with Kate."

Kate's face mottled with red and she glanced at Hogan accusingly. Silently he shook his head and shrugged his shoulders, signifying his innocence. How the devil had Axe known? she wondered. Had she and Hogan been that transparent about their feelings? She turned her attention back to the men. Hogan held out a hand to Thor.

"Any friend of Axe's is a friend of mine," he said, shaking hands. "You can mark off your claim anywhere around here. Axe can show you where our claims are."

"*Ja,* tank you," Thor said. "I von't be any trouble. You'll see. I haf my own supplies and I'm good cook."

"I'll appreciate some help," Kate said. The men started unloading the sledges and Kate went inside to add more barley and meat to her stew. She'd made only enough for Hogan and herself. Their idyll was over. No more meals eaten alone at her calico-covered table, eyes filled with unspoken words of love, desire rising so they left their food untouched to make use of the bed in the corner. She sighed and pulled out her sourdough crock and started making bread.

"Met a man named George Sawyer," Axe said over supper. "Said to tell you he sends his regards, Hogan." Kate didn't at first remember the man on the boat, but she saw the look of anger cross Hogan's face.

"Was Fletcher Meade in town?" he asked quietly, but Kate wasn't fooled by his quiet manner. His hand was white-knuckled around his cup.

Axe shook his head. "Sawyer claims to have split with Meade. 'Course the speculation in town is that he's up here scouting things out for Meade."

"More than likely," Hogan growled. "You can't trust a snake like Meade."

"Folks are up in arms. Not enough supplies came in on the last ship to last 'em through the winter. They think Meade had the supplies off-loaded in Skagway and is sellin' 'em to the new miners comin' in."

"How dreadful!" Kate exclaimed. "People could starve before the army can send in more food."

"Aye, and that's the fear," Axe said. "Mounties are stoppin' people in the passes. If they ain't got six months' worth of food supplies, they're sendin' 'em back." Kate sat wide-eyed, contemplating the seriousness of the situation. Thanks to their prudent shopping on their trip to Dawson, she had enough staples. With careful use they could make it through the winter, but how could she rejoice in that when there were others who might go hungry? She could see the thought in the faces of the men as well. Some miners had brought in their women and children. How would they feed their families?

"Frenchy's joined up with Sawyer," Axe said in such a still voice that all three of them looked at him. They knew he was bothered by the Frenchman.

"Did you see May in Dawson?" Kate asked gently.

Wearily he shook his head. "I know she was there, but she never showed herself to me." He paused. "It ain't like May to be so shy about things."

Kate glanced at Hogan, not knowing what to say to ease the old man's fears. Hogan's features were pulled into a grim scowl and Kate knew he was still thinking of the unscrupulous dealings of Fletcher Meade and his men. The old bitterness washed over her as she thought again of Gilly's death. If he'd not been wounded, he might have gotten clear of the avalanche. She'd never know that for sure, but her hatred for Fletcher Meade was as strong as ever.

Now Frenchy had joined him and become one of the ruthless men who did his bidding. What would happen to May? Suddenly Kate was frightened at the thought of the Indian woman being with the Frenchman.

"She'll be all right, Axe," she said gently, although she didn't believe it for a minute. "May knows how to take care of herself." She didn't say that May chose to stay with Frenchy and therefore could choose to leave should she wish. That thought would offer no comfort to Axe either.

The weeks that followed were busy ones for all of them. When the weather allowed, Axe and Hogan worked steadily on the shafts they'd driven. In between, they helped Thor stake out his own claim and begin a pit. Amiably the big man worked beside them, blindly trusting their advice and adding his considerable strength to any task that needed doing around the clearing.

Wood was cut and neatly stacked against the outside of Kate's cabin. The men hunted and buried a good cache of meat deep in the frozen ground. Digging through the snow along the creek, Thor gathered stones and built a fireplace in the cabin he shared with Axe, but still the men came to Kate's cabin to share meals and an evening of talk.

Thor had brought an accordion, and now their evenings were filled with music. His voice was pleasant as he sang ballads from his homeland. If Kate could not understand the words, the romance of the tune was enough. Hogan would bow to her elegantly and lead her onto the small space of rough plank floor. For a time Kate and all of them were able to forget the howling wind outside their door and the snow piling nearly to the roof. For a while they were back in a gentler place where a woman's tinkling laughter mingled with the strains of music.

The times Kate liked best were when the other men had left and she and Hogan were alone. Hungrily they would rush into each other's arms. Lovingly they would touch, glorying in the texture of the other's skin and hair, the heat of the other's body, until passion consumed them and they were oblivious of everything else.

If her nights were filled with magic and love, her days were lonely. With Thor there to help, the men worked all three claims as a team. With the creek freezing and winter deepening, they moved the rocker up to the cabin. It wouldn't be used again until spring. Kate was out of a job. Hogan insisted she stay indoors out of the deadly cold, so she spent her days mending their parkas and breeches, searching out even the tiniest rip and tear, for the numbing wind would find it and freeze the skin in no time. Axe had tanned several hides, so now Kate busied herself making shirts and mittens. With the smaller pieces of leather she made several pouches for their gold dust, embroidering Hogan's initials on one.

Sometimes, restless at being shut in, she'd stand outside the door watching the men as they moved about. Hogan would wave to her, his dark eyes telegraphing his love and desire for her. Kate knew he longed for their lazy afternoons of lovemaking as much as she did.

Still, there were moments of laughter and surprise, moments so intense with feeling that Kate knew she'd remember them all the days of her life. She wished Gilly were here to share them. Had this been the way it was in all those gold camps he'd lived in? Had he known the pride of surviving under the harshest of conditions and the camaraderie of men sharing hardships and impossible dreams? Was this, then, the reason he'd never come back to her? She could almost begin to understand. Here was a world complete unto itself. She began to see why the sourdoughs who'd come looking for gold had stayed. For them the world was divided into two places, the Yukon and the Outside.

Hogan cut a piece of clear ice from the creek and set it into Kate's window. In dismay she watched, then stood marveling that it let in light and she could see out. Carefully she folded the deer hide and put it away. In the spring when the snow and ice had melted, she'd have to cover her window with the hide again, in the hope it would keep out the pesky mosquitoes. She was surprised that the ice window didn't melt from the heat of her stove.

Once again she hung her calico curtain. Christmas was approaching and she was glad she'd chosen the bright red color. It made the cabin seem more festive. She longed for more company, and then, as if the gods had heard, her wish was granted.

They came on a blustery, snowy day when even the mercury froze and the men had given up their plans to hunt for fresh meat. Two partners upriver had been driven out by the cold and lack of food. They were making their way back to Dawson, pulling their own sledge for lack of a dog team.

"We saw your smoke," one man explained, unharnessing the straps that yoked him to the heavy sledge and holding out a hand. "Tagish Dan. This here's my partner, Innis."

"Pleased to meet you," Hogan said, shaking his hand.

When the introductions had been completed, Tagish Dan shuffled his feet a little. "I kind of figured we could wait out the storm with you, if you didn't mind."

"Come on in," Hogan invited. "We've got plenty of room."

"Looks like we're in for a big blow, all right," Axe said, looking at the leaden sky. "We're much obliged for your company."

"*Ja*, you bed down vid us in our cabin," Thor was quick to say, and Kate was grateful for his thoughtfulness. As much as she'd longed for company, she still treasured her time alone with Hogan. Happily she studied the newcomers.

Tagish Dan was a typical example of the sourdough, bearded, long-haired, with eyes that seemed to have attained that piercing keen-eyed look particular to men who'd lived for a long time in the wilderness. His partner, Innis, was a slightly younger version.

Both men were quiet at first, especially when Kate was around, and she sensed their reserve in the presence of a woman. Yet at all times they exhibited a gentlemanly courtliness to her. Kate outdid herself preparing a meal that night. The men had shot a caribou a few days before, so she made steaks and sourdough bread and put out the last of her butter.

"This sure tastes good, ma'am," Innis said, carefully smearing a dollop of the precious butter on his bread and popping it into his mouth. Kate noticed he exhibited the same thoughtful conservation of food that Axe and the rest of them had practiced. It came from living in the frozen wilderness and not being sure how long supplies would last.

"A man sure gets tired o' the taste of caribou butter," he said, shaking his head. " 'Course, when it's deep winter and they ain't anything else, you get so you like it."

"Caribou butter?" Kate asked tentatively.

"Yes, ma'am," Dan said. "Ain't you ever made caribou butter?"

"No, I haven't," Kate replied, looking around at Axe and Hogan. Was Tagish Dan pulling her leg? she wondered.

"It ain't hard, ma'am, and it'll sure get you by till you can get the real thing. If you've still got the horns to that there caribou you served tonight, I reckon I could show you."

Kate glanced at Hogan, who rose and went outdoors to gather up the antler rack of the last caribou he'd shot.

"Yes, ma'am, them'll do right nice," Tagish Dan said, and gathering up her dishpan, went outside the cabin and scooped up a pan of snow. He placed it on the stove, then cut the antlers into strips and set them to boiling. "That's it, ma'am," he said. "Just let it boil for two nights and a day, then set it outside the door to cool, and you'll find yourself with an inch or two of caribou butter." He smiled, obviously pleased to have imparted this bit of knowledge to a cheechako. He'd repaid her for the meal she'd served him.

The storm they'd been anticipating rolled into the Yukon valley, the chinook winds spending the full force of their fury against the sturdy little cabins. Snow fell in huge flakes that obscured the view of even the creek. Kate knew if they stepped very far away from the cabins, they might become lost. The men were no longer able to light the fires and thaw the ground. They stood staring out Kate's ice window.

"Look here," Hogan called. "See that tree bowing under the weight of the snow? I'll bet you an ounce of gold it'll snap before Kate's bread rises."

"You're on," Innis shouted, digging out his gold pouch. Axe and the other men got theirs, a gleam in their eyes. For the rest of the day they placed bets on any and everything—how long it would take the snow to accumulate to the top of the window, how long it would take a small cockroach to reach the door, a log to burn down, and on and on, until Kate gritted her teeth.

"No more," she snapped.

"Come on, men, let's go over to the other cabin," Axe said with an injured air.

"*Ja,* I haf a deck of cards," Thor said eagerly. Silently Kate watched as the men filed out. Only Hogan remained behind, and then only for a moment, to plant a hasty kiss on her lips.

"I'm sorry I yelled at everyone," Kate whispered, wrapping her arms around his lean, hard middle.

"It's all right," he said. His big hands cupped her shoulders and massaged lightly. "You're getting cabin fever, that's all. Take a nap or something and we'll stay out of your hair.''

"Where are you going?" she asked, hurt that he meant to leave her.

"I'll just be next door." He dropped a light kiss on her eyes and nose.

Kate took a deep breath, drawing in the warm masculine smell of him. "Don't go," she whispered huskily. "I bet I can please you very well before that log in the stove burns down." Hogan's chuckle was low and deep in his throat and his arms tightened around her, molding her to him. Kate felt that molten fire run through her veins at the thought of their lovemaking.

"I bet I can beat you getting undressed," he said, and each raced to shed his clothes and leap under the blankets. The blankets were cold, causing goose bumps on their skin. Kate wound her legs around Hogan's, running her feet up and down his calves until she found a warm spot behind his knees. Hogan brushed his hands along the length of her, and just that quickly the chill left her body.

His touch blazed a trail of fiery want. His fingers explored the softness of her breasts, the hard pebbly nubs of her nipples, rolling them gently between his thumbs and fingers until she gasped with pleasure. His wayward hands plunged downward, kneading her soft belly, and further downward to feel the heat of her inner thighs and the pulsating moistness of her. Kate's fingers curled around his aroused shaft, marveling at the size and smooth warmth of it, then impatiently she guided it to herself, her eyelids dipping closed at that first exquisite awakening as he plunged against her.

"Wait," she cried, hands clasping his taut buttocks to hold him still, sure that if he moved she would fly apart.

"I can't wait, Kate," he grunted, and began the lunge and parry that brought her panting and whimpering to a shattering climax. They clutched each other tightly, eyes clenched shut, mouths open slightly to gasp in air as they waited for the world to right itself. Slowly they descended to the warm reality of their bed and the cabin and the wind outside. The log in the stove cracked and fell apart.

"I believe I won my bet, sir," Kate murmured, smiling sleepily.

"The odds were against me," Hogan whispered, cradling her closely. "They always are if it means resisting you." Kate barely heard him. She closed her eyes, drifting in a cocoon of warmth and contentment. Hogan smiled down at her, but she was already fast asleep.

When she woke, she was alone. More logs had been added to the fire, but the cabin was empty. She knew Hogan was next door and tried hard not to be hurt that he'd gone off to play cards and gamble with the men. Shivering, she rose and dressed quickly. He'd be back soon, she reminded herself. But he didn't return. Thor came to the cabin to get the kettle of stew she'd made, and the men ate while continuing their game. Kate sat on alone, her anger mounting. Daylight faded to darkness. The stove lid banged as Kate threw in more logs and slammed it shut. Her anger grew by the minute, but Hogan didn't return to know she was angry, and finally Kate went to bed. Sometime during the night he crept into bed, his long arms reaching for her, pulling her close to share her warmth, but Kate pushed him away and clung to the side of her bed.

"Shorry, Kate," he whispered drunkenly, and began to snore.

"Ohh," Kate cried in disgust, and pulled all the covers around herself. Hogan rolled on his side and brought up his knees, curling into a ball to conserve body heat. Kate lay tense and furious, but sometime in the night, as the fire burned down and the chill crept in, she relented and spread the blankets over him.

Hogan looked shamefaced the next morning, and well he might, she thought angrily, determined not to let him off easily. Quickly, as if sensing her disapproval, the men finished their flapjacks and hurried back to the other cabin. The blizzard seemed to have increased in fury, but not any more so than Kate's temper, Hogan guessed. He stayed behind, waiting until the door had closed behind the others.

"Kate, I'm sorry about last night," he began meekly. "You have a right to be furious."

"Me? Furious?" Kate said with a shrug of her shoulders. "Why on earth should I be furious?"

"You mean you're not mad at me?" he asked gratefully. Rising from the table, he crossed to the stove where she was putting dishwater to heat. "Kate, you're quite a woman," he exclaimed happily, wrapping his arms around her. At least he would have if her sharp elbows hadn't flown out from her sides to ward off his arms. Startled, Hogan studied her tight face. "I thought you said you weren't mad," he began tentatively.

"I'm not mad," Kate said crisply, her nose pointing into the air in that old prissy, disapproving way that made him feel like an errant schoolboy. "Madness doesn't run in my family."

"You know what I meant," Hogan said, knowing he deserved this. "I thought you said you weren't angry."

"I didn't say that," Kate said precisely. "I asked why I should be angry. It's not the same thing at all."

"You're playing with words, Kate," Hogan said, starting to feel some irritation himself. Dammit, she didn't fight fair.

"I thought I was," she replied. "I just wanted to know if YOU knew why I should feel angry."

"I said I did. Now, dammit, if you're angry, why don't you just come out and say so?"

"I know what you want to do, Hogan O'Shea, and I won't participate in this," Kate snipped, opening the stove door so she could shove in more wood.

"I'm trying to say I'm sorry."

"You're trying to pick a fight so you don't have to feel bad about your behavior *and* so you can have an excuse to go back next door and play cards with the other men today."

"I don't need an excuse to play cards," Hogan bellowed. "I'm a grown man. I've always come and gone as

I want and I've never let a woman dictate to me, ever, no matter how much she swished her skirts at me."

"Swished her skirts at you," Kate shrieked. "Why, you lummox. I've never. It was you—you came into my cabin and . . . and took advantage of me."

"Took advantage of you." Hogan sneered. "You wanted me, Kate. For once, why don't you tell the truth about your feelings?"

"All right, I will," Kate shouted, and slammed the door shut. "I'm mad, mad as hell. I knew it was a mistake to try to stay married to a . . . a man like you. You're stubborn and selfish and self-centered and thoughtless and . . . and . . ." She sputtered to a halt.

"Thank you. Thank you very much," Hogan roared. "At least I'm not a henpecked pantywaist, which is the kind of husband you want and deserve." He picked up his coat and slung it on.

"Where are you going?" Kate demanded.

"I'm going next door to play cards and have a conversation with people who are reasonable and logical and don't try to order me around. If you decide to apologize to me . . ."

"Apologize?"

"If you decide you want me, just come over and swish your skirts."

"Swish my skirts?" Kate cried, but the door had already slammed shut behind him. Through the ice window she could see him hunch his shoulders against the wind and reach for the guide rope they'd run from one cabin to the other.

"I'll never apologize to you, Hogan O'Shea," Kate declared. "And I'll certainly never swish my skirts at you again." Energized by her anger, Kate had the dishes washed in no time, then set about cleaning off the shelves Hogan had built for her, and shaking the bedding she shared with Hogan, and sweeping out the snow Hogan had left behind. As she worked she listed every fault he possessed, every weakness of character, every flaw, and when she was done, she threw herself across the bed and wept like a child. Hogan found her crumpled in a ball on top of the covers, shivering because the fire had burned down.

"Kate, I'm sorry," he whispered, smoothing back the fiery tendrils that clung to her damp cheeks. "I'm everything you said I was and more. I should be horse-whipped."

"No, I'm the one who's sorry," Kate cried, flinging herself into his arms. "I have a terrible temper and I say horrid things and I really don't mean them."

"I shouldn't have left you alone like that. You were lonely and felt left out."

"I was lonely for you," she wept, her cheek against his.

Hogan pulled her onto his lap and rocked her gently. "Shhh, baby, don't cry," he crooned. "It's hard on a woman out here, with no female company. I should have thought of that."

"You only wanted to join the other men," Kate hiccuped. "No need for both of us to be lonely. I'm s-sorry."

"No, no, don't say it." Hogan planted tiny little kisses on her wet cheeks, her lashes, her nose, her mouth. "Don't make me feel worse than I do already. I don't deserve you, Kate."

Her heart was singing. "I don't deserve you," she said, returning his kisses fervently. "I don't know what I'd do if you ever went out that door and didn't come back."

"I never will, Kate. God, I couldn't. I can't breathe without you. I love you. I love you." He hugged her tightly. They sat holding each other for a long time. There was no need for more, no need for lovemaking. They made love with words, with tenderness, with their hearts and minds. Now was the tenderness of new lovers who'd suffered their first quarrel. All the ones that had gone before didn't count, only this one. Only this one had hurt so deeply and made them cling to each other in regret for the things said and not meant.

Only later did Hogan stir. Darkness had fallen outside the ice window. "I'd better see to the dogs," he said. "Axe may have forgotten."

"I'd better start supper," Kate said, then paused.

"Today is Christmas Eve," she said in a hushed whisper.

"Merry Christmas, Kate."

"Merry Christmas, Hogan," she sighed, snuggling against his broad chest.

"It's our first Christmas together," he said softly, and smiled down at her. "But it won't be our last, Kate. You're stuck with me for the rest of your life. Do you mind?"

"As long as you come when I swish my skirts," she answered pertly. Laughing, he released her and slapped her playfully on the backside. Kate grinned. Some things about Hogan would never change, and thankfully so.

While Hogan tended to outdoor chores, Kate washed her face and changed into a fresh gown, wishing she hadn't been so disgustingly practical back in Seattle. She longed for something bright and pretty to wear instead of the dark, serviceable gowns she'd brought. She brushed her bright hair until it shone, and let it hang free, caught back by a bit of ribbon she'd taken from a petticoat. Hogan's eyes lit up when he saw her. His warm kiss was interrupted by Thor.

"I come vor the stew. Ve eat in our cabin again tonight," he said, beaming.

"Not tonight, Thor," Hogan said. "Tonight is Christmas Eve. The men should come to supper here in our cabin."

"*Ja*, is goot. I tell them," Thor said, and hurried out. His head reappeared in the doorway, his blue eyes twinkling. "I bring accordion. Ve sing songs about the little baby."

"*Ja*, Thor. That vould be goot," Kate cried, and hurried to prepare the best supper ever. When all the men were inside the small cabin, there was little room to work, but Kate didn't mind. There was an air of festivity, which was better. Thor played and the men sang while Kate set the small table and prepared the meal. She wished she had some rum and bear fat to make a plum duff. It was Christmas Eve and she wished she could serve something special. She thought of the parties and socials given back in Missouri and her face lit up in anticipation. Quietly she got out the sugar and molasses and set a pan to boiling on the stove. By the time supper was ready, so was the pan of syrup. Kate set it outside to cool while she dished up the caribou steaks and rice.

"Thank you muchly for the meal, ma'am," Tagish Dan said politely, wiping at his mouth. "You're shore a fine cook."

"That's right, Miss Kate," Innis said, grinning at her.

"You boys can't go yet," Kate said, going to the door. "We aren't finished."

Like little boys they waited, their faces mirroring various emotions. Home was a long way off and the magic and wonder of Christmas Eve with all its surprises had long ago faded. Yet they waited. Kate retrieved the kettle, tested the contents, and gave a nod of satisfaction. Bringing it back to the cleared table, she whisked away the cloth, put out a clean board and a pan of caribou butter.

"Butter up, boys, we're going to have a taffy pull," she ordered with a grin. In consternation they looked at her. They shifted their weight from one foot to the other and glanced at one another.

"I don't know, ma'am," Innis began doubtfully. Even Axe seemed to be pulling back. Hogan watched Kate, not wanting her to be hurt if the men didn't go along with her idea.

Suddenly Thor stepped forward and scooped up some butter in his big paw. He rubbed it into his palms and looked down at Kate. "Vat next?" he asked, and Kate felt like kissing him.

"Just grab hold of this stuff and start pulling it," she ordered, pouring out the thickening molasses mixture. "Innis, grab the other end."

In wonder Hogan watched Kate bustle from the table to the stove to the door and back again, all the while ordering and directing the men. Before she was finished they were all involved right up to their elbows, with buttered cheeks where they'd wiped at their faces.

Bits of taffy clung to their shirtfronts and hung in their long beards. Reluctance gave way to enthusiasm, reticence to laughter, and when at last the mass had been pulled and pushed and pounded into some semblance of taffy and cut into chunks, they sat back and sampled their results with immense satisfaction. Now the men felt easy with Kate, joshing her as they would each other and thumping her shoulders.

Cards were brought out. The men vied to teach her to play poker. Soon Kate was betting and bluffing with the best of them. Hogan stood to one side, watching the proceedings with humor sparkling in his dark eyes. When the piles in front of the men had dwindled and Kate's had grown, they looked at each other with dawning comprehension. They'd been had!

"You knew how to play already," Tagish Dan accused, and Kate's eyes sparkled with acknowledgment.

"My father taught me when I was a little girl," she confessed.

Hogan's laughter rang out and he moved to stand possessively behind Kate, his big hands resting lightly on her shoulders. "Gentlemen, you never had the pleasure of knowing my father-in-law. Kate is Gilly's daughter, all right."

"You gotta give us a chance to win back some of our poke," Tagish Dan said good-naturedly.

Kate handed him the cards. "Gentlemen, deal!" she answered.

Cries of "Taffy Kate" rang out amid the laughter, and Hogan knew she'd been accepted. Tales of this evening would be repeated and expounded on and she would come to be known by all but him as Taffy Kate. He'd never think of her as anything but his Kate, his glory woman.

14

The blizzard continued for several days, its fury unslacked. The days had shortened dramatically now. A peculiar gray light of dusk lay over the land even at noonday. In spite of their dwindling supply of oil, Kate was forced to light the lamp hours before bedtime and keep it burning later in the morning. Sometimes she simply left the door to the stove open and worked by its meager light. Hogan and she slept longer hours now. The men in the other cabin, unable to travel or to work their shafts, also rested, emerging only to hunt food or attend to the most necessary chores. It seemed to Kate the dogs felt as morose as she about this bleak period. Their howls filled the night with a cacophony that slowly corroded Kate's resolve. Animal lover that she was, she soon grew to hate the wolflike creatures that made her nights so unpleasant. Sometimes she longed to howl out her loneliness with them; then Hogan would come to put his arms around her and she would feel lonely no more.

"It's time for a change," he said one day, watching Kate's wan face. "When the blizzard lets up and the snow packs a bit, we'll take the sledge and dog team and go to Dawson."

"Oh, Hogan, can we? Won't it be dangerous?" Her eyes were wide with excitement, like a kid's, and he couldn't help laughing at her.

"We'll have to wait for the blizzard to end," he warned her.

"I know," Kate answered, "but do you really think we can make it?"

"With the dog team, we can."

"The dog team," Kate repeated, and hurried to the ice window to look out at the furry balls with renewed fondness. She was sorry for every hateful thought she'd had about them.

"You know, Kate," Hogan said, wondering if his suggestion had been such a good idea, "things won't be the same in Dawson along about now. Remember what Axe said when he came back last fall? The people there will be on strict rations. We'll have to take our own food."

"Of course," Kate replied. "Perhaps if you and Axe can do some hunting before we leave, we can take back extra meat."

"Perhaps," Hogan said. "Hauling it to Dawson would be the problem."

"I could walk," Kate answered. "Axe made me a pair of snowshoes and I've been practicing with them. I could crawl to Dawson if I had to."

Hogan laughed. "Me too, baby, me too."

At his words, Kate felt a niggling prick of fear course through her. Was he looking forward to seeing Roxanne again? She looked at his smiling face and tried to push away her fears, but they were there, and like the stubborn dryas plants that bloomed right behind the snowmelt, they grew and multiplied. Furthermore, her suspicions were fast becoming a certainty that she carried Hogan's child. How would he feel about that? she wondered.

The blizzard let up two days later. Snowdrifts reached nearly to the roof, the rope strung between the two cabins nearly buried in places. Axe and Thor went off to hunt for badly needed fresh game, while Tagish Dan and Innis dug out their sledge and supplies. For the next two days, while they waited for the powdery accumulation to pack down so it would be hard enough to travel over, they mended snowshoes and checked the lacings on their sturdy sledges. They would all travel in a group to Dawson.

Kate's excitement over the coming trip was tempered by her growing concern about Roxanne and her anxiety about Hogan's reaction to her news about her pregnancy. Once Hogan saw the beautiful dance-hall girl again, would he regret his dalliance with his wife? Would he expect Kate to accept the fact that he would be with Roxanne? Surely he wouldn't. Just the thought that Hogan might want to make love to Roxanne Blayne made her blood chill. Then she remembered the first night he'd come to her. He'd said he hadn't been with Roxanne in Dawson, and she'd believed him, blindly. Had she been a fool? Had he lied? She had to trust him. She had to trust the passion and love between them. She had to believe he would want their child as much as she did. She'd tell after their trip to Dawson, she decided, and felt better.

Excited nonetheless about their trip, Kate washed a gown and hung it to dry behind the stove. She'd wear leggings to Dawson, but once there she wanted to be pretty for Hogan. She glanced around the cabin, taking stock. Stew simmered on the back of the stove and fresh bread rested on one of the shelves. The men wouldn't return from their hunting until dark. There was plenty of time to bathe and wash her hair. Throwing a shawl over her shoulders, she went outdoors to gather buckets of snow. As she set them on the stove, she was surprised to hear someone at the door.

"Come in," she called, thinking the men had returned early and she'd be hard put to get a bath after all. But no one entered the cabin. Once again a thud landed against the door. It shook on its leather hinges. Alarmed now, Kate took a step forward. Was someone injured and unable to open the door? Her heart flew to her throat, clogging her breathing. Hogan! She raced across the cabin to throw open the door, her frantic gaze searching the beaten snow in front of the cabin, but all was black. Not even the light seemed to reflect on the snow. It took her a full minute to realize that something was blocking the opening. Slowly she raised her eyes until she was eyeball to eyeball with a huge black bear.

Its mouth opened, revealing yellowed teeth and a slavering tongue as it roared a warning. Kate took one step backward and slammed the door in the animal's face. Breath held, eyes wide and startled, she waited. All was silent on the other side of the door. Perhaps it would go away, she thought. Hadn't she heard tales from the sourdoughs around the fire about bears that wandered into camp and wandered out again? Suddenly a mighty crash sounded against the door. This wasn't to be one of those times. The door shook on its hinges, one side sagging woefully. The battering noise sounded again.

Terrified, Kate backed up. Any moment the door would give, and there would be nothing between her and the bear.

Frantically she looked around. The snow she'd gathered for bathwater had melted. Steam rose from it. Snatching up a bucket, she hurried to the door. Hesitating only to gather courage, she threw it open and tossed the contents of the bucket at the bear. He roared in pain and backed away. Whirling, Kate ran to the stove and grabbed the other bucket and rushed back to the door. The bear was charging again. Once again Kate flung the hot water at him and slammed the door shut.

The bear bellowed his pain, pawing at his snout and rolling in the snow. Weakly Kate leaned against the door, trying to still her pounding heart. The bellows seemed to fade. Perhaps she'd driven him away. She listened, pressing her ear against the door. There was only an occasional grunt. Suddenly the door panel jolted against her with a force that sent her flying across the cabin. The bear roared its displeasure, its long nails raking across the rough planks trying to find a hold to tear them away. Kate was unaware of the tears that wet her cheeks. In terror she looked around the cabin. Only the pot of stew was left. She lifted the pot and made her way to the door.

The bear had abandoned his assault on the door and was scratching at the ice window, his paws cutting wide, deep swaths in its thick, smooth surface. Cautiously Kate opened the door and peered around the jamb. The bear caught sight of her and with a roar lumbered toward her. Kate sent the pot of stew sailing toward him. As she ducked back inside, she saw it hit him in the head. Momentarily stunned, the bear halted. Once again, all was silent without.

Creeping to the ice window, Kate peered out. The bear was engaged in eating her stew, his snout right down in the kettle. Soon he'd be finished with it. Would he attack again? She had to do something now while the bear was occupied. Perhaps she could sneak out and run into the woods. She dismissed that as a foolhardy notion. The cabin afforded her some protection. In the woods there was none, and if she became lost, she might freeze to death. How long before the men returned?

Her frantic gaze fell on the stock of Hogan's gun. He hadn't gone hunting with the other men. He was somewhere along the creek with Thor, marking the big man's claim. With trembling hands Kate dug out the rifle. Was it loaded? She didn't even know how to check.

The rifle was heavy. With both hands she brought it up, forced the hammer back, and swung the door open. Her knees were shaking so hard she feared they wouldn't support her. Taking a deep breath to steady herself, Kate sighted down the barrel and fired. The report was loud. The rifle slammed back against her shoulder so hard she nearly dropped it. With a grunt the bear lifted its head and stared into the cabin.

She hadn't killed it! Now it took a hesitant step toward her.

Frantically Kate tugged at the lever to eject the old shell casing. It was tight and resisted her efforts. The bear roared and lumbered toward her. Panic made her breath come in quick, raspy whimpers. With a cry, she shoved down with all her might and saw the empty shell roll across the floor. Please, God, let it be loaded with a new shell, she prayed, and took aim again. The bear was at the door now. He never paused, but rushed into the tiny cabin, his slavering mouth open in another menacing roar. Squeezing her eyes shut, Kate pulled the trigger and steeled herself for the recoil. This time it knocked her backward. She screamed as she fell over a stool. Scrambling to her feet, she crouched in a corner before looking for the bear. He lay on the floor before the stove.

Kate drew a wavering breath and waited, but the bear didn't move. She was afraid to go around him in the tiny space, afraid he might not be dead after all. The cold wind blew snow into the room. Kate shivered uncontrollably, but stayed where she was.

"Kate! Kate!"

"Hogan!" she screamed. "I'm in here."

Suddenly he was at the door, his face wild with fear, his eyes taking in the dead bear and Kate huddled in her corner. He rushed across the room and took her in his arms.

"My Gott!" Thor exclaimed, looking at the bear and back at Kate.

"Are you all right?" Hogan asked. Numbly she shook her head.

"Get it out of here," she begged, and her voice shook.

"What happened?" Axe exclaimed from the doorway. Tagish Dan and Innis were right behind him. When they saw the bear, they halted in their tracks.

"Well, I'll be damned," Axe declared. "Good thing you were close by, Hogan."

"I didn't shoot it," he answered.

"Well, who—Thor?"

"No, by gum, Kate got that bear," Thor said with as much pride as if he had indeed shot it.

"Well, I'll be a dadburned horn-toed weasel," Tagish Dan commented. "Look at that, fellas. Not only did Kate kill that thar bear, she laid it out on her hearth real pretty for a rug."

The other men laughed. Kate burst into tears.

"What's wrong, little miss?" Dan called, his mirth dying away.

"I . . . I . . ." Kate hiccuped. She hated to admit how frightened she'd been. "I threw the stew at him. Now we have no supper," she bawled. Once again the men laughed.

"Little miss, you've just provided us with some of

the best eatin' a man could ask for. We'll just slice us off a few bear steaks for supper tonight.'' The others nodded cheerfully in agreement. Kate dried her tears and tried to still her wildly beating heart. She didn't even look as the men dragged the carcass outdoors. Of one thing she was very certain. She would not be having bear tonight. She doubted if she'd ever be able to eat again.

They left for Dawson three days later. The day before they left, Hogan and Axe shot two caribou. One they'd cut up for themselves to use on the trip; the other they tied to Tagish Dan's sledge. They'd take it to Dawson along with Kate's bear. It wouldn't be nearly enough, but it might help a starving town.

Dawson was prettier in the winter. Mounds of snow hid the roughness of the buildings and the human waste that had littered the streets. Even the streets themselves were more appealing. The sea of mud had frozen solid, and the accumulation of winter snow was packed hard. For half the year Dawson sported decent thoroughfares. Kate hated to think what they would be like later during the spring thaw. With the frozen tundra just beneath the surface, there would be no place for the melted snow to go.

But if Dawson was different, prettier in appearance, it was also surely different in temperament. The bawdy gaiety of the summer was gone. Now men stood in the saloons grimly downing glasses of weak, watered whiskey and homemade hooch purchased from the local Indians. Some miners, unable to find gold, fed their families by setting up crude stills made from old rifle barrels or any other available metal.

Kate missed Iris Garrett's presence. The big affable woman was at her husband's trading post back at Fort Reliance. The log cabin once set aside as a parlor for genteel ladies had been given over to a needy family who'd arrived too late to build their own cabin. Housing seemed to be as big a problem as lack of food for Dawson inhabitants. Other miners, starved and frozen out as Tagish Dan and Innis had been, now flocked to town hoping for little more than some bed space and a little food each day until the supply boat came in. Some vowed to leave this godforsaken place as quickly as they could; some tightened their belts over rumbling stomachs and gave it no thought. There was gold here, and here they would stay.

Starving Indians had also made their way to Dawson. Not allowed into the town after the stores closed, they thronged the streets in the daytime, begging for crusts of bread or a drink of the watered-down hooch. Even mothers with small children sat in doorways, seemingly impervious to the cold as they nursed their babies. The pinched, hungry faces of the children broke Kate's heart. If the weather and living conditions were hard for able-bodied men, they were devastating for small children, who were dependent on their parents.

Hogan found them a place to spread their bedrolls in the back room of the barbershop. Gratefully Kate stored her things and looked around. There was very little floor space left. Well, she'd wanted to be with people again, and she was certainly going to get her wish.

They delivered the food to Father Luke, who had opened a hospital and shelter for homeless, starving children.

"The man who spawns a child to this kind of hell deserves to die a similar fate," Hogan said tightly.

"Don't you want children?" Kate asked.

"No," he said brusquely and implacably. Kate felt something tear at her heart.

"Come on," Hogan said. "We've done enough good deeds for the day." He led the way down the frozen street to a saloon. Kate couldn't help noticing that it was not the Lucky Lady. He was taking no chance on meeting Roxanne again. She wasn't sure if she was pleased or upset at his behavior. Then she stepped inside the poor establishment and her ire rose. Axe and the other men had gone to the Lucky Lady. Obviously it was far superior to this dank, joyless place. Why should Hogan be forced to skulk over here by himself, just to please her?

"I prefer the other saloon," she said firmly, and before he could stop her, she stepped back into the street.

"Kate, where are you going?" he demanded.

"I'm going to the Lucky Lady," she said reasonably. "Isn't that where Axe and Thor are?"

"Yes, but—"

"But what?" Kate stopped and faced him.

"Kate, Roxanne's there," Hogan said softly, his dark eyes worried as they met hers.

Kate's heart melted with love for this big man who was so willing to give up his wild ways to please her. "Do you love me, Hogan O'Shea?" she asked, her green gaze holding his steadily. For an answer he wrapped his arms around her and kissed her in full view of anyone who might be in the street. Kate felt her knees weaken as they always did when he touched her.

"Does that answer your question, Mrs. O'Shea?" he asked, releasing her mouth. His arms still trapped her in an immense bear hug.

Happily Kate nodded. "Let's go into the Lucky Lady with our friends," she said.

"Whooee!" Hogan's wild cry was joyous, his face alight with happiness. His arm was possessive and reassuring around Kate's waist as they entered the door. The men drinking at the bar or playing cards at the tables glanced up. Kate paused, her courage running out. Back in Missouri she'd never dream of entering such an establishment, but here in the Yukon there was no other place to go unless she wanted to sit in the back room of the barbershop. Now she pasted a wobbly grin on her face and searched the room for Thor and Axe.

"There she is, men," Tagish Dan cried, standing up and raising his glass in a salute. "That's the little lady I was telling you about. Taffy Kate! She'll shoot your dinner, cook up the best meal you ever et, and win all your money at poker. Before you can say,

'Thank you, ma'am,' she'll have you buttered up and pulling candy.''

The men laughed and raised their glasses. "Taffy Kate!" they roared. Kate hung back, embarrassed by the attention, but Hogan pulled her toward the bar.

"What'll you have, folks?" the bartender asked.

"Kate?" Hogan turned to her. The room quieted. The grinning men waited as if everything she did was of high interest.

Kate was aware of their attention as she groped for something to order. She'd never been and never would be a drinker. It went against her grain. Now she looked the bartender square in the eye. "Could I have a cup of tea?" she asked primly.

The men around howled with glee, passing the word to those in back. "Tea—she ordered a cup o' tea," they chortled. Yet Kate sensed there was no malice in their actions. She was a lady, a rare lady who shot bears and made taffy, and if she ordered a cup of tea, that was all right with them.

The bartender looked at her solemnly. "I'll have a cup for you in no time," he promised, and motioned to his helper, who scurried away out of the bar and to the nearest home. In due time a cup of tea was forthcoming. Hogan drank the hooch and chuckled to himself. He didn't notice the blond-haired woman who watched from one end of the bar.

Roxanne Blayne had been looking for Hogan ever since Axe came in. From the doorway she'd seen him kiss his wife in the middle of the street. Biting back the jealous rage that distorted her pretty face, she'd withdrawn here to the corner of the bar and waited. As the men toasted Kate O'Shea, relating her exploits—for the hundredth time, it seemed to Roxanne—her anger had grown.

Studying the tall man hovering over Kate, Roxanne had noted the possessive, protective air, the silent exchange of glances that spoke of shared secrets and intimacies, and she knew the Hogan O'Shea who'd come to Dawson this time was far different from the frustrated man she'd tried hard to seduce on his last visit.

Bitterly she downed her drink. The Kate O'Sheas of this world seemed always to get what they wanted. They were ladies without trying, as if the epithet had been stamped on their foreheads at birth, while she must travel a far different path with bitter rewards at its end. Roxanne ordered another drink and stared morosely into the weak amber liquid. Images of too many gold camps, too many sweating, boastful men dogged her. Here at Dawson she was growing rich, and she'd even entertained visions of becoming a lady herself, with fancy feathered hats and rich gowns, strolling along on Hogan O'Shea's arm.

Well, she thought determinedly, she might have her dream yet. That washed-out old maid wouldn't have him. She wasn't woman enough for a man like Hogan. Roxanne would just have to remind Hogan of what he was giving up. She chose not to think of their last night in her room, when she'd disrobed to no avail. This time . . . This time—Roxanne smiled—she had some new tricks up her sleeve. Frenchy had shown her a few things. She'd use them on Hogan. She'd make him her slave, then she'd humiliate Kate in front of the whole town, just as she'd been humiliated.

The miners waited until Kate had her tea and then surged around her. "Come join us, Kate," they wheedled, holding up a deck of cards. At first Kate shook her head, horrified that they'd asked; then she laughed. She felt freed of all the tight constraints of Missouri society. She was Taffy Kate, learning her way in the Yukon. Pulling out the poke of gold dust Hogan had given her upon their arrival, she walked to a table and plunked it down.

"Gentlemen," she said. Once again there was a roar of approval as the men jockeyed to get to her table. As the stools were filled, men lined up behind each one. They'd wait on the chance one of the players would have to leave before the game ended. Kate looked around. Hogan stood leaning against the bar, his eyes alight with laughter as he watched her. Kate returned his grin and picked up her cards. Gilly had taught her well. She outplayed and outbluffed nearly every man at the table. With every hand she won, every ounce of gold she took from them, the men congratulated her, seeming to enjoy the privilege of losing to Taffy Kate.

When Kate looked up from one particularly fancy piece of playing, she saw Hogan talking to Roxanne Blayne. Her smile wavered for a moment as she seesawed between jealousy and trust in Hogan. After all, hadn't she been the one who insisted on coming into the Lucky Lady? She'd known Roxanne would talk to Hogan. Now she must trust him, trust that he was even now telling her he loved his wife and wanted nothing more to do with her. Kate turned her attention back to her game, but when she looked again, Hogan and Roxanne were gone. Her gaze flew to the narrow stairs leading to the second floor. There was no sign of them. Were they even now in Roxanne's bedroom? Kate lost the next hand.

"How are you, Hogan?" Roxanne said softly at his elbow. She'd waited until Kate was absorbed in her game, then sidled along the bar to the big man. Hogan jerked and looked around, then cast a quick glance at Kate.

"Roxanne," he said stiffly. He threw down his drink as if in a hurry to leave.

"I've missed you." She touched his clean-shaven chin with her fingertip, then let her hand trail down his shirtfront suggestively.

"Look, Roxanne, I told you the last time, I'm married now."

"I remember what you told me about your marriage," she said evenly, looking at him from underneath her lashes. "You needed me then, baby. Don't you need me now?"

"Roxanne . . ." He took hold of her wandering hand and placed it back on the bar far away from him. "I love Kate," he said quietly. "You and I had some fun together, but that's over for me."

"Poor baby." Roxanne pouted. "Now you don't have fun."

Hogan made no answer to the insinuation. He turned

as if to leave, but Roxanne blocked his way with her full body.

"Looks like your wife has got you hog-tied," Roxanne jeered in frustration. "I never thought I'd see the day Hogan O'Shea let a woman wear the pants. What's wrong, Hogan, won't she let you gamble with the boys? She is."

Still she couldn't taunt him into a response. He strolled away from her and she hurried after him, catching him near the door. "Hogan, I'm sorry," she cried, making her voice all soft and pleading, her eyes tearful, and her body pliable as she leaned against him. "It's just that I'm so disappointed. I thought we had something special between us. After that last time."

Hogan's head jerked up. "The last time?" he asked. Roxanne studied his face. The poor fool wasn't sure what had happened the last time. He'd been too drunk. Now she nodded her head, lowering her lashes to squeeze out two big tears. They rolled down her cheeks. "You said you loved me," she whispered. Then, raising her eyes to his face beseechingly, she gripped his arm. "You made love to me, Hogan, as if you meant never to stop. We . . . we did things together that . . ." She paused and looked away as if embarrassed.

But Hogan wasn't watching her. His gaze was turned to the red-haired woman seated at the table. "I told Kate . . . . I promised her . . ." Abruptly he turned back to Roxanne. This time it was he who gripped her arms, but his touch, though gentle, was not loving. "I'm sorry if I said things I shouldn't have," he said firmly. "If I misled you, I was wrong. I love Kate. She's my wife, and nothing can change that."

He fumbled in his pockets and brought out a pouch of gold dust. "I'm sorry," he said, pressing it into her hands. "I love my wife." His words were final and undeniable. He walked away, and Roxanne knew he'd meant what he said. She looked at the pouch of gold and felt like flinging it after him. Then she spied the dainty stitching and the initial in the corner. The pouch had been made by a woman, and with loving hands.

A roar of approval brought her bitter gaze back to Kate O'Shea. Perhaps there was still a way, she thought, tossing the pouch absently. Roxanne Blayne didn't give up easily once she'd set her mind on something, and she'd set her mind on having Hogan O'Shea.

Kate was tired. She rubbed her forehead and tried not to twist around to search the room for Hogan. She trusted him, but she didn't trust Roxanne Blayne. Now she pushed back her chair and rose. "Gentlemen, I'm finished," she said. "Thank you for allowing me to play."

"Thank you," they chorused, which brought another smile to Kate's face. Before her were three pouches of gold dust, not counting the one she'd started with. She picked up the leather pouch and held it aloft for them to see before pocketing it. The men grinned and looked at the other bags. She'd won them fair and square. They wouldn't have had any patience with a player who couldn't hold his own with them. They'd made no concessions for her being a woman or Taffy Kate.

"Now, what you goin' to do with your earnings, Taffy Kate?" someone called.

"I have an idea," she answered. Her hand fluttered to her flat stomach and her smile widened.

"If you're fixin' to buy drinks around, I ain't got a hankerin' for tea," someone called, referring to the unwritten law that a winner must buy drinks.

Kate laughed with them. "Is the town mayor here?" she asked. A portly gentleman pushed his way forward.

"I'm the town mayor," he said, pushing his hat back from his face and glancing around the room. "Thomas Brown at your service, ma'am."

Kate picked up the bags of gold and held them out to him. "I'd like to donate my winnings, Mayor Brown," she said quietly, "to Father Luke's hospital for women and children who have no man to care for them, no one to provide food. I'd like to pledge to send game at least once a week, and I hope some of you men will do the same." They roared their agreement.

"That's mighty generous of you, ma'am," the mayor said.

"It's no more than the generosity I've seen from other men and women here in the Yukon," Kate said sincerely. Once again the men cheered. Kate had given them something better than a drink. In the midst of hunger and lethargy, she'd reminded them of who and what they were. She made them feel proud of themselves, for being part of the sea of humanity that clung stubbornly to life where nature had proven downright inhospitable. Impulsively they pulled out their bags of gold and added them to Kate's offering.

"We're much obliged to you, ma'am," the mayor said.

When the cheering died down, Kate drew out the bag from her pocket. "Drinks are on me," she said, and stepped back as the thirsty miners bellied up to the bar. Kate glanced around and saw Hogan leaning negligently against a back wall, his face full of pride as he watched her. A slow grin crossed his face as she straightened and made his way to her. His hand was warm on her arm.

"You're only adding luster to your name, Taffy Kate," he said teasingly, and all the doubts and misgivings Kate had felt disappeared in the blink of an eye.

"There's only one name I care about," she said huskily. "That's Mrs. Hogan O'Shea." His arm encircled her waist, pulling her close. "Is there anyplace we can go to be alone?" she whispered longingly.

Hogan's grin tightened. "I think I know a place," he said conspiratorially. He led her out the back door and along a row of houses. As he paused beside one, Kate heard music and laughter. "Uh, Kate," he said, shuffling his feet. "This may not be the best place, but it's warm and private, at least for an hour."

"That's all I ask right now," she said, laughter bubbling inside her. She'd already guessed what this place was. Hogan knocked against the rough plank door. It was thrown open by a large woman in a bright red gown of some shiny fabric. Its bodice was somewhat soiled and limp.

"Hogan," she cried when she spied him. Throwing her fat arms wide, she gave him a bear hug. "What are you doing here? You want a woman?" She looked over his shoulder. "Who've you got there? Where's Roxanne? Don't tell me you wised up and dropped that little harlot."

"Mame, I want you to meet Kate, my wife," Hogan said.

"Your wife! Well, I'll be." Mame looked her over carefully; then her eyes, staring out from the fat folds of her cheeks, grew hard. "You'd better treat him right, love. He's a good man."

"I know, Mame." Kate said, and glanced at Hogan. She wasn't aware that all the love she felt for him was evident on her face. Mame noted it, though, and nodded her head in satisfaction.

"How'd you know I was here?" she asked, turning back to Hogan. "Me and the girls just got in on the last boat before the river froze."

"I saw your sign the minute I hit town," Hogan said. "Mame, we need a room, a little privacy."

The big woman's face split in a knowing grin. "Why, sure, Hogan, anytime. You just follow me." She led the way through the main room, cluttered with too much furniture and too many bodies as men sat with half-clothed women waiting their turn at a room. "If I had fifty more rooms, I'd keep 'em filled," Mame said. Attached to the main cabin was a dogtrot of sorts, connecting it to another small cabin that had been divided into four tiny bedrooms. Mame stopped before one of the doors and pounded on it. "Time's up," she called. There was a scuffling inside, and in no time the door flew open. The woman gathered the revealing robe around her, eyeing Hogan boldly as she walked past. The man who followed her hastily shoved his shirt into his trousers. The beatific smile on his face testified to his satisfaction.

"There you are, Hogan," Mame said graciously.

"Take all the time you need. There are clean sheets in the chest."

"We'll need an hour," Hogan said, "and can one of the girls bring bathwater?"

"I'll see to it," Mame said. "I've brought a real tub from Seattle. It earns me almost as much money as two of my girls."

"Thanks, Mame." Hogan felt in his pocket. His face darkened for a moment; then he turned to Kate. "Uh, I seem to have lost my pouch." Kate took out hers.

"Ain't no need for you to do that," Mame said. "You done me favors enough, Hogan. Call this my wedding present."

Still he pressed the gold dust into her hands. "You take this, Mame," he said. "I've got plenty more where that came from. You put this by for a rainy day, you hear?"

Mame shook her head. "That gal's damn lucky I ain't younger, else I'd claim you for myself."

Hogan slapped her playfully on her wide backside. "I've had a hard time keeping my hands off you, Mame," he said, sending her away with a laugh. Now Hogan turned back to Kate, and the laughter died. Passion darkened his eyes. "Mrs. O'Shea," he said, holding out his hand and bowing slightly. Before Kate could curtsy, he'd gathered her up in his arms and carried her into their tiny room.

Kate's laughter was light and carefree. "I shudder to think what would have happened if I hadn't passed Mame's inspection," she teased. "And all this time I thought I had only Roxanne to be jealous of. How many more Mames are there, my wayward husband?"

"You don't have any reason to be jealous of anyone, Kate," he whispered, pulling her into his arms. His mouth slanted across hers hungrily, his tongue probing. Readily she opened to him. Their deep kiss was interrupted by a discreet knock at the door. Two scantily dressed women entered, carrying a tin-lined wooden bathtub between them. Kate squealed with delight when she saw it. Other girls entered with buckets of water. Even before they'd filled the tub, Kate was shucking off her leather breeches and shirt and the long johns beneath. The gown she'd brought was still in her pack at the barbershop.

"I take it you mean to go first." Hogan grinned, enjoying the sight of his wife's pale, slim body. He seldom saw her nude, although they slept that way at home. To avoid the chill of their cabin, Kate always threw off her clothes and scuttled under the covers. Now Hogan let his glance wander lazily over her figure. She was perfectly formed, he saw, from the narrow delicate shoulders to the slim hips, tapering legs, and the graceful arch of her narrow feet. Watching her, he felt the bulge in his pants harden and grow.

Kate had lowered herself into the tub, her face expressing the ecstasy she felt as the warm water rose around her. She leaned back against the sloping sides and stretched out her legs, closing her eyes rapturously. Then, as if remembering Hogan, she opened one eye and crooked a finger at him. "Why don't you join me?" she said seductively. Hogan didn't wait for another invitation. In no time, he had his clothes off.

"I'm not sure if there's room in the tub for all of us," Kate said sassily, eyeing his erection.

"Then you'll have to do something about it, won't you?" Hogan said, swinging his long legs over the edge. Water sloshed on the floor as Kate made room for him. Picking up the bar of soap, she made a thick lather and smoothed it over his skin. Hogan leaned back and closed his eyes, letting her work her magic on him. She lathered and soothed and caressed every part of his hard lean body, and he felt the tension build inside him, but when her soft hands found their way to his manhood, softly cupping and swirling soap along his hardened shaft, he groaned and pulled her hands away.

Laughing, Kate leaned forward, reaching far behind him to find the washcloth. Her firm wet breasts brushed enticingly against his erection. Hogan groaned again and opened his eyes. Two green orbs dancing with silvery lights laughed back at him. She knew what exquisite torture she was putting him through. Hogan reached forward, grasped her waist, and lifted her. Smoothly she slid over him, encasing his hot pulsing flesh in her own. Her knees rested on either side of him and her back arched as she settled herself more tightly against him. Hogan felt the fire build and the room darken. His lean hips plunged upward in the warm moistness that was Kate. She met him with a savage need of her own that soon brought them to climax. Lethargy followed, a slow, sensuous returning to reality. Kate lay spent and exhausted across his chest.

Hogan picked up the soap and washcloth and gently, tenderly washed her sweet body. His hands moved over her and he felt his desire rise again. Swinging Kate up in his arms, he stepped out of the tub and carried her to the bed.

"Hogan," she sighed as he placed her against the pillows. He lowered his mouth to hers, as he scattered kisses across her chin to the softest, most sensitive curve of her throat, then dipped down to the hard-peaked breasts. He sipped the moisture left from their bath, then captured the swollen nipples between his teeth and suckled until she groaned and opened her knees in hopeless surrender.

Hogan trailed kisses down the delicate midriff to her navel, tongued it until she giggled and jerked away, then down to the joint where thigh met hip, and on to the soft, sensuous inner thigh and the sweet, sweet womanhood of her. He lowered his mouth to her, his tongue plundering the sweet depths until Kate arched and cried out. Then he rose, and standing at the edge of the bed, his knees between her thighs, he thrust himself into her willing flesh. Once again he knew a joy and fulfillment he'd never found with any other woman. Kate arched to meet him, giving and taking equally, reaching and attaining the same shattering climax that shook him to his very soul.

Standing outside the door, shamelessly listening, Mame nodded in satisfaction. At last Hogan had found his woman.

One of her girls approached, a besotted man in tow.

"This room is unavailable," Mame said, "for the rest of the night." That, she thought, was her wedding present to Hogan O'Shea and his wife. Her fat neck quivered with excitement. Imperiously she waddled away, her smile beatific.

15

"Kate, about the pouch you made . . ." Hogan said the next morning.

Kate gave him a swift kiss. "I'll make you another," she said. "Don't worry about it." She held up the bag of gold dust he'd handed her. They were standing over their sledge. Hogan had hidden an extra pouch of gold dust there, and now he'd divided it between them. "I'm going to try to buy some supplies, maybe a new coffeepot and some extra flour. I understand they have plenty of that."

"That's what Mame said this morning," Hogan answered. "I doubt you'll get little else in the way of food unless you want to pay double."

Kate weighed the bag of gold dust and shook her head. "I don't mind the paying," she said, "but I hate to think I'm taking food from someone else. With the flour and the game you bring in, we can make it."

"Scurvy's going to be the main problem now," Hogan said grimly, and lashed down their bedrolls. They'd be leaving as soon as they purchased supplies. Originally they'd planned to stay longer, but, locked in the misery of winter and threatened starvation, the town was lackluster, without the gaiety they'd sought. Now they longed for the tranquillity and comfort of their little cabin.

"I'm to meet Thor and Axe at the claim office," Hogan said as they started up the street. "We'll be back at the sledge in about an hour." With a hurried kiss they parted. Kate trudged toward the general store, the snow crunching under her shoepacs. She dreaded the trip home, yet she wanted to go, despite the power of their passionate night. To remember Hogan's lovemaking even now, in the somber light of day, made her knees grow weak and her body tingle with renewed desire. Kate began to hum. No matter what hardships befell them all, she could endure because Hogan was there beside her. She felt invincible, optimistic, beautiful. A soft smile lit her face when she stepped inside the general store. Other customers turned to answer her smile. They'd heard of Taffy Kate and of her feats. If their old-fashioned notions told them a woman shouldn't gamble, they couldn't condemn Taffy Kate. She'd donated every ounce she'd won to an orphans' and women's fund. As Hogan had predicted, she'd only added luster to her name.

Now women who might otherwise have shunned her for her gambling hurried forward to shake her hand and introduce themselves. Shyly Kate acknowledged their kind words and at last was free to browse among the tables laden with goods. There were still pickaxes and dress goods and pots and pans and shoepacs and all manner of paraphernalia, but not as much as in the summer. There were also tins of food jealously guarded on the shelves behind the counter, and sacks of flour sitting everywhere. The potatoes were already growing soft and moldy; the bacon, cut in long yellow strings that had earned it the contemptuous name of yard bacon, was an inadequate supply for the winter.

Kate chose a new coffeepot and a new flannel shirt for Hogan and a tin of lilac-scented talcum powder for herself. She should buy something for Thor and Axe, she thought, standing undecided before the counter.

"Good morning, Jake. Give me a tin of those peaches," a cool voice said at her elbow, and Kate glanced up at the blowsy yellow-haired woman. Roxanne Blayne's eyes looked puffy, as if she hadn't had enough sleep, and lines of dissipation ran from the sides of her nose down to the corners of her mouth. The woman was not nearly as young as Kate had at first supposed, nor was she as pretty as she'd remembered. Roxanne felt Kate's gaze and turned to face her.

"Good Morning, Miss . . . I can't seem to remember your name," Roxanne said. The men gathered around the stove in the back of the store, straightened and listened. Some of them remembered how Taffy Kate had knocked Roxanne into the mud last summer, and now they related the incident with some enjoyment. There were guffaws of laughter that brought a flush to Roxanne's cheeks, but she kept her chin high, her look one of haughtiness. Jake set the can of peaches on the counter. His dislike for the blond whore was all too evident.

Kate felt sorry for her, despite her cattiness. "Mrs. O'Shea," she said in answer to Roxanne's comment. "And I do hope we can come to be friends, Miss Blayne." Kate held out her hand to the woman.

Roxanne looked momentarily taken aback; then she smiled, a cynical, insinuating smile that never reached her eyes. "Why, how generous of you," she said without sincerity. "There are few women able to be friends with their husbands' . . ." Deliberately she let the sentence dangle, and all in the room knew what she meant. Now it was Kate's turn to flush. Still, she kept her gaze steadfastly on Roxanne's smug face.

"I'm aware you and my husband were once friends," she said quietly. "But that is in the past."

"Is it?" Roxanne smirked, and taking out a pouch of gold dust, placed it on the counter to pay for the tin of peaches. "Take it out of that, Jake," she ordered imperiously, and pushed the pouch forward as if to draw attention to it. Involuntarily Kate's gaze dipped, and when she took in the bag she'd made for Hogan, she felt the blood drain from her head. It made her light-headed and put a roaring in her ears.

"Where did you get that bag?" she asked, gripping the edge of the counter.

"This one?" Roxanne asked haughtily, as if she might not answer such an impertinent question, then shrugged negligently. "One of my customers left it with me last night. I did him a favor."

Kate spoke before she thought. "That's Hogan's bag." Although the men around the stove couldn't hear the words, they could sense the tension between the two women.

Roxanne let a lazy, satisfied smile curve her lips, and raised her voice. "That's right, Hogan gave it to me. As I said"—her gaze flickered up and down Kate contemptuously—"I did him a favor."

"You're lying," Kate said in a tense voice. "Hogan was with me last night."

"Hogan was with me while you were so busy playing Taffy Kate of the Yukon," Roxanne said derisively. "A man like Hogan doesn't like to see a woman act like a man." She let her fingers trail along the ribbon holding her bonnet and ran her tongue around her lips in a purely lascivious gesture. The pain in Kate's eyes was quick and intense. Roxanne felt a thrill of triumph course through her. Kate was aware that the whole store had stopped to listen. She squared her shoulders and looked Roxanne in the eye.

"As I said," she began, repeating Roxanne's words, "I don't believe you. Hogan was with me last night. And I can assure you, Miss Blayne, he had not spent himself on a whore first, at least not one of any consequence." Roxanne's face flamed. The men guffawed. The women tittered, horrified by Kate's boldness, yet pleased that someone had finally put one of the arrogant whores in her place. Kate's eyes remained steady on Roxanne's mottled face. As the laughter swelled around them, Roxanne picked up the peaches and the gold pouch and nearly ran from the store.

Without acknowledging the bawdy snickers, Kate gathered up her purchases and with as much dignity as possible left the store. But she felt no sense of triumph. Why had Hogan given Roxanne the bag? she wondered. Had he indeed gone to Roxanne first? Kate knew his tireless hunger and his sexual prowess, but could even Hogan have made love to her so thoroughly after having been with Roxanne? She thought not, but some small part of her wasn't sure.

So wrapped up was she in her own thoughts that she didn't at first notice the Indian woman until she bumped into her. "I'm sorry," she mumbled, and shifting her parcels to a more secure hold prepared to move on. Something in the quick movement of the woman to avert her face made Kate look again. "May," she breathed. "May." She caught the fleeing woman's shoulder and turned her around. "May, it's me, Kate."

The small figure no longer resisted, but stood with her head bowed, the hood of her ragged parka pulled far forward so her face was hidden.

"How have you been, May?" Kate asked. "We've thought about you so often."

There was no answer save for the slight nod of May's head.

"We've missed you. Axe has missed you," Kate tried again.

"Axe miss me?" May asked in a low, tentative voice. What was wrong with the girl? Kate wondered. She'd always been so bubbly and forthright. Now she shrank back as Kate took a step forward.

"Of course he misses you," Kate said, gripping her shoulder. "May, why won't you see him and talk to him while we're here?"

"No, no! No see Axe," she cried, backing away. She turned to flee, but Kate reached out and grabbed hold of her parka. The hood fell back. "No," May cried, hiding her face in her hands, but not before Kate had seen the ugly scars and bruises.

"May, my God. Who's done this to you? What happened?" She stared at the Indian woman, unable to comprehend; then slowly understanding came, and with it disbelief and anger. "Did Frenchy do this? Answer me." She took May's shoulders and shook her.

Without moving her hands from her damaged face, May nodded. "Sometime. Sometime his friend Sawyer."

"And your beautiful hair!" Kate whispered, remembering the shimmering blue-black strands that had hung nearly to her waist. It had been hacked off just below her ears. One small chafed hand smoothed back the ragged, greasy strands in a mute testimony of grief and shame.

"Frenchy say I bad. I witch. Take medicine bag, cut hair. Take power away like shaman."

"That wretched man! Why do you stay with him?" Kate demanded. "Why haven't you left?"

"No place go." May's voice was muffled, coming as it did from behind her shielding hands. Even those bore marks, as if she'd tried to fend off her attacker.

"You could have come back to us," Kate said. "You know you could have."

May shook her head. "Not know at first where you are. Later . . ." She paused, hunching her shoulders even more. "May ashamed Axe see her this way."

"Is that why you ran away from him that day last summer?" Kate demanded. The black head nodded again. Feeling a helpless fury, Kate wrapped her arms around May. "You'll never go back to Frenchy again. You're coming with us."

"No, Frenchy find. He kill May. He kill Axe."

"He can't," Kate scoffed. "When Axe sees what he's done to you, he may kill Frenchy." For the first time May lowered her hands and looked up. Kate nearly recoiled at the damage she saw. May's face had been battered so severely that one cheek was swollen almost beyond recognition. Her lips were cut and crusted with dried blood. One eye was swollen shut. Old bruises mingled with new on the once pretty face. Kate felt her stomach lurch with pity.

But May gave no thought to herself. Her eyes were beseeching as they met Kate's. "No tell Axe. Pretend you no see. Go away now." She turned to go.

"I can't go away and leave you like this," Kate cried in protest. "I'm your friend, May. I want to help you."

"No friend," May said, waving her away with her hands. "No want friend." She darted away between two cabins. Kate dropped her packages and gave chase, but when she reached the back alley, May had disappeared. Thoughtfully she went back to retrieve her packages, and made her way back to the sledge.

Hogan saw her coming, and the smile of welcome

died. "What's wrong, Kate?" he cried, coming to meet her.

"Oh, Hogan, I've seen May," she said, grateful for his strength. Breathlessly she told him of her encounter with the Indian woman. Hogan swore under his breath and turned toward Main Street.

"Where are you going?" she asked.

Hogan turned to face her. "It's time we took care of Frenchy LaRoche."

"Hogan, wait," Kate cried in fright, suddenly understanding why May would rather suffer the man's beatings than have Axe in danger.

"What is it, Kate?" Hogan asked impatiently. His eyes were hard and determined, his jaw a jutting unswerving line.

Slowly Kate shook her head. "Just be careful," she said. "He's got Sawyer with him." Without another word he headed down the street. Kate stood watching him, then, galvanized to action, raced up the street after him. He had already reached the vacant field where Axe and Thor were busy harnessing the dog team. Kate saw them exchange a few words, and then both men fell into step beside Hogan. The three of them made an invincible wall as they stalked toward the Lucky Lady Saloon. Kate began to run.

She was out of breath when she reached the saloon, and had to push her way through the unwashed bodies that pressed forward to hear the ensuing argument.

Hogan was standing before Frenchy and Sawyer, legs spread, weight balanced lightly, taut and alert and aggressive. "Get up off that stool, you bastard," he growled, "and see if you've got the balls to fight a man."

Frenchy looked surprised and wary. His gaze flashed to George Sawyer and back again. "*Mon ami,* I have no reason to fight you," he said, wetting his lips with his tongue. Kate thought the gesture looked like that of a snake about to strike.

"I'll give you a reason," Hogan said, and stepped forward to deliver a punch to Frenchy's jaw. The man fell to the floor and lay rubbing his jaw.

"Ah, hah," Frenchy laughed with false humor. "You pack a good punch, heh. But, my friend, why do you do this to Frenchy? Did I not open my home to you? Was I not your friend?" He kept up a line of questions, a smile on his face while he sized up the big man. "So why do you do this to Frenchy, eh? There is no reason, *n'est-ce pas?*"

He could well guess what had brought about this hostility, but he wasn't about to admit it to them.

"May would think differently," Hogan said. "Get up and fight, you scum, or do you only have the stomach to beat up women?"

"Hogan, *mon ami* . . ." Frenchy held out a hand as if to ward off any further attack while he got to his feet. "I don't know why you're so upset over this. It is not like she is a white woman. She's just a little Indian girl—" His words were cut off by the slash of Axe's fist.

"Let me take care of him, Hogan," Axe said, and swung again. In a sense of fair play, Hogan stepped back, although he watched closely. Frenchy outweighed the old man by a good seventy-five pounds and was considerably younger. Faced with Axe as an opponent rather than the bigger man, Frenchy lost his affability. His face grew ugly as he stepped forward and swung. Axe ducked and swung again, his fist landing against Frenchy's nose. Axe let the momentum of his swing carry him forward, and came up with his boot, kicking Frenchy hard in the crotch. With a howl Frenchy doubled over, cradling himself with his hands. His knees gave way and he slid to the floor. George Sawyer edged off the stool, a blade flicked open, and he sidled toward Axe.

"I wouldn't if I were you," Hogan said, wrapping his arm around Sawyer's neck from behind. Sawyer made a gagging sound and dropped the knife. Kate rushed forward and picked it up, while Thor raised his mighty fist and brought it down on the head of a man who'd edged forward from the crowd to help his cronies. Other men jumped into the fracas and began slugging one another.

"Whoee," Axe cried, and leapt forward to land a punch on a receptive chin. Kate could only stare in surprise at the frail little man. She'd never seen Axe move so decisively before. He was like a dynamo.

"Kate!" Hogan appeared out of the melee. "Get to the sledges and finish hitching the dog teams."

"What about May?" she insisted.

"We'll get her, but be ready to leave, fast." He ducked a wild swing and swiveled to land a quick, hard punch. The man went down like an ox. "Go on, get out of here," he ordered, and Kate couldn't help noting the same gleam in his eyes as in Axe's. They were crazy, all of them, she thought, wending her way through the struggling, wrestling bodies.

"Kate!" She turned to see May crouched against the side of the building.

"May!" she shouted joyously. The glass window behind them shattered. "Come on. Let's get out of here," Kate yelled, taking May's hand and running back toward the river, where the sledges and dogs were waiting. "Quick, help me harness the dogs." With fumbling fingers the women laced the harness straps through the rings and snapped them to the sledges. When both teams were hitched, Kate ran to quiet the lead dog of Hogan's sledge until the men came.

"I go back now," May said wistfully, and took a step backward.

"No, May, you can't," Kate cried. "Axe fought for you. You can't go back to Frenchy now."

"Axe fought for May?" the Indian girl exclaimed in dismay.

"Yes," Kate assured her. "Axe and Hogan and Thor. That's what all this ruckus is about. You have to come with us. You have to, May. We want you." Kate held out her hand beseechingly. What would happen to May now if she didn't come with them? Frenchy would make her pay for his humiliation.

May smiled, a heartrending, lopsided thing that stretched the swollen side of her face. "I come," she said. "I be Axe's woman."

"Kate!" Hogan's yell pulled her head up. The three

men were running toward her, a pack of men pursuing them. "Get going!" He waved them on.

"Let's go, May," Kate shouted. "Mush!" She snapped the reins of her dog team. May ran down to the other sledge and picked up the reins. Kate's sledge lurched off, bumping and catching at every little rough mound of snow. She'd forgotten to ice the runners! Too late now. They flew out to the center of the frozen river. She could hear the men pounding along behind.

Hogan drew near, gasping for breath. Kate ventured a look. His face was bleeding; his teeth were clenched in a grimace. She couldn't tell if it was from pain or the effort of running.

"Hold it," he said, glancing back over his shoulder. Kate drew her dog team to a halt and looked back. The pack of men wasn't pursuing them out onto the river. They stood on the bank, shaking their fists and calling threats.

"Don't you ever come back here, Hogan O'Shea," one of them shouted.

"You owe me for bustin' up my place," another yelled. Wheezing for breath, Hogan chuckled. Thor and Axe ran up and joined him. The three men looked at each other and roared with laughter, slapping each other's shoulders in a manner Kate had come to recognize as ritualistic. She snorted in disgust.

"What have you men got to be so happy about?" she demanded. "We'll never be able to show our faces in that town again. After all I did to try to create some goodwill for us."

The men looked at her in surprise and burst out laughing again. "Ah, Kate," Hogan said between hearty chuckles. He walked over and put his arm around her. "They don't mean it, love. Those men like a good fight as much as any of us. They'll welcome us back next time we come."

"*Ja*, especially if we come vid Taffy Kate," Thor said.

"Oooh, you're all reprobates," Kate cried, but it was impossible for her to remain angry in the face of their good cheer. Over Hogan's shoulder she could see

Axe approaching May. Tenderly he looked at the Indian girl's face and took off his own gloves and gave them to her. May looked at him for a long moment, then laid her head against his chest. Kate's heart swelled. No matter if they never returned to Dawson again. They had May back!

"Good-bye, Taffy Kate," someone onshore called. "See you next time."

"Good-bye," she called. Smiling through the sting of tears, Kate waved back. She felt Hogan at her elbow as he took the reins.

"We forgot Kate's bathtub," he said suddenly.

"Bathtub?" Kate asked.

"I bought it from Mame," Hogan answered absently. All three men looked back toward town. "Do you think we could?" Hogan asked hopefully.

Axe shook his head. "Better get it next time."

"*Ja*, next time," Thor agreed sadly.

"Next time," Kate echoed, and all the way back to the cabin she thought about the wonderful bathtub left behind in Dawson.

16

Their lighthearted mood was short-lived. Halfway home, May collapsed, unable to go on. Carefully the men placed her in one of the sledges, shouldering the supplies onto their own backs. Kate thought fleetingly of her bathtub and was glad it had been left behind. Anxiously she hovered over May. The young Indian woman had nursed Gilly and her through their wounds and fevers. Now was Kate's turn to help May.

Their progress was slowed so they were forced to siwash along the trail and begin again the next morning. Kate made a broth for May, who couldn't eat, and the men guessed she was in far worse shape than they'd thought. Kate was thankful to see the fork of their creek and their snug little cabins.

"Bring May to our cabin so I can tend her," Kate ordered, and hurried in to start a fire. She added logs lavishly, wanting to heat the room quickly. She dared not remove May's outer garments until the cabin had grown warmer. She hurried out with a pail to gather snow, and placed it on top of the stove to melt.

"How is she?" Hogan asked, bringing in some of the supplies and stashing them in a corner.

"I don't know," Kate said worriedly, "but we can't lose her now. Not when we've just got her back."

Hogan's big hand cupped her shoulder and steered her against him. "She'll be all right, Kate," he said gruffly. "She's just run-down. You'll soon have her fixed up with some of your good cooking." Kate knew he was trying to cheer her up, and it would do May little good if she walked around with a gloomy air.

"Where's Axe?" she asked, pulling away and wiping at her eyes.

"He took his gun and went off into the woods."

"He's gone hunting now?" Kate asked in disbelief.

Hogan shook his head. "Not hunting, Kate." They stared into each other's eyes for a moment, thinking of the old man and his fears. He never voiced them, never showed them. He simply went off into the woods to be by himself.

"May'll get better. She'll be all right," Kate said fiercely.

"I know she will," Hogan said quietly. "I'll bed down with the men until she's well again." Numbly Kate nodded.

When she removed May's parka and leather leggings and the pitiful thin dress beneath, she was appalled at what she found. May's body was covered with large welts and bruises that spoke of many beatings, but it was the wasted, thin look of the young limbs and ribs that shocked her. May looked as if she'd hardly eaten anything since she left them. Kate bathed her and pulled on one of her own nightgowns.

May was shivering as with the ague long before Kate was finished. Her teeth clicked together in a rapid staccato that only increased Kate's fear that she might die. Kate hurried to pile on extra blankets and forced some hot chicory coffee laced with whiskey down her throat. Still the shivering continued. If only she had a brick or two to heat. She hurried next door and spoke to Thor.

"*Ja*, I help," he agreed, leaping to his feet and dismantling some of his fire pit. Unselfishly he hauled the large stones next door, where Kate heated them, wrapped them in cloths, and laid them at May's feet and along her sides. At last May's shivering ceased and she fell into a long exhausted sleep. Kate began a stew on the back of the stove, shaving off bits of frozen meat and placing them in the pot of melted snow. Then she added some barley and some wild onions she'd gathered in the summer.

Summer! Would it ever come again? And how brief

it was when it came, gone almost in the blink of an eye. This land was no place for men and women and children. It was a place of perpetual winter, of snow and ice and death. They weren't meant to be here mining gold. Nature herself had thrown every obstacle into their path, but still stubborn men allowed greed to rule their heads, existing like animals in their efforts to survive another winter.

"Kate?" Hogan said at her elbow. She spun around. She'd been so deep in thought she hadn't heard him come in. "Are you all right?" He saw in her eyes all that she'd been thinking and feeling. Apprehension furrowed his brow. Many men went winter mad out here. "Don't dwell on things too much, Kate," he warned gently. "It'll drive you mad if you do."

"We must be mad to stay here like this," she said, and her voice was taut, as if she were exercising immense control. "What good is gold if we must live like savages and die in the bargain?"

"May won't die," Hogan reassured her. He took hold of her shoulder, but she shrugged away from him. "You're tired and hungry. You'll feel better after you've had a meal and some rest."

"Yes, I'll be all right," she agreed, and this time there was a remoteness to her that troubled him. He made no move to touch her again. She'd get through this. She had to. It was something they all faced alone, and either they found their private well of strength to go on and endure the harsh solitude, or they succumbed. Kate was strong. She wasn't a quitter. She'd make it.

In the days and nights that followed, Kate wondered if either she or May could survive. She fought her own depression as valiantly as she fought May's illness. May's skin had taken on a yellow pallor and she couldn't seem to rouse herself enough to eat. Kate tried to feed her some caribou meat, but May was unable to chew it. Her gums were swollen and had begun to bleed. Kate tried to still her fears, and said nothing, not wanting Axe to worry any more than necessary. But the day she threw back the covers to bathe May and saw the sores on her legs and her blackened toes, she screamed in horror. The men heard her and came running.

"Vat is it?" Thor asked, running in first. Hogan and Axe were right behind him. Kate's grief-stricken face drew them to the bed, where they bent to examine May.

"Scurvy," Axe said.

"Scurvy?" Kate whispered. She swallowed hard and looked back at May. "I didn't know." Her eyes were wide and startled as she looked from the men to May. "What can we do? We have no fruits or fresh vegetables."

Without a word, Axe left the room. Kate glanced at him sharply.

"Have we got any potatoes left?" Hogan asked.

"A few," Kate answered quickly. "Will they work?"

"They did with the Irish peasants," Hogan answered, kneeling by the bed to take a closer look at her gums. "Boil up some potatoes, mash them up so she can swallow them without chewing."

"Yes, all right," Kate said, hurrying to the corner where she kept their small supply of potatoes.

"Don't peel them," Hogan called. It seemed to take forever to wash the shriveled vegetables and set them to boiling. In the meantime the men continued to examine May and discuss her fate.

Where was Axe? Kate wondered, and felt anger at the old man for rushing off into the forest when May needed him the most. But before the potatoes were boiled soft, Axe had returned.

"Boil this up and make a tea," he said, handing Kate a piece of spruce bark.

"Will it work?" she asked fearfully.

"Aye. It's what the natives use." He crossed to the bed and leaned over May.

"We may have to amputate that toe," Hogan said. "We don't want gangrene to set in."

"Let's wait and see if the spruce-bark tea works," Axe said. "I've seen worse than this."

With tears flowing unchecked down her face, Kate crept to the foot of the bed. "If I'd only known," she whispered brokenly. "If I'd only recognized the symptoms."

"Kate, you can't blame yourself," Hogan said, coming to put an arm around her.

"If I'd just said something to you, but I thought I was saving you from worry."

"You were being unselfish, as always, Kate," Hogan said gently, burying his face against her hair. "Don't blame yourself. This was done to May long before we rescued her. If we blame anyone, it has to be LaRoche. He didn't take care of her. He let her half-starve while he sat in the Lucky Lady buying drinks and acting like a big shot."

"Oh, Hogan, what if she dies? What if we all die out here? How would anyone know? We can't get help, even in Dawson. God truly has forsaken this land."

"Shh, my love," he whispered, casting a quick glance at Thor and Axe. The men glanced away and tucked the covers around May.

"Is the gold worth this suffering?" she demanded against his shoulder. "Is it worth going cold and hungry and being so alone? Is it worth seeing children starve? What kind of people are we to endure this, to punish ourselves like this? What's happened to the decency of man toward others? Gold corrupts us all."

She was becoming hysterical. He could feel it.

"Kate!" He shook her slightly, his hands strongly gripping her arms. She ceased weeping and looked at him. "Not all men are like LaRoche," he said softly. "Think of the Garretts and Axe and Uly and a dozen other men and women you've met since we got here. Think of yourself, giving away your winnings to be sure Father Luke's children will be fed. Gold does corrupt—those who were corruptible to begin with. Men like that flock to the gold camps whether they're in California or Alaska, but out of all the human misery comes good things. Wildernesses are explored, towns built, and men forge strong bonds that last forever just because they are decent men." He hugged her to him again.

"I know how you feel about the children. They're innocent victims. Their parents should be horse-whipped for bringing them up here. I swear I'll never bring a child into this world." Kate felt as if she were turning to stone. With all the concern over May she hadn't told him yet about the baby. Hogan rubbed her arms, trying to warm her, but she could never be warm again, never laugh in the sunshine or know joy again. She let her arms fall away from him, and he glanced at her in surprise.

"I'll bring in some more firewood," he said, and closed the door softly behind him.

Kate made a soup from the boiled and mashed potatoes and carefully spoon-fed it to May, who at first refused it, then ate. Patiently Kate fed her the spruce tea. In the days that followed, she carefully hoarded her supply of potatoes, using them mostly for May, adding them to a stew for the men and herself only when she feared they might be afflicted with the same disease. Every morning she checked her own gums for swelling and bleeding. And every night she said a silent prayer for the health of the tiny life she carried.

At last the fevers abated and May's weakened body began to fight back. One morning she opened her eyes and smiled at Kate. That afternoon she was able to sit up against a pillow and eat while Kate spooned up the potato soup for her. The next day she was stronger, so Kate let Axe and the other men come in to talk to her for a while. Their rough humor made May giggle in her old way, and Kate noted the color in her cheeks. The awful yellow pallor had faded and the sores on her leg were healing. Even the blackened toes seemed to have healed, though their color still wasn't back to normal.

Finally the day came when May grumbled about the monotony of her potato diet and demanded some bear steaks. Kate laughed and felt happier than she had in weeks. Her patient was getting better. May sat up in bed, watching Kate move around the tiny cabin. Her dark eyes had grown troubled as she watched Kate.

"Kate not happy?" she asked, and Kate forced a smile.

"I'm very happy now that you're well," she said, going to sit on the edge of the bed. "We were so afraid you weren't going to recover. That dreadful man!"

"Frenchy very bad man," May said simply, her eyes lowered to the coverlet; then she raised her head and her smile was radiant. "May glad be back with Kate and Axe." Kate gripped her hand, tears stinging her eyes. "Should never stay with Frenchy," May went on reflectively. "First, he funny. Make May laugh very lot. Then he mean. Hit May, no give food, make May go with other men. May say no. Axe no make May. He say Eskimo way, I go." She shrugged. "May go, do what he say. Men give Frenchy money. Many men. Some kind, like Frenchy at first. Make May laugh. Some hurt May." She lay back against the pillow as if exhausted by her narration.

"You never have to worry about him anymore," Kate assured her. "Hogan and Axe and Thor took care of him."

"May see Hogan and Axe hit him like he hit May. May happy." She smiled, her dark eyes studying Kate. "Kate not happy."

Kate glanced away from her. "I am," she said, and could think of nothing more to perpetuate her lie.

"Kate not happy with baby?" May tried again.

Kate jerked her head up. "You know?" May nodded, beaming.

"You mustn't say anything," Kate said urgently. "Promise me, May."

"May promise," the Indian woman said, not sure why Kate wanted to keep such an event to herself. In her tribe babies were welcomed unless they were female babies, which were sometimes disposed of, even though the authorities had said they mustn't. Now she waited, but Kate couldn't go on.

"Kate not want baby?" she prompted. "May give something. Baby gone."

"Oh, May, no," Kate cried in anguish. "I want this baby very much. It's just that Hogan doesn't want a child here in the Yukon, and neither do I."

"Eskimos have many babies in Alyeska," May said in puzzlement.

"And many of them die," Kate blurted out. "Even now I don't know how my baby is being affected by what I must endure here. What if I get scurvy or become ill? How will I have my baby without a doctor? How will I take care of it through another winter? Oh, May, I'm frightened." Kate put her hands over her face and began to weep.

May watched her in dismay. She'd never thought of Kate as a woman to cry as other white women did. Even when her father had been killed she'd borne it stoically. Finally May shook her head. White women would always remain a mystery to her. They did not lament or tear their clothes and hair when there was a death and grieving was allowed, even enjoyed, but they cried over something like having a baby. May did understand fear, and she knew that Kate was not a cowardly woman, so she put an arm around her friend and patted her shoulder soothingly.

At last Kate's sobs quieted and she wiped her eyes with the hem of her skirt and looked up shamefaced. "I'm sorry, May," she said. "I guess that's been building for a long time."

"Kate better?" May asked anxiously, and Kate nodded, even forcing a tiny smile.

"Kate's better," she repeated, and found she did indeed feel stronger, more hopeful, now that May was recovering. When the men returned from digging in the pits, they found May sitting up and Kate's face once more alight with laughter. Hogan felt relief ripple through him. He'd been worried about her. Axe invited Thor to bring out his squeeze box, and all of them grinned at the look on May's face when he began to play and sing.

The days that followed were easier for Kate. May steadily improved. Now in the evenings Axe and she huddled in the corner of the room talking in low voices, and one night they slipped out of the cabin and disappeared. Kate knew they'd returned to the other cabin. Their reconciliation was complete. Hogan grinned at Kate from across the room, but for some reason her heart felt leaden. The wellspring of passion she'd once known with him seemed forever dead. That night Hogan rejoined her in her bed, wrapping his long arms around her and pulling her possessively close.

"God, I've missed you," he whispered against her ear.

"Thor!" Kate reminded him of the big Swede, who had spread a pallet near the stove in their cabin in order to give Axe and May some privacy.

"Thor be damned," Hogan growled softly, and pressed against her urgently. Kate pushed down the rising desire her traitorous body signaled to her and drew away from him. Hogan lay so still, she knew he was hurt and puzzled by her rejection. But as much as a part of her wanted to throw herself into his arms and seek his lips in a probing, arousing kiss, another part of her shrank from him. She lay stiff and still, trying to sort through her confusion.

She was angry and hurt and frightened. Now that May no longer needed her, she could deal with the doubts that had plagued her about Roxanne Blayne. Were her claims true that Hogan had gone off with her at the Lucky Lady? Kate had refused to believe Roxanne back in Dawson, sure of Hogan's love, but now, as the long weeks had slid by and they'd had no time to talk, those doubts had grown.

And what of the baby? Hogan had made it very clear he had no desire to bring forth a child in this frozen, harsh world, and he was right, but the baby was here, growing inside her, and that brought her back to her other fears. Already she felt the changes in her body that signaled a tiny being was growing there, secure and warm for the time being, but what about later, when the baby was born?

She lay thinking of her room back at Aunt Petty's. It had a wonderful large window that let in the morning light. Everything was clean and bright and comfortable. The doctor was just down the street and could be fetched in a few minutes. Aunt Petty would have delighted in making baby clothes, and they would have hauled down the old crib from the attic, the one Aunt Petty and Mama and even Kate herself had slept in. Homesickness washed over her.

Aunt Petty was gone now, and so was her comfortable house with the big well-lit rooms, but Kate must do what she must for her child. The baby was dependent upon her and no one else. Now she took a deep breath.

"In the spring I'm going back," she said softly. She felt Hogan's body go rigid.

"Kate!" he cried hoarsely. His big hand settled on her shoulder. She could feel the heat of it through her nightgown. "You don't mean that, love," he coaxed. "You're just suffering from cabin fever. You've been cooped up in here taking care of May, but that's over now. She's well. You can come and go as you wish."

"I've told you where I wish to go," she said softly.

His hands ceased their massaging motion on her arm. "Is it me, Kate, something I've done?" he asked wearily. "I know I've been preoccupied, but with May in here with you, I worked myself hard so I could sleep at night. I've gotten used to having you near me."

"You've done nothing," Kate said, and it was true. She'd known what kind of man he was, that he was a wanderer who wanted no attachments, no demands made on him. And he'd made it clear how he felt about having a child. Their idyll had come to an end. "I'm ready to go back." Her words were spoken with such quiet finality that Hogan felt his heart squeeze painfully.

"I know I'm a rough man, Kate," he said humbly. He'd never begged before. "I've tried to change, to be a better man for you." She had to bite her lips not to cry. "I'm willing to do whatever you want me to do, Kate." His voice broke.

"Don't you see it's no good?" she said, sounding angry and impatient, when inside she just felt bruised and unhappy. "You can't change and be something you're not, any more than I can. This was just an interlude, a reaching out because no one else was there for us."

"I didn't want anyone else," Hogan said so loudly now that the steady rhythm of snores from the floor was disrupted. "Kate . . ." His hands reached for her, hauling her around so she must face him in the dark. She sensed him hovering over her as if he could read her face.

"I'm sorry, Hogan," she said, and began to weep silently. Only the trembling of her body gave away her pain.

"Shhh, don't cry." His words were soothing, his touch on her hair gentle. It tore at her heart. "You're distraught, Kate. Think about it some more. There's time. Spring is a long way off."

"But if I decide to go?"

"I'll take you back," he said, and wrapped his arms around her, cradling her against his big chest. "I'd never hold you against your will, Kate." He stared into the darkness with sightless, tear-filled eyes. Kate wept against his shoulder. Finally her sobs quieted and her body grew lax. "Kate," he whispered against her ear. A gentle sigh answered him. She'd fallen asleep. He held her against him, rocking her gently and kissing away the salty tears that streaked her cheeks. The wind moaned outside the cabin, low and insistent, and once again Hogan felt its cold loneliness seep into his soul.

The howling chinok winds and snow blizzards began to lessen. The men were able to work every day in the pits, hauling up dirt and gravel until they reached bedrock, then starting a new pit to repeat the process. Mounds of dirt stood along the riverbank, waiting for the spring thaw so they could wash out the gold.

After that night when May had gone to Axe's cabin, Hogan never shared Kate's bed again. The morning after, as he'd stood in the doorway, his mittens and fur hat clutched in his big hands, Kate had told him she preferred he sleep with the men in the other cabin. He'd said nothing, but his lips had tightened to a thin line in his haggard face and his fists had knotted in the fur cap.

"Whatever you want, Kate," he'd said, and gone out. May had returned to share the cabin with Kate. The men still came over for their meals, but now no music was played, no laughter rang out against the cold darkness pressing in on them. Kate avoided Hogan's eyes as she handed him his plate. He never pressed her. He simply waited, and Kate sensed a growing anger within him. The men often retired early to Axe's cabin, and Kate knew they'd begun to gamble again. May usually joined them, and Kate was left alone. She knew they were all puzzled and hurt by her attitude, but she couldn't change the way she felt.

She closed herself inward, holding the baby to her heart, concentrating on its well-being as if she could will away all dangers. She longed to tell Hogan. She imagined his face lighting up with the news, imagined the joy in his eyes, but then came the image of his face as he'd looked at the pitiful children in Dawson, and the harshness of his voice as he declared he would never have a child. She thought of Roxanne and the pouch Hogan had given her. Had she need for more proof than that? How carelessly he'd given away her gift to him. How little it had meant to him. In her melancholy the pouch came to symbolize her love for Hogan. He held both in low esteem, it seemed.

Now the snow became gray and dirty, yellowish in places, signs of treacherous footing, Axe reminded them. Beneath its crust the snow was soft. Spring was coming! The thought should have made her happy, but it didn't. She'd told Hogan she wanted to leave in the spring, and he'd made no effort to dissuade her. Did he want her to go after all? Was he tired of her? Did he even now long for Roxanne? Kate hugged the knowledge of the baby to her. Her full gown and the shawl she wore against the chill amply hid any thickening of the waist. Kate kept her secret well. Her anger against Hogan had waned, replaced now by a sad resignation.

"Kate . . ." His voice drew her head up from the

small gown she'd fashioned from one of her petticoats. Hogan stood in the doorway, his shoulders blotting out the light behind him. He looked as large and substantial as one of the hemlocks growing in the forest. Blankly she looked at him, automatically noticing that his dark hair fell across his forehead, that the scar on his cheek was nearly faded now, that his eyes were dark and liquid as they gazed at her. Hastily she stuffed the little gown beneath her shawl.

"What is it, Hogan?" she asked quietly, and watched as he stepped inside and slammed the door shut behind him.

"We have to talk," he said, striding across the room. "I've waited, thinking you might come to me."

"There's really nothing more to say between us," Kate answered. "I've told you the way I feel."

"I thought you might have changed your mind."

"No." The air was tense in the room. Kate wanted to look away from him. One eye watered from the strain of meeting his gaze.

"Are you sure, Kate?" he began, and to forestall any persuasion on his part, she got to her feet.

"Very sure," she answered. "You were right the first time, Hogan. I don't belong here."

"Do you hate it so much, then?" He waited. She let her silence be his answer. "What about us?"

"We'll keep our agreement. You're free to go on with your life as you wish. Once I return to Missouri, you'll never hear from me again."

He'd been about to cross the room and draw her into his arms. Her words, uttered so coolly, so reasonably, stopped him cold. He whirled and stalked out of the cabin, closing the door behind him with a bang. Slowly Kate slid back onto her stool. Beneath her shawl her knuckles were white from gripping them so hard. She brought out the little gown. It was wadded and wrinkled now, and seemed woefully inadequate. Burying her face in it, she began to weep bitterly.

How could everything go so wrong? *Do you hate it so much?* he'd asked, and it seemed he meant himself, not just the Yukon. How she'd longed to throw herself into his arms and plead for reassurance, but Hogan's words couldn't comfort her now. They were not enough. His strength wasn't enough to pit against the fierce land. It wasn't that she hated the Yukon. She was just fearful of its wild, untamed beauty. She hated what it did to people.

Spring came with a roar as river ice melted and rushed away toward the sea. A year ago they had struggled along that river, fought its swift fury to travel here. Now they watched as the raging waters swept over the banks.

"Get back to the cabins," Hogan shouted as they stood down by the river watching ice float by, carrying trapped animals or bits of flotsam before it. Hogan waved and yelled again. Kate saw the urgency in his face and glanced at May. Wide-eyed and fearful, they scurried back along the creek bank to the cabins. Hogan and Axe were already there hauling out bedding and handing it up to Thor on the roof.

"What are you doing?" Kate cried, rushing forward.

"The river's flooding. Kate, get some food, hurry," Hogan ordered, and obediently she gathered up the pot of stew simmering at the back of the stove and the fresh bread she'd baked just that morning. She threw it into one of the canvas bags and handed it up to Thor.

"Get some fresh water," Axe yelled to May, who was already scrambling up onto the roof.

"I'll get it," Kate called, and handed up some water buckets.

"Climb up," Hogan said, indicating the ladderlike arrangement of logs at one corner. He gave Kate a boost up to the first step, then turned away to give the camp a final check. Above, Thor leaned down to catch her hand.

"Oh, I forgot something," Kate cried, thinking of the tiny white baby gown she'd tucked into one of the shelves.

"Kate, come back," Thor cried, but she was already sliding down the makeshift ladder. Inside the cabin she found the folded garment and slipped it into her pocket. Quickly she ran back to the ladder. Water lapped at her feet. The river had already crept back to their cabins in that short period of time since Hogan called his warning. Automatically she looked around for him. He was down by the pits, trying to secure the equipment. Someone should go to help him, she thought, and took a step forward. The water was already past her ankles. Kate waded across the clearing to him.

"What do you need done?" she called.

Hogan's head snapped up. "Get back to the cabin," he shouted. His angry gaze left her face, looking at something beyond her shoulder. Kate saw the anger turn to fear, and glanced backward. A wall of water rushed toward them. Kate felt Hogan's iron grip on her shoulder just before the icy waters knocked her to her knees.

"Hogan," she cried, and tried to get to her feet, but the water rushed them forward over the creek and toward a stand of trees.

"Hang on, Kate," he called, not relinquishing his hold on her. "Try to grab hold of that tree." Kate flung out her arms, her hands gripping the slender trunk of a cottonwood. The bark scraped her bare skin. One finger bent at an odd angle. Pain shot through her hand; then the finger went numb. Kate's grip on the scrubby tree nearly broke, but she dug in her nails and hung on. Terror-stricken, she looked around for Hogan. He was clinging to a nearby tree.

"Hang on, Kate," he called. The icy water swirled around them, trying to wrench them free of their precarious hold. Kate was shivering uncontrollably now. Soon she wouldn't be able to hang on.

Hogan looked at her worriedly. "We've got to get out of this icy water," he said, looking back at the cabin. His expression lit up. "Hold on just a little while longer, Kate. Thor's coming. Can you make it?"

Frightened, she nodded. She wasn't sure if she could or not. Hogan peered at her closely. Her lips were already turning blue.

"Talk to me, Kate," he said. "Tell me how you're doing."

Again she nodded.

"Tell me, Kate," he shouted. "Yell it out to me."

"I . . . I c-can't," she stammered, concentrating on clinging to the cottonwood. "I . . . I'm so c-cold. My hands are numb."

"Don't let go, Kate," Hogan shouted urgently. Caught in her own world of misery, she didn't respond. "Dammit, Kate. I told you to hang on," Hogan bellowed. "I'm tired of wet-nursing you, Kathleen Moira O'Shea. You hang on to that tree."

"I am," Kate shouted back, irritated by his bossiness. "Don't worry about me, Mr. O'Shea. I'm able to take care of myself and my b—" Surging water swamped her just in time. Kate spat out dirty river water and took a deep breath. "Just take care of yourself."

"You never listen to me," Hogan yelled back. "If you'd just done what I told you and climbed up on the roof with the others, we wouldn't have this problem."

"I was trying to help you," Kate shouted back. "I don't know why I bothered. Small thanks I get."

He could see her clinging to the tree with more strength now. He hid a laugh. Get Kate mad and she could survive anything. "If I'd needed your help, I'd have asked for it," he scoffed derisively. "Next time—"

"Next time don't bother to ask," Kate yelled, "because I'll never lend you a helping hand again. You can just get swept away for all I care."

Thor was to her now. Kate turned to face him. He had a rope tied to his waist. Now he tied it around the tree and turned to Kate.

"Ve go back now, *ja?*"

"*Ja!*" Kate said. "But what about Hogan?"

"Go on, Kate," Hogan yelled. "When you get back to the cabin, I'll tie the rope around my waist and Thor can pull me in."

Thor shook his head. "*Ja!* Is best."

"Let's go," Kate said, and slid her arms around the big Swede's shoulders. He started out, pulling himself toward the cabin by the rope. In spite of her fear, Kate kept looking back at Hogan where he bobbed against the stunted trees. He'd always seemed so invincible to her. Now the broad panorama of sky, mountains, and flooding river dwarfed him, made him mortal, puny, like other men. Kate laid her head on Thor's shoulder so she wouldn't have to look at Hogan anymore. She felt like weeping, torn between her love for Hogan and her love for her unborn child. She blinked back the tears. She had to be strong. She couldn't lean on Hogan anymore.

They were at the cabin now, and Thor handed her up to May and Axe. "Take off wet clothes," May ordered, and held a blanket while Kate peeled away the icy clinging garments. The two men had turned back to help Hogan. Kate could see him in the distance. He'd untied the end of the rope and now was being pulled through the churning waters toward the cabin.

No sooner was the last piece of wet clothing gone than May swaddled Kate into blankets and urged her into a bedroll. They couldn't build a fire here on the board roof. Gratefully Kate sank into the blissful warmth of her makeshift bed. Her hand hurt abominably. May returned with a couple of small sticks, shaved from the roof boards, and tied them around Kate's injured finger. By that time Hogan was back. He was shaking from the cold, and Kate watched as May helped him strip down and wrapped him in blankets as well.

Hogan glanced at Kate. "Are you all right?" he asked. Kate nodded.

"How's your hand?" Silently she held out her hand for his inspection. He took off the splints and examined the finger, moving it gently. Kate jumped and cried out. "It's broken, Kate," he said, and turned to May. "Bring the whiskey bottle."

Kate looked at him distrustfully. "What are you going to do?" she asked fearfully. Her green eyes were enormous in her pale face.

"We have to set that finger, Kate. We don't know how long we'll be here on the roof. You don't want it to start healing like this. It'll always be crooked and not bend for you."

"You're going to do it?" she asked, swallowing hard.

"I have to. Take a sip of this." He held out the bottle of whiskey.

"Can't you wait until we see a doctor?" she insisted weakly, then held out her hand. He'd already listed the reasons why they couldn't wait.

"It's going to hurt some," Hogan said, and his face was as pale as hers must be. "I'm sorry." Before she could answer, he took hold of the finger and pulled. Pain shot up Kate's arm. She screamed. Tears flowed from between her tightly squeezed lids. She felt faint and wished for unconsciousness, but it never came.

"There, I think it's back in place," Hogan said, taking up the splints again. Carefully he tied them into place, wrapping them with leather strips so the whole hand was held rigid. When he was finished he turned to look at Kate. Every freckle on her face stood out in stark relief. "Take some more whiskey," he said softly. "It's going to ache for a while longer."

Painfully Kate nodded, unable to speak. She cradled the injured hand against her chest like a helpless wounded bird. She lay on her back, staring up at the gray sky while silent tears ran down her temples and into the fur of her makeshift bed.

"Kate," Hogan began, but she turned her face away from him, not wanting him to touch her ever again. She didn't see the hurt in his eyes, but May did.

"Kate feel better later," she said consolingly, and Hogan could do nothing but be patient. Getting to his feet, he walked to the edge of the roof to stand by the other men while they stared out at the devastation.

"Goot thing the cabin held, *ja?*" Thor asked with his eternal optimism.

"We built it to hold in a flood," Axe said. "Nearly every spring this river floods its banks. It'll be down in a day or two and everything'll be back to normal."

Normal! Kate thought bitterly. What was normal in this place? She held her tongue, turning her anger and pain in on herself, nursing it, using it to whip her resolve. She would leave here and never come back, never. The gold be damned. She hugged her arms around her stomach. No one had noticed yet that the once flat planes of her midsection now had a slight curve, a tiny burgeoning that signaled her baby was growing. But Kate had noticed, and now she let her hands cup protectively around that curve, soothing her child, reassuring it.

Love welled through her such as she'd never felt for any other being, not Aunt Petty or Gilly or even Hogan himself. It was mother love, the strongest and fiercest kind of all. It would carry her away from this place of deprivation and isolation, back to a place of civilization where she could find the care she and her baby would need. Her mother love would carry her away from the man who was her life. Her life, not her child's.

She owed her child a better chance than he would have here in this wilderness. Kate closed her eyes tightly, shutting away the sight of Hogan's strong rugged figure silhouetted against the sky and floodwaters. Once again he seemed invincible, but she knew differently. She'd seen him struggling against nature's fury. She'd sensed his fear, fear for her, but fear nonetheless.

Eventually she slept. May and Hogan decided not to waken her for some of the cold stew. She looked pale and exhausted lying there against the rough blankets. Hogan touched her cheek, wishing she could know, even in sleep, all the love he felt for her. Why had she become so aloof, so withdrawn from him? Why? He blinked rapidly against a sting of tears. He was reduced to this, he thought, crying like a baby over a woman, yet he'd never go backward to the man he had been before he knew Kate. She was his glory woman. The thought warmed him as no blankets could. Through the night he sat beside her, listening to the river water lap against the sides of the cabin, watching ice floes glide by like silent ships sailing majestically toward the sea.

It took two days before the water receded enough for them to come down off the roof. Two days and two nights of clinging to the tiny roof, of having no fire, no hot food. Kate couldn't eat the greasy cold stew they'd saved. She munched on the stale bread and thought of the shriveled potatoes they'd forgotten in the corner of the cabin. On the third morning they woke to find they could reclaim their camp. Eagerly they climbed down and walked about in the muddy yard, trying to work their stiff joints. Kate and May examined the cabins, shaking their heads at the sodden, muddy condition of them. Wearily Kate picked up a bucket and headed to the creek for water. Instantly Hogan was beside her, taking the bucket from her good hand.

His dark eyes studied her. "You're going to have to take it easy until that hand heals," he said, motioning to the arm draped in a makeshift sling. "May and the rest of us will clean up."

"Thank you," Kate said quietly, her manner aloof.

"Everything's going to be all right, Kate," Hogan tried again. "Spring is here. The worst is over."

"For a few months, and then the cycle starts all over again."

Hogan said nothing, lowering his eyes almost shamefacedly, as if she'd accused him of some wrongdoing.

"Spring is here." Kate repeated his words. "And you promised to send me back once spring came."

Hogan's head jerked up. "I thought you might have decided to stay," he said hopefully. "Look around you, Kate. It's not so bad. The land is beautiful, even now with the flood."

"It isn't the land that holds you here, Hogan," she spat, her green eyes glinting with anger. "It's the gold. You're willing to risk your life every day for love of a few glittering nuggets."

"There's more than a little gold here, Kate. It's there in those mounds of dirt we've dug up. I know it. I feel it."

"Oh, Hogan . . ." Kate gripped the front of his

shirt. "Give it up. Don't you see what's happening to you, to us, all of us? We find enough gold to tantalize us to stay, enough gold to go to Dawson once or twice a year to buy just enough food to keep us alive through another horrible winter. I don't want to become like those old sourdoughs and their wives, beaten down by the land and the cold, content just to survive. I don't want that to happen to you. Come away with me. Please."

Hogan was silent for so long, Kate held her breath waiting for his answer. Slowly he shook his head, and her breath hissed from her in frustration and disappointment.

"I can't, Kate. I'm not good for anything else but mining gold. It's all I've ever done in my life. If I quit now, it would be like admitting I'm a nobody. I'm a man. I'd do anything for you, Kate, but this. I can't quit, not when we're so close." He gripped her arm, his big hand wrapping around her frail wrist. "Stay with me awhile longer, Kate. Believe in me."

Kate took a step backward, afraid to be too close to him, to feel the heat of his body calling hers, to see the love and pleading in his strong face. "I can't," she cried, her voice rising on a plaintive note. "Not anymore. I want to go back. Now, today."

Hogan held her with his gaze, with his grip on her arm. He'd pressed her hand against his chest, and she felt the rapid thud of his heart. For a moment she thought he meant to refuse her request; then his shoulders slumped in defeat. He released the grip on her hand. "Get your things together," he said raggedly. "I'll get the boat ready to go." Now that the words were said, now that the going was a reality, she felt doubt spear through her; then her stomach, empty and cramping from lack of food, filled with bile. Before he could see her retch, she whirled and ran away from him, going blindly to the cabin.

It didn't take her long to gather up her meager belongings. Tearfully May helped. Wordlessly the two women embraced. Somberly Kate shook hands with Axe and Thor, and then Hogan was helping her into the boat. Kate waved to the people onshore, but only Thor waved back. They set off downriver, letting the current carry them along swiftly. Little was said between Hogan and Kate. Both seemed to hold their emotions tightly in check. By dusk their boat bumped against the wharves at Dawson.

Hogan saw her safely to the new hotel that had been erected since their last visit. Then, with a final tug at his hat, he bade her a wordless good-bye and stalked away down the street. Through tear-filled eyes Kate watched as he turned into the Lucky Lady. He'd lost no time in returning to Roxanne Blayne. Miserably she entered the hotel. She'd never felt so alone in her life.

17

Once again Dawson had changed. Gone was the hopeless mood of winter. Spring had come, and with it a new rush of people. Like an aging whore wishing to gain an air of respectability and to hide the ravages of hard living, the city's face was undergoing a renovation. Store owners erected fancy storefronts over the original cabins.

With the river open, miners had surged into town to spend the gold they'd spent the winter mining. The click of dice and the whirl of the wheel filled the air day and night. Kate felt lonely in the midst of such teeming humanity. Then one day Clay Lawford and Uly came to town with news of their rich strike.

"I'll tell you, Kate, it was the loneliest winter I've ever spent," Clay said as they lingered over a supper of bear steak and flour dumplings in the hotel dining room. She hadn't seen Uly since the day of his arrival. He spent most of his time at the gaming tables.

"I know what you mean," she answered Clay. "It was the same at Sweetwater, even with May there." She'd already told him of May's dramatic rescue.

"I'm never going out again," Clay stated adamantly.

"But what about your claim?" Kate asked in dismay.

"I'll hire someone to do the digging for a share of the profits."

"Can you do that?" Her eyes were large and emerald green and Clay found himself wondering for the thousandth time what she was doing here without Hogan. He sensed a deep sadness in her. He brought his attention back to her question.

"There are plenty of men who haven't been lucky. They're glad to share someone else's fortune." He leaned forward and smiled into her eyes. "Enough about gold. Have you seen the theater group that's come to town? I hear they're extraordinary."

Clay was a gallant and attentive escort that evening and in the days that followed. Though the river was free of ice, a steamer would take several weeks to make its way to Dawson, often not arriving until mid-July. As much as she enjoyed his company, Kate felt a vague uneasiness about their time together. She was a married woman, and her current plans to leave made her no less so. Somehow, she hoped Hogan would give in and join her for the trip back to Seattle. She'd heard nothing from him since he'd first brought her to Dawson.

Iris Garrett was a godsend. She came into Dawson three weeks after Kate's arrival, and her down-to-earth humor and common sense were like a tonic.

"You'll not stay in this cesspot of human corruption and degradation," she declared grandly. "The trading post is just eight miles away and the steamer stops as well. You'll be far better off there than in Dawson getting into mischief." Kate knew Iris disapproved of her seeing Clay Lawford.

"That's very kind of you," she began, "but I don't want to impose—"

"Besides, I could use the company." Iris brushed aside her words as if she hadn't spoken. "I haven't talked to a white woman since the last time we were in Dawson, leastwise not one that said anything worth listening to. You'd be doing me a heap of a favor."

"I'd love to come," Kate said, and thought what an understatement that was. Despite Clay's attentiveness, she'd been lonely and uncomfortable sleeping alone in the hotel, where people came and went at all hours of the night. To go out, she must pass through the lobby, where men ogled her and tried to engage her in conversation. With Roxanne, Cheechako Lil, the Virgin, and myriad other whores available to them, they still had a need to seek out a lady, and especially Taffy Kate.

Her exploits were still recounted. Kate had grown tired of their elaborate courtliness and contrasting boisterous ways. They reminded her too readily of Hogan and Axe and all the other sourdoughs she'd met since coming to the Yukon. Now she packed up her belongings once more and followed Iris Garrett down to her boat which would carry them to the trading post at Fort Reliance.

The trading post was like any other along the Yukon. Hastily set up to meet the needs of the hordes of miners pushing into the Klondike, it had improved little since. The rough log buildings were sturdy and warm in winter, cool and dank in summer. The original hard-packed earthen floor had given way to one of rough planks. Large glass windows had been cut in the front to display wares. Otherwise the trading post stood as it always had, foursquare and substantial in the middle of a wilderness.

The Garretts' living arrangements had been built off the back and were surprisingly roomy. The bottom floor comprised two rooms, one large and open, which was used for cooking, eating, and visiting. A cot in one corner accommodated extra guests. The second room was a bedroom used by Iris and Bud Garrett.

A ladder led to a spacious loft. Since Iris and Bud had no children, the loft was used as additional storage and its meager hoard of food carefully guarded. Though winter was over, it might still be months before a steamer could make its way through the Bering Sea and up the ice-choked Yukon River. The summer before, the town of Dawson had been reduced to a diet of flour and water for a few weeks. Now, with careful doling out of the last of their supplies, the Garretts hoped to avoid the near-starvation that had occurred before.

"I hope you'll be comfortable on the cot," Iris said. "We could move it up to the loft for you, but I don't think you ought to be climbing that ladder in your condition."

Kate spun around to look at the older woman. "Is it so apparent?"

"Only to another woman," Iris answered kindly. At the sad confusion in Kate's eyes, she bustled toward the stove and set a kettle on to boil. "Now, you just store your gear on that shelving back in the corner and come sit by the fire. I'll have us some tea in no time."

Gratefully Kate did as she was told. The dull ache in her heart lessened somewhat at Iris' comforting ways. Kate hated to admit that part of her unhappiness came from missing May and Axe and Thor. She wouldn't allow herself to think about Hogan.

Kate settled into the routine at the post, even helping to wait on customers, miners straggling in from their claims for much needed supplies, and Indians who paid in furs or bits of nuggets they too had dug from the ground. Kate got so she knew some of the regulars who came in and joked with them easily. Those who'd known her before affectionately called her Taffy Kate, and the other miners picked it up. Seeing a good thing, Iris and Kate made up a plate of the molasses candy and put a tray out on the counter. They were surprised at how quickly it sold.

As long as she stayed busy, Kate was all right, but at night, alone in her cot, her thoughts turned back to the Sweetwater Creek camp and Hogan. The creek cabins held all the people who were important in her life. Now that she'd had some time away from them, they seemed eminently dear to her, and the isolation and hardships of the winter were quickly forgotten in the glory of a hillside blossoming with golden dryas and daisies. The hemlock forests would be all green with new leaves, the tree trunks and forest floor made velvety with green moss and gray-green lichens.

If she returned to Missouri, she would be alone—safe and comfortable, but alone. How could she be so willing to settle for a secure, dull life back in Missouri after experiencing the exhilaration of the Yukon and of Hogan O'Shea? She began to consider going back to the cabin. She could tell Hogan about the baby, and perhaps he would want it after all. Perhaps he would throw his arms around her and welcome her back. Then she remembered the winter and May weak and shaken with fever while her limbs erupted in sores and her toes turned black from scurvy, and she hesitated. She must think of her child. All the gold in the Yukon couldn't buy him food if there were none to buy, nor would it buy warmth from the blizzards and fifty-below temperatures, or safety from the icy floodwaters in the spring.

"You're working too hard," Iris said one day. "We need a break. We'll go to Dawson. I understand some packers are bringing in goods over the mountain passes."

"Go without me, Iris," Kate said. "I'd prefer to stay here."

"Nonsense!" Iris brushed aside her protests. "No one will guess you're expecting a child, if that's what you're worrying about. Them skirts and that shawl keep you hidden. You need a change."

"Thanks anyway."

"Hogan O'Shea might be there."

"That's what I'm afraid of."

Iris' shrewd expression faded. She'd felt sure that would entice Kate, for if ever she'd seen a woman in love, Iris was sure that woman was Kate. She still held out hope that Kate and Hogan would get back together. Sighing in frustration, she turned away. But the morning she was dressed and ready to board the *Yukon Queen*, the little steamboat they used to ply the river, Kate joined her without a word of explanation. Iris knew without asking that she was going to Dawson in hopes of seeing Hogan again.

The little steamboat chugged the eight miles up the river and tied up at a wharf in Dawson. Kate's face was eager as she followed Iris over the gangplank and up Main Street. Nearly six weeks had passed since she was last here, but the town had once again undergone a metamorphosis. More buildings had been thrown up hastily for the miners who continued to stream into the town. Its population had doubled. There were now ten saloons in town, some no more than tents. The sound of sawing and hammering filled the air as men rushed to put up buildings helter-skelter. But nothing could change the muddy streets, although logs had been embedded in the mud and rough planks laid across them to provide better footing.

The town had indeed changed. Besides the saloons, new gaming halls had gone in, and the raucous call of dealers and the disappointed shouts of men who'd not enjoyed the benevolence of Lady Luck could be heard even in the streets. And all this so early in the morning. Kate and Iris looked at each other. They passed Mame's place. Mame and her prostitutes had been moved back away from the main street of town now into a place called Hell's Half Acre. Cribs, small boxlike buildings with wide front windows where the women sat displaying their wares, lined these back streets. The whores were no longer allowed on Main Street until evening, but the miners with gold in their pockets and little to spend it on save wine, women, and gambling found them at all hours of the day and night.

Clucking her tongue in disapproval, Iris led Kate past these back streets and up the incline to the log cabin where Father Luke had set up his hospital. The gaunt priest was bending over the bed of a patient when he glanced up and saw Kate. Immediately he left the bedside and rushed forward to greet her.

"Kate," he cried, gripping her hands. "It's good to see you. How is your finger?" She'd gone to have it examined when she first arrived.

"Hello, Father," she replied. "Well, I believe. How is the hospital? Have you enough supplies and food?"

"There's never enough, I fear," Father Luke said wearily, and when Kate began to open her bag, he pushed her hands away. "There's no need to give us more gold dust now. You have been most generous. No, we have plenty of that, but there are no medicines or foods to buy yet."

"Iris heard that some packers had gotten through over the Chilkoot."

"Ah, yes," the priest sighed. "They've come bringing gewgaws, frivolous things of no value. Another piano, handsome new clothes. Look in the shops as you pass by. You will see new feather hats, starched collars, gold eating utensils, silver teapots. There is little tea left to serve, but anyone who wishes to purchase a tea service can serve it with style. Bah! Why did they not bring in potatoes or tinned fruits and medicine?"

The two women remained silent in the face of his passionate denouncement.

"Look, look here, what I must do to fashion plaster." He showed them how he'd dipped strips of muslin into a flour-and-water paste.

"Does it work?" Iris asked in her blunt manner.

Father Luke shrugged. "It works better than nothing." After visiting awhile longer, Kate and Iris retraced their steps to the shops along Main Street. Decry the frivolousness of packers though the priest would, Kate couldn't help gazing into the shops, marveling at the new merchandise. A new French couturiere had set up shop in the place where Mame had once had her business. On impulse, perhaps drawn by the memories she had of Hogan and herself here in one of the back rooms, Kate stepped inside.

"May I help you, *mademoiselle?*" inquired the tall elegant Frenchwoman, who eyed Kate's slender figure. "I am Madame Remy."

"*Oui,*" Kate said breathlessly. "I wish to have a new gown made. Is it possible?"

"*Mais oui,* I have several bolts of material from which you may choose, and I can start immediately."

"I have particular specifications for my gown," Kate explained, and paused, not knowing how to convey what she wanted.

The Frenchwoman's knowing eyes dipped to her waist and stomach. "*Je comprende.* I understand. A tuck here and there which can be let out as needed and taken in again as needed." The seamstress took out a tape measure and slipped it around Kate's waist.

Kate chose a blue-and-gold damask material that Madame Remy agreed to make up in a gown of simple lines with a bolero jacket and leg-of-mutton sleeves. The skirt would be cut with clever box pleats to conceal the extra fabric needed to accommodate Kate's pregnancy later. The gown would be ready in less than a week, and Madame Remy agreed to send it down to the trading post.

Kate and Iris left the shop and sauntered along the street, enjoying the sunshine on their shoulders, the firm boardwalk that held them away from the mud, and the shops with their windows filled with wares. It was almost like being home, Kate thought, only better. After being deprived of such civilized amenities as shops and pretty gowns for so long a time, her appreciation of them now was far greater.

"Oh, look, Kate," Iris cried. "There's the perfect bonnet to match your new gown."

Kate looked into the shop window and drew in her breath as she spied the blue felt bonnet with arching plumes of black ostrich feathers.

"The color's perfect for you," Iris said, and dragged Kate inside. Kate looked around, awed by the quantity of merchandise. Ladies' boots lined one wall, and gowns and petticoats hung along the other two. Kate took no time to look around. She went directly to the hat in the window.

"Would you like to try it on, ma'am?" the salesclerk asked.

"Yes, I would," Kate said, her eyes shining. She held her breath while the woman lifted the hat off its box and brought it to her. Carefully Kate settled it on her head, tipping it rakishly so the feather brushed against her cheek.

"It looks wonderful on you, Kate," Iris gushed. "You must buy it."

"Oh, Iris, I don't know," Kate said reluctantly. "I still have to buy my ticket, and there are . . . other things I'll need to get." She was reluctant to mention the baby clothes she'd have to buy once she returned to Seattle.

"Nonsense," Iris said, and turned to the woman behind the counter. "How much is the bonnet?" she demanded imperiously. The woman told them, and Kate gasped.

"Two hundred and eighty dollars!" Quickly she took off the hat. "I'm sorry," she said, and handed it back. In disappointment she turned away to the shelves that held other items of clothing. For the first time she became aware of another customer in the store. Roxanne Blayne, her blond hair beautifully coiffed, her face carefully made up, and her gown impeccable even after crossing the muddy streets, stood watching her.

"Hello, Taffy Kate," she said, and laughed low and husky. She made the name sound like that of one of the whores of Pleasure Alley. In the months since Kate had seen Roxanne, she'd gained a measure of fame herself. She'd become one of the favorites of the miners, singing bawdy songs in her husky contralto voice and dancing with them until they nearly dropped.

She seldom took a man to her bed anymore, unless he was a very special customer, like Swiftwater Bill, who'd had the good fortune to strike it big and now hired other men to mine his gold while he spent hours inside the saloons and gambling houses of Dawson. He had taken an interest in Roxanne and she'd done everything she could to promote that interest, laughing at his crude jokes, entertaining him in her rooms, singling him out when she was onstage, playing to his enormous ego. Her efforts had paid off handsomely. She was one of the best-dressed women in town, and best of all, Swiftwater Bill had claimed her services almost exclusively as his. He paid well. Now, with an arrogance that stemmed from her substantial and increasing wealth, Roxanne glided across the floor.

"I'd like to try on that hat," she said in a clear, ringing voice that Kate couldn't help but hear. Fussily Roxanne settled it on her head and stood peering into the mirror, studying her reflection one way and then another. "Yes, yes, I like it," she said, and turned to Kate. "What do you think?"

"It . . . It's a lovely hat," Kate mumbled, and wished she'd never come into the shop.

"It is, isn't it?" Roxanne said, tipping her head to one side and smiling at her reflection. "Do you think Hogan will like it?" Her bright gaze caught Kate's in the mirror, gauging her reaction.

Kate strove to hide her hurt. "I . . . You'll have to ask him that."

"I believe I'll take it," Roxanne said ever so brightly. "I want to surprise Hogan when he comes. He loves to see me all dressed up. He says he can't stand women who go around in those horrible drab old things." While she chattered, she opened her bag and pulled out the hide pouch with Hogan's initials stitched into it. Kate took an instinctive breath and tried to let it out slowly, while she felt her knees trembling. Shaking gold dust onto a scale, Roxanne pulled the leather thongs together tightly so none would escape, and lightly tossed the bag.

"Hmm, I'm running low. I'll have to get more from Hogan the next time he comes. He's so generous." Deliberately Roxanne made no reference to Swiftwater Bill and the real source of her new wealth.

"Kate!" Iris said, and only the sharpness of her tone kept Kate from swooning. Taking hold of her waist, Iris guided Kate out to the boardwalk and along the street until they were well away from the shop and Roxanne Blayne. Iris guided her into a saloon and ordered a drink, ignoring the curious stares of men who weren't used to seeing ladies in their midst.

"Oh, Iris," Kate said, blubbering into her handkerchief. "He's been to Dawson to see Roxanne, but he couldn't come on to the trading post to see me."

"Maybe he didn't know," Iris began, but Kate shook her head.

"I left word where I'd be. He just doesn't want to see me again. He doesn't love me." She raised her ravaged face to Iris. "Perhaps he never did."

"Pshaw! I never heard such rubbish," Iris said, and

could think of nothing more. Silently she cursed Hogan O'Shea. He'd never find a finer woman than Kate. That selfish Roxanne Blayne would only take all his gold and leave him with nothing.

"I never asked you before, Kate," she said now, "why it was you left. Was it Hogan what sent you away, or did you leave on your own?"

"I . . . I left," Kate cried into her handkerchief. "I was frightened for my baby."

Iris nodded. She could understand that. Hadn't she buried her only child along a wild river in the Washington territory years ago? But that wasn't a reason to leave your man, not in Iris' estimation. Now she leaned forward and gripped Kate's arm.

"Now, you listen to me, Kate O'Shea," she snapped. "You just get yourself on back to Hogan and tell him about this baby and explain how come you was so afeered. He'll understand, once he knows. He'll take you back."

Kate shook her head. "I could never go back to him now," she said bleakly. "He's been unfaithful."

"You left him little choice."

"He could have come after me. He could have tried again to persuade me to come back. Instead he went to Roxanne. No, I won't ever go back to Hogan."

"Welcome to the Lucky Lady," a voice said pleasantly. Startled, Kate looked around. She'd been so absorbed in her misery that she hadn't noticed where Iris had brought her. Now she raised her eyes to the well-dressed gentleman standing before her and gasped.

"Clay Lawford!" Quickly she wiped her tear-streaked face and stood up.

"It's good to see you again, Kate," he said, glancing with an amused air at Iris Garrett. He was well aware the older woman didn't like him. "Are you back to stay or just for a visit?"

"Only for the day," Iris snapped, pointedly glaring at Clay's hand gripping Kate's.

"We came to do some shopping," Kate said, and smiled to soften Iris' sting. "You're looking elegant."

He no longer wore the rough miner's garb from the last time she had seen him. Now he was dressed in a well-tailored suit and fancy vest.

"Do you like it?" Clay asked, turning from one side to the other to give them the full benefit of his resplendent wardrobe.

"Humph, you look like a gambler," Iris said unyieldingly.

"Iris," Kate remonstrated.

"I do believe you're right, Mrs. Garrett," Clay said, unperturbed. "Do I look like the prosperous owner of the Lucky Lady?"

"Clay, you didn't," Kate cried in delight. He constantly surprised her.

He nodded. "I did. Uly lost his share of the mine in a gambling bet, so I bought the saloon. Uly and I are running it now. If the miners want to gamble, I intend to provide them with an honest place to do it."

"Oh, Clay, you are such a good friend. Uly was wise to take you as a partner," Kate said and hugged him.

His face sobered. "I'm always here as your friend too, Kate, if you ever need me."

"She don't need another friend. She's got me," Iris interjected, pursing her lips in obvious disapproval.

Clay grinned and bowed to her. "I'm here if ever *you* should need a friend, Mrs. Garrett," he replied. The grin died away, and for a moment Iris glimpsed the fineness of him. Like others before her, she found herself liking the young man. Still, she felt compelled to speak to Kate once they'd left the Lucky Lady and were making their way back to the *Yukon Queen*.

"It'd be mighty easy to have your head turned by a man like Clay Lawford," she observed.

Kate glanced at her. "Clay is a good friend. He could never be anything more."

"He's in love with you, you know."

"I know," Kate replied. "But I don't think I could ever love another man the way I loved Hogan."

Iris heard the pain in her voice and shook her head in wonder at the blind pride of the young.

* * *

The lack of food grew worse and the Indians were the hardest hit. They came in from the wilds to beg for food at the trading post. Iris gave them what she could, but her supplies were growing dangerously low. They all ran the risk of starving if the steamboats didn't make it down the river soon. It seemed incongruous to Kate that in the midst of summer's beauty and warmth they might starve. This season of joyful, riotous color offered no sweet harvest to stave off disaster. The paradox of that was not lost on Kate. It was the end of June, and daily outlooks prowled along the river bends, straining to catch a glimpse of the first steamer.

"Quentin and me's goin' down the river apiece to take a look-see," Bud Garrett said one morning. "We may be gone a few days, so don't worry none about us."

"All right," Iris agreed, and she and Kate stood at the wharf waving the men off.

"I'm right glad you're here at a time like this," Iris said. "This can get to be a real lonesome place when a woman's alone."

"I know what you mean," Kate said, thinking of the time when May had been with Frenchy and she'd been alone with Hogan and the other men. Even caught up in the wonder of Hogan's love, she sometimes had grown lonely for another woman's companionship.

Few people came to the post now. There was nothing to sell them when they did. Late in the afternoon, Tagish Dan came by, and when he learned that Quentin and Bud had gone downriver, he frowned and scratched his jaw. "I reckon it ain't likely nothing'll happen to you afore he gets back," he said. "But I'd make sure everything's locked up tonight. They's rumors some renegade Indians is out terrorizing the outlying camps, trying to steal their food and whatnot."

"Thanks for the warning, Dan," Iris said, and Kate marveled at her calm manner. But that night Iris took extra precautions to lock up and to place the heavy bars over the doors. The night passed without incident, and the women felt easier the next day. But near dusk, while walking along the riverbank, Kate caught a glimpse of movement across the river, and her blood ran cold. She took no time to second-guess herself or scoff at imagined dangers. She remembered the night on the trail when Lean Elk and his men had attacked the camp and tried to carry her away. Now she gathered up her skirts and walked as calmly as she could manage back up to the trading post. She arrived all breathless and trembling just as Iris was about to light a lamp.

"Don't," she gasped in warning. "Indians."

Iris looked at her pale face and blew out the match. "Where?"

"Across the river."

"Are you sure?"

Kate nodded. "They were skulking about in the trees. It was only by the merest chance that I caught sight of them."

"Maybe they mean us no harm," Iris muttered hopefully.

"If they meant no harm, they would come out in the open," Kate said. Iris crossed to the mantel, where two rifles hung. Kate pushed herself away from the wall and went to the drawer where extra shells were kept. Without talking, the women moved about in the twilight, barring the doors and shuttering the windows. Then they settled down to their lonely vigil.

Kate had lost track of time. Her eyes hurt from straining to see into the shadows, and her shoulders and back had grown stiff. Still, she didn't move away from the crack in the shutters.

"Kate!" Iris hissed from her post.

"I saw it," Kate answered, blinking her eyes once to clear her vision, to make sure the movement in the yard hadn't been the shadow of a tree moved by the wind. The shadow glided forward, followed by another and still another. The Indians were nearly to the post porch.

"Iris, don't call out to them," Kate warned. "We'll just shoot over their heads the first time, and maybe it'll scare them off. They won't be sure if the men are here or not."

"They must know the men are gone. The *Yukon Queen*'s gone."

"They won't know if we have some other men protecting us though," Kate said quietly.

"You're right." Iris took aim down her rifle barrel and got ready. "Here they come."

Kate's hands were slick with sweat. She tightened her grip on the gun barrel, remembering how it kicked, remembering the bear, remembering Lean Elk. She'd survived all these, and she would survive this.

There were three of them. The first dark shadow stepped up on the porch. Kate took a deep breath, held it, and pulled the trigger. She heard the report of the gun, felt it kick her shoulder, and nearly dropped it. Across the room, Iris fired. There was a cry of surprise outside. Kate peered through the shutters and saw the three Indians leap off the porch and disappear below the riverbank.

"We routed them," Iris said gleefully. She was already reloading.

"Do you think they'll come back?" Kate asked, doing the same.

"I don't know. We'd better not take a chance." Once again the two women took their posts. For hours they waited. Terror gave way to fatigue, and Kate's head bobbed as she fought sleep.

"Let's take turns trying to get some rest," she suggested finally, and one dozed fitfully while the other watched. Near dawn, the Indians returned. This time they came in a double line of five or six men each. The rest of them followed in no order behind.

"Iris," Kate cried. Instantly Iris leapt up from the floor and grabbed her rifle. "They're coming again," Kate said unnecessarily. "Looks like there are about fifty of them."

"Land o' Goshen!" Iris exclaimed softly. "We'll never be able to outfight that many."

"I know," Kate said. Her blood was hammering in her head.

"Wonder why they're walkin' like that?" Iris muttered.

Kate strained to make out the dark shadows in greater detail. The Indians looked as if they were carrying something large and solid between them. "It's a log!" she cried. "They're going to ram the door. Start firing."

Once again the women pulled their triggers and staggered from the recoil, then fired again. "I think I hit one," Iris called jubilantly. With trembling fingers they reloaded their rifles, casting quick glances through the shutters. Their barrage had stopped the Indians' advance. Two of them lay on the ground, while the others milled uncertainly. Kate's gun was loaded. Once again she steadied the barrel against the shutter and squeezed the trigger. An Indian slumped and fell to the ground. His companions looked around in confusion, then, dropping the log, ran back toward the river.

Iris cheered. Kate put her rifle down. She was trembling with fear and exhaustion. "I think we drove them off," Iris said. "Are you all right, Kate?" Anxiously she looked at her friend.

"I'm fine," Kate lied, and clenched her cold hands together to still their shaking. "We'd better keep watch, though."

"You rest awhile," Iris ordered.

Kate made no argument. Nausea washed through her as she huddled on the floor beneath the window. She'd shot a man. Even now he lay out there in a patch of dawn light, bleeding to death. She longed to run out and tend to him, to reassure herself that it was only a flesh wound, that the man would live and she would not have to meet her maker with this sin on her soul, but she didn't dare. For all they knew, the Indians might have only taken refuge below the riverbank. Tensely the women waited until full light. Timidly they unbarred the door and stepped out onto the porch. From behind the trees and bushes and sheds, Indians stepped forward into the yard. They held high a white surrender flag.

"We talk," the leader called.

"Talk," Kate said, and brought her rifle into full view, letting it rest in the crook of her arm.

"Me Little Bear. We come to post as friends," the leader said plaintively. His hair was long and straggly over his shoulders, his hide leggings thin and dirty.

"Friends don't come creeping in the night," Iris Garrett said stoutly.

"We come now in daylight," the Indian said, and smiled, his dark eyes crafty and sly in his narrow face. "We come for potlatch."

"We ain't havin' a potlatch," Iris said.

"Have potlatch," the Indian ordered imperiously, pounding his walking stick against the ground.

"No potlatch," Iris said. "Go away."

"Better angle toward the door," Kate said softly. Aloud she called to the Indian, "We have no food for a potlatch."

"We do not believe white woman," Little Bear shouted angrily. "Have potlatch. We be friends, go away without anger."

"You must go away now," Iris called, and edged toward the door. Little Bear had taken a few steps forward. Now Kate saw a movement out of the corner of her eye and whirled and fired. An Indian who'd crept out from the side of the trading post had lunged forward. Her shot stopped him in midair. He fell at their feet.

"Get inside, get inside," Kate chanted, and she and Iris ran into the trading post and slammed the door shut, barring it tightly. Quickly Kate moved to the window and placed her gun barrel against the shutter. She took careful aim and pulled the trigger. The bullet kicked up the dust in front of the Indians in the clearing, just as she'd intended. She couldn't bear to kill another man unless she had to. Iris followed suit, and the Indians leapt aside and once again melted away into the woods and behind any available covering. Breathlessly the two women waited. They'd taken no time for supper or breakfast this morning, and now, as the hours passed, their stomachs cramped and their lips were dry and parched from lack of water.

"Keep watch and I'll get us something," Iris said. Kate nodded and shifted slightly to ease the ache in her back. Her gaze never wavered from the front clearing. Iris was gone for only a short while before returning with cups of hot tea and stale bread spread with a little caribou butter. Despite her heaving stomach, Kate took it and nibbled, still keeping her rifle aimed into the front yard. The hot tea revived her somewhat. The women took turns relieving themselves in the chamber pot, then settled at their posts. There had been no sign of the Indians since their morning confrontation, but Kate had little doubt they were still there. The menace of their presence still stirred the air, raising the hair along her arms. Where were the miners who sometimes dropped by? she wondered. Where were Bud and Quentin? Where were Hogan and Axe and Thor? She wished them all here. But she and Iris were alone. Alone!

Dusk lay in long dark pools of shadow in the clearing and turned the river's surface to a mirror. Robins chirped in trees nearby. A soft breeze blew through a stand of cottonwood, rattling the leaves; then all was still again. Kate felt the tension grow between her shoulder blades, and she stood at attention, her eyes once again scanning the riverbank.

All was quiet—too quiet, too still. They waited, and slowly grew aware of the smell of smoke wafting through the rooms.

"Kate, they've set the building on fire," Iris called, leaning her rifle against the wall and running to the living area. The logs in one corner were already blazing. The two women grabbed up the water buckets and emptied the contents on the fire, but it had little effect. Grabbing up blankets, they began to beat at the flames.

"It's too late, Iris," Kate called. "We can't put it out." A sound at the front of the building brought her back to the shuttered windows. The renegades had once again surged up the riverbank and taken up the log with the intent of pounding down the door. Kate snatched up her rifle and began firing wildly into their midst.

"Iris," she screamed, and the other woman came running. "Close the door between the two rooms," Kate yelled. "It'll keep the fire out of here for a while."

Screaming like demons out of some terrible nightmare, the renegade Indians overran the post yard, shouting and yelling. One leapt upon the porch and grabbed the barrel of Kate's gun, trying to yank it away from her. She struggled, then pulled the trigger. The gun exploded point-blank into his face. Blood filled the holes that once had been his eyes. Kate screamed and retched onto the floor at her feet. Sweaty and trembling, she leaned against the wall, trying to control her body's heaving rejection of the bread and tea she'd had earlier, and all the while her vision was filled with the gushing blood of the dead Indian.

The sight of the mangled Indian seemed to stop the rest of the renegades. They fell back, their dark gaze moving from side to side as they tried to discern if someone other than the women inside could have wrought this terrible wound. The fire would soon draw people from Dawson or Klondike City. With a silent signal from their leader, they fell back from the burning post and slunk back to the river, where they climbed into their canoes and paddled away.

Inside the trading post the women coughed against the smoke and fumes of the fire. They should leave the building, but the horror of what awaited them outside was far worse than the horror inside, so they remained with eyes tearing and lungs bursting from want of fresh air.

"Here they come again," Iris cried, and Kate pushed herself off the floor, wiped her running nose and eyes on her skirt, and put the rifle back in place against the shutters. She tried not to think about the Indian lying on the porch. Squinting against the smoke, she took aim as the men surged up the riverbank. Rapidly she blinked to clear her vision, then blinked again.

"Iris, they're not Indians," she cried. "It's Hogan and the men from Dawson."

"Praise be to God," Iris said fervently, and helped

Kate unbolt the heavy door. They pulled it open and ran out into the sweet, fresh air.

"Kate!" Hogan called, his face radiant when he saw her. He ran forward and caught her in his arms. The other men ran to grab up buckets and put out the fire. "Thank God you're all right," he whispered. "When we saw the fire, we thought we were too late."

Hogan knew he should go help with the fire, but Kate was in his arms and he couldn't bear to put her aside. His arms tightened around her and he buried his face in her hair. All around them was noise and excitement as men battled the blaze, but Kate barely noticed. She lay against his chest, drinking in the familiar smell and feel of him. His arms were a haven around her. His unshaven jaw was rough against her brow. She closed her eyes while tears streamed down her face.

The fire was soon brought under control and the men stood with beaming soot-smeared faces, still spoiling for a fight with the renegades.

"Reckon they slunk off in the night, the cowardly bastards."

"Shore looks like the ladies held their own," another man observed, nodding toward the bodies of two dead Indians that had been pulled to one side, away from the fire.

"We ought to've roasted 'em." Tagish Dan spat contemptuously.

"Ain't no need to cook their food for 'em," Axe said stoically, and Kate turned away to be sick. Immediately Iris ran to put an arm around her.

"How'd you men know to come down here?" she asked to change the subject.

"I got to talking to some other fellas down at the Lucky Lady," Tagish Dan recounted. "When I heard how these renegades've been attacking outlying camps and posts, I expressed concern about you ladies left all alone down here. Hogan heard us talkin', and right away he says we got to git down here and check on you. The whole bunch of us just jumped into our boats and come on down."

"We're so glad you did," Kate said, looking at Hogan gratefully. "I don't know what we would have done. We were near the end of our strength. I'm sure the Indians would have gotten through the next time they rushed us."

Several of the men smiled at each other. "The Indians were gone when we got here, Kate," Hogan said mildly, his own face wreathed in smiles.

"You two ladies plumb scared the dickens outta them," Tagish Dan cried, and the men behind them good-naturedly called their congratulations.

"Well, I reckon this ain't much good for sleepin' in tonight," Iris said, staring at the scorched, smoking building. "Will you men give us a lift back to Dawson?"

"Sure thing, Miz Garrett," a couple of them said.

Kate looked at Iris, who stood ruefully studying her home and store. Her feet were firmly planted in the muddy yard, her fists resting on her hips, her gray-streaked dark hair falling around her shoulders, her gown tattered and soiled, her face soot-smeared. No one had ever looked more capable, more indomitable than Iris. Kate's heart went out to her and she hugged her briefly.

"I'm sorry about your home," she said softly.

"Shoot, it can be rebuilt. Soon's Bud and Quentin get back here, we'll get started. We'll be ready to open again by the time the steamer pulls in with new supplies. In the meantime, hadn't you better talk to Hogan and tell him about that baby? He deserves to know. He loves you."

"Do you think he does?" Kate asked softly, her heart skipping a beat.

Iris nodded. "He come all the way up here to save you."

"He would have done that for anyone in trouble."

"His face wouldn't have looked all white and pasty like a man who's about to see his worst nightmare come true," Iris snapped. "Now, you cut out all the doubtin' and you forget about that saloon girl back there in Dawson. She don't mean a hill o' beans to him. Now, go tell him about that baby."

Kate's face was anxious as she went to find Hogan. He was standing with a cluster of men, but when he saw her approach, he broke away and came immediately to take her hands in his.

"What can I do for you, Kate?" he asked. There was a brusqueness to his manner that disconcerted her.

"I . . . I wanted to thank you for coming down here the way you did," she answered, stalling for time while she found a way to break the news to him. This wasn't the best time or place. Perhaps she'd be wiser to put it off.

He bobbed his head in acknowledgment. "I'll make arrangements for you at the hotel," he said. "It should be for only a week or two. The boat's due in anytime."

His words fell like lead around Kate, wounding her as the Indians had been unable to do. He wanted her to go!

"That's all right," she answered proudly. "Clay will put us up."

"You can't mean you'd stay at the Lucky Lady?" Hogan cried in consternation.

Kate arched her eyebrows. "Why, of course we will," she answered calmly, as if she were speaking of the finest hotel back home. "And please don't let my presence there deter you from your comings and goings, Mr. O'Shea." She saw Hogan's mouth tighten.

"I see you lost no time in going back to Clay," he said flatly.

"Clay offered me help, should I need it," she replied airily.

He grabbed hold of her arm. "If you needed help, I was there."

"I had no way of knowing that. I haven't seen you since you brought me to Dawson."

He let go of her, almost flinging her arm away from him. "This is the real reason you stopped loving me, isn't it, Kate?" he demanded. "You found out Clay

Lawford was back in Dawson and that he'd made a rich strike."

Kate stared at him, thunderstruck that he could have so low an opinion of her. Without thinking, she drew back her hand and swung as hard as she could, enjoying the stinging pain as she connected with his jaw. His cheek grew red; his eyes hardened.

She hardly knew he'd retaliated, so quickly had he moved, until she felt the dull sting against her own cheek. Her eyes watered and she shut them for a moment. When she opened them again, Hogan had swung around and was stalking toward the river landing. Kate placed a trembling hand against her hot cheek. She could hear the mutterings of the other men and knew they'd witnessed her humiliation. Tears filled her eyes and she fought against sobbing outright. The pain in her heart was far greater than any to her smarting cheek. The group of men broke up and headed toward the boats. Some hung back, waiting for the women. Iris came to put an arm around Kate.

"Oh, Iris, how could he have humiliated me like that in front of everyone?" Kate sobbed, and knew inside herself that his slap hadn't been the reason for her pain at all.

"Seems to me you slapped first," Iris said. "You don't slap a man like Hogan. He shouldn't have done it, but neither should you. Seems to me you two are so intent on hurtin' each other lately, you don't think about the lovin' anymore."

"He doesn't love me. He can't if he's seeing Roxanne Blayne."

"Did he tell you that?"

"No, but he didn't deny it," Kate wailed. "And he said I left him for Clay Lawford because he's made a rich strike."

"Umm, men can be the biggest fools sometimes," Iris said, and urged Kate down toward the boat landing. Hogan's boat had already disappeared around the bend. The men made room for Iris and Kate in the remaining boat.

"Reckon I'd best leave a message for Bud so he

don't worry none when he comes back," Iris said, and using a knife borrowed from one of the men, carved a message into the planking of the wharf.

"All right, boys," Iris cried. "Take me to Dawson. If I can't have any food to sell or eat, I might as well go buy me some of them pretty gewgaws I seen last time I was there."

With a mighty roar of approval the men pushed off from the wharf and pulled on the oars. The boat slid upstream toward Dawson, the new "San Francisco of the North."

18

Clay never hesitated when Kate told him of all she and Iris had been through. "You can't stay at the hotel," he said. "That's no place for a lady. Follow me." He led them out the back door and across the alley to a spacious log cabin.

"I won this in a poker game the other night," he explained, lighting a kerosene lamp. It threw the room into bright relief. "J. D. Adams owned it. He was one of the first men who struck it rich up at the Bonanza Creek claims." He looked around. "I hope it's to your liking."

"Oh, Clay, this is wonderful," Kate cried in delight as she took in the finely carved pieces of furniture that filled the parlor. A satin-covered settee and matching chairs sat before a stone fireplace. There were glass-sided armoires filled with delicate glass and china, and lamps with delicate painted shades. The genteel opulence was disconcerting after the roughness of the trading post and the cabin she'd shared with Hogan. Opening off the parlor was a bedroom, and Kate could see a high carved walnut headboard and matching chests. The kitchen was reached through a short dog-trot to a smaller log cabin built in back. "It's a mansion," Kate cried, thinking she hadn't seen such luxury and comfort since leaving Seattle more than a year before.

"Stay for as long as you need to," Clay said.

"What about you?" Kate asked, her eyes thoughtful and caring.

"The Lucky Lady stays open all night, and I have

a room at the top of the stairs," Clay said. "You ladies will have your privacy."

"You've been most generous."

"Not at all, Kate," Clay said, twirling his hat nervously between his hands. "If it hadn't been for you and Hogan rescuing me from that ice last year, I wouldn't be here now. I'm glad to be able to return the favor."

He spoke so earnestly that Kate crossed the room impulsively and quickly placed a kiss on his cheek. His hands came up as if he meant to take hold of her and prolong the contact, but she drew away again.

"Well, if there's anything I can do for you, Kate . . ." Bowing slightly, he turned toward the door.

"Thank you, Clay," she said. Her hand on his sleeve caused him to pause and gaze deeply into her emerald eyes. He wondered if she realized how beautiful she was with her freckles and high cheekbones and the intelligence and pride evident in every glance. But that was part of the beauty of Kate, that she gave no thought to her looks. She wasn't like other females. "Clay?" she said softly when he continued to stare at her.

He shook himself and placed a hand over hers where it rested on his sleeve. "I'd do anything for you, Kate, just remember that," he said, and left the cabin. Kate stared after him a moment, surprised at the intensity of his words. She'd never thought of Clay as anything but a friend, yet she was remembering the declaration he'd made to her on the banks of the Yukon River more than a year ago. Sighing, she turned toward the parlor again, her pleasure in the beautiful cabin diminished somewhat by the thought that she might cause Clay more pain simply by being here.

"Ain't this a grand place?" Iris said, lighting a fire in the stone fireplace. "I remember J. D. Adams when he made that first strike. My, he was a jubilant man that day. He sent back to Seattle for all this furniture. He bought the best of everything and had it hauled up here, then invited everyone in to see his new home. He was going to ask one of the saloon girls, Gert Manahan, to marry him, but she turned him down. He locked up the place and went on back out to his mines. He don't hardly ever come back to town, and Gert, well, she took the boat back to San Francisco last summer. Said she couldn't stand the cold winters up here."

"I don't blame her," Kate said, and went to crouch beside the fire. Although it was the end of June and the days were hot, the nights were chilly, so the fire was welcome.

"You still got your mind set on going back Outside?" Iris asked.

Kate nodded. "Now more than ever."

Iris studied her pale face and the dark circles beneath her eyes. Something was bothering the girl badly, and Iris guessed it was a tall rawboned Irishman.

"You might better think about it some," Iris said. "Be sure that's what you really want to do."

Kate stared into the fire, not even noticing the tears that spilled down her face. "I have to, for the good of my baby," she said softly. "Oh, Iris . . ." She turned and laid her head on Iris' lap. "All I could think of all winter was: what if something happens to my baby up here and there are no doctors or hospitals?"

"Things happen Outside even when there are doctors and hospitals. Besides, we got doctors here in Dawson, and Father Luke's hospital."

"But no supplies," Kate said. "I love Hogan, but I can't risk the life of our child, and . . . and Hogan doesn't want a child, not up here."

"Pshaw, I never saw a man that wasn't tickled pink to think he'd got himself a child. His manly pride takes over, no matter what he says."

"Do you think so?" Kate asked, raising a flushed face. One by one Kate voiced her fears, fears nurtured through the long bitter winter, and one by one Iris brushed away her concerns, reassured her that civilization was on the doorstep, just a shipload of goods away. Kate wiped her eyes, feeling better for the good cry and the advice. But no matter how commonsensical Iris was, she couldn't explain away Hogan's hateful words concerning Clay or his continued involvement with Roxanne Blayne.

Kate's lips tightened with pride and she got to her feet. Iris shook her head and sighed. Hogan and Kate were too much alike in their stubbornness and pride. She just hoped they came to their senses soon. Once Kate stepped onto that boat, it would be too late. It would be a year before she could return to Dawson, and a year would give Roxanne Blayne all the time she needed to comfort a lonely man. Iris sighed and went to see if the kitchen larder was as generously appointed as the rest of the cabin.

Bud Garrett and Quentin Finley returned the following day and came immediately to Dawson, where they were directed to Clay's cabin. Bud's ruddy face was positively white until he caught sight of Iris.

"I'm glad you're all right, old woman," he said gruffly, without even taking her into his arms, but Iris seemed to understand his undemonstrative ways. She smiled and made him a cup of coffee. Surreptitiously Kate watched them, seeing the simple unspoken ways they declared their love for one another, and she felt saddened that she and Hogan would not grow to this same comfortable understanding and acceptance. Their flame had burned too brightly to ever revert to complacency. When they were in the same room, they'd been compelled to touch, to express all the sweeping emotions they felt. Now Kate turned away from the sight of Bud and Iris, leaving them to their privacy while she went to the bedroom to lie down for a while.

The baby was growing. She was six months along and beginning to show now, although her shawl still hid her condition. But Kate could feel the other changes within her body. She tired more easily and seemed never to get all the sleep she wanted. Afternoon naps were becoming a daily part of her routine.

One afternoon Clay came to call while she was lying down. Kate heard his voice and quickly got up.

"Clay, how good of you to visit us," she said, hastily adjusting her shawl.

He turned his concerned gaze on her. "I was just leaving, Kate. I didn't mean to disturb you if you're unwell."

"I'm fine. Sit down and I'll make some tea for us," she reassured him with a brisk smile. He noted the paleness of her face and the circles beneath her eyes, and he wasn't fooled.

"Please don't trouble yourself," he said quickly. "Sit down with me, Kate. I want to talk to you."

Piqued by his serious tone, she did as he asked, settling herself on one of the Victorian chairs. Carefully she spread the full skirts of her new gown before giving him her undivided attention. The bright blue brocade of her gown was a perfect foil for her brilliant hair and emerald eyes. He thought he'd never seen a more beautiful woman.

"What is it, Clay?" Kate asked, alarmed by his warm gaze. She didn't want to hurt Clay, but she sensed she might be forced to.

"Kate, I . . . I've made no secret of the way I feel about you," he began. "I told you when we first came out here."

Kate gripped her hands tightly in her lap, knowing what was coming and loath to hurt him when he'd been so kind. "I remember," she said softly, "but I was already married."

"I . . . I know I'm saying this awkwardly," Clay rushed on earnestly, "but my feelings haven't changed for you, Kate."

"Clay, please." Kate put a hand on his arm to halt the outpouring of words she knew would come. "My status hasn't changed. I'm still a married woman."

"But you and Hogan aren't together anymore. I thought your marriage was over," he pressed.

Kate lowered her gaze to her tightly clenched hands. "It is, to all intents and purposes," she said dully, "but the consequences of my marriage can't be ignored."

Puzzled, Clay studied her face. "Are you thinking of a divorce? I'll stand by you every step of the way."

"Wait, Clay," Kate protested. "I haven't considered a divorce."

"Then I don't understand," he said. "What consequences?"

Taking a deep breath, she put aside the shawl and rose from the chair. Slowly she paced the room, finally turning to face him. His gaze hadn't left her face. "I'm carrying Hogan's child," she said softly. Clay leapt to his feet. Now his gaze dropped, and he measured with a glance the thickening waistline, the bulging front of her skirts. For a long moment he was silent. Kate could see the pain in his face, and her heart was filled with pity for him. Didn't she, too, know how painful it was to love someone who didn't love back? Steadfastly his eyes met hers again.

"That bastard!" The words exploded from him. "How could he abandon you at a time like this?"

"It's not like that, Clay," Kate said, crossing the few feet to grip his arm. "Hogan doesn't know about the baby. I haven't told him, and I do beg your silence about this matter."

"Why?" Clay gripped her hands in his.

She looked away, once again feeling guilty for something she knew couldn't be helped. "Hogan doesn't want a child," she said lamely, "and now there's Roxanne Blayne. I don't want to hold on to him just because I'm having his baby." She pulled free of Clay's grip. "It's such a mess. I should never have married Hogan. I see that now."

"Kate . . ." Clay gripped her shoulders, pulling her backward so she rested slightly against his chest. "I meant what I said. If you decide to divorce him, I'll stand beside you through it all. We could be married as soon as it was over. We could go back east, and no one need ever know."

"Dear Clay," Kate said, sagging against him, relishing the strength of a man for one brief moment; then she pushed away. "This is something I must do on my own, first. You needn't worry about me."

"She's a lady who can take care of herself, haven't you heard?" a deep voice growled.

Iris stood in the doorway, her market basket over her arm. "Look who I found on the doorstep," she said flatly, her snapping brown eyes studying Kate and Clay. How she wished she'd made some noise before opening the door and stepping inside with Hogan on her heels.

Kate whirled away from the accusing lights in Hogan's dark eyes. Walking to the chair where she'd sat, she flung the shawl around her shoulders, draping its folds over herself with nervous fingers. How long had Hogan been standing there? she wondered. How much had he heard? Had he noticed her condition? She thought not, for even as she turned to face him, he was still glaring at Clay Lawford.

"You don't wait long to move in on a man's wife," he was saying belligerently.

"Kate's not your wife anymore," Clay answered. Kate heard the growl low and menacing in Hogan's throat and saw an answering hostility in the flare of Clay's nostrils. The two men squared off to each other, eyes glaring, fists clenched at their sides for now, but it was only a matter of time before they were raised.

"Stop it," Kate cried shrilly, "both of you, or I'll have nothing more to do with the lot of you." The men backed down. Their stances relaxed, although their jaws remained clenched and their brows were pulled low in scowls. Kate looked from one to the other.

"Clay, would you mind leaving me alone with Hogan?" she asked, and saw the wounded look on his face. Without another word he picked up his hat and left the room. Kate heard the door close behind him.

"Well, I've got to get to my marketing or we won't have supper," Iris said, and followed Clay.

Hogan continued to stand in the center of the room, glaring at Kate. Uneasily she moved away to the mantel. Her fingers were pale and cold as she gripped the poker and jabbed at the burning logs.

"Why have you come?" she asked finally, when

she'd poked at the fire as much as she dared and had placed the cast-iron rod back on its hook.

"I brought something for you." Hogan crossed back to the entry hall. For the first time Kate noticed the large satchel. He placed it on a table, opened it, and stood back.

"What is it?" she asked curiously.

"Your share of the gold so far. Take a look."

In wonder Kate walked to the table and peered into the satchel. Glass jars of glittering gold dust and nuggets rested against rusted tins and hastily sewn leather pouches filled to near-overflowing.

"All this is mine?" she asked disbelievingly. Slowly she sank into a side chair.

"This is from only the first half of the shafts we dug out in the winter. We're still washing out the dirt, but I was afraid to wait any longer before bringing you your share. The boat will be in any day, and I didn't want you to go off to Seattle without adequate gold."

"Adequate gold!" Kate exclaimed, rising to look into the satchel again. "Hogan, there's enough gold here for me to live very comfortably for the rest of my life."

"You're a rich woman, Kate." He paused. "We're all rich."

"I could buy Aunt Petty's house back," she said dreamily. She didn't see the stricken look that crossed Hogan's face.

"Will you and Clay be living there together?" he asked nastily. At his tone, Kate's chin came up.

"Perhaps," she said haughtily.

"I wish you every happiness." Hogan spun on his heel.

"And I wish the same for you and Roxanne," Kate snapped.

Hogan whirled back to face her, his face mottled, his clean-shaven jaw jutting. "Kate . . ." he said through gritted teeth.

"Yes, Mr. O'Shea?" She made her voice syrupy sweet, knowing it irritated him, but inside her heart was pounding. She longed to run across the room and throw herself in his arms. But the thought that Roxanne Blayne had been held in those arms aroused a jealous monster within her that Kate had never guessed existed. Had Hogan kissed Roxanne as he'd kissed her? Had he made love to her the same way? Fool, she thought silently. You know he has. Her chin went higher. "If there's nothing more, Mr. O'Shea, I'll bid you good day. Thank you for bringing my gold."

But as Kate's anger was fanned, Hogan's cooled. Now he took a tentative step forward. "Kate . . ." he began huskily. The sound bothered her, it scraped across her nerve endings, it reminded her of talk whispered in the dark after lovemaking. "Kate, if you decide not to take the boat . . ."

"I will, of course."

"Well, dadblameit, you don't have to," Hogan said, crushing his hat in his big hands. "If you decide you don't want to marry that . . . that pantywaist Clay Lawford—"

"Clay is not a pantywaist. Shame on you for calling him that. He saved your life once."

"All right," Hogan snapped, "I know Clay's a good man. I reckon that's why you set such store by him, but, Kate, we . . . I . . . I know you had it tough with me. I know it's hard and lonely for a woman out there, and I'm not all refined and educated like Clay is." Hogan took a breath and swallowed. His pride went down hard. "I thought you loved me, Kate. I thought we had some good times. I . . . " He paused, groping for words he couldn't find. He cleared his throat. "I wish you well, Kate. I hope the gold buys you everything you want. I hope you'll be happy."

"Oh, yes, the gold," Kate said, casting a disparaging glance at the satchel. "A king's ransom. Why shouldn't I be happy with so much gold? The gold never meant as much to me as it did to you and Gilly."

"I know," Hogan said, and his shoulders sagged. "Well, good-bye, Kate. Be careful. Fletcher Meade and his men are here in Dawson. He's as mean and deadly as he was back in Skagway. Keep the news about your gold quiet until you get to Seattle."

"Fletcher Meade's here in Dawson?" she echoed disbelievingly. "Thanks for the warning." She was concentrating so hard on her memories of Skagway and Gilly's accident that she didn't hear the door close as Hogan went out.

"Hogan?" she called, but only silence answered her.

Fletcher Meade's presence was quickly felt in Dawson. Within a week he'd won the Golden Nugget Saloon in a poker game and had set up his own faro tables and roulette wheel. When the miners of Dawson heard he was serving free drinks every third round, they flocked to his establishment.

Never mind that the drinks were watered and that he charged twice as much as the Lucky Lady and other saloons in town. Gold flowed into the pockets of the miners and out again into Fletcher Meade's. The goal of every man and woman who worked for Fletcher was to extract from the miners, by any means legal or illegal, as much gold as possible. Bartenders grew their nails longer so that when they dipped into the miners' pouches, gold dust became embedded beneath their nails.

Likewise the waiters learned to keep their hands wet for the same reason. Clinging gold dust was carefully harvested into chamois pockets. As a miner poured out a measure of dust from his pouch in payment, his elbow was jostled. Scales were tampered with, wheels fixed, dice loaded, and all against the miner. Dancehall girls barely danced once around the floor before leading the miners to the bar for another drink, and when the miner had had enough watered drinks to get drunk, his dust was measured out of his pouch with an ever more generous hand, so that he was soon led out onto the street, all his gold spent.

Clay Lawford had established himself early on as a scrupulously honest proprietor, and many miners continued to frequent his saloon, but the takings were lean for a while. Then Roxanne defected, lured to the Golden Nugget by Fletcher Meade's handsome face and pretty promises. Swiftwater Bill had lost his fortune and Roxanne. Now she and Fletcher became an item, and they played their fame to the hilt. Roxanne sang all her sultry love songs directly to Meade, and he, knowing her love of chocolate, bought up all the chocolate in Dawson. This was no mean feat, for although gold dust was left lying about carelessly, chocolate was kept under lock and key.

At last the supply boats arrived. Their whistles rent the air and everyone rushed down to the wharves to help unload the goods. The rest of the day free drinks and an orgy of feasts were supplied to one and all.

"Madness," Iris said, shaking her head. They stood on the sidewalk out of the rush of men. Kate glanced along the street, which seemed to boil with writhing, teeming humanity. Gold-fevered new arrivals spilled into Dawson, their faces eager.

"Cheechakos," a voice said contemptuously, and Kate turned. Fletcher Meade stood at the other end of the boardwalk with Roxanne Blayne clinging to his arm.

"Good for business," the blond saloon girl said calculatingly.

Meade smiled down at her, his hard eyes glittering. "A woman after my own heart." He chuckled. "You never let anything stand in the way of making money."

"Nothing else is as important," Roxanne acknowledged, simpering up at him. Yet her eyes were as cold and hard as his. An unholy alliance, Kate thought, watching the pair. Anger shot through her as she remembered Gilly. Rumors had already begun to surface of Meade's techniques, and many of the old-timers were beginning to avoid his place. That meant he'd have to go after the unsuspecting cheechakos.

As if drawn by Kate's steady perusal, Meade turned to face her, his eyes hard and unwavering as he regarded her. Kate had the sensation of being observed by a deadly snake that might strike at any moment. Still, she did not lower her own gaze, allowing him to see the anger and hatred she bore him.

"Kate, come away," Iris said, not knowing the reason for Kate's defiant stance, but fearing repercussions nonetheless. Reluctantly Kate turned and followed Iris.

"Who was that woman?" she heard Meade ask behind her, and Roxanne's mocking laughter before she replied.

"I've seen her before," Meade mused, staring thoughtfully after Kate's rigid back. Then Roxanne tugged impatiently at his sleeve, and he smiled coldly. "All right, my dear, let's go bring in the fools."

"Iris," Kate said, digging in her heels, "I can't just walk away and let those two do to these unsuspecting men what they did in Skagway. I have to warn them."

"There's nothing you can do," Iris replied. "Men will learn their own lessons." But Kate was already walking purposefully toward the wharves. Reaching the end of the boardwalk, she climbed up on a wagon.

"Attention!" she called, but no one looked at her, nor did the roar and bustle desist. Kate looked around and called to a miner she recognized. "Hank, may I use your gun for a moment?"

"Shore you can, Kate," he said, and handed up his pistol.

Kate aimed it skyward and pulled the trigger twice. The shots reverberated down the streets. Men stopped their cavorting and turned to look at her.

"It's Taffy Kate," some yelled, and fell silent again as their friends scowled.

Kate gingerly handed Hank's gun back to him, then faced the crowd that had gathered. "Welcome to Dawson City," she began, and waited until the cheer had died down. "We wish you well in your endeavors." Another cheer sounded.

"Quiet, Taffy Kate's talking," someone bellowed, and the noise died down.

"I would be remiss if I didn't warn you of some of the dangers that exist here." The miners, old and new, fell somber. "Death will stalk your every waking step. It's in the freezing cold of winter. Prepare well before the snows come. They'll begin in less than two months' time. It's in the poor food supplies. You'll suffer scurvy, frostbite, dysentery, starvation, and madness. And death and violence and cheating await you here in Dawson. Be prudent. Be especially careful of Fletcher Meade and his gang, who will take everything you have. Beware of men offering to give you free advice or free maps to the gold mines. Beware of the Golden Nugget Saloon and the crib girls in Pleasure Alley. They'll rob you so that you have nothing left to buy much-needed supplies."

"That's a lie!" a voice roared from the boardwalk, and Kate turned to see Fletcher Meade bearing down on her. Frenchy LaRoche and George Sawyer, guns riding low on their hips, flanked him. Roxanne ran along behind, trying to keep up. Her pretty face had lost its calculating look and now showed malice.

"It's not a lie." Kate faced Meade. "You robbed men in a similar manner in Skagway. My father was one of them, and when he made a protest, you shot him." Kate turned back to the miners. "Meade and his men lie and cheat and strong-arm anyone who would resist them. I've heard of men killed by Meade's thugs for no other reason than that they tried to warn others." She swung around. "Is that what you intend to do to me, Meade?"

Meade's handsome face was twisted in an ugly snarl. "Get her down from there," he told his men, and they started toward Kate. The miners, of one voice, growled their warning. Frenchy and Sawyer hesitated, glancing back at Meade for instructions. A Northwest Mountie stepped forward, planting his feet firmly in the mud as he stared at the two men.

"In Dawson, we allow people to speak freely," he said. "Folks around here wouldn't take kindly to anything happening to Miss Kate."

The two men eased back, glancing around at the threatening faces of the miners.

"Come on," Fletcher said, furious that he'd been faced down. Whirling, he stalked away.

"Come down off that wagon and fight with me," Roxanne cried. "You called me a whore and I don't take that from anyone, especially not an old maid."

Her words were cut off as the wagon on which Kate

stood lurched forward. Fletcher Meade cracked the whip a second time over the heads of the mules and they leapt ahead. The wagon jerked. With a scream, Kate tumbled forward into the muddy street, while the wagon bounced away. With no one at the reins, the mules plunged unchecked through the streets. Women screamed, and men cursed and scattered, running to catch the team. But Kate never heard the commotion. She was lost in a dark, swirling void of pain.

19

Kate's first thought was for her unborn baby. She curled her knees, trying to protect herself. The mud had cushioned her, but not enough. The impact of the fall knocked her breathless and sent a sharp pain through her abdomen. Mindless of the muddy street, she gasped and lay still, trying to garner her strength, trying to beat back the waves of nausea that threatened to overtake her.

Roxanne stood on the boardwalk sneering down at her. "So the high and mighty have fallen," she jeered in delight, remembering the humiliation of a similar fate. "How sweet to see you lying in the mud where you belong. You may think you're better than me, Kate O'Shea, but you're not." She paused as Kate glanced up at her, face drawn in a grimace, eyes filled with agony. Kate's hands cradled her stomach. With the shawl lost in the fall, there was nothing left to hide her condition.

"Help me," she gasped, and gritted her teeth against the nausea. When she looked up again, Roxanne's figure wavered and danced before her. "My shawl . . ."

Roxanne's face blanched and her eyes looked soft and vulnerable for a moment. "Please, my shawl," Kate begged, and intuitively Roxanne guessed she'd been hiding her pregnancy. Kate whimpered as another spasm of pain hit her. When she could speak again, she turned appealing eyes to Roxanne. "Get Iris," she whispered. "I need help."

Before Roxanne could move, men rushed forward to Kate's aid. With rough, well-meaning hands they set her on her feet. Kate moaned. Her knees buckled and she slid downward into the mud again.

"She's hurt. Carry her," Roxanne ordered, and stepped out into the muddy street to gather up Kate's shawl and cover her with its concealing folds.

Kate's white hands gripped the shawl. "Thank you," she whispered. "Don't tell anyone." Roxanne had no time to answer, no time to promise.

"Kate!" Iris Garrett pushed her way through the throng of men. "Are you all right?" At Kate's nod, she rushed on. "I got swept along by those men. I thought they were going to trample me." She caught sight of Roxanne and drew her chin up haughtily. "You just get away from her, you white trash," she railed. "Haven't you and that scoundrel you've taken up with done enough?"

Kate put out a hand to halt her words. "Roxanne was helping me, Iris," she said weakly.

"Where do you want us to take her, ma'am, the hospital?"

"No," Kate mumbled. "Take me back home."

"Home," Iris ordered imperiously, and the whole crowd surged as one toward the cabin Clay had given them.

Roxanne watched them go, then stepped back on the boardwalk, scraping away the mud on her new slippers. So Kate was pregnant and she didn't want anyone to know, most especially Hogan. Roxanne swiped at her dirty skirts and stared back up the street. Kate didn't want her to tell him, so she wouldn't.

Roxanne smiled. She wouldn't even tell Fletcher. She wondered how to make the best use of the information, or if Kate had already done it for her. Soon Kate would leave, and Hogan need never know he had a child. Rumor had it the Sweetwater claim was a big one, maybe as big as the Bonanza and the Eldorado. Hogan would be a rich man and he'd need someone to help him spend all that gold dust—and she wouldn't share it with Fletcher Meade. Roxanne hated men who had to be in control. She'd tolerated Meade's authority only because he was useful to her at the moment. All that would change if she became Hogan's wife. No, she saw no reason whatsoever to share this new bit of information. She chuckled in spite of her ruined shoes, and with a light step made her way back to the Golden Nugget.

Kate drifted in a white mist of pain. It tore at her middle and she writhed on the bed, trying to escape, but to no avail. A wind blew, wild and dry and cold, a chinook wind, a mistral that brought misfortune and death. Kate moaned before its power. She stood again on a windswept ledge of the Chilkoot pass while the wind tore at her. She called for Hogan, but he wasn't there as he once had been, to hold her close and help her beat back the shadowy terrors. Piteously she wept, calling his name.

Then the low moaning sound of the wind changed. She was back in the cabin and there was a dark shadow at the door. "Hogan," she cried, and ran forward, but the dark form lumbered forward menacingly. Kate halted, her breath caught in her throat. "Hogan?" she whimpered, but the figure wasn't Hogan. A great black bear reared up on its hind legs, its massive hulk towering over her. "Hogan!" Kate screamed. The bear swung his huge paw. Kate felt pain sweep through her middle. "Hogan!" she screamed before darkness claimed her.

"Poor thing's exhausted." Iris' voice floated above her. "She had a bad time."

"Kate," a dear familiar voice cut through the mist. Hogan had come at last! Everything would be all right now. Blissfully she sank into a deep sleep.

When she awoke, the room was in shadows. Weakly Kate moved her head and looked around. A large figure slumped in a chair, his big head resting on his palm, his shoulders sagging. Kate recognized the dark shock of hair over the broad brow.

"Hogan," she whispered gratefully. He was here after all. She must have dreamed all the rest—the gold, the baby, and Dawson City, all of it. They were still here on the Chilkoot bluffs and Gilly had just been swept away. Tears slid weakly down her cheek and onto her pillow. But something was wrong. Above her head was not the slender sapling pole holding up the gray canvas. Puzzled, Kate stared at the lacy white canopy, struggling to understand where she was and what had happened to her. She must have made some sound, for the figure in the chair moved.

"Kate," Hogan whispered, and came to stand beside the bed. His face was haggard, but there was a barely restrained joy in the smile he gave her. "We have a son, Kate, a son!" Then it all came flooding back, Fletcher Meade and her fall from the wagon.

"The baby," she whispered. "Is he all right?"

"Ah, he's right as rain, Kate." Hogan knelt beside the bed and pressed a fervent kiss on her hand. "Iris said he came too early but he's healthy enough. He'll make it. I've never loved you so much as I do this moment."

"How did you know?" Kate asked, confused and wary. Was she still dreaming after all?

"Iris sent for me. She said you called for me over and over. She said . . ." He paused and buried his face against her shoulder. "Oh, God, Kate, I've been a fool. All this time I've thought you wanted Clay Lawford. Iris said some women just can't take the solitude at a time like this. She told me how frightened you were for the baby's well-being. I know I didn't make things any better for you, declaring I didn't want a child. I'm like a lump of coal, with about as much sensitivity. Can you forgive me?"

Kate's fingers automatically went to the dark locks spilling over his brow. She smoothed them back, closing her eyes with joy at touching him again.

"I love you, Kate," he whispered raggedly. He placed his face next to hers on the pillow and she felt his shoulders jerk in a spasm of weeping. "So many times I've thought I'd lost you. I tried not to think about you, tried to pretend you'd never come into my life, but it didn't work. I've only been half a man without you. I couldn't sleep, couldn't eat. The only thing that kept me sane was going into the pit and digging until I couldn't move except to fall down on my cot. Don't ever leave me again, Kate,'' he whispered brokenly.

"I won't," she said, and wanted to speak to him of her own pain at their separation, but she was tired, so tired, and her throat was too clogged with tears. Wordlessly she tugged at him, urging him up on the bed beside her, and when he'd cradled her body next to his, she took a deep shuddering breath and drifted off to sleep. Later must come explanations, reassurances that Roxanne had meant nothing to him, that he truly wanted his son, that he hadn't returned to Kate just because of the baby, and so much more, but for now it was enough that he was here, holding her in his warm strong embrace. For the first time in months Hogan breathed easily and finally slept, but even in sleep his arms never relinquished their hold on Kate.

"Oooh, he is so beautiful," May said when Axe brought her to visit. She held the tiny hand and cooed at the baby for hours on end. Axe, too, seemed touched by the child's presence. Tears misted his watery old eyes and he turned away to blow his nose into his handkerchief. Kate felt her heart lurch. How she wished Gilly could be here to see his grandson. Hogan noticed the woebegone look on her face.

"Cheer up, love," he said softly. "I'm sure Gilly is seeing his little namesake."

"Oh, Hogan, do you think so?" Kate asked, then paused. "Namesake? Do you mean it?"

Hogan nodded. "What else could we name him?" he said softly. "Gilly gave me a lot when he was alive, but the best thing he ever gave me was you, Kate."

Tearfully she melted against him, resting her cheek against his broad chest while she cried.

"Kate, what did I say? What's wrong?"

"Nothing's wrong," she cried. "Everything's perfect."

Puzzled by this bit of inconsistency in his practical Kate, Hogan did the best thing he could, wrapping his arms around her tightly and simply holding her. It seemed to Kate her joy knew no bounds. Things had been explained away between them. Mouth gaping, Hogan had only stared in disbelief when she asked him about Roxanne and the pouch. When he'd finished explaining, Kate had felt foolish, and when he'd told her how he'd never been able to return to Roxanne or any other woman after having Kate, she had wept and begged his forgiveness for doubting his love. The weeks following Gilly's birth were a time of healing for both of them. Tactfully Iris managed to make herself scarce except when needed to help with little Gilly.

Boats came and went while Kate was convalescing. Additional supplies had been brought in, so the town reveled in a new aura of prosperity. No one would starve for a third winter. Few of the citizens of Dawson were aware that by the time the steamers returned next summer, the town would already be past its heyday, as a new strike was discovered on the black sands of Norton Sound at a place called Nome. Secure now with a plentiful supply of food, whiskey, and gold, the old thoughtless gaiety returned and the warning Kate had risked so much to give had fallen on deaf ears after all.

Kate was unaware of it. Her every waking thought was of her tiny son. Born prematurely, he didn't seem to understand the conditions of frailty for such a newborn. He thrived on his mother's milk, demanding frequent feedings. In no time his cheeks plumped out and his limbs gained strength. His eyes were dark, almost black, from the beginning, and stubborn shocks of black hair sprouted on his little round head. Iris and Kate doted on him shamelessly. If not for her own joy in her new son, Kate might have felt jealous at Hogan's attention to the baby each time he arrived from Sweetwater. But after he'd jostled his son and exclaimed over his growth, Hogan always turned to her, his eyes brimming with love as he pulled her against him and nuzzled her cheek.

Kate's heart was full. Only one problem remained. After each visit, Hogan still returned to his claim. As her body healed, Kate longed to have him near her all the time, to be a family full-time instead of the few visits he made. She was determined to speak to him about it, and knew her time was running out.

The *Miranda Lynn*, a tiny steamer, pulled up to a wharf in Dawson in mid-August. She would spend only a few days in port before leaving again. She had to make it back to the Bering Sea and south before the waters froze, or risk being trapped. Kate sent word to Hogan to come immediately.

"Kate, what is it?" he asked, striding into the cabin without knocking. Kate had just finished nursing Gilly and he lay sleeping, warm and heavy in her arms, the nipple of her breast still gripped between his gums. Hogan paused, drinking in the sight of his wife and baby in such an intimate pose. Tiptoeing forward, he crouched before them, cradling Kate's legs between his knees. "Is everything all right?" he asked. "When I got your message I thought the baby was ill."

"He's fine," she whispered, fondly gazing at her son. "He's just been a little glutton." Gently she pulled her nipple from the baby's mouth. His lips were rosy and damp from her milk.

"I can't say I blame him," Hogan said huskily, his hungry gaze lingering on her pale full breast. The nipple was still hard and pronounced from the baby's nursing, the skin of the surrounding areola puckered. "God, Kate, you're beautiful." Leaning forward, he placed a kiss on the exposed curve of pale breast. Kate's heart beat erratically.

"Hogan," she sighed, feeling desire sweep through her. It had been so long, too long. Her fingers wound through his dark curls, holding his head to her. Little Gilly stirred in his sleep and Hogan drew back, his smile dark and sensuous and questioning.

"I'd better put him in his crib," Kate whispered, not answering the plea in Hogan's eyes. She saw the disappointment on his face, but he rose and gently took Gilly from her. Kate adjusted her clothes, watching as he held his tiny son, nuzzling the baby softness of him, drinking in the baby smell of talcum. How gently he handled Gilly, how proudly he looked at him.

Kate smiled to herself and followed them to her bedroom.

"He's a dear wee thing," Hogan said, standing beside the crib, staring down at his son. "No man could ask for more than I've got right this minute, Kate." He put his arms around her shoulders and pulled her close.

"I'm sorry to hear that," she said softly, letting her words trail off. "I'd hoped . . ."

"Hoped what, love?" Hogan asked, ever attentive to her moods.

Kate let a wickedly sensuous smile curve her lips. "I'd hoped you'd want more, much more," she said softly. Mixed emotions played across his chiseled features, then a light flared in his black eyes.

"Don't tease me, Kate girl," he growled. "You see before you a desperate man."

Taking hold of one of his big hands, Kate placed it against the soft mound of her breast, relishing the heat and weight of it there. "No less desperate than I, my love."

"Kate!" Her name was a moan low in his throat. His hand curved possessively around her breast. "I won't hurt you? Are you sure?"

"Positive." She giggled, feeling girlish and breathless and sexy and beautiful all at once. Hogan did that to her. With adoring eyes she gazed up at him. He let out a whoop and swept her up in his arms.

"Shhh, the baby," Kate admonished as Gilly stirred in his crib. Conspiratorially they waited, both willing their son back to sleep, while the need inside them built. Finally, his dark eyes smiling into hers, Hogan tiptoed toward the bed, Kate held high in his arms. Desire spiraled through her and she wrapped her arms around his shoulders and laid her head in the crook of his neck, drawing in the heady fragrance of this large rugged man. He smelled like the outdoors, like the spruce trees from their forest, like the fresh sweet water of their creek, like home. Kate felt a jolt at that thought, then pushed it away, wanting only to concentrate on the wonder of their union.

Hogan placed her on the bed and stood over her, his dark eyes drinking in the beauty of her. She hadn't refastened her bodice and now it gaped open, showing the sweet curve of breast and shadowy, mysterious depths of cleavage. The look in Hogan's eyes changed to heated passion. Kate felt her blood quicken, hot and pulsating, in her breasts and between her legs.

"Hurry," she gasped. Sitting up, she began wriggling out of her clothes. Hogan stood beside the bed, shucking his pants and shirt. He was ready, his shaft hard and elongated. Kate reached for the hot smoothness of his erection, curling her fingers around it. Hogan moaned as she gently slid her hand along the length of him. Smiling, wanting to give him pleasure, wanting pleasure and release for herself and the turbulent needs within, Kate leaned forward and placed her tongue against the hot round tip. Hogan moaned, his head thrown back in ecstasy. She could see the cords in his neck stand out as he strained toward her. Delighted with his response, Kate took all of his pulsating member into her mouth, running her fingers playfully over the dark sprinkle of hair on his tense muscular thighs. Hogan shivered as if with the ague. His strong hands took hold of her shoulders, pressing her forward for a moment as he savored this new surprise from Kate; then he was pressing her backward onto the pillow. His eyes glowed. "I can't wait, love," he murmured. "It's been too long." His hands glided over her, his fingers slid along her flesh, seeking entrance to her, checking to be sure she was ready for him, and then he hovered above her. Anxiety for her well-being mingled with his terrible hunger. With wordless whimpers Kate urged him down to her, welcoming him, wanting him with an equal intensity. At his first surge against her, she gasped and closed her eyes.

"Oh, God, Kate, have I hurt you?"

Unable to speak for the ecstasy that spiraled through her, Kate could only answer with an arching of her body to deepen their contact. Her fingers threaded through his dark hair, bringing his head down so his mouth met hers in a long kiss. Planting his palms on either side of her, Hogan pushed up so his hips could rotate in sweeping lunges that brought moans from Kate.

He no longer mistook them for pain. Her pleasure in his lovemaking was too evident, too quickly met by her own plunging hips. With quickening thrusts he ground against her until a fine dew clung to their bodies and their breaths came in quick gasps. They were no longer a part of a room, the town. They had entered another world that was at once new and old to lovers, a world that spun crazily out of control. Together they reached for the spinning vortex of that world, and claimed it in a blazing kaleidoscope of color and motion.

Hogan collapsed against the pillow at Kate's side, half-lying across her, their bodies still joined. Dizziness swept over him and he lay gasping for air. Beside him, Kate's breasts rose and fell. Her skin was dewy and moist from their lovemaking. Slowly she turned her head and met his gaze.

"I wanted it to last longer, love," Hogan said gently, grinning at her with a special intimacy she'd missed all these months. "But I don't think I could have lived through it."

"It was perfect," Kate said, and paused. "Of course, we do have all night."

Hogan swept her against him, settling her in the old position in which they'd always slept. "The rest of our lives," he vowed softly. Too sleepy to answer, Kate closed her eyes, a soft dreamy smile on her lips.

As dawn crept through the window, Kate lay satiated and exhausted, yet unable to sleep. The long days of a Yukon summer were intruding upon her time with Hogan. As if sensing her restlessness, he opened his eyes and studied her face in the pale gray light. His big hand sought hers beneath the covers, found it and interlaced his fingers with hers. A little smile crept over Kate's lips as she turned her head on the pillow.

"Why so melancholy, love?" he asked softly, his free hand smoothing the richly hued tendrils from her cheek. The light outside the window had brightened some now and he could see the dark shadows beneath her eyes. She seemed so fragile to him, yet he remembered how she'd stood shoulder to shoulder with him on the trail and at the cabin.

"I'm not sad," she said quickly, and stretched luxuriously, like a cat. "I think I must be the happiest woman in the world. I have you again, and Gilly is healthy and growing."

"You are a rich woman, Kate O'Shea," Hogan reminded her.

"Ummm, I am." Kate turned to nuzzle her face against his neck. Her hands wandered over him wickedly.

Hogan's laughter was deep in his chest, but he captured her roving hand. "If you're looking to be a widow, Mrs. O'Shea, that's a good way to go about it." Kate's fingers curled around his. "Besides, I was talking about the gold."

"Oh." The smile faded from Kate's eyes. She disengaged herself from him and pulled the covers high beneath her chin.

"All right, Kate, let's have it," Hogan said indulgently. "You've been dying to tell me something ever since I walked in here yesterday."

Perhaps he was receptive, Kate thought, peeking at his face. Maybe he would listen to what she had to say. Enthusiasm for her own plans made her bounce upright and settle herself against the propped-up pillows. The covers had fallen to her lap, but Kate seemed not to notice. Impatiently she pushed aside the long fiery strands of hair so they fell over her shoulder, curling provocatively over one ivory breast. She sat pondering what she was about to say, unconscious of her nudity. Hogan was all too aware of it, but he forced his attention to whatever surprise Kate had for him now. Her first words made his heart thud heavily and the blood leave his head.

"Hogan, I want to go Outside," she said. "The last boat will leave in a few days. If we hurry, we can be packed and ready to board."

"Whoa," he said, holding up a flat palm to halt her flow of words. "I thought you meant to stay here in Dawson for the winter."

"You know I've always wanted to go back to Seattle," Kate said. "I've only delayed this long because . . . because of . . ."

"The baby," Hogan said flatly.

"Yes," Kate answered. "I mean, partly, but long before that first boat came in, I was wavering. I don't think I could have left without you."

Her earnest expression eased the tight ache in his chest. "Then why leave now?" he asked stubbornly.

"Hogan, don't you see? We could never lead a normal life here in Dawson. We can't bring up Gilly in a good environment here. This place will always be filled with gold-fevered men and women who think of little else but digging a few nuggets out of the ground so they can come down here to Dawson to gamble and drink it away. That's no life for a child, for a family."

"We don't have to be a part of that, Kate. Besides, what about our claim? You should see how people are flocking to the Sweetwater. They're saying it's bigger than—"

"Yes, I know. I've heard it too," Kate said flatly. "Bigger than the Bonanza or the Eldorado. You could sell it, though. There are men right here in Dawson, men with money, who'd gladly buy it from you."

Hogan shook his head. "I'd never get what it's worth."

"But you'd be free of the dirt and grime and hard work of digging it out of the ground. You'd be out of the danger of someone jumping you to steal your gold or a wild animal attacking you or of freezing to death or starving to death." Her voice had risen angrily.

"Kate," Hogan said, shaking her slightly, "I can't walk away now. Mining is all I know. I have no other skills. Besides, Axe and I started out together."

"You and I started out together," she reminded him sullenly. "Oh, give it up, Hogan. We have enough gold in that bag you brought me to live comfortably. We could go back to Missouri. You could open a business, maybe a livery or a smithy. I could teach. We'd be back where people are civilized, where Gilly can go to school and get an education and learn to be a gentleman instead of one of these rough, illiterate . . ." She paused as the import of what she was saying washed over her. She turned a horrified, apologetic face to him. "I didn't mean that the way it sounded," she began lamely.

"Yes, you did, Kate," he said calmly, too calmly. His cold manner was more frightening than anger would have been.

"Hogan, I just meant I want a different life for us, a better life than we'll ever have here."

Swiftly Hogan swung his long legs over the edge of the bed and reached for his pants. "You're a snob, Kate," he said with cold fury, shoving his legs into his pants. Kate watched helplessly as he snapped them around his lean waist. Even now the sight of his big body excited her.

"I'm not a snob," she said, "and I don't want to make you angry or to hurt you. I just thought it was time to leave rather than face another long harsh winter here in the Yukon." Her voice faltered.

Hogan paused, studying her averted face. Dropping his boot on the floor, he reached for her. "I know the winter was hard for you, Kate," he said softly. "I understand. But you were pregnant last year, and pregnant women can get a little queer out here without someone to talk to. You're not pregnant now and you have Iris. There are more women here than there were last year, and there are a hospital and a school. Dawson is growing."

"It's only temporary," Kate said stoically. "Look at Circle City and any number of towns that have sprung up when gold was found. When there's a new find, the people just pick up and move on."

"Not me, Kate," he answered with finality. "I like this wild country." He held his hands out, palms up, as if they held all the words he needed to tell his feelings. Then he shrugged in futility. "It suits me," he said simply. "I'm at home here. I've never felt like that any other place. Here I'm not measured by how much education I have or my family background. I'm measured by the kind of man I am. Try to understand, Kate. I can't go back and be what you want me to be. I can try, but I already know I won't make it." He paused and paced across the room before whirling to face her again.

"Up here I can be whatever I want to be. There are no limitations set by another man or woman. That's exciting, Kate, more exciting than washing a thousand dollars' worth of gold through the rocker." He paused, and when he spoke again his voice trembled. "Please stay." His voice was humble, his eyes dark with fear at losing her. "I'll give up everything to go Outside with you, if that's what you insist on doing, but somehow I know it's wrong for us."

"What will you do here?" Kate demanded, her heart twisting in her chest. "Will you just go on grubbing in the ground for more and more gold? We can't spend what we have now."

"No, Kate." His big hands captured hers, his dark eyes lit with excitement. "We'll help open up this land. I want to build a railroad right over the Chilkoot Pass."

"A railroad over the Chilkoot?" Kate asked wonderingly. "Can you do that?"

Hogan laughed, tossing his dark hair back in his exuberance. "I know a man who'll build a railroad anyplace you tell him. I once worked for him. Now I want to hire him. Kate, I want to be a part of the future of this land. Stay here with me and you won't be sorry. I promise."

Suddenly Kate remembered him sailing across Lake Linderman, the wind whipping his hair as he defied the gods and nature. He was right. He'd never fit back in Missouri. He was too big in body and thought and dreams and daring. Tears stung her eyes. Rising on her knees, Kate flung her arms around him.

"I love you," she cried. Fiercely she kissed him; then the laughter died from her eyes and she sat back. "But I have a premonition."

Laughter rumbled from deep in his chest. "You and Gilly," he said indulgently, "and your premonitions."

"Don't laugh," she said, piqued at his dismissal.

"My sweet Kate," he mumbled against her hair. "Stay with me, Kate." She could feel his big body trembling.

"I'll never leave you, never," she whispered fiercely. "If you want to say, we'll stay. I don't care about the gold or the railroad, but I want you to be happy."

"If you're here, I will be, you and little Gilly." Hogan pressed her against his chest and rocked back and forth. As if hearing his name, Gilly stirred in his crib and let out a shriek. Hogan laughed, spinning around, head thrown back, Kate clasped high in his arms. "I suppose I'll have to share you with this greedy little fellow."

"I'm afraid so," she said, but lingered for a moment, savoring the feel of his big body and the last remnant of their night together. Then, as her son let out another cry, she hastily pulled on a dressing gown and went to tend the needs of the second male in her life.

She hadn't a chance with her fancy dreams of a normal life Outside, she thought, staring down at the tiny carbon copy of Hogan O'Shea. Somehow it no longer mattered, but the premonition still clung. Kate pushed it away. In the distance the steamer's whistle blew imperiously. In a few days it would sail out of the harbor, but Kate and her men would not be on it.

20

As the *Miranda Lynn* prepared to leave, Kate was too busy to even notice. The decks of the little steamer were already littered with bags of gold, left unattended, for their very weight alone made them safe from theft. Some miners were returning home rich men, some were going to taste the fleshpots of the outside world before returning, and some, broken and ill, were giving up. The day after Hogan left, Kate went off to the dressmaker. Now that she had her slim figure back, she wanted something new to show it off the next time Hogan arrived. Besides, if she were to remain in Dawson as one of its richest citizens, for surely she and Hogan were, she could afford a few nice gowns.

Bud Garrett and his brother-in-law had rebuilt the trading post and now Iris moved back, vowing to come to visit as often as possible. Kate hugged the older woman, remembering all they'd been through together. Although Iris would be only a few miles downriver, she hated the parting. Before he left, Hogan had prevailed upon Clay to agree to sell the cabin. Kate would spend the winter in her new town house.

Likewise, Axe bought a cabin down the street for May. The Indian woman was ecstatic to own her house. She had new gowns made as well, and bought a lacy parasol, which she carried no matter where she went. Any other place, she might have been a laughingstock, but in Dawson she was just one more of the colorful characters that created its history.

At the Sweetwater cabin the men would cook for themselves and come to town when they could. It wasn't the best of arrangements from Kate's way of thinking, but her protests were futile. Hogan was determined she not spend another winter so far from people and hospitals and stores. For the sake of Gilly, Kate finally agreed. The separations from Hogan seemed interminably long.

The days were growing shorter, the winds out of the north whistling with maniacal promise of the coming winter. Cottonwoods and scrubby oaks bloomed gold and rust red along the river. Flocks of geese and other water fowl flew overhead, sounding their warning of impending winter. Kate had a warm winter cape made for herself out of thick wool, as well as woolen shirts for Hogan. Iris and she spent the lengthening fall evenings knitting warm afghans and baby blankets. May brought little Gilly a parka with a hood she'd made from the fur of a lynx. Its edge had been trimmed with the soft white fur of a snowshoe rabbit. Everyone prepared for winter. Everyone remembered.

It was, strangely, a time of contentment for Kate. She'd made her decision, and if she'd had to compromise her own dreams, she had only to look at Hogan and little Gilly together to know that dream was meaningless without both of them.

One night as Hogan and Kate put the baby in his crib and turned to each other hungrily, their kiss was interrupted by a pounding at the door. When Hogan hurried to answer, he found Axe waiting on the steps.

"Better come quick," the old man said. "There's trouble."

"What is it?" Kate asked while Hogan shrugged into his coat.

"It's Thor. He's got himself smitten over one of Meade's cheap floozies. She enticed him into the Golden Nugget, where she's been filling him with whiskey ever since. 'Bout an hour ago he started gambling. You know Thor. He ain't got no head for it. He's lost nearly every ounce of gold he dug out of the ground last winter."

"Let's go," Hogan said, taking down his gunbelt.

"Hogan," Kate cried in sudden fear for him, "don't

TOMORROW'S DREAM

go. You know how Meade is. He'll have you killed. He set a trap for you once."

"Don't worry, Kate," he said, buckling the belt beneath his coat. "I'll be careful, but I can't abandon Thor. He's too gullible. Meade'll kill him."

"Don't go," Kate cried, but he'd already headed out the door. She stood watching the men disappear down the street. The dark shadow of her premonition pressed in on her. She thought of her father. Fletcher Meade had caused his death as surely as if he'd been there on that mountain that day. She'd nearly died and lost her baby because of this evil man. She couldn't just stand by and let something happen to Hogan and Axe.

Throwing a cape over her shoulders, Kate plunged into the snowy street. Hurrying to May's cabin, she pounded on the door frantically. "Kate, what wrong?" May asked, her eyes round and frightened. She must look the same way, Kate thought fleetingly.

"May, watch Gilly for me, please. I have to follow Hogan. There's been some trouble with Thor."

"I watch Gilly," May said, and hurried down the street toward Kate's cabin. The snow seemed to clutch at Kate's feet, holding her back. Once she slid and fell to her knees. Snow had begun to fall again. She arrived, breathless and wet, at the Golden Nugget just behind Hogan and Axe.

Pushing inside, she paused, caught by the tension that gripped the room. The tinny thump of the piano had died away. The dice were tossed and lay forgotten. The roulette wheel fluttered to a halt. All eyes were riveted on the drama at the other end of the room. Hogan and Axe stood over a poker table. Roxanne Blayne stood at the bar, resplendent in a red silk gown with jet-black beads. Frenchy LaRoche and George Sawyer were at either end of the long polished bar.

In odd contrast to the strained mood, Fletcher Meade lounged back in his chair. Thor was seated across from him. A saloon girl stood behind Thor, a mirror out, a powder puff clasped near her chin as if she'd been frozen in mid-action. The place in front of

Thor was bare, all his gold gone. A piece of paper lay in the center of the table.

"Hogan," Thor cried heartily, waving him over.

"Let's go, Thor," Hogan said quietly.

"Your friend's in the middle of a play." Meade spoke for the first time. "He can't leave yet."

"He won't be doing any more play in this saloon," Hogan said, reaching for the paper in the pot. With a flick of one hand he opened it and read, then glared at Meade. "It's deeding Thor's claim over to you." Hogan's lips tightened and he spoke through clenched teeth. "It won't work, Meade," he rasped out. "You'll never get your hands on a piece of Sweetwater Creek."

Meade shrugged. "It was his idea, O'Shea. I can't help it if your friend's a bad poker player."

"Helped along, I'm sure, by your whore," Hogan said.

"Here now, who're you calling a whore," the girl cried plaintively. "I'm a decent woman."

Her words were cut off as Hogan grabbed hold of her arm and jerked her forward. She went sprawling across the table, the mirror falling from her grasp.

Thor had been sitting dumbfounded, too drunk to make any sense of what went on around him. Now he looked blankly at the man he'd always admired.

"Hogan, vhy you do dat? Ruby's goot friend of mine."

"Your good friend is helping to cheat you," Hogan said, picking up the mirror for all to see. A murmur ran around the room.

Thor looked from the girl to the mirror and slammed his fist on the table. "By damn," he swore, getting to his feet. He swayed drunkenly, his eyes blank, and fell forward over the girl. She screamed and wriggled away. Meade sat up straighter, his face suddenly ugly.

"That's it, O'Shea. Your friend's just folded. I won." With a triumphant smirk he held out his hand for the deed. "You know the rules."

"I'm playing Thor's hand," Hogan said. Meade's sneer faded, but he couldn't refuse with so many miners looking on. There were already angry mutterings over the mirror. He nodded in capitulation, and signaled unobtrusively to his man at the bar.

Hogan picked up the hand and barely glanced at it. "I'll bet Thor's claim against your stake, plus I'll raise you the Sweetwater One claim."

The men in the room gasped. Kate took a step forward. Hogan had just bet his own claim—their claim. Surprise rippled through her. A flutter of red silk drew her attention for a moment, and she saw Roxanne pick up a whiskey glass and toss back the contents. Her eyes never left the two men at the poker table. There was another movement as George Sawyer slid along the bar to a more strategic spot. Roxanne Blayne drew the whiskey bottle toward her and slowly poured another drink.

Kate drew a shuddering breath. The stakes were high, too high for Meade to ever let Hogan out of the saloon alive. Frantically she looked around. Why hadn't she thought to send someone for the Northwest Mounties? She couldn't leave now, not knowing Hogan was in such danger. Axe had disappeared with Thor. Kate felt bitterness well up inside her. What good did it do to save Thor's life if it cost Hogan his?

"I'll call you," Meade answered, and pushed forward the heavy bags containing Thor's gold.

"That's not enough," Hogan said calmly. Meade's eyes flickered like a deadly snake ready to strike.

"There's a fortune there," he said.

"But it's not enough. Everyone knows the Sweetwater's one of the richest claims around. Either call or throw in your hand." Hogan's hard gaze bore into Meade's. Kate saw the man's face flush with ugly color. He didn't like being made to back down.

"I'll throw in the Golden Nugget, if that's acceptable," Meade said with affected casualness, but Kate could see the vein in his temple throbbing furiously.

"I'll accept it," Hogan said, and drew out two cards from his hand. "I'll take two," he said.

Grinning, Meade picked up the deck.

"Deal them from the bottom," Hogan said in a quiet deadly voice Kate had come to recognize. He wouldn't allow himself to be cheated as Thor had been. Once again Meade's triumphant grin turned to a scowl. His eyes were narrowed to slits as he flicked a glance at the end of the bar. The miners had pressed forward. Hogan took out his gun and laid it on the table. "Deal us both cards from the bottom," he said softly.

Sweat ran down Meade's elegant jaw. He tugged at his collar and glanced around. He had little choice, he saw, and with a shrug and a smile meant to disarm, he dealt as Hogan had directed. The miners swore and muttered among themselves as two aces were turned up in front of Hogan. Meade dealt himself three cards. Once again there were cries of speculation and surprise as a king and two tens turned up.

Meade looked smug. "Full house," he said, turning over his remaining cards.

"Four aces," Hogan said, and turned over his cards. "You lose, Meade."

"You cheated," the gambler shouted.

"Did I?" Hogan asked mildly. "Check the deck, boys."

One of the miners stepped forward and spread the remaining deck. "Ain't no other aces in this deck," he said. "Looks like he got them all."

"Maybe so," Hogan said. "Maybe I missed one. Maybe I missed the one up your sleeve." He grabbed hold of Meade's arm and slammed it down on the table. In full view of the miners he reached up Meade's coat sleeve and pulled down a card.

"Seems there was another ace, after all," he said. "Looks like one of us was cheating. Which one do you suppose it was?" The miners laughed at his humor, although their expressions when they looked at Meade promised retribution.

A movement at the bar made Kate glance up. "Hogan!" she screamed as George Sawyer brought his pistol up and aimed at Hogan's chest. It was too late, too late, Kate thought in anguish. He had no time to draw and fire. Everything seemed to be happening in slow motion. Another movement, a blur of red silk, was followed by the swing of a whiskey bottle. Roxanne brought the bottle down on George Sawyer's arm and his shot went wild. Startled, he turned, and seeing Roxanne with the dripping remains of the broken bottle, swung his arm in a wide arch. His fist slammed against her face and she fell backward.

"Sawyer," Hogan called, and the man spun around to meet him. His gun fired wildly, tearing into the wooden post near Hogan's head. Kate screamed again. Deliberately Hogan fired. With a look of stunned surprise twisting his face, Sawyer gave a grunt of pain and crumpled to the floor. The saloon door flew open and Axe ran in, followed by the mounted police.

"What's going on here?" Lieutenant Fuller of the Northwest Mounted Police demanded.

"Arrest this man," Meade cried. "He came here and killed one of my men."

"It was self-defense," the miners called. "Sawyer shot first."

Fuller knelt beside George Sawyer and examined him for a pulse. "He's dead, all right." He rose and faced Hogan. "Want to tell me what happened?" All the men chimed in. Kate pushed her way through the crowd.

"I insist you do something, Lieutenant," Meade was saying.

"Let's have a miners' meeting and try them both," one of the men cried. "Meade was caught red-handed at cheatin'."

"If we try Hogan, we try Meade," they cried.

Meade looked around at the shouting, angry miners. "You're the law here," he said to the mountie. "Do something."

Lieutenant Fuller shrugged. "It's out of my hands," he said. "Although this is technically under our jurisdiction, we've cooperated with the miners in their legal systems. We've found them to be fair in their dealings."

"You can't listen to what this bunch of rabble have to say," Meade shouted, looking around. Frantically he waved to Frenchy LaRoche, but his man was already slinking out the back door.

A miner pounded on the bar. "I move we call this meetin' to order right now," he shouted. "We're here to try Hogan O'Shea for the murder of George Sawyer."

"Self-defense," the miners roared.

The self-appointed chairman turned to Hogan. "This committee finds you innocent of the charge of murder on the grounds of self-defense. You're free to go." Once again there was a roar of approval.

"Next on the agenda is the trial of Fletcher Meade, who's been charged with cheatin' at cards."

"Guilty," the men roared.

"You've been found guilty of the crime of cheating at cards," the chairman said, "and are ordered to leave Dawson City within two days' time."

"Hip, hip, hooray!" the men shouted.

"Boys, as the new owner of the Golden Nugget Saloon, drinks are on me," Hogan called, and the men cheered and scrambled to the bar.

"Hogan," Kate called, fighting against the push of men.

"Kate!" he cried elatedly, catching her up in his arms. "Did you hear, we got rid of Fletcher Meade. He's been ordered out of town."

"Yes," Kate answered gleefully. "Oh, Hogan, I was so afraid you'd be killed."

"Hogan!" Tagish Dan yelled, and waved him to the bar.

"I have to go," Hogan said to Kate hurriedly. "Can you get home all right?"

"Don't worry about me," she answered, forcing a smile to hide her disappointment over their shortened evening.

"I may be late." Hogan grinned and leaned forward to whisper in her ear, "Wait up for me." His hard, quick kiss held wicked promises. Then he was gone, quickly lost among the boisterous, jubilant miners at the bar.

Before she headed home, there was one thing she must do, Kate thought, and looked for Roxanne. But the saloon girl had disappeared. Kate caught a flash of red silk at the door. Her arm around a defeated Meade, Roxanne was chattering breathlessly, trying to cajole him. Kate followed them out onto the street.

"Roxanne," she called. The couple paused and looked around. Fury made Meade's once handsome face ugly. Roxanne looked startled and apprehensive. Kate hurried toward them. "I just wanted to—"

"Haven't you done enough?" Roxanne demanded, coming back along the boardwalk to meet her. In her barely suppressed fury it seemed she might launch herself at Kate. "You and that Hogan O'Shea," she hissed. "I hate you both. If I'd had a gun I'd have shot you both myself."

Stunned, Kate could only stare openmouthed at the woman. The look on Roxanne's face didn't coincide with the venomous words she had hurled at Kate.

"Stay away from us, you sanctimonious do-gooder. You've been trying to get Fletch out of town ever since he arrived. Well, you've finally succeeded. You should be happy. Go on. Get away from me. I don't want to hear another word from you." *Please,* her eyes begged, *don't give me away.*

For the first time Kate came close to liking the girl. Playacting was a small price to play for Hogan's life. Raising her chin haughtily, Kate gave her a scathing look. "Your behavior speaks all too well for the kind of woman you are," she said, hoping she'd made her tone convincing enough for Meade's ears, hoping that Roxanne understood the double meaning. With a twitch of her skirts she walked away.

Now that the need to pretend was past, Kate pondered over Roxanne's actions. Obviously the girl was frightened of Meade's revenge. But why had she taken the risk? Kate halted, her hand gripping a post. Roxanne Blayne was truly in love with Hogan!

Jealousy swept through Kate at the thought that Hogan had been intimate enough with the saloon girl to elicit that kind of passionate loyalty. Slowly she walked back to her cabin. She should be grateful that Roxanne had saved his life and not think of the reasons why, but jealousy dogged her every step.

The Golden Nugget changed hands with barely a halt in business. If Kate had hoped that being a saloon owner would keep Hogan in Dawson, she was soon to learn otherwise. He quickly sold the saloon to a gambler who'd come in on the *Miranda Lynn*, with the provision that the cheating of miners would stop. Having witnessed the miners' justice, the new owner quickly agreed. The scales with their unequally balanced weights were thrown out and a new bartender and dealers were hired. Hogan donated the profit from the sale of the saloon to Father Luke's hospital.

Meade remained conspicuously out of sight, but Frenchy LaRoche began to brag in the Lucky Lady and other bars that he would soon take over the Golden Nugget himself. The new owner grew increasingly nervous as Frenchy's threats got back to him. Some feared he might take the *Miranda Lynn* right back out. Kate was distressed by the news. If Frenchy scared away the new owner and took over the Golden Nugget, she had little doubt he would simply be a front for Fletcher Meade. There was nothing to prevent Meade from moving downriver and setting up his crooked operations again.

"Don't worry, love," Hogan reassured her. Prudently Ruby, Thor's dance-hall girl, had already disappeared, and some thought she was hiding until the *Miranda Lynn* was ready to sail. Good riddance, they agreed.

It wasn't Ruby's helping Meade cheat at cards that was so unacceptable. Everyone knew the dance-hall girls engaged in a little chicanery, and the gold dust flowed so rapidly through all their fingers that they didn't begrudge a working girl her due. It was all part of a gold-mining town. The miners were grown men and could choose not to frequent the saloons and cribs. No, their objection was that Meade had gotten too greedy. He'd tried to take by illegal means a miner's claim, and the girl had helped him. No one looked for her or threatened retribution. It was just clearly understood that like Meade, she would leave on the next boat.

Thor, the gentle, naive giant, woke with a fierce taste for revenge, so Hogan and Axe bundled him back to his Sweetwater cabin until he could cool off. Everyone began to breathe easier.

The night before the *Miranda Lynn* was to sail, the temperature fell. The captain of the craft chomped at his cigar and cursed himself for delaying so long. If they didn't head south in time, they could be trapped by ice. He climbed the bank and made his way to a saloon to drown his worries in whiskey.

Down on Sweetwater Creek, Hogan and Thor washed through the last of their gold, bagged it, and added it to the growing pile in the storage cabin. They'd panned nearly a thousand dollars today, an incredible amount.

"Looks like it'll snow again," Hogan called, standing on the creek bank and smelling the air. He loved it out here. There was a crackling freshness that bit at a man and made him know he was alive. He raised his face to the large fluffy flakes that had begun to fall, opening his mouth to taste them. They even tasted better up here.

"*Ja*," Thor answered. "Geese fly south." He pointed to a dark flying wedge against the dusky sky. The flock passed out of sight, but their garrulous voices could be heard long after they passed. Like a Sunday social meeting, Hogan thought, and grinned. Only a few more days and he'd go back to Dawson to see Kate. He hadn't been able to spend any time alone with her the last visit, and he had a powerful hunger for her. He thought of her long white neck that reminded him of one of those swans she wouldn't allow him to kill when they first started on the trail. He chuckled at the memory, then winced and fell to the ground as a pain rippled through him.

He'd been shot! He clutched at his shoulder, rolling over until he landed up against a pile of dirt.

"Thor!" he shouted.

"*Ja*. I heard," the big man called. He was over to Hogan's left.

"Where'd the shot come from?" Hogan called softly.

"The creek," came the answer. "Vhere's Axe?"

"Hunting," Hogan said, and pulled a bandanna from his pocket and pressed it against his shoulder. "We've got to get to the guns."

"They're in the cabin," Thor said. "Vant me to get them?" He tried to move closer, but gunfire pinned him down, kicking up the dirt pile.

Hogan shook his head, staring into the gathering shadows. "They've got you spotted. Try creating a diversion for them and I'll run to the cabin."

"*Ja,*" Thor agreed.

Hogan saw him crouch, ready to move when the word was given. He gave a quick thumbs-up sign for luck and crawled on his belly toward the cabin. The snow and dirt kicked up all around him. Hogan hugged himself tight against the ground, playing dead while he waited for the fusillade to end.

Another shot rang out, but since it landed nowhere near him, Hogan assumed Thor had made his move. Gathering himself, he leapt for the door of the cabin. Bullets thudded into the heavy wood planks. Hogan crouched behind the door while his attackers turned their full force on the cabin. Lead embedded itself into the door and walls. Broken glass fell inward from the window. Hogan cursed. They'd just had the glass put in.

When he was fairly sure no bullets could penetrate the walls, he dashed across to the gun rack, taking care to dodge the open window. Grabbing up his gunbelt, two rifles, and shells, he ran back to the corner and loaded both rifles and strapped on his pistol. He had to get out of the cabin. They could keep him pinned down in here and toss in a torch. He'd be burned alive. He had a horror of that kind of death.

Frantically he looked around. Axe had fashioned a hall tree of sorts, a plain log with a board nailed to it on which they'd hung their garments. Hogan wrested it forward to the window and placed his jacket and hat on it. Propping one of the rifles on it with the barrel extended, he called out, "Fletcher Meade!"

The potshots halted and he could imagine the men with the guns looking at each other uneasily, wondering how he knew. "You'll never get away with this, Meade. The people in Dawson will do more than run you out of town. You'll be hanged."

"They'll have to prove it was me," Meade called back.

"I'll tell them how you jumped our claim and fired on us," Hogan shouted.

"You ain't gonna be alive, none of you," Meade called back, and laughed wildly. Hogan chose that moment to fire into the bushes along the creek. Then he shoved the coatrack forward and dived for the door. Once again bullets ripped into the side of the cabin, but this time they were aimed at the window. Hogan threw open the door and somersaulted out into the snow. His body continued to roll until he came up against a mound of dirt. His shoulder ached and he could feel blood trickle down his arm. He willed away the pain. It was too distracting. He had to be alert and get a weapon to Thor.

"Thor," he called out, but there was no answer.

"He's dead, Hogan," Meade called. "My men are good shots, and he was such a big target. They couldn't help themselves."

"You bastard!" Hogan yelled, and fired into the bushes. Meade laughed again. They'd moved farther up the creek. Cautiously Hogan wriggled forward, his eyes straining to penetrate the darkness. A flash of red on the right made him throw himself to one side. Bullets hammered into the ground where he'd been.

Slowly he worked his way in the direction Thor had taken. He might be wounded and need help, or he might be all right and biding his time. Someone moved in the bushes behind him.

Cursing silently, Hogan froze, wishing his dark clothes didn't make such a contrast against the snow-covered ground. Was it only a few minutes ago he'd tasted a snowflake?

Someone was ahead of him, and the man behind was pressing tighter. He'd be caught between the two of them. Hogan crept forward on his elbows to a log and slithered over. Its surface was slick with snow-covered moss. Carefully he raised his head and looked around. One of Meade's men was crouched behind a spruce tree. Silently Hogan circled, happy now about the snowfall, for it muffled his footsteps. Meade's man was so busy watching the creek bank, he didn't hear Hogan until he was right on him.

"What the devil?" the man said, but a big hand clamped over his mouth, shutting off his words.

"I'm over here, you sons of bitches," he yelled, and fired, using the captured man as a shield. Guns blazed and Hogan felt the man's body jerk at the impact of bullets. But Hogan's eyes never wavered from the line of deadfall where he'd seen the flash. Deliberately he took aim and fired. A man cried out. He'd gotten one. That was the last thought he had. Pain tore through his back and side. His gun slid from his limp hand as he slowly collapsed to the ground. He felt something soft and warm beside him. He'd found Thor.

"Hogan," Thor gasped. The side of his face was covered with blood. "Hogan," the big man whispered. Hogan opened his mouth to answer him, to give him a warning, but no words came. He seemed trapped in a vacuum where sound and feeling were gone. Yet he sensed that Meade's men were approaching.

"I got 'em both," a man cried jubilantly.

"One of them's still alive," Frenchy LaRoche said, kneeling over Thor. The shadows danced and jumped as the men made room for Fletcher Meade. He bent over Thor, grasping a handful of hair to pull his head up.

"Listen to me, you big dumb Swede." Meade sneered. "I've got your gold after all, yours and Hogan's. My men are loading it into the boats now. Hogan should have left well enough alone. Now you're both going to pay for what he did to me back in Dawson." He let go of Thor with a contemptuous gesture that made the big man's head bob helplessly.

"Kill him," Meade ordered. Grinning, Frenchy stepped forward and placed a gun against Thor's temple.

Hogan tried to cry out, to raise his hand. He cried a warning, but it was silent. Frenchy pulled the trigger and Thor flopped back in the snow.

Walking past Hogan, Meade kicked him viciously. "Shoot him again too, just to be sure," he ordered. Hogan saw Frenchy's grinning face as he hovered against the pale night sky. Slowly he pulled back the hammer and took aim.

A shot ripped through the night, thudding into a tree nearby. It was followed in rapid succession by others. Meade and his men spun around, looking for this new source of gunfire.

"Must be Axe," Meade muttered in a low voice. "Come on out, Axe," he called. "We have Hogan and Thor. That's all I came for. I don't have any fight with you." Another fusillade was his answer. Once again the cottonwoods quivered as bullets hit them. Wood chips flew and one of Meade's men gave a grunt and went down. Only Meade and Frenchy remained. They crouched low, peering into the shadows.

"Cover me until I get to the boat," Meade ordered, but Frenchy's big hand clamped over his arm.

"Non, mon ami," he said. "You will take the boat, no? And Frenchy will be left here alone. We go together."

Meade's face was ugly. He brought up his gun and pointed it at Frenchy, but LaRoche had already aimed his gun at Meade's chest.

Meade forced a smile. "Come, Frenchy," he said affably. "It's just you and me now. We'll divide the gold evenly, right? First, we'd better get out of this."

"Mais oui," Frenchy said. "I'll show you the way. We'll quickly lose this old man." They melted away in the darkness. Hogan lay staring at the sky, willing his arms to move, but they felt paralyzed. Meade and Frenchy were getting away, and he was helpless! He

heard the boat scrape against the sandy bottom, and the creak of oars. More rifle shots came from back in the woods, and then Axe was there beside Hogan.

"Hogan . . . Thor!" he whispered. Hogan willed himself to make a sound, although the words came out like grunts. "Hogan!" Relief was evident in Axe's voice as he rolled him over.

"Whiskey," Hogan muttered, and Axe pulled out the flask he always carried. The raw liquor cut a path down Hogan's throat. He sputtered, coughed, and lay back, feeling the alcohol take affect. He drank more, willing himself to numbness, willing himself to move.

"They got Thor," Axe said, regret clogging his throat. He and the big man had become good friends. Once Thor had saved his life. Axe hadn't been able to do the same. Failure lay bitter in his mouth, but he had no time to grieve. When he judged Hogan drunk enough from the whiskey, he helped him to his feet and half-carried, half-dragged him up to the cabin. Swinging him onto the bed, Axe hurried to light a lamp and start a fire. Hogan had passed out, which was best, for he was going to have to dig some to get out the bullets.

Hogan came to sometime during Axe's probing, but he never uttered a sound. He simply gritted his teeth and steeled himself, concentrating on his hatred for Meade and LaRoche. Sweat stood out on his brow. Besides the bullet wound in the shoulder, Hogan had also been hit in the back and side. One was just a flesh wound, but the other had come perilously close to his spine. He'd been lucky.

Axe packed the wounds to stop the bleeding, and wrapped them. He was barely finished when Hogan pushed himself to his feet, weaving dangerously.

"You can't go anywhere tonight," Axe said, watching him.

"I have to," Hogan grunted, strapping on his gun with one hand. "The last steamer sails tomorrow morning. Meade plans to be on it. I plan for him to miss it." He shrugged into his coat.

"I'm going with you," Axe said, and reached for his rifle.

"Let's bring Thor up to the cabin so the animals don't get him." Hogan picked up his own rifle and turned away. Within a few minutes they shoved off in Axe's canoe. It would be dawn before they reached Dawson.

The *Miranda Lynn*'s whistle rent the air impatiently. The captain was anxious to be gone. The townspeople walked down to the wharf to see the ship off and to call final orders for outrageous items to be brought the following spring. Good-naturedly the crew kidded back, while Captain Smith kept a stern eye on the loading of passengers and their gear.

It was a cold, crisp day. The muddy streets had frozen once again and now the new-fallen snow lay clean and white. Kate and May had brought Gilly out for some air and because they couldn't stand to miss the excitement. This was the last boat, the last chance to leave, and those staying behind thought of home and family on the Outside. It would be a long winter before another ship came up the river. The only way out would be the formidable Chilkoot Pass, and four hundred miles of harsh wilderness lay between them and the pass. They pushed away their misgivings and shouted gruff jokes.

Kate and May walked along Main Street, enjoying the hustle and bustle. Wrapped snugly against the damp coldness, little Gilly slept in his mother's arms. Now and then she nuzzled her cold nose against his soft warmth.

"Hogan come," May said brightly, and pointed down the street toward the wharves.

"He's back early," Kate cried in delight, and hurried toward him. He didn't see her until she was almost upon him. His face was pale, his chin covered with stubble. His stance was fixed and rigid as he stared at the gangplank of the *Miranda Lynn*.

"Hogan," Kate called. He jerked around, his hand flying to his gun. Startled, she halted and stared at him, the laughter fading from her eyes. "What's happened?" she whispered. "Are you ill?" He looked even worse close up.

"Get out of here, Kate," he growled, taking hold of her arm and trying to steer her away.

"Hogan, I don't understand. What is it?" The black premonition was rushing toward her. Danger beat against her bright secure world. "What are you doing? Where are Axe and Thor?"

"Kate, I'm looking for Meade. He attacked us last night, shot Thor, and took our gold. I can't explain more than that. Take Gilly and get out of here, Kate. Now!"

"Hogan!" Axe called out a warning, and he whirled around. Meade and Frenchy LaRoche were trying to board the *Miranda Lynn*. Each of them carried a heavy canvas bag obviously filled with gold. Frenchy's face blanched when he saw Hogan. Meade dropped his bag and drew his gun. Hogan's gun appeared in his hand so quickly it took Kate's breath away.

"You'll never get to spend that gold, Meade," he said grimly. "You're about to die."

Blindly Meade fired, his bullets going into the crowd. People screamed and tried to duck. One bullet struck Hogan in the thigh. Behind him, he heard Kate scream. Steadying himself, he took aim and fired. A bright red stain blossomed on the front of Meade's jacket. A look of surprise crossed his face. The gun slid from his nerveless fingers and his knees buckled. Before Meade hit the ground, Hogan had cocked his gun and turned to face LaRoche, but the wily Frenchman had once again slipped away in the confusion.

Holding his thigh, Hogan turned toward Kate and felt a great roaring in his head. Kate was on her knees in the street, bent low over something, a hoarse keening moan coming from her throat. Her dark red skirts were a sharp contrast against the snow. But it wasn't her gown, he thought hazily. It was blood!

"Kate," he cried, hobbling toward her. She heard his cry and raised her head to stare at him, her eyes filled with anguish, her face distorted with horror. She clutched a small bundle to her breast. Darkness roared toward Hogan, but he refused to give way to it.

"Kate?" he whimpered. The blood lay bright red in the snow between them.

"Our son is dead," she said dully.

21

"No!" Hogan's cry echoed down the street. He lurched toward Kate and his son. Caught by the drama being played out before them, people fell silent and stared at the huddled figures of Kate and her baby. May hovered nearby, weeping, her hands pressed to her mouth in wordless grief.

"Kate, it can't be true," Hogan pleaded brokenly, but the despair on her face was too heartrending.

"Our son's been shot," she said tonelessly. Slowly her eyes focused on him. "You! Murderer! You killed him with your lust for gold. Murderer!" Her voice rose in a scream.

"Don't, Kate," Hogan whispered, holding out a hand as if to ward off the terrible pain of her words. In her grief, she was unrelenting.

"Murderer!" she spat. Her eyes were filled with revulsion and rage. Feeling her hate like a thick wall separating them, Hogan fell to his knees in the snow. One blood-covered hand reached out for his son.

"Don't touch him," she cried, springing away from him as if he were something evil. She cradled the small bundle against herself protectively. Her cloak was smeared with blood, his son's blood! Hogan groaned and gnashed his teeth.

Kate's voice was like cracking glass in its cutting intensity. "I should never have listened to you. I should have taken the first boat back to Seattle. I let you talk me into staying so you could fill your pockets with more gold. Was your gold worth our son's life?"

"Kate, I'm sorry, so sorry," Hogan wept brokenly.

"I detest you," she hissed. "I wish you were dead,

do you hear? I wish Meade had shot you instead." She crouched over him, her green eyes glittering with hatred. With a bitter twist of her mouth she spat on him. Hogan made no move to wipe away the ugly smear.

"Don't ever come near me again," she whispered, "or so help me God, I'll kill you myself."

She turned away and a weeping May came forward to help. Kate sagged against her, shoulders jerking in a horrible spasm of sobs. Slowly the women made their way down the street. Hogan stayed where he was, kneeling in the snow until finally his large body bowed and curved inward upon itself, upon the pain and loss he'd suffered. He lay whimpering, and men looked away, moved at the sight of the rawboned giant's misery.

Grief was replaced by rage and a need for revenge. Hogan wished Meade were still alive so he could have the satisfaction of killing him again. His keening cry halted. Remembering, he raised his head from the muddy slush and looked around. A name roared through his head and he opened his mouth and bellowed it to the leaden, snow-filled skies: "Frenchy!"

The name echoed through the town. Men drew back from the mad-looking creature crouched in the snow. Axe moved forward, holding Hogan's gun.

"He got away, son," he said sympathetically.

Hogan raised his face to his friend. "Good," he said briefly, and staggered to his feet. "I'm going to find him and kill him."

"You're in no condition, son," Axe said. "You've been shot up pretty bad. Go see the doc first and get patched up."

"It doesn't matter," Hogan said brusquely. He grabbed his gun from Axe and holstered it. His eyes were half-mad and feverish as he looked around.

"Your leg," Axe began. "You can't get far on it like that."

"I'll make it." Hogan's face bore a grin, feral and grim.

"You'll die out there like that," Axe said with rising agitation.

"Not before I get LaRoche," Hogan growled. "Get out of my way, old man. I don't need you for what I'm about to do."

A woman standing on the boardwalk heard his words, and now she rushed after Hogan. "You can't go off wounded," Roxanne Blayne cried, clutching at his sleeve. "At least get a dog team and some supplies. Hogan!" He hadn't even acknowledged that she was there except to shake off her hand. Helplessly Roxanne turned back to Axe. "Go after him," she cried. "He can't die out there."

"Aye." The old man nodded. "I'll get some supplies and trail him."

The satchels of gold Meade and Fletcher had dropped still lay unclaimed in the snow. Men walked around them. None would claim another man's earnings. Besides, the gold was tainted now with misfortune and bad luck. It might rub off on them. Roxanne hired one of the drunks to bring the bags to her own cabin. She'd keep them for Hogan until he came back. Please, God, she prayed for the first time in too many years, let him come back alive.

May helped Kate into the house and finally took the small bundle from her clasp. Kate slumped into a chair, head bowed. Tenderly May laid the baby on the table, then gasped with disbelief as the tiny lashes fluttered. "Gilly," she cried, but his eyes remained closed. Kate looked at her, startled.

"He's alive," May cried. "Kate, he's alive."

"What?" Kate ran forward to look at her son. A wary joy filled her eyes. With trembling fingers she removed the warm furs and blankets that bound him. Something rolled out of the mound and landed on the floor. Neither woman paid attention to it. Hastily they washed away the blood and examined the tiny body. The bullet had entered the left side from the back and exited in the front. May's small sensitive hands pressed gently, feeling for broken bones and examining for internal injuries. She brought out her medicine pouch and packed the wound with spiderwebs and shaved inner bark from a tree. Kate stood aside, letting her work. She never once thought of summoning one of the town's doctors. She trusted May.

All night they tended the small body, but there was no improvement. The day after the shooting, Iris arrived at the cabin.

"I come as soon as I heard," she said. "They brought word down on the *Miranda Lynn*. I had Bud bring me up in the *Yukon Queen*. We're here for as long as you need us."

Kate took one look at her big homely face and burst into tears. "Oh, Iris, he's going to die. My baby's going to die and I can't do anything for him."

"Here now," Iris said, gathering Kate into her arms and rocking her as Aunt Petty had done when she was a child. "We'll have no more of that," she said finally. "What we all need is a cup of tea. I aim to spell you some in lookin' after that baby, the poor little fella."

So the vigil began. For days the women watched over the baby, taking turns at rest. Gilly had not regained consciousness, and Kate despaired that he ever would.

"He'll be all right," Iris said fiercely. "He's just gatherin' his strength. Sleep's the best thing for him." But even her steadfast courage began to fade with each day that passed. Then three nights later as Kate sat beside the little crib, her eyes red from weeping, she heard a movement. Gilly's eyes were open and his fist pummeled the air impatiently. Opening his mouth, he gave a lusty yell.

"May, Iris," Kate called above his shrieks. "He's awake. He's going to live." The other two women came running, hastily wrapping their dressing gowns around them against the creeping cold. Laughing, they hung over his crib, delighting in the sound and fury of this tiny life they'd fought so hard to save.

"What's wrong with him?" Kate asked worriedly. "Is he in pain?" Iris placed a hand on the baby's stomach and nodded. "I expect he's hungry," she said. "You'd best feed him."

"Oh," Kate sighed, lifting her son from his crib and settling into a chair. As she guided his impatient mouth to a nipple and felt the strong sucking pull of him against her breasts, she laid her head back and wept tears of thanksgiving. Fondly Iris watched her friend, then motioned to May, and the two women crept back to bed. It was only later, when Gilly was once again sleeping and Kate was kneeling by his crib, loath to leave him, that she thought of Hogan and those last hateful words she'd flung at him. Where was he now? she wondered. She must send word that his son was alive after all.

Frenchy had never been a woodsman, had never understood the barest laws of nature in the Yukon. Blindly he plunged away from the town and the flaming death of Hogan's guns. Now he floundered, exhausted and cold. And behind him, growing ever closer, was the sound of a dog team. Hogan, that son of a devil, was on his trail. Frenchy pushed on. He'd been traveling for three days now, trying to follow the river back up to the Chilkoot Pass. If he could get to Skagway, Soapy Smith and some of his men would hide him out until he could get a steamer to the Outside.

Frenchy stopped to rest, his breathing quick and shallow in the cold thin air. Pushing back his hood, he listened. The dog team was still an hour behind him. He was safe for the time being. He swung around and angled toward a stand of spruce trees. A dark shadow moved among them. Frenchy grabbed his gun and froze in his tracks, his eyes searching among the trees fearfully. Once again the wind carried an echo of the dog team. Grinning, he relaxed his stance. He was jumping at shadows. It was easy for a man to get spooked out here. He holstered his gun and moved forward.

"Aigh!" The cry was torn from his mouth by the wind and flung toward the mountaintops. Eyes wide with terror, Frenchy stared at the figure before him— Hogan O'Shea, no longer looking human. His eyes blazed with fever and revenge. Spittle gathered at the corners of his mouth, like that of a mad dog. He wore no hat and no mittens, and yet he seemed impervious to the snow and wind. Ice had caked in his dark brows and made a frozen cap of his hair. Blood had frozen stiff on one leg. His skin looked gray, as if all the blood had already drained from his body. A specter from the dead couldn't have looked more terrifying. Only his eyes, his terrible eyes, were alive.

Whimpering, Frenchy backed up. "It wasn't me," he whined, and was aware of the hot liquid that spewed along his legs and wet the front of his pants. He'd soiled himself. "It was Meade. Meade did it all. He was angry that . . . that you'd caused him to be run out of town. He wanted to get even with you and Thor."

"Take out your gun!" Those feverish red eyes never left his face as Hogan deliberately pulled his gun from its holster and pointed it at Frenchy.

"Non, non," LaRoche cried, holding out a hand. "I swear, it wasn't me. Aigh!" His words were cut off as Hogan's bullet tore through his shoulder.

"Take out your gun and fight me like a man," Hogan said again. His gaze never wavered, his lips barely moved.

"I can't fight you, *mon ami*. I know you are a better shot than Frenchy, eh? It would not be fair." LaRoche laughed ingratiatingly, as if they shared a common joke. "You are a reasonable man, Hogan. I tell you this. I have never done anything against you. Meade was the one. He shot Thor. I watched him. If you want me to testify against him, I will."

"Meade's dead." The words were said without emotion. "Take out your gun."

"Mon ami!" Frenchy's false smile faded and he tried another tack. "I ain't going to pull my gun. I'm giving myself up to you. You have to return me to Dawson for a trial."

"You've already been tried," Hogan said. His head snapped up at the sound of an approaching dog team. While his attention was diverted, Frenchy made a grab for his gun and leveled it at Hogan. He pulled the trigger and felt the gun leap in his hands, but Hogan never moved a muscle. Fear crossed Frenchy's face as he considered the possibility that he was indeed facing a ghost from the other world.

With contemptuous leisure, Hogan aimed his gun. "Your time is up," he said, and pulled the trigger. Unerringly his bullet entered Frenchy's heart. The Frenchman was dead before he hit the ground.

Axe heard the gunshots and swung the whip over his team's head, urging them on to greater speed. They were tired. Hogan had pushed forward harder than Axe had anticipated he could with his wounds. As nearly as Axe could tell, he'd taken no food or water since starting, unless he'd eaten snow. Now the gunshots told their own story. He'd found the Frenchman. Axe swung the whip again. The spruce woods were just ahead.

Frenchy LaRoche had died with his arms outflung, knocked backward by the impact of the bullet. His black eyes stared unseeingly at the gray sky. Hogan had simply crumpled and lay in a heap near one of the trees. Quickly Axe rolled him over and felt for a pulse. There was a flutter, weak and unsteady, but there. Levering his wiry old body under the big man, Axe dragged him to the sledge and laid him on it. He cast another glance at the sky. The temperature was dropping steadily. The sky was menacing. Snow was falling again. He weighed the chances of making it back to Dawson and estimated the cabin was closer. He had to get Hogan back to shelter before the storm hit in full force.

"Mush," he shouted to his team, and turned southwest toward the Yukon River. The wind was at his back.

The winds howled down from the Arctic Ocean, cold and harsh. On the main street of Dawson men scurried from one building to another as quickly as possible. The women in the crib houses on Pleasure Alley no longer sat in their open doorways, but huddled near their stoves. Nonetheless, business was good, for the miners, unable to return to their claims, found their way to the cribs out of boredom and a sure knowledge that nothing was as warm and comforting as a willing woman's body. Other miners gathered around the stoves in saloons and general stores, swapping tall tales with one another. New legends had been formed during the past year. Hogan O'Shea and his expertise with gun and fist were among them, as were the continued exploits of Taffy Kate. The miners were hardly surprised to hear that Kate's baby had lived. They would have been more surprised if he hadn't.

Snug in their warm cabin, Kate and the other women coddled the baby and spent long hours talking. Their friendship was deep and abiding by now.

"I reckon Bud and me ought to be headin' on back to the tradin' post," Iris said one day. "The river's going to freeze one of these days."

"You were so kind to come," Kate said, but Iris could see her thoughts were on something else.

"Have you sent word to Hogan about his son yet?"

Miserably Kate shook her head. "Oh, Iris, I don't know yet what to do. If I tell him, if he comes here, I may . . . may . . ."

"Go back to him?" Iris prompted.

Kate nodded. "I can't bear any more, Iris, the lonesome winters, the danger, the greed, and for what? All for gold. It means nothing to me."

"But it means something to Hogan," Iris said wisely, "so it has to be important to you as well."

"Not if I don't let it. Not if I choose not to stay," Kate said, twisting her hands in her lap. "I want to leave this place. I'm not cut out for this kind of life."

"Oh, pshaw, Kate," Iris snorted. "You're a strong woman. When you make up your mind to something, you stick to it. And I've never seen you look happier than you were this summer when you had Hogan and Gilly. What do you suppose you're going to do with yourself in the Outside? Without Hogan, will it be that grand?"

Kate turned away without answering, for she'd asked herself those same questions over and over. She looked around the spacious, well-appointed cabin. It had been her home. She'd felt loved and cosseted and happy here, because Hogan was here. Hogan!

"I don't know where he is," she said. "He's disappeared. Tagish Dan said he followed Frenchy out of town."

"So you have given him some thought," Iris said. "I'd begun to wonder, Kate O'Shea, if you were going to let that foolish pride of yours get in the way."

"As soon as he returns, I'll tell him about Gilly," Kate said. "But I can't promise anything more than that. Not now. I love Hogan. I guess I'll never stop loving him. But we're too different in our thinking and our goals. I'm not sure we can ever live together happily." Impatiently she turned away. "It's all so confusing, Iris. I don't know what to do."

"You've got time, child, to figure it out," Iris said.

But time had run out. A miner coming downriver brought word that Hogan was in bad shape and might not make it. Axe was bringing him in. Anxiously Kate waited, peering out the window a dozen times a day. But when Axe's dog team pulled into town, he was alone.

"Axe, where is he?" Kate whispered, her eyes huge in her pale face.

"He was too weak to risk bringing him on in," Axe said, coughing and wheezing. "I left him at the cabin. He's in a pretty bad way." Axe looked in a bad way as well. His thin chest rattled with each racking cough, and when he tried to walk, he collapsed on the floor. He'd expended all his energies getting help for his friend. May had already retrieved her medicine pouch. As Clay and Tagish Dan carried him off to bed, he put out a hand to detain them while he spoke to Kate.

"Hogan may not make it," he rasped out.

"No," she cried. Suddenly all her doubt had melted away. It was one thing to contemplate a life without Hogan as long as he was alive and well. But to exist in a world where he did not was unthinkable. Frantically Kate snatched up her warm cape. Her glance flew to Iris.

"Can Bud take me upriver to the Sweetwater?" she asked anxiously. "We can bring Hogan back on the steamer. It'll be faster and more comfortable for him."

"Shore he can," Iris said without hesitation.

"The river may freeze any moment," Clay said, coming back into the room. "You'd be ice-bound, swept under."

"I have to take that chance, Clay," Kate answered. "Hogan may die otherwise." She turned back to Iris. "If we don't make it," she began, "if the steamer is wrecked, there's gold stored in my bedroom to buy another."

"I'm not worried about the boat," Iris said. "Go to your man."

"Gilly—" Kate began.

"May and me'll watch over him. You go on, now."

"Thank you," Kate said, and gave each of the women a warm hug. Then she was gone, out into the night, pushing against the cold wind and slashing snow. It hit against her face like tiny hard pebbles. Kate barely felt it.

The *Yukon Queen* pushed away from shore and Kate wondered how Bud could see to navigate. But he'd plied this river often enough in the past years, and he held the little craft steady in deep water. Dusk had fallen already, the banks but a shadowy haze on either side of them. Kate stood at the cabin window, straining to see ahead and so call a warning should a snag appear. Ice was forming along the river's edge, and Kate prayed some miracle would occur that would hold the ice at bay. They were drawing closer now. She could feel it in her bones. Now a new worry assailed her. What if she missed the mouth of the creek? What if they sailed on past? She bit her lips until they bled.

Then disaster struck. With the coming of darkness, the temperature dropped quickly. Ice began to form on the prow of the boat. Bud tied a rope around his waist and leaned far over the edge to chop away the ice. It did little good. With a mighty groan, the river capitulated to the restraining cap of ice. The sturdy little boat gave a final shudder and sat still, while all around her the ice popped and groaned as it grew thicker.

"What are we going to do?" Kate cried.

"We'll have to get off," Bud said. "When the ice gets thick enough, it'll crush the boat, but we have to wait until we're sure the ice is strong enough to hold us."

"Surely if it can stop a boat, it's strong enough now," Kate called.

Bud nodded and pointed toward shore. Water still swirled beneath thin layers of ice in some spots. "If we step into one of those, we'll go under. We'd best wait awhile." So they paced the deck while the little steamer groaned and shuddered in its death throes and the ice tightened its deadly grip on the river.

"Now!" Bud cried. Throwing their packs of food and medicine overboard, he turned to Kate. "Quick, over the edge." Obediently she swung her legs over the rail, sweeping her full skirts out of the way. She wished now she'd taken a few precious minutes to change into leggings and a parka. She pitched forward onto the ice, landing on her hands and knees. But she was unable to scramble away. Her skirts had caught against the railing.

"Come on," Bud yelled. "Get away from the boat." Kate heard a squeal of wood and metal and felt herself pulled backward. The force of the ice had caused the boat to list to the starboard. "Run, Kate," Bud yelled.

"I'm caught," she cried, and tugged at her gown. The sturdy wool held. "Bud, I need your knife," she screamed, trying not to panic. She could feel herself being drawn across the ice again. But Bud was beside her now, his knife already open. He slashed at the wool, and with a final rending sound, Kate tore free of the boat.

"Run," Bud called, and Kate leapt to her feet and gathered up the packs. She cast a quick glance over her shoulder and stopped in her tracks, mouth gaping in a scream that never left her throat. Bud had fallen, and even as he struggled to his feet, the little boat shifted. The ice where Kate had lain trapped cracked. A section tipped upward, spilling the rest of their supplies into the icy waters.

"Bud!" Kate screamed, and ran a few steps toward him.

"Go on, Kate. Get to shore," he cried, regaining his footing. Kate clutched the precious pouch of medicine she'd hung over her shoulder. Their extra food supplies were gone. The ice floe that had once held their packs settled back into place as neatly as a lid being put over a boiling pot. In horror Kate stared at the cracks radiating outward. The *Yukon Queen* was being crushed by the ice, its prow sliding upward while its stern dipped below the freezing water. The deep crack that had claimed their supplies snaked across the icy surface, giving birth to other cracks. In terror Kate ran toward shore. Bud was close behind. They could never outrun it, Kate knew. At any moment she expected the ice to tip and dump them both into a watery grave. Then who would save Hogan? His life depended on them.

With one last superhuman effort, Kate threw herself forward, leaping those final few feet to shore. She landed with a thud that knocked the breath from her. Without pausing to draw another, she wriggled madly up the embankment until she knew at last she was safe from the river's icy fingers. Now she lay panting, heedless of the cold snow against her face. She was vaguely aware of Bud's hoarse breathing, but she was too breathless to acknowledge his presence. Fervently she said a prayer of thanksgiving that they were alive. Her gaze fell on the gaping hole in the river ice. The *Yukon Queen* had slid beneath the water's surface.

"Oh, Bud, your boat!" she gasped.

"We're alive. That's what counts," he answered, echoing her thoughts. "Come on. We have to move or we'll freeze."

A will to survive made her get to her feet. She had no idea how far they were from the cabin, but if they followed the river they would reach it eventually.

Checking the medicine pouch, she pulled her heavy cape tightly about her and set out after Bud.

It seemed they walked forever, stumbling through the predawn darkness. Often Kate fell over logs hidden in the snow. She nearly gave up, but each time, she struggled to her feet and followed Bud's trudging figure. Dawn was streaking the northern sky when she caught a wisp of smoke in the distance. Sobbing in relief, she began to run, feeling the cold slice through her lungs.

"Kate!" Bud called in warning, and she forced herself to stop, holding on to a sapling while she struggled for breath. Then, willing herself to a steady, even pace, she sedately followed Bud.

No matter how far they walked, it seemed, the smoke was no closer. For a while Kate even lost track of it, and panic nearly overcame her. She had no feeling, no expectations, no hope. She simply put one foot in front of the other, pushing herself forward, when all she wanted to do was sink down in the snow and sleep. When they stumbled into the small clearing, she had to blink and look around, unable to recognize the frozen creek bed. Then she saw the cabins through the trees, looking small and forlorn in the great white wilderness. Nothing had ever looked as wonderful in her life.

"This is it!" she cried, and forced her frozen feet to move, her gaze fixed on the smoke emerging from the chimney of her little cabin. It was where warmth and life and the man she loved waited.

Without knocking, she yanked the drawstring and walked in, a smile on her face, words of love and encouragement on her lips. The woman bending over the bed raised her blond head and stared at her.

"Hello, Kate," Roxanne Blayne said. She had her arm around Hogan's shoulders, lifting him to give him a drink. Now she laid his head back on the pillows. Hogan never opened his eyes. He mumbled something incoherent and tossed on the bed in the throes of a fever.

"You!" Kate gasped, stepping into the room. "How did you get here?"

"I hired an Indian guide to bring me out when I first heard Axe was bringing Hogan in. I knew he'd have to stop here." She tucked the covers back around Hogan, her touch possessive and sure. Kate's heart ran cold. "Where's Axe?" Roxanne asked.

"He's back in Dawson. He took sick on the way. He couldn't have made it back."

"Then who came with you?" Roxanne asked, glancing at the door.

"Bud Garrett," Kate answered. "He's coming. We tried to come upriver in his boat, but the ice caught us. His boat was sunk." Bud had entered the cabin now, and without a word crossed to the stove. His face was pale, his eyebrows hoary with frost.

"You came the rest of the way on foot?" Roxanne asked incredulously.

Kate nodded. "So you've been here all this time caring for him?" She'd begun to shiver, now that she was in the warm cabin.

"Yes, I have," Roxanne answered calmly, and rose from the side of the bed. "You'd better get out of those wet clothes or you'll be sick too."

"Not yet," Kate said, and walked to the bed. Tears stung her eyes and nose as she stared down at Hogan. "How is he?" she asked quietly.

"He's been wounded four times, in the shoulder, back, side, and thigh," Roxanne said, demonstrating a thorough knowledge of Hogan's body, but there was no triumph in the words. "He was caught in the storm without food or water for several days and he has a fever." She raised anguished eyes to Kate. "I don't know what else to do for him."

Kate pulled off the small pouch of medicines she'd brought. "May sent some herbs and roots for teas that will bring down the fever. He needs to be warmer. Are there any more blankets?"

"Over here." Roxanne moved to pile on more blankets.

"We need to build up that fire. We can't let him get chilled."

"I'll get some more wood," Bud said, picking up the ax. "After that, I'll see about hunting for food." After Kate changed into a dress Roxanne lent her, the women worked to make the sick man comfortable, and when at last they paused to share a cup of tea, Roxanne looked at Kate and smiled. "You really do deserve all those legends made up about you. You're very brave."

"I don't know about that," Kate answered. "I just knew I had to get to Hogan." She fixed her gaze on her teacup while she searched for words. "I said some horrid things to him back in Dawson. I have to tell him they're not true. I . . . I hope it's not too late." She didn't see the regret wash across Roxanne's face.

Rising, Roxanne crossed to the stove and stirred the stew. "You love him very much, don't you?" she asked softly.

Kate glanced up at her, startled. "Yes, I do," she answered. "But then, so do you." She watched Roxanne's shoulders stiffen in denial, then slump.

"I have from the first moment I saw him," she said, coming back to the table. "I met him in Colorado. He was mining for gold with a bunch of other men. Your father was there. None of them were having any luck. Hogan was different from the other men. The rest of them just naturally seemed to turn to him to be their leader. We had some good laughs in those days. I guess I . . . well, I just never thought he was the marrying kind." She glanced at Kate. "Otherwise, I would have tied him up myself." She looked down at her hands. "Ah, hell, who am I kidding? Hogan and me, we had some laughs," she repeated softly, "but he never loved me, not like he does you."

Kate's heart leapt at the words.

"He never came to me after that first night you came looking for your father back in Seattle. Oh, he'd laugh and joke in his old way, and he always treated me like a lady, but when I saw how he was with you . . . well, I could see it was different. You were a real lady. I was a saloon girl—a whore."

"How did you ever go into this . . . this business?" Kate asked, not wishing to offend, but curious about Roxanne.

The saloon girl shrugged deprecatingly. "I was brought up on a dirt-poor farm back in Indiana," she said. "I hated it. We never had shoes except in the winter when it got cold. I wanted more. I wanted pretty gowns and shoes to wear every single day of my life. I wanted to laugh a little and not worry that there was too much rain or not enough. When Papa died, I just walked into town, hooked up with a gambler, and I never went back. I stayed with the gambler for a time; then one morning I woke up and he'd left. He took everything, all the pretty clothes he'd bought me, everything." She shrugged. "So I started earning money the only way I could." She glanced down at her full body. "It's paid off well enough. I'm a rich woman now."

"Then why go on?" Kate asked. "Why not live differently?"

Roxanne shook her head. "Nah, I'm good at this. I got a few more years left in me. Then I'm going to retire." She drew a deep breath. A mocking smile curved her lips. "Maybe I'll go respectable after all."

A moan from the bed drew both women from their chairs. Kate flew to Hogan's side, kneeling beside his bed. "I'm here, love," she whispered, washing his face with a rag dipped in cool water.

"Kate . . . Gilly!" His cry filled the room.

"Shh, my love, Gilly's well. He's alive," she reassured him over and over, but doubted he heard, for his restless thrashing seldom let up. In the days and nights that followed, Kate feared she might lose him after all. Then one day the fever broke and she knew he'd make it.

"Kate," he whispered, staring at her, and this time his eyes were aware.

"Hogan," she cried, going to take his hand. "Oh, Hogan, my beloved."

"Don't hate me, Kate," he croaked weakly, his dark eyes pleading. "I'm sorry." He paused and drew in a deep breath, rolling his head from side to side while tears flowed down his cheeks. "Oh, God, I'm so sorry about Gilly. My son!" He wept. "My son!"

"Gilly's alive, Hogan," Kate said softly. "He didn't die."

He turned a disbelieving face to her. "Is that true?"

"I swear he is," Kate said, laughing. "You know May. She was able to stop the bleeding and beat the fever. He's alive, Hogan. We're going to be together again. I promise you."

She saw the black despair in his eyes turn to joy, and he reached for her hand, holding it tightly. "We'll never be apart again. Never!" she said fiercely. "I love you, Hogan." Now it was Kate who wept, burying her face against his shoulder, giving way to all the tension and fear she'd lived with during the past two weeks.

Hogan brought a shaky hand up to smooth her brilliant hair. "Gl-glory woman!" he whispered, and his eyes closed in sleep. It was the first time she'd heard the name he'd often given her in private, but she had little trouble recognizing the love and pride behind the words. She laid her head against his shoulder and wept. Great hoarse sobs of relief tore from her throat.

Roxanne stood by the stove, tears raining down her cheeks. Kate raised her head and looked at the saloon girl, then quickly got to her feet and put her arms around her. Together they stood sharing the joy as they'd shared the burden of nursing and praying over the man they loved.

Finally Kate put on her coat and went outside to sit on a stump and give thanks for God's mercy. Twice now she'd nearly lost the people she loved, and twice a miracle had occurred. She felt humbled and awed. With new eyes she studied the cold harsh beauty around her. The storm had passed on by. Spruce trees, their branches drooping under their burden of snow, rose majestically toward the clear sky, their magnificence eclipsed only by the awesome mountain peaks in the distance. Beneath its new mantle of snow, the earth rested, waiting for that short intense season when all things would spring to new life. In the spruce forest a shadow moved, and Kate knew it was either a caribou or a bear in its endless search for food and life. Why had she thought this land barren and dead? Life was even more precious here, for it was more hardily won. She and Hogan were part of it, a part of the struggle, a part of the triumph.

She was still sitting on her log when she saw two dog teams approaching along the river. Springing to her feet, Kate ran to meet them. Clay Lawford and Tagish Dan pulled their sledges to a halt.

"Oh, I'm so glad to see you," she cried breathlessly.

"Kate, thank God you're alive," Clay said, hugging her. "Word came back to us that the *Yukon Queen* was wrecked in the ice. We assumed you and Bud were dead."

"Thanks to Bud's quick thinking, we escaped," she said.

"You mean Bud's still alive?" Tagish Dan asked in disbelief. "Shoulda known that old possum wouldn't die. Iris'll be mighty happy to hear that. She's been a-grievin' some, I can tell you."

"How's Gilly?" Kate asked, anxious to hear some word of her son.

"He's just fine. Iris's practically taken over the care of him, just to take her mind off her grief. She'll be overjoyed to hear you're safe."

"We brought some supplies," Clay informed her. "We weren't sure how long we'd have to stay."

"We can use them," Kate said gratefully. "How's Axe?"

"He's been down with pneumonia. May is babying him and he's grumbling. He tried to come with us, but we persuaded him it was best if he didn't. We weren't sure what we'd find when we got here." Kate knew they'd expected to find a dead man.

"Come with me. I have a surprise for you," she said, laughing jubilantly.

Hogan slept most of the time the men were there. Jealously Kate hovered over him, tucking in the covers, making sure the lamplight didn't shine in his face. But he woke in the evening and smiled at the beaming faces around him. When his sweeping gaze reached Kate, it went no further. Love flickered in his eyes, and Kate's heart soared.

Clay and Tagish Dan stayed for two days before starting back. Kate had decided that Hogan would be better off recuperating at the cabin before making the long, hard trip overland, so Tagish Dan and Bud went hunting and managed to kill a caribou and a lynx. That, along with the supplies they'd brought, would give Kate and Hogan enough food to last for several weeks if another storm left them stranded. The men also buried Thor, thawing the ground with fire before scraping out a shallow grave. Kate stood by his graveside and thought about the gentle man who'd brought so much laughter into their lives. The Yukon, and the greedy men who'd flocked here, had once more claimed the life of a loved one, but this time Kate wasn't bitter. The greedy, evil men spawned by the goldfields were few when compared to men like Thor, Bud Garrett, and all the others. With a lighter heart than she might have expected, she turned back to the cabin. Thor was buried in a beautiful land, just as he would have wanted.

"I'll be going back to Dawson with the men," Roxanne said after the small funeral.

"I don't know how to thank you."

"Don't," Roxanne answered, and looked at Hogan, who lay sleeping. "I'm not like you, Kate. I don't do many selfless things in my life. I want to remember this one for a long time."

Kate took her hand and squeezed it gently. "I think we could have been friends," she said, "if things had been different."

"If things had been different," Roxanne repeated. Picking up her bundle and drawing on her parka, she paused in the door for one last look at Hogan. Seeing Roxanne's face, without the artifice of paints and powder, Kate thought she'd never looked prettier. Without saying anything more, Roxanne stepped out into the

TOMORROW'S DREAM

cold air. The snow crunched under her shoepacs as she walked to the sledge and settled herself. Kate stood in the doorway watching the men hitch up their teams. Clay walked back to speak to her.

"Are you sure you want to stay all alone out here?" he asked anxiously.

"I'm not alone," she replied serenely. "I have Hogan."

"Good-bye, Kate," Clay said with an air of resignation. Pity welled in her for a moment, then was quickly gone. Clay would find someone else.

"Give Iris my love," she called to Bud, who nodded. She waved until their sledges slid onto the thick river ice and disappeared around a bend. It seemed to her, watching them go, that this was the end of one era in all their lives. Old dreams were behind them. Tomorrow's dreams were still to be found. She chuckled. If this was a premonition, at least it was a happy one, she thought wryly, and turned back to the cabin, where Hogan waited.

Hogan was recovering rapidly now. It had been more than a week since Tagish Dan and Clay left and Hogan stayed awake for longer periods of time. Kate sat by his bedside for long hours, bringing him up-to-date on all that had happened—Gilly's recovery, Axe's pneumonia, the loss of Bud's boat. Hogan told her about Frenchy LaRoche's last hours and she turned aside so he wouldn't see the quiver of fear and guilt that filled her at the thought of how close he'd come to death. He'd been wounded, needing her, and she'd spewed hatred and anger at him. Every day of her life she'd wish those words had never been uttered.

She was heartened and amused one day while bathing Hogan when his member stirred and burgeoned beneath her hands. Startled, she glanced at him and found his dark eyes regarding her wickedly.

"Not yet, Hogan O'Shea," she said firmly. "Those wounds aren't healed well enough yet." But that night she slept wrapped in his arms and awoke to find him kissing her ardently. She was able to resist only by rising and starting a fire in the wood stove. Hogan was growing impatient in his role as invalid, but she would decide when the time was right.

Ten days later, Kate brought down the tub he had bought from Mame the year before. Setting it beside the stove, she heated melted snow and filled it. Hogan's eyes followed her actions with growing curiosity. At last she was ready, and standing in full view of him, with the lampglow outlining her slender figure, she slowly unbuttoned her gown and let it fall to the floor. Her long underwear quickly followed.

"Kate, what are you doing to me?" Hogan groaned.

Smiling, she stepped into the tub and picked up the soap. "I'm taking a bath, my love," she said innocently. She washed her hair thoroughly, with arms raised high so her pert breasts stood out. Then she slathered soap over her arched neck and downward over her breasts. Her hands covered the pale mounds, her fingers gliding over the dark rosy nipples. She could see Hogan's chest rise and fall as his breathing deepened.

Smiling seductively, Kate let her hands drift lower, smoothing down over her rib cage and the trim dip of her waist. Rising on her knees, she soaped her flat belly and the tangled red-gold nest of feminine hair. Ignoring the groan from the bed, she took up the cloth and with the same slow, sensuous motions washed away the soap, sluicing water over her shoulders, breasts, and belly. Suddenly Hogan's frustrated moan turned to a primeval growl and he threw the covers aside. Startled, Kate looked around.

"What are you doing?" she cried. "You can't get out of bed. Your wounds . . ."

"The hell with my wounds," he said, and swung his long legs over the edge of the bed. Save for the white bandages at his thigh, waist, and shoulder, he was completely nude, and Kate's breath drew in sharply when she saw his erection. Boldly he strode across the room to the tub. Quickly she stood up and reached for a towel, fumbling as she tried to draw it in front of herself. The towel was snatched away. Black eyes raked over her. She could feel the dark male heat of him. Her heartbeat fluttered erratically. She'd pushed him too far.

"I was coming to bed," she said wanly.

"After you drove me thoroughly crazy," he said unforgivingly, and swept her up in his arms.

"Hogan, your injuries . . ."

"Are not nearly as bad as what's going to happen to me if you don't do something," he threatened.

Kate laughed and wound her arms around his neck. "I'm willing to do whatever it takes to nurse you back to health," she said softly, then ducked her head, hiding her face against his neck in embarrassment at their bold love talk.

"Kate, my love, was there ever another woman like you?" he asked, delighted to find some prudishness still left in her. Before the night was ended, he made her blush many times over, but she never faltered in her responses to him. She was Kate, his Kate, his glory woman.

About the Author

Although Peggy Hanchar travels with her husband, Steve, they return often to their lake cottage in Delton, Michigan. She has four children, and in addition to writing romances, she quilts and sketches with pastels.